GHOSTWALKERS

BOOKS BY JONATHAN MABERRY

DEADLANDS: Ghostwalkers

The Wolfman

THE JOE LEDGER SERIES
Patient Zero
The Dragon Factory
The King of Plagues
Assassin's Code
Code Zero
Extinction Machine
Predator One
Joe Ledger: Special Ops
Kill Switch

THE PINE DEEP TRILOGY
Ghost Road Blues
Dead Man's Song
Bad Moon Rising

Darkness on the Edge of Town:
Stories of Pine Deep

THE ROT & RUIN SERIES
Rot & Ruin
Dust & Decay
Flesh & Bone
Fire & Ash
Bits & Pieces

THE DEAD OF NIGHT SERIES
Dead of Night
Fall of Night
Dark of Night

THE NIGHTSIDERS SERIES
The Orphan Army
Vault of Shadows

DEADLANDS

GHOSTWALKERS

JONATHAN MABERRY

TOR

A TOM DOHERTY ASSOCIATES BOOK
NEW YORK

DEADLANDS: GHOSTWALKERS

A Tor Book
Published by Tom Doherty Associates, LLC
175 Fifth Avenue
New York, NY 10010

www.tor-forge.com

Tor® is a registered trademark of Tom Doherty Associates, LLC.

ISBN 978-0-7653-7527-8

Our books may be purchased in bulk for promotional, educational, or business use. Please contact your local bookseller or the Macmillan Corporate and Premium Sales Department at 1-800-221-7945, extension 5442, or by e-mail at MacmillanSpecialMarkets@macmillan.com.

First Edition: September 2015
First Mass Market Edition: August 2016

Printed in the United States of America

0 9 8 7 6 5 4 3 2 1

This one is for all my readers—old and new—who seem willing to follow me down any weird trail I decide to take. Thanks for sharing the ride. God only knows where we'll go next!

And, as always, for Sara Jo.

Acknowledgments

Thanks so much to Jeff Mariotte for asking me to ride with him through the Deadlands. Thanks to my agents, Harvey Klinger and Sara Crowe, and to the good folks at Tor Books.

Thanks to the Deadlands roughriders: Shane Hensley, Matt Cutter, and the crew at Pinnacle Entertainment; C. Edward Sellner, Charlie Hall, and the Visionary Comics posse; Tom Doherty, Greg Cox, Stacy Hill, Diana Pho, Patty Garcia, and all the roustabouts at Tor.

DEADLANDS

GHOSTWALKERS

PART ONE

Blue Fire

———◆———

To fear death, gentlemen, is no other
than to think oneself wise when
one is not, to think one knows what
one does not know. No one knows
whether death may not be the
greatest of all blessings for a man,
yet men fear it as if they knew
that it is the greatest of evils.

—SOCRATES

Chapter 1

Grey Torrance sat on his horse in the dark shade of a tower of rock and watched a posse try their damnedest to kill a Sioux.

They were going about it with a will, Grey had to give them that. Clearly they'd given it some thought. Put some effort into. Making a job of it.

The Sioux?

He seemed to have the same work ethic when it came to not being killed. Riding hard until they shot his little pinto out from under him. Then climbing onto the big piles of rocks left over from when sheets of ice covered this whole land. The Sioux kept deviling the riders, cutting through narrow clefts in the rock, picking his way up trails a goat wouldn't risk. Tumbling rocks down on his pursuers. Even set a small brush fire. The man was using all the tricks.

Grey thought it was highly entertaining.

Kind of a shame the Sioux had no chance at all.

Not with six mounted men. Not out here where he could stall but he couldn't really escape.

Still, it was fun to watch.

Grey took a piece of jerky from his pocket, bit some off, and chewed slowly, letting the salt coax spit from his dry mouth. He wasn't entirely sure the jerky was beef, but as he'd taken it from a dead man's saddle it wasn't something he could verify. It kept him alive, though.

That and a handful of beans and a water skin he'd filled from a dreary little stream.

Alive, and until now, unhappy.

This lifted the day from nothing to something.

One man on foot trying to escape six on horseback in a country that was made for dying. The hills were a broken tumble of tan rocks that looked like they'd been dumped here at the end of the sixth day of creation. When God was just too damn tired to build anything else, so he tossed it all across Nevada and said to hell with it.

Maybe he thought the Devil would want it.

No one else much did.

Hateful, ugly place where the scorpion was king and water was worth more than gold or ghost rock.

It wasn't a place for the living.

It was a desert.

A boneyard.

A dead land.

He chewed and watched as the Sioux raced for the shelter of a massive tumble of rocks and started to climb. Some of the rocks stood straight up like the arms of buried giants. Some lay flat and stacked. Three of these formed a kind of rough terrace, with two smaller platforms and a big one up top. Be hard as hell to make it up that top shelf, but as Grey watched the Sioux seemed to be trying just that. The Sioux raced across the lowest table, leaped up and out, and caught a twisted root of a Joshua tree. The root was as withered as the tree, which leaned drunkenly over the edge of a higher shelf. Grey narrowed his eyes, trying to understand the point of the Sioux taking that risk. Even if he got to the next shelf, the posse could simply fall back and wait. There was nowhere else to go. That second shelf stood alone, like a tiny mesa, offering no shelter or . . .

The Sioux snaked out his hands and caught the vine.

Clutched it firm, then immediately began to climb. He was clearly making for the dense shadows under that bigger top shelf and Grey wondered why the six pursuers didn't just shoot him down. At that range they could shoot to wound and have a good chance of getting it done.

But they didn't seem to want to kill or injure the Sioux. They wanted him alive.

Now . . . why was that?

As the fugitive climbed up the vine toward the lip of the higher shelf, Grey found himself chewing on the question as much as on the jerky.

Why would six white men go to such lengths to capture an Indian unharmed?

That was damn odd, even for a part of the country that was odder than most. If it was one man Grey could put it down to heatstroke or some personal grudge. But this was six men. Well-armed, and from their bulging saddlebags, well-provisioned.

And wasn't that damned interesting?

Grey reached down and stroked the long neck of his horse. His newly acquired horse. The animal's coat was the same shade of dusty blue as the hair of Grey's grade-school teacher back home in Philadelphia, so he'd named the mare Mrs. Pickles. Picky for short. Nice horse.

Picky blew softly and shook her head. But she, too, was watching the drama below. She seemed every bit as curious as Grey was.

"So," Grey murmured, "what do you think?"

Picky lifted her head as if listening.

"We could turn northwest and leave these fellows to their own adventures."

Picky made no move.

"Or we could be busybodies and go interfere where we ain't wanted."

The horse blew again and stamped the rock with a hoof. She did it so hard it kicked up a spark.

"That's what I thought you'd say."

Grey thumbed the restraining thong off the end of his pistol and loosened the Winchester in its scabbard. He absently touched the knives in boot-top and belt. Then, as he did a thousand times a day he turned and looked over his shoulder.

There was nothing there.

Behind him was more of the blasted and blighted Nevada wasteland. The road he'd come was a random zig-zag through different states, different nations, different climates.

Different wars.

He knew, with all his intellect and experience, that no one was following him. He was good at leaving no trail to follow. So, he knew that there was no one back there. No one hunting him, as the posse down there was hunting the Sioux.

He knew that.

Just as he knew that he was wrong.

Partly wrong.

No man followed him, that was certain. No posse, no hunting party, no Agents or Rangers.

What was back there, riding his back trail somewhere in the dust and distance, was not a man. Or even a group of men.

No, you couldn't call them "*men*."

Not anymore.

They'd been men once upon a time, though. They'd been men before they died.

Before he killed them.

The ghosts of his crimes were relentless.

Grey took a breath and forced himself to turn and study the landscape before him, not the wreckage behind.

He swallowed the last bit of jerky, took a long drink, nodded to himself, and then kicked Picky lightly in the sides.

"Come on, girl," he said, "let's go see if we can't get into trouble."

Which is what they did.

Chapter 2

By the time Grey reached the floor of the broad valley the Sioux was scaling the wall that led to the topmost shelf. He had a fair piece of work ahead of him and Grey didn't envy the task.

Below, the posse had all dismounted. The men tied their horses to a stunted juniper and left the smallest man among them to guard the mounts. The others spread out to look for a way up. Two of them circled around out of sight while the remaining three set to climbing. As Picky drew closer, Grey could see that they weren't going about it the right way.

One fellow was trying to climb one-handed while holding his rifle in the other, and he was making a piss-poor job of it. Another was trying to muscle his way up, showing off by chinning himself on edges of rock and making big leaps. It was impressive for a few seconds, but under this sun and wearing jeans, a heavy canvas coat, boots, and a gunbelt, the fellow was wearing himself out. By the time he reached the second of the two highest shelves he was moving at a breathless crawl.

The other two were not climbers at all, but at least they went about it with caution.

While all this was happening the Sioux seemed to be either unconcerned with their approach, or he was looking for something. Or, Grey thought, maybe the man was plain loco.

The Sioux dropped to all fours and began spitting on

the ground. Grey could see him suck in his cheeks and hock spit over and over again. Once the Indian took a wrinkled water skin from his belt and upended it, squeezing out the last drops. Instead of swallowing them, he bent forward and let the water dribble from between clenched teeth.

"Yup," said Grey quietly, "that boy there's lost it."

Then something flashed up on the hill.

Bright and sudden and very strange.

As the Sioux spat once more there was a burst of intense blue light beneath him. For just a split second it was like the man knelt over a skylight to a room lit with blue fire. It erased all shadows and was so bright Grey threw a hand up to shield his eyes.

But when he peered between his fingers the light was gone.

From the sides of the hills he could hear the pursuing men cry out. First in fear and then in anger.

"What in the hell was that?" Grey asked the empty air.

Picky nickered uneasily and Grey patted her neck, but he was frowning. What had the Indian done to cause that flash?

He waited to see if there was another flash.

There wasn't.

However the memory of that one moment of azure light lingered. It burned in his eyes as if he'd stared too long at the sun, and only slowly, slowly faded.

Whatever it was, there was nothing natural about it, he was certain of that.

And there was nothing out here in the desert that could easily explain it. Not amid a pile of ancient rocks dropped by a glacier before the red man even hunted these hills. There wasn't even any water to reflect sunlight, not that water on brown rock under a yellow sun would flash with a blue as bright as cornflowers.

He pulled Picky up short on the far side of a jutting

shoulder of sandstone and slid quietly out of the saddle.
The small man guarding the horses was on the other side
and he was masking all sound by yelling encouragement
up to his companions. He had a truly poisonous mouth
and cursed his companions, called them goat molesters
and worse. Damned them to hell and wished seven kinds
of torment on them.

Grey was bored by the patter, so he screwed the barrel
of his pistol into the man's right ear and said, "Hush
now."

The man hushed.

The man froze solid.

Grey took a fistful of the back of the little man's collar to keep him from rabbiting. The man held his arms
out to his side.

"Good," said Grey amiably. "Take your pistol out like
it's red hot. Yup, just two fingers. Nice, that's the way to
do it. Put it on the ground. No, no, don't be moving
quicker than common sense tells you to. Good, good.
Now back up and let's go have a quiet chat, shall we?"

With the gun in place, Grey used his hold on the collar to walk the man backward around the shoulder of
rock. Then he pushed him toward the wall.

"Hands on the wall, feet wide. Yeah, like you're trying to hold it up."

Grey patted him down, removed a small two shot
over-and-under derringer and a skinning knife and
tossed them into a tangle of cactus paddles. Then he
spun the man and thrust him hard against the hot stone.

His prisoner was nearly a foot shorter than Grey's six-
two and easily sixty or seventy pounds lighter. A skinny
man with a bad sunburn and worse breath. He had rough,
big-knuckled hands, though, which spoke of years of
hard labor. A farmer or a miner. Nothing else would do
it. His face was young but his eyes were old and they
didn't seem to want to meet Grey's.

Grey stood very close, the gun barrel an inch from the man's tobacco-stained teeth. The fellow went crossed-eyed trying to look at it.

"Now," said Grey, smiling an affable smile, "let's start with your name."

The man hesitated for a beat, then said, "Riley."

"First name?"

"That is my first name."

"Give me the whole thing, then."

"Riley Jones."

"Uh huh. And, do you want to tell me who you are and what's going on here, Mr. Riley Jones?"

Riley turned his head and snarled. "We're sheriff's deputies and you're interfering with a criminal apprehension."

"You saying you're a deputy?"

"Yes I am."

"Where's your badge? I must have missed it, or'd you forget to bring it along?"

Riley licked his lips. "We were deputized by the sheriff. This here's an official posse."

He pronounced it "*O-ficial.*"

"*Deputized?* Ain't that interesting as all hell. Remind me now . . . which sheriff's department has jurisdiction way the hell out here?"

"Reno."

"Maybe you need to buy a map, son, but you're a long damn way from Reno."

Riley Jones licked his lips again. "We . . . I mean . . ."

"Take your time," suggested Grey. "Think up a good answer. Let's see how much we both like what you have to say."

On the other side of the rock and above them on the shelf Grey could hear the grunts and curses of the other pursuers. They were discovering that the route taken by the Sioux was considerably tougher than it looked, and it had looked plenty tough to Grey. He would not have tried it without rope and some time to plan.

"Who are you, mister?" demanded the prisoner.

"I'm the ghost of George Washington, father of our country come to reunite these dis–United States," said Grey. He tapped the edge of the barrel against the man's upper lip. "I believe it's your patriotic duty to tell the whole unexpurgated truth."

"Unexpur . . . what?"

"No lies."

"I ain't lying," insisted Riley. "The sheriff's got special powers from the territorial governor himself."

"*Special powers?*" Grey smiled. "Bullshit."

"Hand to God. Like I said, we're out here on official business."

Grey kept his smile in place but he began to wonder if he'd made a mistake. The moral high ground felt a little shaky beneath his feet.

"You want to tell me what that bright blue flash was?"

Riley's eyes shifted away immediately. "I didn't see no light."

"Sure you did. Everyone for twenty miles must have seen it. Bright as can be, right on top of that rock. Right under that Sioux you men have been chasing. How could you not see it?"

Riley squared his shoulders. Very carefully. "What's your interest, mister?"

"In the blue light? Common curiosity."

"No. Why'd you step into something ain't your business?"

"I saw six men chasing one. Didn't look fair."

"You saw six white men chasing a red injun."

"I don't care if he's bright purple. Six to one?"

"You always bring more men than you need to for a posse. That's how it's done."

"Posses usually have someone in charge," said Grey.

"Someone with a badge, and so far I'm not seeing one. What I am seeing is a bunch of damn fools trying to kill themselves while pretending to catch an unarmed Sioux."

Riley sneered. "You're one of them injun lovers, aintcha? Gone sweet on some squaw and now you're standing up for all them savages?"

"You got a lot of sass for someone with a gun halfway down your throat."

A voice behind him said, "And you got a lot of balls drawing on a deputy of the law."

There were two simultaneous sounds. The soft, warning nicker of Mrs. Pickles. And the metallic click as a pistol hammer was cocked back. Then the cold barrel of a pistol was pressed into the hot flesh of the nape of Grey Torrance's neck.

"Ah," said Grey, "crap."

Chapter 3

Turn around slow," said the voice. "Riley, you get his gun."

The little man snatched the Colt .44-40 and shifted to the right to cover him with it as Grey turned to face the newcomer. The second man was as tall as Grey but not as broad in the shoulders and much wider in the hips and gut. Not fat exactly, but solid. He was one of the two men who'd circled behind the rocks. Grey figured the man must have found no way up and come back sooner than expected.

It was Grey's bad luck and, he knew, his own damn fault for being careless.

And, for all that, it was typical luck, as far as he was concerned, because lately he hadn't had much of any other kind. He tended to ride that narrow path between no luck and bad luck.

Now he had guns in his face and all of his luck seemed to have run out.

The big man wore a long-sleeve denim shirt and canvas gloves with the fingers cut off. He stood holding a Manhattan Navy pistol in a rock-steady hand, the black eye of the barrel staring right at Grey. A British Bull Dog revolver was tucked into his belt, ready for a quick grab. He stayed close, his finger inside the trigger guard.

Grey smiled at him, raised his hands and said, "Howdy."

"Shut up and tell me who the hell you are," growled the man.

"Um . . . can't really do both."

"What?"

"I can't shut up and tell you—."

"You trying to be smart?"

"Trying to be helpful," said Grey. "Just like to know which of those two things you'd like me to do."

"Careful, Bill," said Riley, "he thinks he's funny as a catbird."

"Don't matter what he thinks. He seen us going after the stash, and that's too damn bad for him," said Bill. "Get some rope and tie him up. Big Curley's going to want to have a long talk with this dumb son of a bitch."

Grey didn't know who Big Curley was, but he guessed it was the large man climbing up after the Indian. He was positive he didn't want to meet him. Especially when hogtied.

No, the situation was rolling downhill on him. Grey felt like sighing and crawling back into his bedroll to see if there was a way to start the day over again. Instead he remembered a Latin phrase he'd read in an old book written by some Roman fellow named Horace. *Carpe diem*.

Seize the day.

Or, possibly seize the moment. Grey didn't really understand Latin.

The message, though, that was easier to grasp.

When a man stands with his hands raised he is admitting defeat. When, as his granddad once told him, a *smart* man does it, he is preparing for action. Grey's hands were up at shoulder level, raised and slightly forward. Granddad said: "Always place your hands so you can see the back of 'em. That means they're like a couple of snakes, ready to bite. So . . . *bite*. But be quick about it or you're going to die looking like you was giving up, and that ain't no way for a Torrance man to go down."

Without changing his expression, without tensing a single muscle, Grey moved.

He whipped his left hand out and slapped the Manhattan pistol away, swatting it like a scared man swats at a wasp. The barrel swung right at Riley, who yelped and jumped backward. In the same second, Grey snatched the Bull Dog from Bill's belt, used the hardwood butt to chop down on Bill's wrist, and then lashed out with the barrel across the bridge of Riley's nose. Two guns hit the ground—Bill's and Grey's own Colt. Riley staggered back with blood exploding from his nose.

Bill, startled as he was, tried to make a fight out of it. He swung a wild left hook that popped Grey in the side of the head hard enough to make all the church bells from Sacramento to Chicago play the Hallelujah chorus. Grey took two quick wandering sideways steps then wheeled around as Bill came after him. The big man was swinging rights and lefts with every ounce of his muscle and mass behind them. Huge punches, the kind that work really well in barroom brawls.

This, however, was not a barroom.

Despite the pain in his head, Grey tucked his chin down on his chest, hunched his shoulders, covered his left ear with a fist, and raised his elbows into the path of the left haymaker. The inside of Bill's right forearm hit the point of Grey's left elbow. The impact was considerable, but it was muscle against bone, and bone always wins. Grey thought he could hear something go crack inside the big man's arm.

He didn't wait for the pain to hit Bill. He did it instead, clubbing out fast and nasty with the Bull Dog. He banged the butt into the center of Bill's forehead once, twice. On the third blow all of the clarity fled from the big man's expression. The fourth put him down on his knees, and a fifth, this one behind the ear, put him flat on his face.

Grey turned to Riley, who was doing some kind of Irish dance while holding his bloody nose and wailing like a banshee. Grey kicked him in a most unsportsman-like way. Twice. Riley joined his friend on the rocky ground and lay there curled like a boiled crawfish, whimpering like a baby.

Grey blew out his cheeks and tried to shake the bell echoes from his head. That bastard Bill could hit, damn him to hell. He knelt, quickly patted Bill down, then fished a piece of hairy twine from his saddlebag and lashed both men wrist and ankle. Bill was totally out, but Grey crouched over Riley and said, "I took you twice, old son. Get loud, warn the others, or make me tussle with you again and I guarantee you won't like what happens. Are we understanding each other here?"

Riley squeaked something that sounded like a yes.

"Good doggie." Grey patted his cheek and stood.

His Colt had landed on hard rock and there was a scrape along the cylinder, but the barrel was clean and the action was as smooth as ever. He slid it into its holster. The Manhattan had fallen barrel-first into soft sand, so he kicked it away. The Bull Dog was a tidy little five shot and that went into his pocket.

Picky was stamping and pulling at her tether, so Grey soothed her with long strokes down her neck, murmuring calming words to her. In truth, though, he was as nervous as the horse. Whatever was going on here was none of his business, and now he was ankle deep in a mess. It felt like standing on quicksand, and Grey cursed himself for making the kind of move that had gotten him into trouble too many times before.

Far too many times before.

He squinted up to try and see what was going on above him, but none of the players were in sight. He could hear the other members of the posse cursing and shouting to each other, which told him that they hadn't yet reached the summit.

The fact that he couldn't see the other men suggested that they had not spotted him. None of their shouts seemed to involve anything but climbing and getting to the Sioux. As for the Indian, there was no sign of him at all. Not a peep, either.

Grey looked at the two fallen men. Riley glared up at him through painful tears.

There was still time to change the course of what was happening. He could gag Riley, cut the posse's horses free, climb onto Mrs. Pickles, and ride like hell for anywhere but right here.

Yes, sir, there was time to do that.

Grey Torrance stood there, looking up.

He could be halfway to what was left of California before these jokers organized a proper pursuit.

Yup. He could get away clean.

But there was the Sioux.

And there was that damn blue flash. What in Satan's own hell was that?

It had to be something really important or these men wouldn't be trying so hard in such a wretched place as this to get it. Grey worked it through in his mind. He liked puzzles and this one had some useful clues.

The posse was after the Sioux but instead of shooting him, they let him climb the rocks. Why? Was there something he had? Something they needed him to tell them? Something that they wanted to force out of him?

That seemed pretty obvious.

The wanted man kept spitting on the ground and he looked like he'd been rubbing at something. Once, down in New Mexico, Grey had spent a couple of weeks as hired security for a professor from the University of Pennsylvania. The professor had been looking for wall carvings left behind by some ancient tribe of people who lived around Clovis thousands of years before the Indians moved in. He sometimes used spit to clear off old dirt and grime to reveal the faint lines etched into rock walls. Was that what the Sioux was doing? Looking for something hidden? But what? Now was a damn poor time to be doing scientific research, and Grey doubted the Indian was a natural philosopher or any kind of university pencil neck.

But he was looking for something, and he seemed pretty damned desperate to find it.

What could that possibly be? A cache of weapons hidden in a concealed cleft? A trapdoor to a hidey-hole?

Maybe.

Didn't explain the blue flash, though.

So, despite his better judgment and a clear path to safety, Grey Torrance began walking toward the rocks.

He got exactly four steps before there was a second blue flash.

This time it was bigger.

Much, much bigger.

It was so bright that it turned the rocks, the desert, and the sky itself into one big blue nothing.

And it was loud.

For one split second Grey thought that the Sioux had found his weapons cache and had set off some kind of explosive device. There was plenty of it around. Tons of it had been looted from the camps of the barons tied up in the Rail Wars. Just as much had gone missing—along with rifles, ammunition, and even cannons—from both sides of the War Between the States.

That's what flashed through Grey's mind in the first microsecond.

Then the sound of the blast pummeled his head even as the force of it picked him up and hurled him into the juniper tree.

It was not the deep rumble of dynamite or the hiss-pop-boom of black powder.

No. Nothing as ordinary as that.

The sound that screamed inside Grey's head as the blue flash filled the world was the ungodly, tormented wail of a thousand lost souls. The sound of the damned shrieking in spiritual agony from somewhere down in the depths of Hell itself.

He hit the tree and bounced off and crashed into a terrified Mrs. Pickles. The horse reared up and he saw a wild eye and then the blur of a hoof.

Then he saw nothing at all.

He felt himself fall and the screams of the damned followed him all the way down.

Chapter 4

Grey Torrance was lost in a dream of dying.

Of running. Of fighting. Or being killed and rising from his own grave. Of fighting again. With guns bucking in both hands. With the smell of cordite in the air and the taste of gunpowder in his mouth.

In the dream his guns never ran out of bullets. They fired and fired and fired. Heavy slugs ripped into the flesh of the men and women who came toward him. Their flesh ruptured and bled as each round struck them, but they did not fall. Their eyes were not eyes. They were hollow pits in which fires blazed. Black blood ran in lines from their open mouths. Their blood-streaked legs kept working, kept moving, kept propelling their bodies forward into the hail of bullets that exploded from Grey's guns.

They moaned as they came. Not from the pain of his bullets. This was something else, something much worse. It was a deeper kind of pain. An agony of the soul that manifested as a wordless cry of despair that was a more eloquent accusation than any words could ever be. You did this to us, it seemed to say. You damned us.

Grey shouted back at them, denying everything. But even to his own ears his words were false and hollow.

Of course they were right.

They were the damned.

What reason could they have for speaking anything but the unbearable, naked, bloody truth?

Grey fired and fired and the moans of the dead rose above him like a wave of sound that threatened to drown the world.

He tried to back away from it, but the wave slammed down on him and consumed him.

Chapter 5

Did I kill you, white man?"

The voice did not belong to the chorus of the damned.

It did not belong to Grey's memories, either.

It was the voice of a stranger. Soft, cultured, accented. British?

That didn't seem right somehow.

Grey's eyes were closed and he wondered if he was dead. He wondered if the Devil was an Englishman. The world was strange, but that would be the strangest thing in it.

He opened his eyes. It hurt to do it. Everything hurt. His eyes, his skin, his bones. Even his hair ached.

"I—don't know," he said in a dusty croak of a voice. "Am I dead?"

There was a pause, and then the voice said, "Perhaps halfway. Not entirely, I'd say."

The world was out of focus and Grey had to blink several times to coax the shapes into some order that made sense. The mingled blurs slowly coalesced into a canopy of juniper leaves, a wall of cracked sandstone, the docile face of Mrs. Pickles chewing a mouthful of grass.

And the face of a man.

Not a white man. Not black either.

It was a red man.

A Sioux.

The Sioux.

The Indian was smiling. He was a few years younger than Grey; about thirty. He had the broad, long nose and strong chin of a Dakota Sioux, probably an Oglala. Long, gleaming black hair tied in pigtails, eyes so brown they looked black. And . . . steel-framed spectacles. Blue-lensed spectacles, in fact, perched on the bridge of that impressive nose.

"Welcome back to the land of the living, old boy," said the Sioux. "Jolly good to know that I have not, in point of fact, killed you."

The British voice came rolling smoothly off that Indian face.

At least fifty possible replies stampeded through Grey Torrance's muzzy brain. None of them seemed able to adequately address that comment, the man who spoke it, or the circumstances surrounding all of this.

What Grey managed to say was, "What the fuck?"

The Indian's smile widened. "Come on, old chap, let's sit you up."

He cupped the back of Grey's neck and took his arm and eased Grey into a sitting position. Hoisting a piano to the second floor of a dancehall using a cheap block and tackle would have been easier. Grey felt simultaneously flattened and swollen. His body felt like a stepped-on sore toe. He cursed a blue streak as he sat up, and one of the things Grey was good at was cursing. He'd learned some vile phrases from a girl he was sweet on down in New Orleans. Nobody could out-curse Shotgun Ginny. No one. Not even a sailor who'd spent time among Malay pirates. Grey always admired that about Ginny. That, and other things.

The Sioux picked up a water skin and handed it to him. It was Grey's own.

"Take a sip. No, just a sip. Let's not be greedy. Eye to the future, what? Besides, it's all we have."

Grey paused with the mouth of the water skin an inch from his mouth. "*We?*"

The Sioux shrugged. He wore thin deerskin trousers and a hand-stitched breechcloth, but for a shirt he wore a stained and dusty blue U.S. Cavalry blouse that was unbuttoned halfway to his breastbone. Loose bracelets of leather and beads hung from each wrist. He wore a gentleman's bowler hat beneath which a scarlet cloth was wound around his forehead. The cloth looked to be silk, and there was a hint of lace—the kind they put on women's drawers.

"Who," asked Grey, "the hell are you? And while you're at it, how is it we're suddenly friends?"

"My name," said the Sioux, "is Thomas Looks Away of the Oglala Tiyóspaye, grandson of Mahpíya Lúta, better known as Red Cloud to you white men."

Grey stared at him. There wasn't a man, woman, or child in the western hemisphere who didn't know who Red Cloud was. He was one of the reasons the Sioux had won back their tribal lands and formed a powerful nation. Grey said, "Wow."

Looks Away chuckled, enjoying the reaction. "And your name, my dear fellow?"

"Torrance. Grey Torrance out of Philadelphia. My grandfather was a wicked old cuss and isn't worth naming."

Looks Away grinned at that. "Well, we don't get to pick our family, do we?"

"Not usually. But . . . how is it you're an Oglala Lakota and you speak like you just stepped off the boat from London?"

"Very likely because I just stepped off a boat from London."

"Okay," said Grey. "What?"

"Oh, it's a long and rather sordid story," said Looks Away, waving a dismissive hand. "And I don't know you well enough to share the squalid details. The quick version is that I went to England as a young buck in a traveling Wild West show and now I'm back."

"Fair enough. Now let's talk about the '*we*' thing," said Grey. "You're helping me and I want to know why. And while we're at it, what in the hell was that explosion?"

"That's also a long story," said Looks Away.

"Well, I'm too banged up to ride and there's not enough daylight to make it anywhere worth getting. Seems like a good time for a tale." Then another of the clouds in his mind blew away and he jerked upright and looked around. "Hey—where are those other fellows? The posse?"

Looks Away's smile faded. He said, "Ah."

"Ah?"

"The sins of those men seem to have caught up with them."

"You kill them?"

"In a word, yes."

"Jesus Christ. Alone? One against six?"

"Well, you helped by stretching two of them out on the ground."

Grey bristled. "I trussed them up to keep them out of it. I didn't mean for some savage to come along and slit their throats."

"First," said Looks Away in an offended tone, "I am not a savage, thank you very much. Clearly not. Anyone can bloody well see that, the braids and buckskin trousers notwithstanding."

"I—."

"Second, I did *not* slit their throats."

Grey relaxed. "Well, that's—."

"I dropped half a mountain on them," said Looks Away.

"You—."

"Though, technically it's not a mountain, more of an outcrop, I suppose . . ."

"You're sun-touched, aren't you?" asked Grey.

"Mm? Oh, no, sorry. Merely digressing into trivialities. I do that when I'm upset. Killing those men has me quite distraught."

"You ever going to tell me what happened or are you going to simply talk me to death and bury me next to them?"

Looks Away straightened and walked a few paces away. He held his arms wide to indicate the big pile of rocks.

"This is what happened to the posse," he said.

Grey looked and now he saw how much it had all changed. The two shelves were gone, the jutting shoulder of rock was gone, and much of the big outcrop was shattered. Chunks of it were strewn across the desert floor. Only a small patch of ground lay mostly undisturbed and in the middle of it stood a placid Mrs. Pickles munching her grass. All around her were massive fragments of sandstone. Close to where Grey sat was a slab of stone as big as a chuck wagon. Beneath the stone, reaching out from one ponderous corner, torn and flattened, was a wrist in a denim sleeve and canvas gloves with no fingers. A thin trickle of blood had pooled out beneath the flaccid wrist and the pale fingers were curled upward like the legs of a dead tarantula.

"Oh," said Grey. "Well . . . damn."

"The men who were climbing up after me were blown to bits," said Looks Away, and to emphasize the grisly point he nodded toward some red and shapeless chunks that were being swarmed by blowflies. Grey felt his stomach turn over. "The other two, the ones you tied," continued the strange Sioux, "could not get up and run, and so . . . well, you see what happened to them."

"So why the hell are you still alive?" demanded Grey. "And for that matter, why am I? And my horse?"

"Why I'm alive is something we may or may not get around to. A lot depends on who and what you turn out to be. You don't have the look of a cowhand. Your gear suggests a *condottieri* of some kind."

"A con-what-er-what?"

"A free companion, a mercenary, if you will."

"Hired gun is the phrase you're fishing for." Grey climbed very slowly and carefully to his feet. He was positive that even his shadow was bruised.

"Hired gun will do," said Looks Away. Then in an overly casual tone, added, "And did you come to rescue me in hopes of my hiring you for services rendered?"

Grey got it now. This crazy Sioux thought that Grey had been attempting to rescue him from the posse and was caught in the explosion. This act of charity in helping Grey was less altruistic than it appeared and more of a fishing expedition for information.

It was an interesting problem.

Did he play along in the hopes that the man would share his secrets? And would there be some gold attached to the deal? Or, was it better to come right out and tell him the truth?

The third option, under other circumstances, would have been to hogtie the Indian and use a little muscle to open him up. Grey had done that sort of thing before, but he dismissed it. He wasn't really that kind of person.

Not anymore.

He stalled by stretching his aching muscles and inspecting his horse. The Sioux waited him out. Grey noticed that there were several pistols and two rifles laid in a row on a flat stone. Within Looks Away's reach. Not at all close to Grey.

Fair enough.

In the end, Grey blew out his cheeks and exhaled a great sigh and decided to be straight with this man. He owed him something for dragging him clear and giving him water. The Indian could have cut his throat and made off with Mrs. Pickles. Or simply stolen the horse and left him here to burn in the desert sun.

So, he turned back to Looks Away.

"Truth is, I'm not a gun for hire. Not at the moment," he said. "And I didn't step into this mess to make a buck. Not that I haven't done that sort of thing before."

Looks Away was not smiling now, and he edged closer to the guns. "Then why did you interfere?"

"Six against one," said Grey.

"Uh huh. Six white men against one red savage. Is that the kind of math you want to sell? That the unfairness and intolerance sparked your inner nobility to take action?"

"Something like that."

Looks Away studied him.

"And," said Grey, "there was that blue flash."

Now the Indian smiled.

"Oh yes," said Looks Away. "There was that."

Grey said, "I heard something when whatever it was blew up."

"Did you?"

"Sounded like all the devils in hell screaming at once."

Looks Away said nothing.

Grey said, "This is about ghost rock, isn't it?"

"Yes," said Looks Away. "And . . . no. It's not as simple as that."

"In my experience," said Grey, "it never is."

Chapter 6

Which is it?"

Looks Away cleared his throat. "How much do you know about ghost rock?"

"A bit, same as most folks. Some kind of rare stone. Burns like coal, but hotter. With more oomph."

"An understatement."

"Lot of folks want it," said Grey. "Lot of folks been killed over it."

"In my experience," said Looks Away, "people will kill each other over almost any damn thing. In England, in Limehouse, I saw two men slash each other to red ribbons over a slut with venereal disease and a face like the south end of a donkey. People kill over scraps of food. And, as a member of the Sioux, I can tell you what you white folks have been willing to kill for."

"Okay, so people are a mess. Not exactly telegraph news. But I've seen ghost rock up close. Twice. It's black with white veins running through it. It doesn't burn with a blue light, at least not that I've ever heard of."

"Yes, well there are more things in heaven and earth, Horatio."

"That's from that fellow Shakespeare," said Grey.

Looks Away laughed. "A literate cowboy. I am in awe."

"A funny Indian," said Grey. "I'm . . . I'm . . ." He stopped and rubbed his eyes. "There was a joke there but my head hurts too much to go looking for it."

They stood for a moment, looking at the smoking pile of rocks. The only sound was Picky munching quietly.

"So," said Grey, "care to tell me about all this? Posse. Ghost rock. Explosion. Start anywhere."

Grey walked over to one of the boulders, reached behind it, and came out with two heavy saddlebags. "These no longer have owners."

He placed them on the ground, squatted down, opened them, and began removing tin cooking pans, a sack of beans, smoked beef, and a silver flask that sloshed when he shook it.

"It's a long story that shouldn't be shared when either hungry or sober," said Looks Away.

Grey smiled. "Fair enough."

They worked together to build a fire on the side of the rock pile farthest from the corpses. From the surviving horses of the posse they found enough water to cook beans and soften the beef, and even enough to make pan biscuits. As the sun tumbled behind the far mountains they settled down to wash badly cooked food down with even worse back-alley whiskey. As he drank, Thomas Looks Away told his story.

"I grew up in the Sioux Nation, of course," he said. "Learned all of the traditional skills from my father and grandfather, and from more uncles than I can count. Hunting, fishing, stalking, fighting. I even did some fighting with patrols along our borders. I'm sure you know how it is, old chap—in this world there's always someone who wants what you have and is willing to take it rather than buy it or earn it."

"So I've heard," agreed Grey with a laugh. They tapped tin cups and washed that truth down with whiskey.

"When I was about twenty, two things happened," said Looks Away, drifting back into his tale. He removed his bowler hat and as he spoke, slowly turned it like a wheel, running the brim between thumb and forefinger.

"First, I had a wee bit of a dispute with one of my cousins. An irascible fellow named Big Water. Hard words were exchanged, then there was a spot of violence, and, well . . ."

"What was the dispute about?"

"What else?" said Looks Away. "What do men always go crazy and fight about?"

"Gold?"

"Women," corrected the Sioux.

"Fair enough."

"We both liked the same girl. Big Water had land, horses, lots to offer."

"And you—?"

"Not to be too indelicate, but I helped her get into the family way, as they say."

"*Helped?*"

Looks Away gave him a roguish grin. "She was a very lovely and painfully naïve little thing."

"And—?"

"Big Water took it amiss."

"Amiss. Is that where the violence came in?" asked Grey.

"It was. I left Big Water a tad dented and felt it was a prime opportunity to see the world. Which I did. I drifted east and in Philadelphia I met a chap who was putting together a Wild West show to take to England. Splendid little fellow by the name of Barnum. He made me a rather enticing offer and before I could say 'heap big wampum' I was on a ship to London. Spent many happy years there playing everything from the Noble Savage to the Wild Savage to the Last of the Red Men. Often in the same show. Along the way I took the opportunity to better myself and even got a degree from Exeter."

"A degree in what?"

"Natural philosophy, with an emphasis on chemistry and geological studies."

Grey sipped his whiskey. "You're a scientist?"

"Amateur natural philosopher I believe is the correct phrase."

"Well . . . holy shit."

"Indeed."

"Let me guess," mused Grey, "that's what brought you back to America. Chemistry and geological studies, I mean. You're prospecting?"

"Correct."

"For ghost rock?"

"Also correct," said Looks Away.

Night had fallen around them like a blanket, leeching away the heat of the day and leaving in its place a moistureless cold. Somewhere out in the blackness something scuttled across the dry sand. Above them the sky was littered with ten billion stars, but even these burning suns looked like chips of ice scattered on a piece of black basalt. Grey got up and took a blanket from his saddle, wrapped it around his shoulders and sat back down. As an afterthought, he walked over to the rock on which Looks Away had arranged all of the guns. He retrieved his own, examined the barrel by firelight, blew through it, dumped out the bullets, and thumbed them back in after inspecting them for grit. Then he slid the gun into its holster. He did not do it with any of the fancy flourishes some men use. Grey was a skilled gunman but he wasn't a showman. He picked up Riley's little derringer and slipped that into his pants pocket. His knives were there, too, and he returned them to belt and boot sheaths. Then he went and sat back down. He was aware of Looks Away watching him with intelligent dark eyes. The Sioux made no comment about Grey taking back his weapons, and that told him a lot about their relationship. Maybe not yet friends, maybe not allies, but definitely two men at peace with one another. Fair enough.

"That explosion," said Grey as he picked up his tin cup, "wasn't ghost rock."

"It was and it wasn't."

"You deliberately beating around the bush, or is that a British thing you came back with?"

Starlight sparkled from Looks Away's white teeth. "A bit of both, I dare say." He poured more whiskey into their cups, stared into his for a moment, sipped, sighed, and began speaking. "A lot of people are studying ghost rock, you know. Not just here in America, but all around the world. It's not unfair to say that it is the most significant scientific discovery of the nineteenth century. It's potentially one of the most important scientific discoveries of all time, and I am not exaggerating when I say that. Of all time."

He let that hang in the air between them. Grey waited.

"Ever since ghost rock was discovered in the Maze out in California," continued the Sioux, "everyone has been looking for it. Men have actually left gold and silver mines in order to search for the ore. Think of that. Abandoning a working gold mine in order to find that damnable black rock."

"Why shouldn't they? Gold can't make a ship sail faster than the wind," said Grey. "It can't make a gun fire twenty times faster than a man can work a rifle lever. It can't make a carriage run without horses."

"Exactly," said Looks Away, nodding. "Ghost rock is all of that and more."

"Hard stuff to find, though. Nowadays, I mean. After the big Quake of '68, folks were finding bits of it everywhere including their own backyards; the supply seems to have dried up."

Looks Away shook his head. "That's not precisely true. A lot of people went to great—very great, I dare say—effort to collect as many pieces of it as they could.

Much of that sundry supply was begged, borrowed, bought, or stolen."

Grey nodded. "Mm. I've heard tales. I also heard they found a crapload of it in the Black Hills. Why aren't you looking for it there?"

"Would that I could," said Looks Away glumly. "But for reasons I've already explained I am persona non grata there. There is a considerable price on my head."

"Really? Exactly how badly 'dented' was this Big Water fellow?"

"Mmmm . . . let's just say that he won't be fathering any children."

Grey winced. "Ouch."

"In my own defense, he did start that fight."

"Uh huh." Grey sipped some whiskey. "You can't get Sioux ghost rock. And . . . ?"

"And it doesn't entirely matter," said Looks Away. "As it turns out it isn't necessarily how much ghost rock one has . . . but how you use it."

"Does this get us around to a big blue explosion?"

"It does."

"Will I like the explanation once we get there?"

"Probably not."

"Are you going to tell me anyway?"

"It seems likely." Looks Away poured the last of the whiskey into their cups.

"Guess I'd better hear it."

Looks Away nodded and took a breath to tell the rest of his tale.

But suddenly he jerked erect, stared past Grey with huge, terrified eyes, and uttered a scream that split the desert darkness into a thousand jagged pieces.

A moment later pale, blood-streaked hands reached out of the shadows and grabbed Grey Torrance and jerked him backward into the night.

Chapter 7

Grey was dragged down and pulled across the rough ground by hands that were as cold as ice. He bellowed in rage and fear and punched upward over his head, trying to hit whoever had him. He felt his knuckles strike home, felt flesh and bone yield to his blows, heard the thud of each punch, but there was no cry of pain, no release from those hands.

His hand flashed toward the handle of his pistol but his fingers only brushed the wood grips as the Colt fell into the dirt.

Grey could hear Looks Away shrieking in terror behind him. Awful growls filled the air.

Desperate and frightened, Grey flung himself backward from the hands that held him, trying to use force and dead weight to stop the pull, and for a moment he saw two figures bent over him. They were silhouetted against the stars but the firelight glowed on the edges of their features. Men. Two of them, dressed in torn clothes, hatless, their hair stringy, their faces dead pale in the bad light.

Their eyes . . .

Empty.

Totally empty.

Not like the hollowed sockets of skulls, but empty of all human light, all knowing, all intelligence. Looking into those eyes was like looking into polished glass.

Their skin was ruined. Slashed and torn. Blood was caked on their cheeks and jaws.

But the wounds did not bleed.

The blood looked old. Dried.

Their flesh hung in streamers and it should have bled.

Should have.

Should have.

Fear stabbed itself through the front of Grey's chest and clamped icy fingers around his heart.

He *knew* these men.

For one terrible, fractured moment Grey was somewhere else entirely. For a stalled heartbeat of time he was not in the Nevada desert at all, but on the muddy banks of Sunder's Ford, deep in the heart of the Confederacy. In that moment the faces leaning over him were those of Corporal James and Sergeant Howell.

They were the faces of dead men.

Of men Grey had failed long ago and left behind.

The ghostly faces of the spirits who dogged his backtrail. The accusing faces of the specters he saw in dreams every night of his life. The ones a fortune teller in Abilene warned him were following and who would haunt him until they caught up with him and dragged him down to Hell.

That's what he saw in one dreadful moment.

And then the moment passed.

He was instantly back in the desert and these were different men. Not James and Howell. Not old friends whose blood was on Grey's soul.

No.

This wasn't them.

But Grey knew them just the same.

Yes, he did.

Not five hours ago he had seen one of these men try to climb a tumble of rocks and do it badly, holding a gun in one hand and reaching for handholds with the other.

And he'd seen the other man stand at the bottom of that rock pile and yell curses and taunts up at his friends.

Their names floated through shock and horror to his mind.

The man who held his left arm was Big Curley.

The man who held his right was Riley Jones.

They stared at him with empty eyes.

The eyes of men who could not be doing this. The eyes of men who should be nothing more than buzzard meat. Feasts for the worms.

But they held him and they bent toward him, their mouths filled with broken teeth.

Open mouths.

Hungry mouths.

Dead mouths in dead faces.

Bending down toward him.

Chapter 8

Something snapped in Grey Torrance's mind.

It was like the chain between handcuffs yielding to inexorable force. It was like a worn piece of rope breaking when a bull jerks his head with absolute defiance.

Like that.

Big.

Sudden.

And all at once Grey felt his muscles release from the frigid rigidity of terror and become loose, become his own again. As the biting mouths of the two dead men dipped down toward his face and throat, Grey moved.

With a howl of fury he rolled onto his shoulders, bending his knees, bringing his feet up, forcing them between those cold hands and his own flesh. Then with a savage grunt he kicked up with all his force. His boot heels smashed into the face of Riley Jones and burst it apart. Shoe leather and hobnailed heels obliterated the chin and sent the remaining teeth flying. The steel spurs ripped bloodless flesh from the raw gray muscle. One eye popped like a grape.

The thing that had been Riley Jones merely staggered back, his neck tilted backward at a curious angle.

The other one kept coming, though.

Grey bashed aside Big Curley's hands, fell over onto his hip, and hammered at the man's knees and calves with a brutal one-two-one-two. Bone cracked like gunshots and the big deputy canted sideways on a leg that looked like it now had two knees, both of which were bent the wrong way. His big body fell hard, and Grey had to roll sideways to keep from having it land on him.

But even as Big Curley crashed to the ground, his hands kept snatching and trying to grab. So did Riley, despite his smashed face. As if pain meant nothing at all.

Nothing.

Grey kicked himself backward, got to heels and palms and scuttled away from the two men.

If "*men*" was even the right word.

Over the course of a hard life Grey Torrance had been shot, stabbed, slashed, kicked by a horse, and thrown from a moving wagon. He'd broken bones and torn his flesh, and though he was a tough and stoic man, he knew for certain that he could not have endured this kind of damage and not reacted to it.

No one could.

No man could.

The two things crept and thrashed along the ground toward him.

Grey dug frantically into his pocket and came out with the two-shot derringer. He thumbed the hammer back and as Big Curley lunged at him Grey fired. The bullet caught the dead man dead center in the chest.

Big Curley twitched.

That was it.

As the bullet punched through his sternum and into his heart, the man merely twitched and grunted.

And kept coming.

Now the world seemed to be completely falling off its hinges. Grey had one round left and he jammed the barrel into the big man's eye socket.

"Die, you son of a bitch!"

He fired.

The close contact muffled the sound of the shot,

rendering it soft and wet. The gun was low-caliber and the bullet did not have enough force to crack its way out of the back of Big Curley's skull. Instead it bounced around inside the vault of hard bone, plowing trenches and tunnels through the man's brain.

All at once the hungry mouth fell into slackness, the body instantly flopped down. There was no intermediary process. One moment Big Curley was trying to grab and bite, and in the next he was limp meat.

Grey stared at the corpse, his relief momentary and polluted by confusion and doubt.

Then Riley Jones flung himself at Grey, ripping and tearing with his claws like a wildcat. From between the torn lips and past the broken teeth came a steady screech like an enraged mountain lion. That scream was not born in any human soul, Grey knew that at once. This was something else.

Something worse even than a dead man who didn't want to stay dead.

This was a monster.

Monster.

The word was jammed sideways into Grey's head as he fired the empty gun over and over again as if will and need could put fresh cartridges into the chambers. Riley swatted it out of his hand and began scrabbling at Grey's throat, trying to tear through the skin with cracked and torn fingernails.

"Get off!" cried Grey as he began punching the man in the face.

Over and over again.

He could feel bones grind and break. He saw the man's face lose what little shape it had. He could feel his own hand beginning to ache, to swell.

With a savage grunt he brought his knee up into Riley's crotch. The blow must have done damage, but it did not stop the thing. Grey grabbed him by the wrists and kicked upward again. Harder. Faster. And as he did so he heaved and twisted.

Riley went up and over and down spine-first onto a slender piece of rock that stood up like the spine of a sailfish.

There was a horrible wet crack as the impact bent him nearly in half the wrong way.

Grey scrambled around to his knees and stared.

Riley kept thrashing.

With a shattered face, with a broken back, with the injuries from the blue explosion still marking every inch of his body, the man kept thrashing.

"Why won't you die, you son of a bitch?" snarled Grey. He snatched up a stone as big as a bread loaf, raised it over his head and with both hands slammed it down on Riley's head.

Again.

And again.

And again.

Until there was no more head to hit.

The kicking legs and whipping arms flopped down and the insane little man lay like a fallen scarecrow. Limbs and body bent in all the wrong ways.

Dead.

Dead at last.

Grey knelt there, chest heaving, sweat running in lines down his face, the bloody rock still clutched in his hands.

He heard a sound, a scuff, and he turned, fearing what was coming for him out of the shadows.

He raised the rock.

His mouth formed the words of a prayer he'd learned long ago and thought he'd forgotten.

A prayer to Mary. Something sinners say when they know they're about to die.

". . . be with us now and at the moment of our deaths . . ."

The figure lurched from shadows into a spill of starlight.

Staggering, torn, pale, and gasping.

A long dagger hung from one hand. Blood, black as oil in the bad light, dripped from the wicked blade.

"Are you alive . . . ?" whispered Grey. "Or have the doorways to hell been kicked open for all times?"

The face that looked down at Grey was filled with shock and horror.

But there was light in those eyes.

Human light.

"Hell?" murmured the man. "I think we're both in hell."

The knife fell from his hand as Thomas Looks Away sank to his knees and vomited onto the desert sand.

Around them the night was vast and black and it loomed above them like the ceiling of some great temple of death.

Chapter 9

For three long minutes the two of them did nothing. Said nothing.

Grey was barely able to think.

Breathing was difficult enough to manage.

Looks Away fell over onto his side and rolled away from the mess on the ground. He lay gasping like a fish and staring up, his hands clamped to the side of his head.

It took a long time, but Grey finally climbed to his feet. It required about as much strength and engineering as hoisting a freight train out of a gully. He tottered over to his Colt and picked it up. The barrel was clogged with sand, so he thrust it into the holster and walked painfully past Looks Away to the rock where the other guns had been laid out. He paused, looking down at the two corpses that were sprawled at the edges of the campfire light. Two more of the posse. One was missing his arm at the shoulder, but the wound was bloodless. A souvenir of the explosion? Grey thought so. The man had a knife buried to the hilt in his right eye socket. The other man's head was crushed by a stone, almost exactly like Riley. The sight was sickening, and Grey turned away.

He picked up the Manhattan pistol, opened it to inspect the barrel and loads, closed it, walked over to where Looks Away was struggling to sit up.

The Sioux looked up and gave Grey a weary, troubled smile. He half laughed and shook his head. "By the Queen's lacy garters . . ."

Grey did not smile.

Instead he kicked Looks Away in the face.

Very hard.

The man flopped backward and Grey swarmed atop him, stepping on Looks Away's right bicep and pinning him down with a knee to the chest.

"What the bloody hell are you—?" began Looks Away, but Grey placed the barrel of the big Manhattan right between the Indian's dark eyebrows. Right at the bottom edge of the red lace bandana.

"No more bullshit," he said in a deadly whisper. "I have been half blown up and attacked by men who all sense and logic tell me are already dead. I don't know what's going on but I believe you do. And by God and all His angels, Mr. Looks Away, you are going to tell me right damn now."

Chapter 10

Looks Away told him.

They sat on opposite sides of the campfire. All of the guns were arranged around Grey. He'd patted the Sioux down and taken everything he had except his clothes.

"This is about ghost rock," said Looks Away, rubbing at the heel-shaped bruise on his face. "I was about to explain it all to you when we were attacked. You didn't have to kick me."

"If you are waiting for me to apologize, then I hope you have a comfortable seat," said Grey. "Besides, it made me feel good. Tell me how this is about ghost rock."

Looks Away grunted. "It's complicated."

"Uncomplicate it for me."

"Have you ever heard of the word 'metallurgy'?"

"Sure. Something to do with metals and such. Making alloys, all that."

"All that, correct. The term was originally used by alchemists because some of the properties of various metals and ores were believed to be magical."

"I don't believe in magic," said Grey, but his comment sounded false even to his own ears. He saw the expression his tone put on Looks Away's face, so he amended. "I believe in God and suchlike. And . . . ghosts. I believe in ghosts. Not sure about a lot of the rest of it. Witches and like that. Met a couple of fortunetellers who were fakes. Maybe one who had something." He shrugged. "I met a whole lot of people who think ghost rock is spooky. The sounds it makes when it burns. Like the screams of the damned."

The Sioux nodded. "Do you think that's what it is?"

"Don't know. Only heard it burned twice. Sounds weird, sure, but if I'd never heard a kettle boil or a steam engine scream I'd have thought that was the sound of the Devil, too."

"There is perhaps a stronger connection between ghost rock and the spirit world than you might think," said Looks Away slowly. "You see, inventors, industrialists, and natural philosophers the world over have been experimenting with the ore to harness its power. There's really nothing like it anywhere."

"So I've heard. So what?"

"So, just as scientists are exploring its potential, so are alchemists."

"How's that work? I thought all that alchemy stuff was hokum that died out a hundred or so years ago."

Looks Away laughed. "Died out? Not even close. It was largely discredited, to be sure, and fairly so because most alchemists were charlatans. Like most fortune-tellers and other snake oil salesmen."

"Con men," suggested Grey.

"Con men," agreed Looks Away. "However, just as you've met one fortune-teller who you thought might have something, there are a precious few among the world's remaining alchemists who also 'have' something. I refer, of course, to those who have made a serious study of what some call 'the larger world.'"

"The spirit world, you mean?"

"Yes and no. For most people the spirit world is a label they slap on everything from ghosts to demons to, say, vampires and werewolves. Most of it is fairy stories for gullible children. Gullible adults, too, I suppose."

"But—?"

"The larger world, as viewed by those select wiser alchemists, refers to a universe where science and magic may well be two sides of the same coin. After all, our science of this modern age would look like magic to someone a century ago." He touched his chest. "Imagine what the first peoples here in America thought of the Europeans with their great wooden ships and muskets. Think about it. Imagine that a red man who is a skilled hunter and tracker, one of the best of his tribe, who is deadly with a bow and arrow, encounters a man in a metal chestplate and helmet who can point a stick and with thunder and lightning, strike down a great elk a hundred yards away. Tell me that red man did not believe he was witnessing true magic."

Grey thought about it, nodded.

"To the settlers who crossed this continent in covered wagons barely half a century ago," continued Looks Away, "what would the steam locomotive have been like? Twenty years ago the thought of a horseless carriage was an impossible pipe dream, and now, with the power of ghost rock, you can see them on the streets of New York and Philadelphia and Boston."

"I see where you're going with that."

"Now, step back and look at ghost rock through the same telescope. It screams when it's burned. Sure, we all see that and it's rather shocking. The weak-minded always want to ascribe something supernatural to the things they don't understand. History tells us that. But what if all we're witnessing is merely an aspect of science that has not yet been measured and quantified."

Grey thought about it, but he slowly shook his head. "I'll buy that as an explanation for why ghost rock sounds like the screaming damned. Chemicals hiss and pop and make all sorts of sounds. Everyone knows that. But that?" He stabbed a finger toward the corpses that were now laid in a row and weighted down with rocks. "Tell me how your science—or alchemy, for that matter—explains dead men getting up and getting rowdy? I shot one of those fellows in the heart and he didn't blink. You hear me? He did not even blink. He just kept grabbing at me, trying to bite me. If that's science and not magic, then everyone's been calling it by the wrong damn name all these years. Maybe it's all magic. That or this is a madhouse and we're all inmates."

Looks Away nodded. "And now you get to my problem."

"Pardon?"

"Until tonight I was fully invested in the camp of people who believed that the qualities of ghost rock were nothing more than science that was not yet understood." He paused and regarded the corpses, then shuddered. "Now I don't know what I believe."

"Welcome to the rodeo," said Grey. "We're both riding the same bucking bronco here. Want to tell me what was the blue flash, and could it have caused this?"

"That's the point where all of my beliefs trip and fall on their face, old chap," said Looks Away. "You see there was a man I met while at university in England. An American scientist and inventor. Rather a brilliant fellow by the name of Percival Saint."

Grey frowned. "Why's that name so familiar?"

"He was an advisor to President Grant," said Looks Away.

"Oh, hell yes. He was a slave as a kid, but he escaped. Took a bunch of other slaves with him and went north."

"That's the man."

"The papers said he went to college and got himself a degree. Went back down South after the Confederate States of America abolished slavery and helped build some factories and design some new farm equipment.

I heard that he's been making weapons, that he's a gun maker."

Looks Away sniffed. "Calling Percival Saint a 'gun maker,'" he said with asperity, "is like calling Michelangelo a 'house painter.' Doctor Saint has more doctorates and degrees than you've had hot dinners. He is a great, great man."

"Well pardon the living hell out of me."

"I met Doctor Saint when our Wild West show visited Sweden. We gave a special performance in October for the birthday of his friend and colleague Alfred Nobel."

"Dynamite Nobel?"

"The same. Our show was held at the Bofers Ironworks factory in Kariskoga where they make the steel for certain types of cannons. The factory used several of Nobel's metallurgic techniques there, and there is a rumor that he plans to buy the company. We gave a show for the staff and several hundred guests. I had arranged with Doctor Saint and Mr. Nobel to use some of their experimental chemical combinations to create a fireworks display that served as our finale. It was all quite exciting."

"And you're drifting away from getting to the damn point," growled Grey.

"Not really. It was during my discussions with Doctor Saint and Nobel that the subject of ghost rock came up. This was a few years ago, mind you, during that big surge to find the stuff. Naturally both men had a great interest in the rock and its potential. They both saw it as a great weapon of war. They had each done some, shall we say, casual experiments with it."

"*Casual?*"

"Did you hear about the big fire in Chicago some years back?"

"Who hasn't? The Great Fire they call it. Back in '71."

"The very one."

"What about it?" asked Grey. "I thought a cow started it. Kicked over a lantern . . ."

"Balderdash. There was no cow in the story at all. At least not one that mattered."

"I don't—."

"All of the reports by those who witnessed the start of the fire," continued Looks Away, "described a great flash of light that was like nothing they'd ever seen." He smiled. "Care to guess what color that flash was?"

Chapter 11

Grey narrowed his eyes. "Now we're getting somewhere. This blue flash ... it's some kind of ghost rock weapon? Is that what I'm pulling from your mosey-round-the-mountain way of getting to a goddamn point?"

"In a word," said Looks Away, "yes."

"Shit. A weapon that raises the dead?"

"Ah, no ... that would be what Doctor Saint and Mr. Nobel refer to as an unfortunate and unforeseen side effect."

"Unfortunate hardly seems to come close to it."

"No," said the Sioux, cutting another uneasy look at the corpses, "it does not."

Grey got the fixings for coffee from his saddlebag. "Might as well have something to keep us up while we talk this through," he said. "I sure as hell don't plan to get any shut-eye while the sun's down."

The Sioux made a face. "I seriously doubt I will ever sleep soundly again."

"Blue light," prompted Grey.

"Depending on how pure a sample of ghost rock is, it can burn with different colors," explained Looks Away. "If there are trace amounts of calcium chloride the fire will burn orange, if lithium, it will burn red, and so on. What Saint and Nobel did was combine ghost rock with chalcanthite, which is a copper mineral. They found that by compressing tiny bits of ghost rock in a ball of cupric chloride, they get a burn of very short duration but with an exceptionally high energetic output. This discharge of energy can be directed through a metal tube such as a rifle barrel lined with copper to make a projectile. It can also be super-condensed within a sphere made of alternating layers of copper and steel to create a high-impact aerial grenade. Are . . . are you following any of this?"

"I'm limping along your backtrail, but, sure, I get the sense of it. Put a bead of ghost rock in a copper ball and you get a big bang."

"Because chalcanthite is pentahydrate—meaning it contains elements of water—the resulting discharge creates a vapor of a distinct azure hue."

"It's blue. Got it. Stop showing off," said Grey, "and get to the part where it raises the dead."

"Ah," said Looks Away, "that's the part that neither Doctor Saint nor Mr. Nobel quite understand."

"Are you messing with me, son?"

"Not at all, my good fellow. I am in earnest. And that is where this whole thing began. As with many of the great discoveries in the field of explosive compounds, this revelation began with a bang. A rather large bang, to be precise. It blew out an entire wing of the factory in Sweden and killed sixteen men."

"Jesus."

"The rescue crews were picking through the rubble— and both Saint and Nobel were right there with them," said Looks Away, "as was I . . . when one of the dead men sat up."

"Shit."

"Everyone was delighted at first because they had counted the man as dead and here he was, clearly still alive."

"Except he wasn't."

"Just so. As Mr. Nobel's assistant rushed to help him, the injured man grabbed him and . . . well . . ."

"Well what?"

"He bit the man's throat out. And, um, swallowed it."

Grey was bent over with his arm extended to pour coffee into Looks Away's cup and instead poured it on the Sioux's foot. The Indian screamed and jumped back, and Grey jerked the pot away.

He did not apologize. Instead he stood there, slack-jawed and horrified.

"You said there were sixteen men killed?"

"Yes," said Looks Away, wincing and slapping at his soaked moccasin.

"Did all sixteen—?"

"Yes."

"Mother of God."

"I seriously doubt either God or His mother was there that day," said Looks Away dryly. He pulled off his moccasin and set it on a rock near the fire to dry.

"What happened?"

"There was a bloody great fight, what do you think happened? Sixteen corpses got up and tried to eat everyone in sight. They killed eleven rescue workers and three of Nobel's laboratory staff before they were brought down by a Gatling gun. It took many, many rounds to do the job, too."

Grey just shook his head. "Those fellows who were killed—the second bunch I mean—did they—?"

"What? Oh, no. They stayed dead. Apparently it's only someone who is killed by this new compound that reanimates."

"*Reanimate*," said Grey, tasting the unfamiliar word.

They sat there and looked at the line of corpses.

"What was up on those rocks?" asked Grey. "What blew up?"

"A cache of weapons made to fire the Lazarus rounds."

"The what?"

"The chalcanthite bullets. After the, um, incident at

the factory, Mr. Nobel gave the compound a name. Lazarus. Named for the—."

"—fellow in the Bible Jesus raised up from the dead. I went to Sunday school. Why the hell would Doctor Saint invent a gun that raises the dead?"

"Oh, dear me, no . . . the gun doesn't do that. It's powered by the gas and, well, somehow that name got attached to the weapon. It's one of several radical designs the good doctor devised. There are others, too. Better weapons. The Celestial Choirbox, the Kingdom rifle—."

"Now you're just making shit up."

"I wish I was. Although I could hardly be described as a pacifist, I prefer to avoid violence whenever possible. I came out here to find these weapons because I have some friends who could use some help. But . . . the cache was clearly booby-trapped and when I opened the vault built into the rocks, it exploded, as you saw. I was behind the lead-lined hatch when the bomb went off and was thrown into a Joshua tree, so I survived. The others did not. And, well, there you have it, old chap. That's my story."

"No," said Grey, "that's only part of a story. How'd you get from Sweden to Nevada? Who booby-trapped the cache? Hell, who put it there in the first place? And why was that posse after you?"

"Ah, yes, that's a much longer tale," said Looks Away, "and to tell it I really would like two things."

"What?"

"Some of that coffee. In a cup this time."

Grey poured it. "And—?"

"I would feel far more comfortable sitting in the dark telling tales if I had my gun back, there's a good fellow."

Grey considered the request as he poured his own cup. Then shrugged. "Sure."

Looks Away fetched his Smith & Wesson pistol and knife. He removed a cleaning kit from his saddlebag and commenced cleaning and oiling the .44 American. Grey thought that was a smart idea and did the same with his Colt.

The rest of Looks Away's story was long and he rambled through it much the same as he had with the first part. After the disaster at the factory in Sweden, Doctor Saint and Mr. Nobel made a private agreement to do some quiet but intense research into the qualities of this new ghost rock compound. Doctor Saint returned to the United States and asked Looks Away to accompany him as his laboratory assistant, guide, and bodyguard. They traveled west as far as the rails would take them and then Saint hired a wagon and horses for the rest of the trip to the broken lands of what had once been California. There, at the edge of the new badlands known as the Maze, they set up shop in a tiny town called Paradise Falls. It was a wretched place of poverty, crime, drunkenness, and near starvation. Water was desperately short and Saint made himself a local hero by paying to have several wagons laden with water barrels brought in. And he used his knowledge of geology to locate several promising underground water sources. Those underground wells, unfortunately, ran through lands owned by a rich and reclusive man named Aleksander Deray, about which nearly nothing was known.

Saint worked for many months to mine ghost rock and develop the new Lazarus weapons. The work was slow, painstaking, and more often than not met with frustration and failure. However he did manage to make a few weapons and seven months ago held a public demonstration of his Lazarus rifles. Dignitaries and military officers came all the way from the Confederate States of America to witness the demonstration. Saint had very little of the proper compound to spare, but the brief demonstration he put on was quite impressive. He was asked to accompany the Southern bigwigs down south to meet with the War Department and President Eric Michele himself. The invitation was very flowery, and there were many gifts and medals bestowed upon Saint. There was no actual apology from any of the CSA or even an acknowledgment of the years Saint had lived as a slave when he was a child. No mention of the generations of Saint families who had lived, toiled, suffered, and died on the plantations. The current administration of the CSA was all about the future, and making friends with learned men like Doctor Saint was part of their attempt to move a solid step out of the dark ages of slavery and into the enlightened era of the coming twentieth century. After all, as one of the dignitaries kept saying, our great-grandkids will be alive to see the New Millennium, and by then no one will ever remember anything as old-fashioned as racism and oppression.

"And Saint believed all that?"

Looks Away shrugged at Grey's question. "Hard to say with him. I rather think he's playing along until he finds out what they really want. He is not a deeply trusting soul, bless his heart. And although he is no one's idea of an 'agreeable' or even affable soul, he is forward thinking. If letting go of the past moves science forward, then he will move with the tide."

"So he went?" asked Grey.

"Indeed he did, and according to his last few telegrams, his demonstrations were quite a success. That's when things started to go wrong, however. Instead of coming directly back here, Dr. Saint made several stops to gather special materials for his work. His last stop was supposed to be Salt Lake City, to collect canisters of smoke from the ghost rock factories. However that's where I lost track of him. I don't even know for sure that he reached Salt Lake. There's been no word."

"You think he was ambushed?"

"If he had any trace of ordinary manners or habits I

could venture a guess, but he's an odd duck. He's gone off on his own several times before, often with no advance warning and little explanation once he returns."

"Which means you don't know whether to sit and wait or plant flowers on an empty grave."

"Just so. I wish I'd accompanied him, if only to keep track of him. He could drive an angel to hard liquor. On the other hand, I haven't been bored. He left me behind to continue the work in Paradise Falls and to try and locate new sources of ghost rock ore that was rich in chalcanthite.

"Some weeks ago," Looks Away explained, "while he was out digging in the hills, the laboratory was raided. Most of the equipment was undisturbed, hidden behind very strong locks. But the thieves made off with many of Saint's blueprints and nearly all of his canisters of compressed ghost rock gas. They also took a journal in which were recorded the locations of several of Dr. Saint's remote testing sites. My employer had small caches of supplies scattered throughout this end of the country and did much of his research in spots where he mined for ghost rock, or where he felt he could field-test his devices without attracting attention. Some of them have pretty dramatic effects. I began systematically going from one to the other and found two sites undisturbed, two empty, and two others booby-trapped."

"Someone's trying to kill you?" asked Grey.

"Me or Saint. Hard to say. It's even possible all of this was an elaborate plan to get me out of Paradise Falls."

"Why?"

"That's a different discussion. What concerns me is their methods. When they broke into Dr. Saint's laboratory, they killed the two men we'd engaged as guards. Slit their throats."

"Those men were friends of mine," continued Looks Away gravely. "All I could do was try to catch whomever was responsible, and they led me on a merry chase I can assure you. It would make a ripping yarn filled with traps, double-crosses, and all manner of devious villainy."

"So the explosion wasn't a trap set by Saint?" said Grey, jerking a thumb toward the shattered rocks.

"I . . . don't know for sure. My guess is that it was another trap set for me by my enemy, but it could just as easily have been something set by Doctor Saint. He's generally a humanitarian—after a fashion—but he does not like having his research tampered with. So, yes, it could have been his booby-trap."

"Nice. He could have blown you all the way back to London."

"Well, he wouldn't have expected me to come out here, would he? He does know about the theft of his journal. And it's not like this cache was something anyone could stumble upon."

Grey's reply was a sour grunt. He found that he didn't much like this Doctor Saint. And he was pretty sure calling the scientist a "*humanitarian*" was a bit of a stretch.

"Why was the posse after you? You get some other girl pregnant?"

"Hilarious, but no. Doctor Saint has rivals and some of them are quite vicious. Not at all above hiring a group of gunmen to end the life of one renegade Sioux. Especially one who has been hunting the men who committed the murders at the laboratory. I daresay I was making a nuisance of myself, buzzing around the edges of this and someone decided to swat me." He slapped his palm flat on his thigh.

Grey listened with great interest, but he watched the Sioux's face for any telltale signs of deceit or evasiveness. Nothing showed, however. That didn't mean that the man was telling the truth, the whole truth, part of the truth, or a pack of lies. Grey had played poker and faro at too many tables not to know that some fellows could keep darn near everything off their face. Even so, he had a sense that what he was hearing was at least partly true.

Partly.

He wondered what this strange English Indian was leaving out. The Sioux returned to his narrative.

"I believe I've been getting close to proving who is responsible," said Looks Away as he sipped the dregs of his second cup. "This was no ordinary theft, I'm sure of it. This was well organized and well financed. Someone important wanted that science and now they have it. I was following a lead and came here to Nevada. Someone swore they saw a blue explosion out here in the desert. Naturally I thought that my enemy's people had raided this cache."

"What exactly was out here?"

Looks Away spread his hands. "This was something Doctor Saint made before I came to work with him. It's not much, just a small bunker built into a natural declivity in the sandstone. He enlarged it and built a small testing laboratory. A one-man station. It was all he needed to test the Lazarus weapons without prying eyes. Doctor Saint hid it very well, and even though I had no key, I know his methods. He always creates a hidden lever that is invisible to the naked eye. The man is as devious as he is brilliant . . ."

"You found it, though?"

"I used some of my grandfather's tricks for finding the hinges. It was a clever trap set to trap a clever man."

Grey remembered Looks Away spitting on the ground and nodded. "Let's say, for the sake of argument, that Saint didn't set this trap himself. Is your bad guy smart enough to set this kind of trap? He'd have to know a lot about how this ghost rock stuff works."

"Oh yes," said Looks Away. "And the more I think about it the more I think it was a trap set specifically for me. Particularly if my enemy was, in fact, able to effectively interrogate the guards before he killed them. He had to know that I would keep hunting, so he lured me here with false clues."

"Lured you specifically?"

"Not to blow my own horn, but yes, I daresay he did. It was a trap that brought me to an isolated spot and one that required geological knowledge and Sioux tracking skills to find. The posse was a nice diversion. Oh yes," said Looks Away, "that trap was very much designed to kill me. My enemy is very, very clever."

"Do you have a name for this clever son of a bitch?" asked Grey.

"Not one I can prove," said Looks Away cautiously. "Merely one I've come to view as the only person with both means and sufficient guile."

"Who?"

He finished his coffee, sloshed the last drops into the fire, and listened to them hiss.

"Aleksander Deray," he said.

"Yeah," said Grey. "Pretty much figured. What are you going to do about it? From what you told me, this Deray character sounds like a bad enemy to have. Lots of money, lots of guns working for him, and like most folks he probably doesn't cotton too well to nosy redskins."

Looks Away shrugged. "What can I do? I can give up, head to the Sioux nation and try to make peace with my family."

"Could you?"

"Dear me, no. I'd probably find myself buried up to my chin in an anthill. If I was lucky."

"Maybe you shouldn't have done that much damage to your cousin's privates."

"Water, as they say, under the bridge."

"Or—?"

"Or, I could go back to California, get the evidence I

need, build a case and turn it over to the proper authorities."

Grey looked at him. "*Proper authorities?* In the Maze? Who in the great green hell are the *proper authorities* in that godforsaken place?"

"Have you ever been there?"

"No, but I heard tales. Ever since the Great Quake, there isn't all that much of California left, and what is left is no place for proper people to live. Lots of bad people doing bad things and what little law's out there is owned by someone else. No, son, I don't think you're going to get any help from the authorities."

"Correct. Which is why it'll just be the three of us," said Looks Away.

"You and who else?"

Looks Away gave him a smile that was every bit as cold, lifeless, and murderous as he'd seen on the dead faces of Riley and Big Curley. The Sioux held up his .44 American. "Messieurs Smith and Wesson and your humble servant."

The fire between them popped and hissed.

Grey Torrance said, "You know . . . I was thinking about heading west to see if there's any kind of trouble I can get into."

"Are you indeed?" asked the Sioux, cocking an eyebrow.

"Yes I damn well am."

They grinned at each other while above them the wheel of night ground on toward the coming dawn.

Chapter 12

Dawn found them miles away from the corpses and the blasted heap of rocks.

Thomas Looks Away sat astride a chestnut mare that had once belonged to Big Curley. Since he had no way of knowing what the horse's name had been, Looks Away renamed her Queen Victoria, but by mid-morning that name became unwieldy so he shortened it to Queenie.

Grey gave Picky a thorough going-over to reassure himself that she hadn't been injured by the madness of last night, and aside from a few scrapes and scratches she was fine. Three of the posse's horses had survived the blast, and they trailed behind, laden with all of the supplies, weapons, and water the men could find.

The chill of the night burned off with disheartening rapidity and the sun began to bake the landscape in earnest. The Joshua and juniper trees were spaced too far apart to offer any hope of shade. The horses moved forward, heads down, in a plodding walk that seldom veered from an arrow-straight line except to go around a knot of creosote bushes or avoid a barrel cactus. A clutch of vultures were hunkered down around a dead bighorn sheep, and once a sidewinder whipsawed through the dry grass.

Grey had lived in a variety of climates all over the country, from the deep snows and biting cold of a Missouri winter to a swampy Florida summer, where the only thing that could move through the humidity were mosquitoes. But this desert was how he imagined the landscape of Hell must be. Nothing out here was friendly, nothing offered either comfort or ease, and everything seemed to want to kill everything else. They passed a tarantula locked in mortal combat with a scorpion, and perched above them on a rock was a horned lizard waiting to eat the winner.

The pace was monotonous, and after a while Grey drifted into a doze. But his dreams were haunted and strange.

In those dreams he walked naked across this desert, and no matter how many days or weeks passed, the horizon never got any closer. When he paused to weep or pick at the sun blisters on his skin, he'd hear a sound and turn to see a whole company of ghosts following behind. They were all broken and dismembered. Fresh wounds gaped on their skin and they left behind them a trail of bloody footprints that vanished into the far, far distance.

These were the same ghosts that had followed him for years, but now their company had grown. Riley Jones and Big Curley led the grotesque parade. Their eyes were as black as polished coal; their reaching hands as pale and mottled as mushrooms.

"Grey . . . ," they murmured. All of them, a chorus of spectral voices that sounded almost like empty wind drifting across the hot sands. "Grey . . . come with us. Come join us."

"No!" screamed his dreaming self. "You're dead. You can't be here."

"Come with us," they cried. "Stop running. You can stop running now. It's peaceful here. It's quiet and cool. You don't need to be afraid."

The words were meant to soothe, to lull, but they were spoken by shattered mouths filled with jagged stumps of teeth. Pale tongues writhed like fat worms in those mouths, and it all conspired to tell the lie behind the soft words.

"No," said Grey again, but each time he said it the power in his voice faded, faded . . .

They kept calling him.

"You're not real!" he whispered. "You're dead. For God's sake stop following me. I'm sorry. God knows, I'm sorry. Leave me alone."

"Never."

"For the love of God, leave me in peace!"

Their voices faded as his panic pushed him up through the waters of sleep. As he broke the surface and came awake with a start, he could hear the last echoes of their ghostly chorus.

"There is no peace," they said. "Not for you. Never for you . . ."

Chapter 13

Looks Away snapped awake and cut a suspicious glance at Grey.

"Did you say something?"

Their horses were still moving forward with the implacable plodding gait that kept them all from dying, out in the relentless sun. Both men had slept.

Grey cleared his throat. "No. I was just studying the terrain."

"Studying the terrain," echoed Looks Away. "With your eyes closed?"

"How would you know? You've been snoring for the last three miles."

"Sioux never fall asleep in the saddle," said Looks Away, offended. "I was contemplating our problem and formulating various plans."

"Sure," said Grey. "While snoring."

"Haven't you ever heard of Zen meditation? That was a mantra."

"I don't know what that is, but it sounded like snoring."

"You," said Looks Away, "are welcome to kiss my ass."

"And you are welcome to—."

Grey stopped and suddenly stood up in the stirrups.

"What—?" began Looks Away, but then he turned as well.

They both squinted into the distance. There, so far

away that it was nearly invisible in the heat shimmer, was something that glittered. Sparks of sunlight flew out from it like they would from fragments of a broken mirror, except these were above the ground.

"What is that?" murmured Looks Away.

"I don't know. Something metal, maybe? Or glass . . . ?"

Looks Away cupped his hands around his eyes and stared hard. "By Jove," he exclaimed, "it's a town."

"A town? There's no town way out here."

"There is now, my dear chap. I can see buildings and one structure that looks for all the world like a theater. Or, perhaps a music hall."

"A music hall? Out here in the middle of no-damn-where?"

"So it seems."

Grey shielded his eyes and stared, too, but all he could see were indistinct lumps. And whatever it was that sparkled.

"You can actually see a town?" he asked.

"I can."

"You have damn good eyes, then."

"Well, my people didn't name me 'Looks Away' because I was nearsighted."

Grey thought about that, grunted, shrugged, and sat down in the saddle. "I know we're on a kind of mission here," he began slowly, "but—."

"Oh, absolutely," said Looks Away and kicked his horse in the direction of the town.

Grey smiled at his retreating back. "Well, okay then."

He nudged Mrs. Pickles and followed.

Chapter 14

The wooden sign across the town's main—and only—arch had two words painted in bloodred letters.

FORTUNE CITY

They paused and looked up at the sign. All around those words someone had nailed hundreds of small hand mirrors to the wood, but the glass in every single mirror was cracked.

"Well," said Looks Away, "I'm not a deeply superstitious chap, but that can't be good."

"Someone's idea of a joke," said Grey, but his tone didn't sound convincing even to his own ears.

Beyond the sign, a single street of hard-packed dirt ran between two rows of buildings. There was a livery, a barbershop that also advertised tooth-pulling, a funeral home, a gun shop, a lawyer's office, six separate taverns, and a brothel that rose like a shimmering tower above the others. The brothel was the only building that was more than a single story, and the top floors had long balconies that wrapped around both sides. There were girls in bright colors leaning on the rails. Down on the street level, hard-faced men and women walked or sat or stood in small groups. Maybe a hundred people. And every one of them was looking at the two strangers on horses.

"Friendly looking," said Looks Away.

"Yeah," said Grey, "like a nest of scorpions."

"Nowhere near as charming as that."

Grey couldn't argue. No one was smiling. No one spoke or gestured. They all stood and looked their way.

"Well," said Grey dubiously, "we're here . . . might as well go on in."

"Said the foolish pilgrim at the outer ring of hell."

"Is that a quote?"

"No, merely an observation."

They nudged their horses and entered the town of Fortune. The people on the streets, or up on porches, or standing in windows watched them with hostile and suspicious eyes. Except for the brothel, every store or business in town looked like it teetered on the edge of financial ruin. Windows were cracked, paint peeled from weathered boards, and in the streets there were unshoveled piles of horse dung that were thick with blowflies.

"Charming," murmured Looks Away.

"Seen worse," observed Grey.

"Where?"

Grey couldn't come up with an easy reply and gave it up as a lie.

The people looked no more vital or healthy than the town. They were dirty, their clothes badly patched and mismatched. Warts and dark moles were common among them, and many had scabs or open sores. Several had limbs missing. Hands, arms, legs. Though Grey thought the missing limbs looked more like defective births than injuries. The stumps were smooth. The people were dressed in clothes of black and gray, of desert brown and dried salt. Dead colors for a lifeless town.

Only the whores on the balcony of the brothel looked whole and healthy. They were dressed in frilled silks and satins. Grey and Looks Away stared up at them, seeing every color in the rainbow, from royal purples to soft blues of Pacific evenings to the shocking yellow of new-grown daffodils. Each of the brothel's ladies smiled down at them. Red, red lips parted to reveal white, white teeth.

"Grey," said Looks Away quietly, "do you see any children?"

Grey shook his head. "Not a one. Don't see a schoolhouse, either."

"I know I haven't been to as many American towns as you have, but is that normal?"

"Son," said Grey, "I think we left 'normal' behind somewhere out there in the desert."

"Ah."

"Keep your eyes open."

"Yes," drawled the Sioux. "Capital idea."

They stopped outside of the brothel. There was a name painted on a silk banner draped elegantly above the big batwing double doors.

Madame Mircalla's Palace of Comfort

Grey swung out of the saddle and tied Picky's lead to a post over a water trough. The horse eyed the water cautiously for a moment, sniffed it, nickered in as close to a sound of disapproval as a horse could make, and reluctantly took a drink. The other horses joined her.

Looks Away lingered in the saddle for a moment longer, looking up at the smiling women. Grey followed his gaze. The women were all young, some barely out of their teens. They were all voluptuous, with soft half-moons of enticing flesh rising above the lace trim of their bodices. Their hair was pinned with flowers and feathers. Their skin was totally unmarked by disease or any imperfection.

A voice in Grey's head whispered a warning.

Get out of here now.

But he ignored it. That voice had spoken too often in

his life, and too often he'd listened. Sure, he'd survived . . . but that survival had always come at a cost.

Doing so took some effort, though, and if he wasn't sunbaked, thirsty, and hungry for real food, he might have heeded the warning.

"You coming?" he asked the Sioux.

"With great reluctance and trepidation," said Looks Away as he swung his leg over the horse's rump and dropped to the ground.

Side by side they mounted the steps. It was cool on the porch. One of the women, a fiery redhead with emerald green eyes, rose from a rocking chair and stood between them and the door. She was a little older than the other girls. Maybe twenty-eight, Grey reckoned. Very pretty and she smelled of roses.

"By the queen's garters," murmured Looks Away.

"You fellows are new in town," said the woman, making it a statement rather than a question.

"Brand new," said Grey. "Passing through."

"From where to where?"

Grey hooked a finger over his shoulder. "From back there to somewhere else."

His answer seemed to kindle a light in the redhead's eyes. She nodded, as if appreciating his caution. Then she swiveled her gaze toward Thomas Looks Away.

"Sioux," she said, again not making it a question.

"Ugh," he said. "Me heap big red savage."

The redhead rolled her eyes. "That's adorable. But I heard you talking a second ago. You sound like someone who's traveled a bit."

Looks Away paused, shrugged, nodded. "A bit."

"Then you'll feel right at home. All of us girls here have been around the block a time or two."

It was so saucy a comment that the two men laughed. The woman laughed, but her laugh was a beat slower and, Grey thought, entirely false. Or, maybe it was that she was laughing at a different joke than the one he thought she'd made. The laugh had that kind of flavor to it.

She said, "My name is Mircalla and this place belongs to me and my sisters." Her voice was soft and she had a faint German accent. "Would you like to come in?"

"If there's cold beer, a hot bath, and a rare steak," said Grey, "then we surely would."

"A bath, a beer, and a bite?" laughed Mircalla. "And maybe a bed?"

"I haven't slept in a bed in so long I forget what a pillow's for."

"Slept? Lordy-lord, gentlemen, surely you didn't come here to sleep."

Everyone laughed again. Same flavor as before. Once again Grey was sure there was some bottom layer to her joke that he wasn't quite grasping.

"I think we can accommodate whatever pleases you," said Mircalla. "If it's your wish to enter, then come on in—we can provide everything a man could ever hope to want."

Before he could comment on it, Mircalla turned, shimmied her way between them, hooked an arm in each of theirs, and began guiding them toward the bat-wing doors.

As they stepped across the threshold Grey flinched. It was a strange feeling, but he did not know what he was reacting to. The brothel was well-lighted and cool, there were aromas of perfume and cooking meat, of beer and firewood. The women inside were all beautiful and they all smiled at the two men.

So, why, he wondered, did he suddenly feel that he wanted to run?

To go back outside.

Into the sunlight.

Mircalla's arm was locked around his and he felt that he was not so much walking into the place as being pulled.

Behind him the batwing doors slapped shut with a loud, hollow crack.

Chapter 15

G rey soon forgot his unease. Mircalla ushered them into an alcove furnished with gorgeous chairs decorated with red pillows. Chinese tapestries hung from the walls, their delicate floral patterns edged with gold fringe. Candles burned in silver sconces and there was a Turkish brass table laden with bowls of fresh fruits and tall glasses of amber beer.

Mircalla detached herself from the two men and pushed them down into chairs. She snapped her fingers and two women entered the alcove, both of them carrying ornately patterned plates heavy with steaks and vegetables from which steam rose like pale snakes.

Grey wanted to ask how the food could have been prepared so quickly, but before he could a crystal beer glass was pressed into his hand by a brunette with burning blue eyes.

"This will wash away that desert dust," she said. "Drink . . . go on, drink deep."

He did.

The beer was ice cold and it felt like liquid paradise as it slid down his parched throat. The woman touched the bottom of the glass and guided it so that he leaned back and drained it. She took it and refilled it. Suddenly he had a knife and fork in his hands—both heavy and ornate—and he was cutting into the tenderest piece of three-inch-thick steak he'd ever seen. Blood oozed hot and red from the meat, and when he took his first bite he thought he would cry. It was perfect. Beyond perfect. So hot, so well cooked, so bloody and delicious.

"Oh, God . . . ," he moaned.

Out of the corner of his eye he saw Looks Away with a blonde on his lap. She was cutting his steak for him and feeding him pieces she held between thumb and forefinger. Her nails were long and painted a dark and gleaming red.

He cut another piece of his own steak.

And drank more of the delicious beer.

He was so dehydrated that the alcohol went straight to his head. The alcove seemed to swirl around him as he ate and drank, ate and drank. Drunkenness came over him in waves, distorting everything. With each new glass of beer the colors around him changed. Became brighter, more garish. There was music somewhere and at first it was soft and subtle, but soon it became grating and harsh.

Off to his right, somewhere else, somewhere down a hole or on the other side of the world, he heard a voice. Looks Away. Laughing. Speaking nonsense words.

Then crying out.

In anger first.

Then in surprise.

And in . . .

Pain?

He felt pain, too, but Grey didn't care. Probably a mosquito or a fly biting him on the neck.

Nothing to worry about.

Nothing to care about.

He bent forward to reach for his glass of beer, but something jerked him backward.

Hands?

That was silly. There was no one here but a couple of girls and they weren't strong enough.

He laughed at the thought of whorehouse girls manhandling someone as big as he was.

The pain in his neck became sharper.

Harder.

Worse.

Wrong.

He could feel heat on his throat. Wet and moving.

Running in lines from where those flies were biting. If they were flies.

He tried to speak, to protest, to ask what was happening. The room spun around him. All of the colors swirled and blended together.

"I don't understand . . . ," he heard himself say.

And then he felt himself falling.

Not forward.

Down.

Down down down.

The colors melted into red and then into black.

And then everything was gone.

Chapter 16

Grey Torrance sat in a chair in the middle of the desert.

The sun was high in the sky but the world was draped in shadows. The wind was cold and blew out of the east in long gusts, like the exhalations of some sleeping giant. In the darkness off to the north was a blighted tree and there were hundreds of crows standing silent vigil on the twisted limbs.

Grey stared at the birds and they stared back.

"Pick a card," said a voice, and Grey jumped, startled. He whipped his head around and saw that he was now seated at a table. It was covered with a heavy brocade in red and gold, and the surface was covered with embroidered dragons locked in death struggles with saints and angels. A woman sat across from him. Mircalla. Or at least he thought it was. She wore a veil over her pretty face, so all he could see was the faint outline of her features.

Before her, on the top of the table, was a slender taper in a silver holder, the flame burning with no heat. And beside that was a deck of cards. They were larger than standard playing cards, and the design on the back showed the death mask of some ancient and beautiful queen. Her eyes were closed and blood ran from the corners of her mouth.

Mircalla wore black lace gloves that had patterns of

flitting bats on them. As he watched she drew her hand across the deck and fanned it out in a graceful arc.

"Pick a card," she repeated.

One of the crows in the tree cawed softly. It didn't sound like a bird. It sounded like the plaintive call of a lost child.

Grey licked his lips. They were as dry as if he had been lying all day in the hot sun. And yet he remembered drinking. A lot. And very good, cold, crisp beer it had been, too. So how could his lips be dry and cracked? Why would his throat be filled with dust?

He looked down at his clothes and they were covered with dust and clods of dirt. He no longer wore the jeans, blue shirt, and black leather vest that he'd been wearing since coming west. His clothes were his old cavalry blues. The dirty-shirt blue he'd worn into battle against the Confederates back when he was a young man, barely out of his teens.

His hands, though, were not the hands of a callow youth. They were not the hands he saw every day now, either. They were thin and wasted. The hands of an old, old man.

Or the hands of something else.

Something from which all vitality, all of the juices of life, had been leeched away.

"Pick a card," said Mircalla once more. "Any card."

"I . . ."

"Go on. They won't bite."

She laughed, and it was a grating sound. Like a knife blade dragged across wet glass.

He recoiled from the sound, but even as he did so his withered hand reached out to take a card. It slid from between the others with a soft hiss.

"Turn it over," she said. "Show me."

He turned it over.

It was a tarot.

It was the death card.

Exactly the card he expected it to be.

But Mircalla made a sound of disgust and annoyance. She picked up the card, regarded it for a moment, and then flicked it away into the wind. The card swirled in a circle for a moment and then vanished.

"Not that card," she said.

"Why? It's mine."

"You need to pick a new card," she said. "That one's been used already."

"I don't understand."

She laughed again. "Of course you don't. Pick another card. Pick one that matters to your future."

"My future? But the death card . . ."

"Has already been played. Don't you know that?" She shook her head. "No, you don't know it. I can see it in your face. You think you only dream about the dead. You think they're ghosts of a guilty conscience."

"They are—"

"Of course they're not," snapped Mircalla. "The dead follow you everywhere you go. You know it on a level too deep for your stupid mortal mind to realize, but it's why you always move on. It's why you're never content to stay anywhere. It's why you don't have friends. Not living ones, anyway." She paused. "It's why you don't love."

"I loved someone once . . ."

"And she follows you, too, Greyson Torrance. Your Annabelle Sampson shambles along with the rest of them."

"No!"

"Just because you don't see her doesn't mean that she isn't there." Mircalla cocked her head to one side. "You never even look for her, do you?"

"She's buried in Pennsylvania. I dug her grave. I was there when they spoke the words over her to send her soul to heaven."

Mircalla threw her head back and laughed.

"Heaven? Heaven? Is that where you think the dead go? To heaven to play harps and bask in the glory of an eternal God. Oh . . . mortal man, you are such a fool. Like so many men I have known. Like so many men who still walk this earth. You go about with your guns and your strength and your certainty that the world is what you judge it to be, and all the time the world moves in different gears. You think you understand how the clock-work of the world operates, but you don't. You're like monkeys staring at a fine watch and thinking it's magic made just for you."

She turned, lifted the hem of her veil and spat into the dust. For a brief moment he saw her naked flesh. Chin and cheek and lips. And he recoiled from what he saw. They were not the smooth features of a beautiful woman. What he saw was withered and cracked, mottled like the skin of some ancient mummy. Mircalla dropped the veil and turned back to him.

"You do not understand the world because you are afraid to know its truths," she said. "Like so many men."

"You're not making sense," he protested.

"No? Turn and look." She gestured to the east and he turned with great reluctance. There, in the direction from which the cold wind blew, there were people. A mass of them, shuffling along, moving slowly. Pale faces and empty eyes.

He knew them.

He knew them so well. And she was there. Annabelle. With her torn dress and broken fingernails. Annabelle.

Oh God, Annabelle.

"This is a dream," he said.

"Yes," she agreed. "This is a dream. But they are not."

"What?"

"The dead follow you, Grey Torrance. They have followed you since you caused their deaths, and they will follow you until you have nowhere else to run. And then they will claim you as one of their own. That is the truth of it. It is the truth you have been running from."

"That's madness," he snapped. "You're a witch and a whore and you drugged me. You slipped something into my beer."

He remembered the pain in his neck and touched the spot. His fingers came away slick with fresh blood.

"You sicced something on me. A snake or a . . ."

"My sisters tasted you, mortal man," admitted Mircalla, "and they wanted to drink deep of you. You may be damned and a fool, but there is so much power in your blood. So much. They wanted to drink you like a fine, rare wine."

"Drink me . . . ?"

Mircalla shrugged. "Men have some uses."

"God! What are you?"

"You wouldn't even know if I told you. Mircalla, Miracall, Millarca, Carmilla . . ."

"You're not making sense."

She smiled beneath her veil. "Pick a card."

Without meaning to, without wanting to, he did.

"Turn it over," she commanded.

Grey glanced toward the east. The ghosts were closer now. Time, he knew, was running out. He had lingered too long, even here in this dream.

He turned the card over.

The picture showed a man hanging by one foot, hands bound behind him, dangling upside down from a gallows. Unlike any gallows Grey had seen, this one was made from living wood and fresh leaves sprouted from it. Despite being so perversely executed, the face of the hanging man was serene and composed, and there was a saintly glow around his head.

Mircalla grunted in surprise. "The martyr's card," she mused. "Interesting. I would not have thought it of you."

"I'm no damn martyr," he snapped.

"You do not know what you are, man of two worlds." She laughed and traced the edges of the card. "The man who lives between the worlds. Yes . . . that's what it says about you. You do not belong to either life or death."

There was regret in her voice.

"That means that I and my sisters cannot have you, Greyson Torrance," she continued. "You are exempt, pardoned. Not from your crimes but from my web. So sad. Such a loss. And I suppose you must have your companion, too. My sisters will be so disappointed."

"What are you talking about?" Grey said, and he could hear the pleading tone in his own voice. "Tell me what this all means."

"It means," she said, "that the universe, for good or ill, is not done with you. I am forbidden to claim you. Your journey is not over. Weary, weary journeys lie before you."

"Make sense, damn you."

"Make sense? You ask something very dangerous of a gifted one, my doomed young man. But you ask and the card compels me to answer and so I will." She bent closer and spoke in such a low voice that he was forced to lean closer in order to hear. "You will walk in the land of the shadow, Grey Torrance. Deep into the heart of darkness. Worlds will turn on the wink of your eye. Worlds will fall in the light of your smile."

"I don't understand any of that."

"No," she said. "You were not meant to. The clock has not struck the hour of understanding."

"But—."

She swept the cards from the table and Grey immediately bent to catch the Hanged Man card. He did so, but when he looked up, the table, the other chair, and Mircalla were gone. He shot to his feet and turned. The ghosts were gone, too.

And then, so was he.

Chapter 17

When he opened his eyes the harsh sun of noon nearly smashed him back into unconsciousness.

He flung an arm across his eyes and rolled over, groaning and sick. His head swam and his stomach felt like it was filled with sewer water in which ugly things wriggled and swam. He coughed, gagged, and finally gasped in a ragged lungful of dry air.

To his left he heard a low, weak groan.

Grey turned and saw Thomas Looks Away laying sprawled and sunburnt on the hard ground. Forty yards beyond him stood a tall, crooked cottonwood, and in the sparse shade cast by its withered leaves stood Picky and Looks Away's horse. Just those two. The other horses belonging to the posse were gone. Grey looked around.

The town was gone, too.

He frowned.

The landscape looked familiar. A pair of hillocks, a dead juniper, an untidy row of chaparral cactus. All of that was the same as it was when he and the Sioux rode up to that painted wooden arch on which had been written the word FORTUNE.

But the town was not there.

He got to his feet and as he studied the land he realized that he was wrong about that.

The town was there.

But it was nothing more than broken timbers laying

bleached in the sun. Nothing more substantial than the charred cornerstone of a building was left. It chilled him despite the heat because this was not a new disaster. Those timbers lay like bones of some ancient thing, half covered by the hungry sands. Somehow the town had died and been reclaimed by the desert.

How long ago, though?

Surely he could not have slept for years, and only many years of the unrelenting sun could do this.

"Madness," he said aloud, and even he wasn't sure if he was making a statement about the world or his own mind.

Behind him, Looks Away groaned again. Grey reluctantly turned from the impossible wreckage and hurried over to his new companion. His foot kicked something and he saw that there was a full waterskin on the ground by where he'd awakened. He uncapped it, sniffed it, smelled nothing more than water and heat. He took a pull, and although the water was warm it tasted as pure as new melted snow to his parched throat. The second sip tasted every bit as good.

Grey knelt beside Looks Away, uncertain as to whether the man was alive or dead. Or, if his luck was holding steady, something *else*. He placed a hand on the man's chest, felt the reassuring *thump-thump* of a living heart, and blew out a sigh of relief. Looks Away groaned softly and his eyelids fluttered weakly. Then, much as the Sioux had done for him after the ghost rock explosion, Grey gently cupped the back of the man's neck and helped him raise his head to take a sip.

"Easy now," he cautioned, "wet your throat with a sip first. There, that's good. Now take a real pull."

Looks Away took the waterskin from him and took two long drinks, then, gasping, thrust it back into Grey's hands.

"By God and all the devils in hell," the Sioux growled

as he struggled into a sitting position. "What the bloody hell happened and where the bloody hell are we?"

"God only knows. Or, maybe it's the Devil who knows." Grey stood up. "In either case, take a look for yourself and maybe you can tell me."

He held out a hand and pulled Looks Away up. Together they walked over to where the FORTUNE sign should have been. Pieces of it lay on the ground, the letters faded to ghosts. Grey watched as the other man turned to look at the landscape and then looked once again at the ancient ruins.

"I don't . . . ," the Sioux began, but let the rest trail off into the dust.

"Yeah," said Grey.

They stood there for a long time, neither man saying another word. What, after all, could they say to this? Nothing in Grey's experience provided him with a vocabulary sufficient to put what he felt into words. Sure, there were words for some of this deep in his soul, but none of those words would fit into his mouth. He couldn't have said them at gunpoint. From the strained, frightened expression on Looks Away's face, he was facing the same challenge. So they left it unsaid.

As one they began backing away from the town. Then they turned and ran for their horses.

However as they approached, Grey saw something that twisted an already misshapen day into an even more perverse shape. There, tucked into a fold of his saddle, was a single heavy pasteboard card.

On the back was a painting of the death mask of some ancient queen, her mouth bloody.

Grey did not want to touch it, and his hand shook as he reached for it.

"What's that?" asked Looks Away sharply. "Is that a tarot?"

Grey said nothing. He took the card and turned it over, though he knew full well what would be on it.

A hanged man.

Looks Away saw it and cursed softly.

Without another word the two men got onto their horses and fled toward the west.

Chapter 18

G rey Torrance and Thomas Looks Away did not speak at all for the rest of that day. Grey knew that they should. It was probably important to compare experiences, to try and make sense of everything.

But he did not want to.

He was afraid of the sense that it would make.

The world had become a strange place. It was like stepping into a dreamscape. Or like entering one of the fantasy worlds in the dime novels he used to read back in the early days of the war. Back when fantastical adventures were a way to turn away from the endless bloodshed, the weeks of drudgery and boredom between battles, the aches of walking hundreds of miles, the diseases that came with bad food and worse water. Back then the stories of frontiersmen braving the wilds and ragtag bands of soldiers defending small Texas forts and castaways finding treasure on deserted islands were all ways to step out of the moment. They allowed for hope of something better, even if that hope was nothing more than purple prose in some writer's fanciful scribblings.

That time had passed.

The war never ended. The nation became so fractured. The dream of a grand America had been torn apart by greedy and hateful men.

And there was something else.

Something that lurked behind the scenes of everyday

life. Something people knew about but never talked about.

The world itself had changed.

Not merely the politics or borders. Not loyalties and plans of empire.

No.

The actual world was different now.

Something had shifted.

It was a darker world. And that thought was true even as they rode beneath this blistering sun. The heart of the world was darker. Its soul was darker.

It wasn't the same world he grew up in.

Grey knew that much of this had started when the big quake tore itself along the fault lines in the West and dragged most of California into the thrashing sea. That alone might have been enough to fracture the world. At least the American part of it.

But it was only the start, and Grey knew it. Everyone knew it.

It was simply that people didn't talk about it. The change, the darkness, was like some kind of secret.

Grey thought about that and realized that he had it wrong.

It wasn't a secret. Not really. Nothing as simple as that. It was more like a night terror. Like a monster hiding beneath the bed. It was something that was not real, but could be real if people were unwise enough to say it out loud. To name it.

To accept that it was real.

That's why Grey didn't want to talk about what had just happened. Not with Looks Away, and maybe not even with himself. Every time his questioning mind tried to look too closely, tried to put labels on the things that had happened, Grey forcibly wrenched his thoughts away. He force-fed new thoughts into his head. He considered the landscape. The clouds. He counted and named the number of cities and towns he'd been to. He mentally recited old lessons from his school days, or snatches of poetry. He mumbled the lyrics to old ballads and alehouse bawdy songs. He named all of the women he had ever known and catalogued their virtues.

He did all of that to keep from thinking about the town of Fortune and the women there. If they were women at all. He tried not to think about the hanged man tarot. He tried to erase the memory of Mircalla from his memory.

He tried and tried.

The more he tried, the more he failed.

The more he failed, the more terrified he became.

He caught Looks Away staring at him as they rode, and for three slow paces of their horses, their eyes met.

Then the Sioux shook his head.

And Grey responded in kind.

The terror in his heart grew and grew.

PART TWO

The Maze

———————•———————

*Science is always discovering odd
scraps of magical wisdom and
making a tremendous fuss about its
cleverness.*

—ALEISTER CROWLEY

Chapter 19

They did not speak again until they crossed into California.

Looks Away grunted and pointed to a wooden sign hammered onto a post someone had driven into the dusty ground. It read:

**SINNERS REPENT
ALL OTHERS TURN BACK
THERE IS NO REDEMPTION HERE**

Clustered around the base of the post and piled into a crude pyramid that reached halfway up its length were skulls.

Human skulls.

Some still had scraps of leathery skin or strands of sun-bleached hair stuck to them, but otherwise the bones were white and dry.

"By the Queen's sacred bloomers," said Looks Away. "That's bloody charming."

Grey slid from his horse and walked in a slow circle around the post.

"Over here," he called, and Looks Away jumped down and came over to see. On the far side of the pyramid were two heads that were much fresher than the others. They both wore their skin and hair, both still had milky eyes in their sockets. Withered lips were peeled back from their teeth as if the owners of these heads had died laughing, which Grey knew was a lie. Skin contracts as the moisture is leeched away.

Looks Away cursed softly as he squatted down to peer at the heads. Both of them had long black hair. Both had prominent noses and wore red cloths around their foreheads. Their skin was a slightly ruddier shade than Looks Away's.

"Apaches," said Grey quietly.

"Yes," murmured Looks Away. "And I sodding well know them."

"You what?"

Looks Away bent forward and spat into the face of each Apache. He took his time, hocking up phlegm and firing it off with great accuracy and velocity.

"I take it you weren't friends," said Grey. "But since when did the Sioux and the Apaches have trouble brewing between them?"

"They don't. Not as such. They are no more representatives of their people than I am of mine. This was entirely a personal dispute."

"Who are they?"

"The one on the left there was known as Horse Runner. His companion was Dog That Barks. Rather an obvious name, don't you think? All bloody dogs bark. It's like saying Cow That Moos." He sniffed. "They were renegades from their tribal lands and when last I saw them they were working as hired muscle."

"For who? That Deray fellow?"

"No. They worked for a land syndicate run by a right bastard of a man named Nolan Chesterfield, a nephew of one of the rail barons."

"Which baron?" asked Grey.

Looks Away caught something in his tone and gave him a sharp look. "Why does it matter?"

"It matters to me."

"Not a chum of the barons, I gather?"

"Hardly," said Grey bitterly. "I worked for a couple of them once upon a time. Got well paid, but somehow I always seemed to come up short on the deal. First one I signed on with was that Chinese fellow, Kang. He was my boss for six months."

"Kang? I thought he only hired his own people."

"His own people don't always blend in with people outside of his own crowd," said Grey, shrugging. "And he needed someone solid to protect his lawyers when they went to dicker with some of the other barons. That was me, for a while anyway, but we had some differences of opinion. So . . . then I worked for that witch Mina Devlin."

Looks Away wore a wistful smile. "Ahhh . . . Mina Devlin. I've seen pictures, heard tales. Reliable tales, mind you. I always wanted to make her acquaintance."

"No," said Grey, "you don't. She may be prettier than a full moon over the mountains, but she will gut you and leave you to bleed just for the fun of seeing it. And people say she's, you know . . ." He tapped his temple.

"I believe the phrase is 'touched by God.'"

Grey snorted. "Touched by someone," he said sourly, "but I don't think God was doing the groping."

"Ah. Even so. She is supposed to be a truly passionate woman." He cut a sly look at Grey. "You . . . wouldn't know anything about that now, would you?"

Grey felt his face grow hot and he immediately changed the subject. "You said these Apaches were providing muscle. Muscle for what?"

"Oh, for whatever needed to be done. If Nolan Chesterfield wanted a tract of land so he could lay down some tracks, he had these two fellows—and a couple dozen others who worked with them—drive off anyone who lived there. Drive off or bury."

"Ah. I've met the type."

Looks Away turned to his companion. "I daresay you

have. I've been wondering about that. When you say you've met the type it makes me wonder if you are, in point of fact, the same type?"

Grey smiled. He could feel how thin and cold his smile was. "That's a strange question to ask, friend. Especially after what we've been through and how many miles we've ridden. You slept ten feet from me for twelve nights and now you wonder if I'm some kind of bad-man?"

"Actually, old sport, the thought has occurred to me before," admitted the Sioux. "I've been trying very hard to figure you out. You have a charming demeanor when you want, but mostly you keep a distance. And your face gives nothing at all away. I'd hate to play poker with you."

Grey shrugged. He was very much aware that he let very little of his personality show through in either word or expression. He generally played the role of a saddle-weary but competent gunhand, and that was true enough in its way. There were layers of his soul he did not want peeled back. He dreaded the thought of anyone seeing the real him. The man who had failed, who had betrayed. The man who was certain that his true road led down-hill to somewhere hotter even than this desert. Nor did he want this Sioux, or anyone, to see the fear that was always vying with his courage for control of his life. So, as he had done for so many years now, he kept his face wooden and his gaze flat.

"Besides, the moment always seemed a bit wrong for bringing it all up. Manners, don't you know."

"And mutual protection, let's not forget about that."

"Let's not. However let's not let a shred of self-interest cloud this particular conversation."

"Okay then. If you have a straight question, ask it."

Looks Away sucked a tooth for a moment. Grey noted that the man's hands hung loosely at his sides, well within range for a quick grab for the pistol butt in his stolen holster. The Sioux's fingers twitched ever so slightly. Grey shifted his weight to be ready to dodge as well as draw if this all turned bad.

"I'll ask three questions," said Looks Away, surprising him.

"Shoot."

"That's a rather unfortunate choice of word, wouldn't you say?"

They smiled at each other. They kept their gun hands ready.

"What's the first question?" asked Grey.

"Have you ever been to the Maze before?"

"No," said Grey flatly. "Second question?"

"Abrupt, aren't we?"

Grey just looked at him.

"Very well," said Looks Away. "Are you hunting for ghost rock?"

"No."

"And you're telling me the God's honest truth?"

"Is that your third question?"

Looks Away shook his head. "No."

"Then I've already answered it once. I've never felt the need to repeat myself."

"Fair enough, and therefore I must take you at your word."

"Seems so. What's your last question?"

Looks Away took a breath. "Are you now, or have you ever been, in the employ of Aleksander Deray?"

"I never heard of the man before you told me about him the day we met. And that," said Grey, "is the God's honest truth."

They stood and studied each other, and Grey felt as if something shifted between them. Looks Away had an almost comical way of speaking, which Grey figured was more than half put-on, but there was nothing funny about the keen intelligence in the man's eyes. They were hard, cold, and sharp as knifepoints. Grey would not have wanted to stare into those eyes on a bad day if he didn't have a well-oiled gun within grabbing distance.

"Well then," said Looks Away.

He watched a slow smile spread across the Sioux's face. It looked genuine, and the man appeared to be relieved. Probably not so much at what Grey had said in answer to those questions, but at whatever Looks Away had seen in Grey's eyes.

And Grey found himself making a similar decision about the strange Sioux renegade.

The sun beat down on them and the horses blew and stamped.

"If I've offered offense, my friend," he said, "then please allow me to apologize. I would take it as a kindness and a pleasure if you accompanied me on my little mission. I will, in fact, pay you for your services and would value both your protection and your company. Here's my hand upon it."

Grey couldn't help but return the smile. "You don't even know how much it costs to hire me."

"Are you expensive?"

"I'm a little saddle-worn but I'm not bargain counter."

"Then by all means state me a price."

Grey did and the Sioux's smile flickered. "Dear me, you think very highly of your skills."

"Others have in the past. I'm giving you my last rate with only a five percent increase."

"Ah," said Looks Away. "Well . . . done and done."

"All right then."

Neither of them moved. Not until the moment had stretched between them. However it was Looks Away who broke the spell and held out his hand. Still smiling, Grey took his hand and shook it. Before he let it go, he asked a question.

"What would you have done if you didn't like my answers to your questions?"

"Shot you, I suppose."

"What makes you think you can outdraw me?" asked Grey.

"Oh, I have no doubt you're a faster draw than me."

"Then—?"

"I anticipated a moment like this, so I took the liberty of emptying your pistol while you were sleeping last night."

Grey's smile vanished and he whipped the pistol out of its holster, pivoted and fired three quick shots at the mound of skulls. The bones exploded as heavy caliber bullets smashed through them.

Thomas Looks Away shrieked. Very high and very loud.

The echoes of the gunshots rolled outward like slow thunder and faded into the desert shimmer.

"And I reloaded them this morning, you mother-humping son of a whore," said Grey.

Looks Away took several awkward steps and then sat down heavily on the sand. "By the Queen's garters!" he gasped.

Grey opened the cylinder, dumped the three spent casings, and thumbed fresh rounds into the chambers. Then he slid the pistol into his holster.

"And that," he said quietly, "is why you're paying the extra five percent."

He turned and walked back to his horse.

Chapter 20

They entered into the broken lands of California and rode into the hills. As they climbed away from the desert floor they left the relentless brutality of the Mojave behind and found small surcease in the shadows beneath green trees. All around them, though, were remnants of what had been and hints of the new realities. Some of the most ancient trees had cracked and fallen, their roots torn by the devastating quakes and aftershocks of the Great Quake of '68. There were deep, crooked cracks torn like ragged wounds through the rocks. Mountains had been split apart. Massive spears of rock thrust up through the dirt. Forest fires had swept up and down the hills, turning forests to ash. Rivers and streams had been changed by the new complexities of the landscape. And not very far across the border from Nevada lay the edge of the world. Instead of the miles upon miles that had once stretched to the bluffs and beaches west of the Camino Real pilgrims' road, a new range of shattered mesas had risen up as most of the rest of California had cracked like dry biscuit and tumbled into the churning Pacific. Millions had died in what anyone within sound of that upheaval must have truly believed was the true apocalypse warned about in the Revelation of Saint John.

Even now, a decade and a half later, the land still looked like an open wound. Grey fancied he could feel the land moan and groan as it writhed in agony.

And yet . . .

And yet, the ash from those burned trees had enriched the soil and now there were new trees reaching up to find the sun. Riots of flowers bloomed in their millions, and even the desert succulents were fat and colorful.

At least that was how Grey saw it for the first day of their journey.

All of that changed the deeper they ventured into the broken lands. The lush growth waned quickly as they climbed a series of stepping-stone mesas that marched toward the shattered coastline. The soil thinned over the rocks and was more heavily mixed with salt from ocean-born storms. The flowers faded to withered ghosts and gasping succulents and austere palms replaced the leafy coniferous trees.

As the hours burned away, Grey found himself sinking into moody and troubled thoughts. His life had taken some strange, sad paths since he had gone to war. And stranger still since he'd tried to leave that war behind. No matter how far he rode the world did not seem to ever wash itself clean of hurt and harm. And everything seemed to get stranger the farther west he went.

Not that the south was any model for comfort and order. That's where his luck had started to go bad.

That's where he began to dream that the dead were following him. That he was a haunted man. That maybe he was something worse.

Doomed, perhaps.

Or damned.

Maybe both.

Even now, as he drowsed in the saddle he could catch glimpses of silent figures watching him from the darkness beneath trees, pale faces that turned to watch as he passed. It would be easier, he thought, if all of those faces belonged to strangers. If that was the case he could resign himself to accept that it was the land that was haunted. He'd heard enough stories—and recently had enough experiences—to accept that any definition of the word "*death*" he once possessed was either suspect or entirely wrong.

After all there were those things that had been raised by the explosion of Doctor Saint's strange weapon. Surely if the hinges of the world were breaking, then the door to hell was already torn off and cast into the dust. It made him wonder about all those wild tales he'd read in dime novels about the lands of the Great Maze. Monsters and demons, angels and goblins. He'd enjoyed those books as exciting and absurd fancies.

Now he wondered.

And he feared.

If even a fraction of them were true, then dear God in Heaven why was he riding west? Why had he agreed to this job? Why was he moving toward the lands of madness and monsters?

As if in answer, the voice of that woman—that witch or vampire, whatever Mircalla was—whispered inside his memory.

You do not know what you are, man of two worlds. The man who lives between the worlds. Yes . . . that's what it says about you. You do not belong to either life or death. That means that I and my sisters cannot have you, Greyson Torrance. You are exempt, pardoned. Not from your crimes but from my web.

And when he had demanded to know what she meant, Mircalla had confounded him more.

It means that the universe, for good or ill, is not done with you. I am forbidden to claim you. Your journey is not over.

But the thing that had frightened him most was what she said about the ghosts he dreamed about every night. He had never spoken of them to anyone, but she had either plucked the thought from him, or possessed a true second sight.

The dead follow you, Grey Torrance.

"No, goddamn it," he said between clenched teeth.

Looks Away glanced at him. "What's that, old chap?"

"Nothing," mumbled Grey. "It's nothing at all."

The lie fit like thorns in his mouth. Looks Away studied him for another few moments, then shrugged and turned away.

They rode on.

Two hours later he and Looks Away stopped there and stared out at what lay beyond. The horses trembled and whinnied. Grey felt his own heart begin to hammer while his skin felt cold and greasy.

"Suffering Jesus on the cross," breathed Grey.

Beyond the mesa was madness.

Beyond the mesa was the world gone wrong.

A world where sense and order had drowned along with mountains and fields.

There, shrouded in drifting clouds of gray mists lay the bones of the earth. Tall spikes and shattered cliffs. Great gaping holes. Monstrous caverns that gaped like the mouths of impossible beasts. And through it, swirling and churning, the ocean reached into the tortured land, slapping at the rocks, smashing down on newborn islands, sizzling into steam as it flooded into deep pits.

Grey had once read a book by a man named Dante that described the rings of Hell.

He was certain he and Looks Away stood looking at the outermost ring.

"Welcome to the Maze," said the Sioux. "And God help us both because that is where we're going."

Chapter 21

Where exactly are we heading?" asked Grey as their horses picked their way down through a series of crenellated canyons. Juniper and eucalyptus trees leaned drunkenly over them, their damaged roots clinging desperately to the shattered rocks. "Does your Doctor Saint have his workshop up in these hills?"

"Yes and no."

"Damn, son, have you ever considered giving a straight answer?"

"Life's not that easy," said Looks Away.

Grey thought about it. Nodded. "So—?"

"We're going back to where this all started."

"You mean to the laboratory where those guards were killed?"

"Yes. Maybe there was something I missed, something that would give me a new trail to follow."

"Worth trying. What's the town?"

"You won't have heard of it," said Looks Away. "Sad little place called Paradise Falls. Way out on the edge of the Maze. Dusty little nowhere of a town."

"Sounds charming."

They pushed on and Looks Away brought them along a chain of trails that linked former trade routes and newer traveler's roads. There was no longer such a thing as a straight and reliable road. Not since the quake. Many times they had to dismount and lead their horses on treacherous paths along the sheer sides of mesas, or in the darkened hollows at the feet of crumbling mountains.

"A goddamn billy goat wouldn't take this road," complained Grey more than once. Looks Away offered no argument.

By the afternoon of the third day they emerged from a canyon and paused on a promontory beyond which was a sight Grey Torrance had never before seen.

The land was as blasted and broken as it had been, but now, past the cathedral-sized boulders and spikes of sandstone a wide blue expanse spread itself out under the sun. The Pacific was sapphire blue and each wind-tossed wave seemed to glitter with diamond chips. White-bellied gulls wheeled and cried. Long lines of pelicans drifted on the thermals, changing direction, taking their cues from the flight leader. After the blistering desert and the heartbreak of the shattered lands, the deep blue of the rolling ocean was like a balm on the soul.

"God . . . ," breathed Grey.

Looks Away smiled faintly. "Looks lovely from here," he said, "but I don't recommend taking a swim."

"Why not? Are there sharks?"

The Sioux shook his head. "I saw a few sharks once. Big ones. Bull sharks, I think. Or Great Whites. Washed up on the beach. Bitten in half or crushed."

"Crushed by what?"

"What indeed?" said the Sioux mysteriously. "This is the Maze, my friend. I'm afraid there are far more things that we *don't* understand than things we do."

"What, sea serpents and cave monsters?" laughed Grey. "Those are just tales from dime novels. There's nothing to any of that nonsense."

The Indian turned and studied him for a long moment. There was a small, knowing smile on his lips, but no humor in his eyes. "As you say."

Grey could not draw him into an explanation. So, in another of the moody silences that seemed to define their relationship, the two men rode down a crooked slope toward a massive cleft in the ground. A rickety bridge spanned the chasm. They stopped at the foot of the bridge and the men slid from their horses to peer over the edge.

"This gorge runs for two hundred miles north and south," said Looks Away as he and Grey squatted down on the edge. "It opened up during the quake."

Below them was a raw wound in the earth. Far below, nearly lost in the misty distance, were spikes of jagged rock that rose from a threshing river. Fumes, thick with sulfur and decay, rose on columns of steam.

"The water comes from some underground source," said Looks Away. "Not salt water, which means that it comes from inland, but I wouldn't dare call it 'fresh.' Anyone who drinks it gets sick and some have died. They break out in sores and go stark staring bonkers."

"Jeez . . ."

Grey stood and nodded to the bridge. "Is that thing safe?"

"It hasn't fallen yet."

"That's not exactly an answer."

"I daresay not." Looks Away shrugged and pointed to the twisted remnants of a second bridge. All that was left was a pair of tall posts and some rotting tendrils of rope. "That one, the Daedalus Bridge, used to cross a lovely little stream of crystal clear water. It was destroyed in the Quake. A man named Pearl organized the building of a second and much longer bridge to span this chasm. Not sure who chose the name, but people call it the Icarus Bridge."

"Wasn't Icarus the one who fell?"

"Yes," said Looks Away, "charming thought, isn't it?"

They remounted. Beyond the far side of the bridge was a small town, though to Grey's eyes it looked more like a ghost town. A cluster of dreary buildings huddled together under an unrelenting sun. Everything looked faded and sunbaked.

"That's Paradise Falls?" he asked.

"Such as it is."

"Swell."

They crossed the Icarus Bridge very slowly and carefully. The boards creaked and the ropes protested, but it proved to be more solid than it looked. Even so, Grey was greatly relieved when they reached the far side.

"And we didn't plunge to our deaths," murmured Looks Away.

"Oh . . . shut up," grumbled Grey.

The road into town was littered with lizard droppings and the bones of small birds. They passed under a sign very much like the one they'd encountered in the ghost town in Nevada. The difference here is that the paintwork looked like it had been done with some sense of style. A little artistry, no less. But it was faded now and there were cracks in the wood and there had been no attempt to freshen the sign. Grey looked up at it.

PARADISE FALLS

Beyond the sign were a few dozen buildings along one main street and on a few, smaller side lanes. Smoke curling upward from a handful of chimneys. Bored-looking horses hung their heads over hitching posts. Withered old men and women sat on porch rockers. A few grubby children played listlessly, tossing a wooden ball through a barrel hoop. They missed more often than made the shot, but their bland expression didn't change much no matter how the game turned out.

"*Paradise Falls?*" Grey mused quietly.

"I know," said Looks Away. "The running joke is that Paradise Fell."

"Not a very funny joke."

"No, it isn't." Perched on the corner of the sign was a bird that Grey at first thought was a buzzard, but as they passed he did a double take and gaped at it. The creature had wings and feathers, but beyond that it bore little resemblance to any bird Grey had ever seen. Not outside of a nightmare at least. The body was bare in patches and instead of the pale flesh of a normal bird, this thing had the mottled and knobbly hide of something more akin to a reptile. The wings were leathery and dark, and there were claws at the end of each that gripped the sign as surely as did its taloned feet. The creature's beak was long and tapered, and it cocked its head to stare at the two horsemen with a black and bottomless eye.

"Christ," whispered Grey, "what the *hell* is that thing?"

Looks Away followed his gaze and shuddered. "Be damned if I know," he said. "The locals claim that after the quake great flocks of them flew out of caverns that had previously been trapped in the hearts of mountains."

"It looks like it flew up from hell itself."

"Yes," agreed the Sioux. Grey hadn't meant it as a joke, and Looks Away did not appear to take it as such. They kept a wary eye on the bird as they passed beneath. The sun was in the east and it threw the misshapen bird's shadow across their path. Both horses, unguided, stepped nervously around that shadow.

That made the flesh on the back of Grey's neck prickle.

The Sioux nodded to the people who had come to windows or porch rails to look at them. "They're simple people, but good ones."

The remark surprised Grey. "You care?"

Looks Away shrugged. "I do. I've lived among them

for months and I know most of them. Granted, few make rewarding conversational partners, but they are honest folk who have had a run of bad luck that was both unearned and unlooked for."

"The quake?"

"That was the start of the bad luck, but it didn't end there. When the land fell into the sea it changed the course of the water. That road we took had been a strong freshwater stream. Pure snowmelt from the mountains. The Paradise River, and it ran to the edge of a drop. That waterfall is what gave the town its name. There used to be thousands of square miles of arable land. Now there are rocks, scorpions, and ugly mesas where nothing grows that you'd care to eat."

"How the hell do they survive?"

The Sioux gave him a rueful smile. "Who says they're surviving, old chap?"

Grey opened his mouth to reply, but a scream suddenly tore through the air.

A woman's scream.

And almost immediately it was punctuated by the hollow crack of a gunshot.

Chapter 22

They wheeled in their saddles and looked off down
a side street. There, at the very end of town, were
several figures engaged in a furious struggle by an
old stone well.

"Shite!" cried Looks Away as he instantly spurred his
horse into a full gallop.

Grey hesitated for a heartbeat longer. This was not his
town and not his fight.

Except . . .

The fight looked too uneven for his tastes. A tall,
thin stick-figure of a wildly bearded Mexican man in a
monk's brown robe, and a woman with curly blond hair
were struggling with six hard-looking men.

"Well . . . balls," he growled, and kicked Picky into a
run. Even his horse seemed outraged and barreled down
the street at incredible speed.

Grey watched in astonishment as Looks Away vaulted
from his saddle and flung himself at one of the biggest
of the six men. They crashed against the side of the well,
spun and fell out of sight. In almost the same moment,
one of the men—presumably the one who'd fired the
gun—slashed the monk across the face with the pistol.
Another man had the woman in a fierce bear hug and
held her, kicking and screaming, off the ground. The
other men were closing in on her, laughing and pawing
at her.

As Picky devoured the distance between Grey and the

fight, the woman lashed out with a foot and caught one of the men on the point of the chin. He backpedaled and hit one of his companions. They both staggered. Then she used the same foot to kick backward and upward. The man holding her let loose with a high whistling shriek and hunched forward, his thighs slapping together about a tenth of a second too late.

Then Grey was among them.

He used Picky's muscular shoulder to crash into the back of the sixth man and the force of that impact picked him off the ground and flung him into the side of the well. He bent double and very nearly went in, saving himself at the last second by clawing at the stone lip.

Grey leaped from the saddle, grabbed the hair of the shrieking man holding the woman, and jerked him backward with such force that the man was bent nearly in half the wrong way. His hands snapped open, sending the woman staggering forward. Grey snapped the handful of hair like a whip and the man flopped onto the ground. He immediately tried to sit up and got as far as the short, hard kick Grey fired at his face. The man flopped back, bleeding and unconscious.

Pain exploded in Grey's kidney and he reeled, but he turned as he did so, crouching and bringing up his arms to block a second punch. It was the bruiser who'd pistol-whipped the monk. He'd rammed the barrel of his Colt into Grey's back and was raising the gun now to point it at the intruder's face.

Grey rushed him low and hard, ducking beneath the gun arm and hooking a muscular arm around the man's waist. He drove forward, plucking the man off the ground and running him three steps into the rocky well. The man let out a huge "Oooomph!"

Grey let him sag down and spun just in time to see the first man the woman had kicked snake an arm around her throat. He had lost his pistol after the kick, but he plucked a skinning knife from a belt sheath and touched the edge of the blade to her cheek.

He was fast.

Grey was faster.

He caught the man's wrist before the blade could do more than dent the woman's skin, then he stepped back and sideways, pulling the arm with him. Grey had received some schooling in the manly arts, but he'd learned more from gutter fights and trench wars. He knew what hurt and how to make it hurt. He jerked the man's arm straight and punched him full-fisted just above the elbow. A bent elbow, Grey knew, was as strong as a knotted tree limb. A straight elbow was as fragile as a breadstick if you knew where to hit. He did.

There was a sharp *snap* and the elbow suddenly bent the wrong way.

The knife fell from twitching fingers and the man let loose a howl that would have broken glass if there was any around.

The woman, clearly not content with the man having a broken arm, spun toward him, kneed him in the crotch, drove a thumb into the socket of his throat, boxed his ears and broke his nose with a very professional short punch.

He went down.

And she spat on him as he fell.

Grey liked that. He grinned.

A fragment of a second later the grin was knocked off his face by a hard punch that caught him on the point of the jaw and spun him halfway around. He staggered back, continued the turn and then stepped inside the follow-up punch. It was the man Picky had crashed into. Not tall, but far bulkier than Grey had first thought. Arms and shoulders like a circus gorilla. He swung big lefts and rights that would have darkened the world if a second one had landed fair.

Grey brought his elbows up and used his own fists to protect his ears. As he plowed forward he let the man ruin his own arms by punching elbows and shoulders; then as he got close enough he leaned in and hit the man in the face and throat, left-right, left-right, and followed it all with an overhand right that put the man down on his face.

Then Grey stepped back and drew his pistol. He thumbed the hammer to half cock and the sound was as sharp and eloquent as if he'd fired the weapon.

"Stop!" cried a voice. "For the love of Jesus and the saints, please stop this!"

Grey turned to see the bearded monk, his cheek torn and bleeding from the pistol-whipping, his nose askew, eyes filled with the tears of pain, standing between him and the thugs. He stood with palms out, pleading with him. With everyone.

The moment froze into a bloody tableau.

The group of men lay or knelt or leaned in postures of exhausted defeat, their clothes dusty, faces streaked with bright blood. Looks Away climbed to his feet on the far side of the well, and the man he'd been fighting with crawled away from him with blood dripping from his nose and slack lips. The woman stood panting, fists balled, blond curls blowing free from her pins, blue eyes blazing with cold fury.

"Please . . . ," begged the monk. "I beg you."

Grey glanced at Looks Away, who gave him a small nod. The woman looked too furious to speak, but even she gave him a nod. And in that moment Grey's heart froze in his chest.

The woman.

Dear God, he thought. She was a stranger to him, and yet there was something so intensely and deeply familiar about her and a name came to his lips.

"*Annabelle*," he murmured.

The woman frowned. "My name is Jenny Pearl."

Grey swallowed hard. It was like forcing down a chunk of broken glass.

Not her, he told himself. *Annabelle's gone and this is another world, another life, another woman.*

The face was different, the body was different, but those eyes.

He wanted to turn and run out of the moment.

There was a smudge of bloody dirt on Jenny Pearl's left cheek. And that hit him almost as hard. There had been blood on Annabelle's cheek when he buried her.

God.

"Please," repeated the monk, intruding into his thoughts and bringing him back from that long-ago grave on a forgotten hillside in Virginia.

Grey took a breath, then nodded, eased the hammer down, and let the gun hang at his side.

"Okay, Padre," he said. "Okay."

The monk exhaled a big lungful of air and nodded. "Thank you, my son. God bless and thank you."

On the ground, one of the men groaned and staggered painfully to his feet. He stood swaying like a drunkard. With a snarl of feral hatred he peeled back the lapel of his coat to show the vest he wore beneath.

Pinned to the vest was a round disk of metal embossed with a star. The words "*Sheriff's Deputy*" were etched into the silver badge.

Grey said, "Oh . . . shit."

Chapter 23

Drop your weapons and raise your hands," snarled the deputy as he laid his hand on the butt of his holstered pistol. "All of you sons of bitches are under arrest."

Grey stiffened. His gun was still at his side. "On what charge?"

"Assaulting an officer," barked the deputy. "How's that for a start?"

"Not good enough," said Grey. "Way I saw it six grown men were assaulting a man of the cloth and a helpless woman."

"I'm not helpless," snapped Jenny and again those eyes flashed at him, full of life and challenge.

Full of life.

Of *life*.

"Point taken. Assaulting a woman," Grey amended, trying to study that lovely face while keeping an eye on the deputy. "Even if that wasn't illegal in itself, six to one is hardly what I'd call fair."

The deputy sneered. "We were in the process of making a legal arrest."

Jenny spat at him. It didn't reach his face, but the effort was impressive. Grey smiled. She was a very pretty woman. Slim, but with an abundance of everything he liked above and below. A face like an angel and, clearly, the temper of Satan himself. Nice. And it was a relief to see those qualities, because even though Annabelle had been willful and passionate, she was a gentle flower and not this desert rose. Plus Jenny could clearly handle herself. If it had only been two men, she might have wiped the street with both of them. Grey liked her at once.

"Arrest?" he asked. "Care to tell me what the crime was?"

"None of your goddamn business."

Grey kept the pistol down at his side, but he thumbed the hammer back to full cock. "I guess I'm making it my business."

The deputy eyed him, clearly weighing his options. The man had his hand on his gun, and maybe he was a quickdraw artist—they seemed to be springing up all over the place these days—but on the other hand, Grey already had his gun out. And Grey knew that to anyone with wits he did not look like a man unfamiliar with gunplay.

"Please," urged the monk. "We can be civil about this."

"Civil?" said the woman. "How can anyone be civil with wild dogs?"

"You watch your mouth, Jenny Pearl," warned the deputy, his fingers beginning to close around the sandalwood grips of his gun. The other deputies were getting to their feet, dazed and stupid with pain. But there was anger and bloodlust in their eyes.

Thomas Looks Away drew his pistol in a smooth, fluid motion and pointed the barrel at the side of the deputy's head. "Jed Perkins, I believe you were born stupid and you've lost ground since."

Deputy Perkins froze.

A shadow passed above them and out of the corner of his eye he saw the same ugly bird he'd spied earlier. With a whipsnap of its leathery wings, the creature came to rest on the top of the well's crossbar. It cocked its head again, turning a dark eye on the drama here on the street. The monk touched the wooden cross that he wore on a cord around his neck.

"Now," continued Looks Away, ignoring the bird and giving Perkins a stern and uncompromising look, "I believe I heard my friend ask you a fair question, son. What exactly were the crimes for which you were attempting to arrest Miss Pearl and Brother Joe?"

Perkins licked his lips.

"Theft," he said.

"Theft?" cried Jenny Pearl. "So help me God I'll nut you and feed—."

Looks Away touched her arm and it cut her flow of threats.

"Theft it was and there's no way you can deny it," countered Perkins. "There's your proof, and it's enough to get you a full month in the mines. Hard labor, too."

As he spoke, Perkins pointed to the base of the well, where two wooden buckets lay on their side, surrounded by a pool of water that was drying quickly in the hot afternoon sun.

"Maybe I'm missing something here," said Grey. "Are you saying they stole the buckets?"

"No, you damn-fool," said Perkins. "Anyone can clearly see they were stealing water."

"Water?" echoed Grey. He looked from Perkins to Jenny Pearl, to Looks Away, to the monk named Brother Joe, and back again. "You're arresting them for drawing water from the town well?"

"Of course," said Perkins. "That well is the sole and complete property of—."

"No, wait," said Grey, holding up his free hand. "We're talking about water? Water as in . . . *water*?"

"What are you? Stupid?"

"No, but I am deeply confused," admitted Grey. "Or maybe *appalled* is the right word."

"That'll work," agreed Looks Away, icily. Miss Pearl nodded.

Brother Joe tried to explain. "Mr. Deray has legal claim to all the water rights in this whole region."

"Why? Is he grazing cattle or sheep?"

"No."

"What's he farm, then, that he needs so much water? Help me out here, brother, 'cause I'm having a hard time getting my hands on this."

"Like I said," laughed Perkins, "you're a fool who doesn't know shit from sheep's wool."

Grey's arm was a blur. He raised his gun and fired a shot into the dirt between Perkins's feet. The bullet ricocheted up and whined away into the distance. The deputy emitted a sharp yelp like a kicked dog and jumped two feet in the air. He landed flat-footed and froze into a hunched statue, eyes as wide as saucers.

"You want to keep a tighter rein on your mouth, son," he said. "Call me a fool again and I'd be just as happy to put the next one through your kneecap. See if I don't."

Perkins's mouth was open but he said nothing. Grey was pretty sure that the man was, at the moment, incapable of human speech. It took some effort to keep a smile off his face.

Brother Joe took a step forward as if he planned to stand between Perkins and Grey should the former incur any further wrath. The action said a lot about the monk's devotion to the heart of scripture. It said a lot less about his awareness of the realities of this hard world. Even so, Grey lowered his gun again. He still didn't holster it, though.

Looks Away let out an audible breath.

Jenny huffed. "You *should* have shot him. That's what people do with mangy dogs."

Grey turned to the other men. He could see that they each wore a deputy badge. His heart sank. However he said, "I see anyone's hand twitch in the direction of their holsters I will kill each and every damn one of you. No, don't look at me like that. I have five shots and my friend has six. If you don't think we can put you down before you clear leather, then have at it. I'm sure there's a coffin-maker in town."

"There is," Jenny assured him.

"So," continued Grey, "you have to ask yourself if there's anything here worth dying for. I'm thinking there isn't."

The deputies did not draw their guns. Brother Joe let out a deep breath of obvious relief.

"Well now," said Grey affably, "how about someone tell me what in the actual hell is going on here? How is it that someone can claim water rights inside a damn town? Pardon my language, ma'am."

"I don't want your damn apologies," she fired back. "I'd rather you had the balls to shoot these shit-heels and be done with it."

Looks Away chuckled. "Ah, I do admire you, Jenny Pearl."

"And you can keep your mouth shut, too, Mr. Looks Through Windows," growled Jenny.

Looks Away affected to look like innocence offended. He said nothing, though, and Grey could see a ghost of a smile on his mouth.

"Padre," said Grey, trying to find a voice of reason in this pack, "what's the story with this water rights thing? Surely you're able to tell the truth. Kind of a professional requirement, as I understand it."

"Don't listen to that old—," began Perkins, but Grey shushed him. Not with a finger to his lips but with the barrel of his big Colt. That shut the deputy's mouth.

"You were saying, Padre—?" encouraged Grey.

The monk cleared his throat. "Please, I don't want any more trouble."

"No trouble at all," Grey assured him. "Just some folks standing around chatting on a sunny afternoon. So . . . if you please . . ."

"Well," said Brother Joe, "what Deputy Perkins says may be true in the sense of the local law. This well is technically owned by Mr. Deray."

"Tell him all of it," said Jenny.

Brother Joe nodded. He wiped blood from his broken nose and pawed it from within the tangles of his beard. There was a lot of it. "That's the thing . . . Aleksander Deray has acquired the rights to all of the water in this part of the Maze. All fresh water, that is."

"All of it?" asked Grey, smiling at the absurdity of it.

"Every drop."

"How's that even possible? This well is inside the town limits. Surely it has to belong to the town." Before he finished both Brother Joe and Jenny were shaking their heads.

"Mr. Deray bought *all* of the water," said Brother Joe.

"You mean he stole it," growled Jenny.

"More like swindled," suggested Looks Away casually. They ignored him.

"All of it?" Grey asked. "What about on the farms? You can't tell me there's no water on any of the farms."

"There's water," said Looks Away. "Not a lot, but it's there."

"Well, there you go, then—."

"Mr. Deray owns that, too," said Brother Joe. "That's what I'm trying to tell you. It's what makes this all so unfair. People are dying for want of water. The livestock and crops are already withered down to nothing. At first Mr. Deray would sell us some. A gallon a day for a family of four. Then it was a gallon every other day. Then a gallon a week."

Grey gaped at him.

Jenny Pearl's eyes flashed with blue fire. "Now Deray says that we can't even *buy* water."

"How does he expect you to live?"

"That, my dear chap," said Looks Away dryly, "seems to be the question. Perhaps one of these fine constables can furnish us with an adequate answer. Shall we ask them?"

Grey took a step toward Perkins who, for all that he was afraid, held his ground. Grey had to grudge him that much. The deputy stiffened and stuck out his jaw in an attempt to look like the symbol of authority he was supposed to be.

"Talk," said Grey.

"This ain't your business, mister," said Perkins. "Or the Indian's."

"I beg to differ," drawled Looks Away.

Grey smiled. "I guess we're making it our business."

"You know you only got the better of us because you snucked up on us and bushwhacked us."

"*Snucked* isn't a word, you illiterate troll," said Looks Away.

"You're saying," Grey said to the deputy, "that things would have been different if we'd made this a fair fight?"

"You're damn right."

"Like the fair fight that was in progress when we arrived? Six men against a woman and a parson who clearly didn't offer any resistance. Which means that it was six men against this woman. That's your idea of fair? Is that what you're trying to sell here?"

Deputy Perkins turned as red as a fresh bruise and wouldn't meet Grey's eyes.

"They was breaking the law."

"You call that a law?" demanded Miss Pearl. "There are children wasting away in this town. People are getting sick."

"That's not my concern," insisted Perkins. "The law is the law."

Grey used the barrel of the Colt to turn Perkins's chin, forcing the man to look at him.

"When armed men enforce a law like that, then the law's no law at all."

"You need to take that up with the sheriff and the circuit judge. They say it *is* the law."

"Fine. Tell me where they are and I'll be happy to have that conversation."

Perkins faltered. "Well . . . you can't."

"Why not?"

"The, um, sheriff's down south in the City of Lost Angels."

"And the circuit judge?"

"Well . . . he won't be back around until March."

"That's a long time," said Grey. "What about Mr. Deray? Maybe I should go have a conversation with him."

Brother Joe gasped audibly. Jenny Pearl took a step back, touching her hand to her throat. They both looked deeply afraid.

A slow and nasty smile crawled onto Perkins's mouth. "Well, why don't you?"

Behind Perkins, out of his line of sight, Looks Away pursed his lips and quietly blew out his cheeks.

Grey Torrance hoisted a smile onto his own face. It wasn't the kind of smile he liked to show to people he thought well of. The smile on Perkins's face leaked away.

"Take your men and get the hell out of my sight," said Grey. "Do it quick and do it now."

"And then what?" said the deputy. "Soon as we're gone you're going to steal some water. Tell me I'm wrong."

"Oh, you're absolutely right. I intend to have a water party. Free water for everyone. Much as they want."

The other deputies milled around, looking at each

other, looking at the well. Looking everywhere but at Grey or Looks Away.

"C'mon, Jed," mumbled one of the men. "This ain't worth taking a bullet over."

Jed Perkins slowly slapped dust from his clothes. He bent and picked up a brown hat with a band of silver conches and screwed it down on his head. The motions were deliberate and exaggerated, as if cleaning himself up after a beating was somehow able to shift him to a moral high ground or some position of tactical superiority. Grey was unimpressed. He'd seen this sort of thing before.

"Get gone," he advised.

Perkins stepped up and for a moment stood nose to nose with Grey.

"You better watch your backtrail, mister," he said coldly. " 'Cause the next time I see you I'm going to—."

And Grey hit him.

It was a left-handed blow. Very fast, and despite being short-range it rocked Perkins onto his heels, knocked the lights from his eyes, and then sat him down hard on his ass.

The other men cried out and started forward and Grey turned smoothly, raising his pistol, pointing it at the closest man. Looks Away stepped out from behind the well and held his gun in a rock-steady brown fist.

"Listen to me," said Grey coldly. "Learn this for the future. If you've just taken a beating, that is not—I repeat *not*—the time to make a threat. Only a complete idiot does that. Like this sorry excuse for a human being."

He punctuated his words with a short, sharp kick that drove the square toe of his boot under Jed Perkins's chin. The man's eyes rolled up white and he flopped back.

"Please!" begged the monk.

Grey patted the air toward him. "It's okay, Padre. This

is over. Deputy Perkins dealt the play. Everyone here saw that. Now you fellows pick this piece of cow dung up and cart him off before I get really mad. Be best for all concerned if no one said anything smart while you were about it. Go on, get 'er done."

The other deputies did not say a single word as they hooked their hands under Perkins's arms and knees, hoisted him up, and went creaking away in a puffing cluster.

Grey and Looks Away held their guns on them until the men flopped Perkins over a saddle and the six of them rode out of town.

The ugly bird suddenly cawed. It was so strange a sound. More like the plaintive cry of a lost child than any sound that could come from a bird's throat. With a snap of its leathery wings it launched from the crossbar of the well, rose ponderously into the air and flew away to the northeast. Whether it was following the deputies or merely heading in a similar direction was unclear. The four of them watched it, and the fleeing men, until they were out of sight.

Then, with a sigh, Grey opened the cylinder, replaced the single spent cartridge, and reholstered his Colt. Looks Away did the same. They turned to face Brother Joe and Jenny Pearl.

Before Grey could say a word, the woman slapped him across the face with all of her considerable strength. It was a lightning-fast blow that rocked Grey's head and spun him halfway around. Then the woman grabbed his shoulder, wheeled him back, grabbed his ears, pulled his head down, and planted a scalding hot kiss on his lips.

Then she shoved him back. Gasping, blinking, totally confused, Grey staggered and might have fallen if Looks Away hadn't caught his arm.

"What," he sputtered, "the hell was that for?"

Jenny Pearl crossed her arms under her breasts and

cocked her head. Her blue eyes seemed to ignite the air around them. "The slap was because you didn't kill that murdering son of a bitch, Jed Perkins." She paused. "The kiss was because you damn sure beat a pound of stupid off his sorry ass."

Brother Joe turned a suddenly scarlet face away and shook his head slowly. Grey heard Looks Away laughing softly.

He rubbed his face and stared down at the woman and had no idea what to do or say.

Chapter 24

Looks Away made formal introductions and that broke the spell of the moment.

"Jenny Pearl," he said, "I would like to formally introduce my new associate, Mr. Grey Torrance. Grey, this is Miss Jenny Pearl. She owns—."

"*Used* to own," corrected Jenny.

"—*used* to own a cattle ranch northeast of town."

"You're a rancher?" asked Grey, rubbing the red welt on his cheek.

"Why?" said Jenny with challenge in her tone. "Can't a woman own a ranch?"

"Sure. But you don't look old enough."

A shadow passed behind the woman's eyes. "It . . . it was my father's place. I took it over when he . . ." She let the rest hang, then added, "I ran near three hundred head before that bastard Deray got here."

"Miss Pearl, please . . . ," said the monk.

"Not talking about it isn't the same as it not being the case," said Jenny; but then she sighed and nodded, withdrawing her anger from the moment.

"And this," said Looks Away, "is Brother Joe, late of the order of the Brothers of Outcasts."

"I heard about you fellows," said Grey, nodding.

Those monks were all, in one way or another, failed shepherds of their flocks. Drunks and sinners, thieves of church offerings, men who had broken their vows of chastity, and others who had dishonored their vows.

Where such disgrace would drive most clerics totally away from the church, a handful of them had come crawling back and begged for a chance to redeem themselves.

They were stripped of most of their priestly powers and allowed to serve without pay, without praise, and probably without much chance of setting things right. Grey had never met one before and didn't give much of a damn for humility, but he admired their courage. As a man who felt the weight of his own sins and worried about the slim chance of salvation and the very real threat of celestial punishment, he hoped the Outcast Brothers would prove that even the most wretched had a fighting chance on Judgment Day.

He said, "Thought you were all down Mexico way, trying to turn the last Mayans into good little Christians. What brings you up here? You a priest of a church 'round these parts?"

"We missionaries go where the Lord sends us."

"God sent you here? Why? You lose a bet with him?"

The joke fell flat and Grey was sorry he'd made it. The monk actually winced as if he was in physical pain.

"Are you a Christian, brother," he asked.

Grey shrugged. "Not sure where I stand on that topic. God and me haven't had any meaningful conversations in quite a long time."

"But you believe?"

"That's a complicated question," said Grey. "The world's big and strange. Maybe bigger and stranger than people thought it was. So . . . I guess I'll keep an open mind. But that doesn't mean you're going to find me in a pew come Sunday morning."

Brother Joe nodded. He was as thin as a rake-handle, nearly bald. He wore a rough brown robe with the hood folded down on his bony shoulders, and rope sandals on his feet. His only extravagance was a beard that was full and wild. His voice had only the faintest echo of the Spanish that had probably been the language of his childhood.

Brother Joe offered a thin hand and Grey shook it. The monk's hand was like dry parchment stretched over fragile sticks.

"Although I abhor violence of any kind," said Brother Joe, "I thank you for what you did. Those men might have hurt Miss Pearl."

"They might have done worse than hurt her," said Grey. "I know men like that. I know that type. Maybe I should have schooled them a bit more on how to treat decent folks."

Jenny smiled at that.

But Brother Joe shook his head. "Judgment and punishment are for God."

"Sure," said Grey, "forgiveness, too. But I'd rather be judged by the Almighty for doing what I think's right than stand aside and let bastards like that make life hell for people. Tell me I'm wrong."

"It's not as simple as that."

Grey put a hand on the monk's shoulder. "Yeah, padre, I know. Maybe carrying a gun makes me a bad man, too. I'll talk that over with Saint Peter if I get the chance. Or maybe my answer will come from a lick from the Devil's riding crop, but I will be *damned* if I stand aside and do nothing. Some men can. I can't."

Brother Joe met his eyes and it was clear that there was much he wanted to say, but they both knew this wasn't the time. Instead he took Grey's hand and kissed it.

"May God's mercy and protection be with you always."

"Amen to that," said Looks Away. "Now, how about we draw some of that water and get off the street? I doubt our Deputy Perkins or his employer will let this matter stand where it is."

"So what? I'm not afraid of them, Looksie," said Jenny.

Looks Away winced at the nickname, but he let the bucket slide down the well. "I'm not afraid of them coming back," he said. "But let's make it later than sooner. I'm fair parched."

"*Looksie?*" echoed Grey, grinning.

"Don't start," warned the Sioux as he cranked up the laden bucket. "You wouldn't be the first white man I've scalped."

There was a sudden rumble, deep and heavy, and they all turned toward the west. Far out over the ocean was a massive bank of dark clouds that Grey could have sworn were not there five minutes ago. It was a storm front, and the clouds pulsed and throbbed with thunder. Lightning flashed within and it looked like red veins in the skin of some great beast.

"Looks like the town's in for a break," said Grey. "Stretch some canvas and catch the rain. Nothing beats a cup of fresh rainwater."

"Not *that* rain," said Jenny softly. "God . . ."

Brother Joe quickly crossed himself.

A wet wind whipped off the ocean and blew past them. It smelled of rotting fish and sulfur. Jenny wrapped her arms around her body and shuddered. Even Looks Away seemed to grow pale and nervous.

The first fat raindrops pinged on the tin roof of the nearest house. Fresh thunder growled at them. Closer now.

High above they heard the shrill and haunted call of that strange bird. It seemed to be pushed toward them on the stiff wind.

Rain splatted down on the street a block away and they watched the leading wall of the storm march toward them. Grey frowned at the storm. It was strange. It was . . . *wrong*. As the belly of the storm swelled outward like an obscene pregnancy, the lightning changed in color. Where a moment ago it had been like red veins, now it changed into a tracery of blue.

Grey knew that shade of blue. He'd seen it in Nevada. He'd nearly been killed by a burst of it.

"Looks Away—," he began, but thunder exploded like artillery fire, smashing all other sounds into nothingness.

Inside the storm, behind the veil of slanting rain, something moved. Something vast, something that writhed like a nest of serpents. And tangled up with the growl of thunder he thought he heard something else. Something that roared with a voice from nightmare.

Looks Away glanced down at the bucket he held.

He let it fall.

"Run," he murmured. Then as the rain thickened and as the sky turned black as sackcloth, he yelled it. "*Run!*"

The four of them turned and ran.

Chapter 25

Running from a storm is like running from a forest fire or the fall of night. At first it seems possible, but then with every step the realities become apparent. What man can do, nature can overmaster.

"Get the horses!" Grey bellowed to Looks Away. "You take Brother Joe and I'll take—."

Before he could finish the statement a gray bulk slammed into him and sent him skidding into the stone well. He rebounded and whipped around in time to see Picky race away from him in a full-out panicked gallop. Queenie was neck and neck with her.

Grey wasted no time cursing the horses. Instead he launched himself to his feet, caught Jenny Pearl's arm, and together they ran. He heard feet slapping on the dampening mud behind him.

"Oh God, Oh God, Oh God," breathed Brother Joe with every step.

"Move your holy ass," snapped Looks Away.

Rain pelted them, punched them, and chased them. Grey could see that the street up ahead was empty. Everyone had fled the coming storm. Two of the rocking chairs still wobbled, proof that their occupants had been there only a moment before.

The howl of the wind was a terrible thing to hear. It was the sound of souls in burning torment. It was the shriek of the tortured damned. As he ran, Grey tried to tell himself that it was the wind, only the wind. That the sound was some freakish side effect of ghost rock that was somehow caught up in this gale. That it was no more dire than the hiss of a burning fuse or the bang of gunpowder. Just a sound.

Only that.

But the rain burned as it struck his skin. It hissed and sizzled as if the storm had come howling up from Hell itself, carrying with it the screams of the dead. The cries of a thing that hated the living for what the quick had and the dead did not. It was a hungry, covetous sound that betrayed a greedy want of life. Or to see life torn down and swept away.

As Grey ran he heard human voices screaming, too. Rising to match the wind.

They came from inside houses. They came from behind closed doors and windows. And they came from the mouths of Thomas Looks Away, Jenny Pearl, Brother Joe.

And from his own mouth.

Jenny grabbed his sodden sleeve and jerked him sideways toward a rain-spattered porch. They raced up the three wooden steps and across the porch. Jenny fumbled in her skirt pocket for a key, stabbed it into the lock, turned it, shouldered the door open, and fell inward, dragging Grey with her. Brother Joe came through next, stumble-running from a push, and finally Looks Away staggered in. The Sioux slammed the door and began slapping at his skin, trying to swat away the stinging rainwater as if it were filled with biting gnats.

Jenny pushed past him and tore a curtain down. "Use this!"

They each grabbed a corner of the frilly yellow curtain and frantically dabbed and blotted themselves.

"It burns," cried Brother Joe. "God, it burns."

"Out of those clothes," ordered Grey. "Now."

Brother Joe, despite his pain, cast an appalled look toward Jenny, but the woman brusquely waved him off and began unbuttoning her blouse. Grey half tore his shirt getting it off. He yanked off his boots and shoved down his jeans. Looks Away was already down to britches and Brother Joe pulled off his robe to reveal a thin and many times patched pair of what looked like a woman's cast-off bloomers.

All three of the men turned their backs on Jenny Pearl and she stepped out of her dress. Grey had a lingering afterimage of her in layers of white, and a bodice with a plunging neckline. There was another tearing sound and he half turned to see her rip down a second curtain and begin winding it around her slim body.

Thunder boomed and outside branches snapped from the oak tree on the lawn. Flying sticks hammered the front of the house.

"Stay away from the windows," warned Grey.

"Looksie," said Jenny, "the shutters."

"Shite," groaned the Sioux, but he ran to the closest window and opened it. Wincing into the spray, he snagged the pulls of the heavy wooden shutters and slammed them closed. Grey did the same with the window on the other side of the door as Brother Joe and Jenny ran to repeat this with the windows upstairs. By the time they were done, Grey and Looks Away had the rear and side windows shuttered. It darkened the house, but it felt far more secure. They grabbed the curtains and rags from the kitchen to mop up the stinging rain.

"Am I burned?" asked Looks Away, probing at his face with nervous fingers.

"Don't take this the wrong way," said Grey, "but your skin's red."

"Hilarious. But it feels blistered."

"It's not. How's mine?"

"The same. There must be something in the rain to cause this, but it doesn't seem to be causing tissue damage."

"Hurts like a bitch, though."

"Yes, it damn well does," agreed Jenny as she rejoined them. Grey became instantly and acutely aware of how transparent white undergarments could be when soaked with rainwater. He tried his level best to look anywhere but at her, and failed miserably. He felt his face burn even hotter, and that had nothing at all to do with the rain.

Outside the rain intensified. Grey bent and peered through the shutter slats. The rain fell in sheets that seemed to march like platoons of ghosts across the street.

"It's starting to hail," said Looks Away, then he stiffened. "Oh . . . bloody *hell*!"

"What is it?" asked Jenny, crowding beside him to peer between the slats.

When Brother Joe joined them, he immediately gasped and clutched his crucifix in a white-knuckled fist. "Dear Lord, save us from the horrors of the Pit."

In silent fear, they stood and watched for long minutes, each of them staring in horror at what was falling with the rain.

Snakes.

And frogs.

Hundreds of them.

Thousands.

The snakes were strange and there were many kinds Grey had never seen. Not desert snakes like sidewinders and rattlesnakes. These were mottled and sinewy, more like sea snakes or eels. And the frogs were tiny and brightly colored. Livid greens and bright blues and shocking yellow. Some of the frogs landed in puddles and hopped away; others struck harder parts of the street that hadn't yet softened to mud. These exploded into red that was immediately washed away. All of the falling animals steamed, though, as if plucked from boiling pots.

Overhead the lightning flashed with blue madness and it cast the entire street into an alien strangeness.

They could still hear the screams and the deeper bellows of whatever vast things they'd glimpsed inside the storm. Huge, stentorian cries rattled the glass in the frames and shook the timbers of the house.

"What's happening?" whispered Jenny. "What the hell *is* this?"

"It's the end of the world," whispered Brother Joe. "This is the Beast come to conquer. God, bless us sinners and shelter us with your mercy."

If Grey expected—or hoped—that Looks Away or Jenny would refute the monk's words, he was mistaken.

Blue lightning struck a telegraph pole on the far side of the street and it exploded into a swarm of splinters. The wires broke apart and drooped in defeat to the muddy ground. Grey and the others cried out and shrank back as jagged splinters thudded into the mud and rattled against the windows like a hail of arrows. One of the panes cracked but did not break. Even so, Grey spread his arms and pushed Jenny and Brother Joe backward. Looks Away flinched away as another azure bolt hit the stump of the telegraph pole and set it alight. The blue flame burned like a torch despite the heavy rain.

"This is madness," breathed Grey.

"Madness," agreed Looks Away.

Outside the storm raged.

It went on and on and on as darkness closed its fingers around the town of Paradise Falls and tightened everything inside a big, black fist.

Chapter 26

After a while the lightning and thunder began to ease, but the rain continued to hammer down. The *thump* of frogs and snakes had dwindled and stopped after the initial cascade. Now it was only rain.

The four of them had long since retreated to the subjective safety of Jenny's kitchen and sat huddled around the table. As the storm eased, their focus shifted from the wrath of a perverse nature and more toward the others in the room. The men became increasingly aware of their state of undress, while Grey in particular remained distracted by Jenny Pearl's lack of attire. With disheveled hair and a curtain for modesty she looked like some fairy princess from an old story. Even in the weird blue light of the storm she was beautiful.

It seemed to take her longer, however, to begin feeling self-conscious. She was clearly not overly concerned about modesty. Not that she flaunted herself, that was clear enough. It was just that she seemed to be a practical woman. Very grounded, and Grey admired that as much as her looks.

However she did finally turn away from the windows and pluck at the folds of cloth she'd wrapped around herself. "I'm going to get dressed," she said. "There's wood in the kitchen. Looksie, why don't you make a fire in the stove and set some water to boiling. Once that's going I'm sure you men can figure out how to dry your clothes. When I'm decent I'll see about eggs or soup.

Maybe a steak, if it hasn't spoiled. And Brother Joe—you'd better get some hot coffee into you."

"I-I'm o-o-o-k-k-kay," said Brother Joe, but his teeth chattered the words into a stutter.

The hard look on Jenny's face softened. "Don't be silly. You're turning blue. If you don't get something hot into you, you'll catch your death."

"I'm f-f-fine," he insisted.

"You're not. You've got no meat on you to keep you warm, you skinny old thing." Jenny chewed her lip in thought, then nodded to herself. "Look . . . my dad's things are still in a trunk in his room upstairs. You boys can sort through and find something to wear. He was of a size, so his stuff will be big on everyone except Mr. Torrance."

"Call me Grey. And, thank you kindly."

She nodded, appraising him. "Come along then. This storm's not going anywhere for a while and it's getting cold in here."

With that she turned and headed up the stairs into the shadows of the second floor.

Grey lingered, glancing at Looks Away.

"That," he said quietly, "is some woman."

"Indeed she is."

"What happened to her pa?"

Brother Joe said, "The D-Devil t-t-took him."

Grey looked to the Sioux for explanation.

"Bob Pearl was a good man. Everyone called him Lucky Bob. He was a real bull of a man, a sterling chap. Tough as leather, but fair-minded and honest as the day is long. He did a lot for the people of Paradise Falls, and after a while it seemed like he was the backbone of the whole town. He hated Nolan Chesterfield and hated Aleksander Deray even more, which is saying something because men like Lucky Bob Pearl seldom give in to hate. He had a big heart, as the poets say."

"What happened?" Grey repeated.

"What happened is that he decided he'd had enough of what was going on, and he went out to see Aleksander Deray about setting things straight," said Looks Away. "He wanted to appeal to him to be more fair with the water leases. However he never made it to Deray's place. Or, at least that's what Deray told people. Lucky Bob's horse was found in a pit near the edge of the drop-off. It was dead, its bones nearly picked clean. I saw the body. The horse's right front pastern was broken. The evidence *suggested* that Bob was riding along the edge and the horse stepped wrong, broke its leg, and fell into the pit. It was a long fall and there were plenty of rocks. Our fine Deputy Perkins concluded that when the horse fell, Bob Pearl pitched over the edge of the drop-off and went down into the salt water."

"His body wash up?"

Brother Joe shook his head and repeated, "The Devil took h-him."

"Devil or not," said Looks Away, "Lucky Bob's body never washed up." He paused. "Around here the sea doesn't willingly give up its dead."

Grey thought about that, remembering the churning water and jagged rocks. And the things that moved beneath those troubled waves. He shuddered.

Then he cleared his throat and changed the subject. "Our horses are out there somewhere."

Looks Away almost smiled. "I daresay they are. And while I value horseflesh as much as the next bloke—and maybe doubly so since I am, after all, Sioux—if you are primed to suggest that we venture out in that rain to corral them, then—."

"Don't!" said the monk without a trace of stutter.

"Not even a little chance of that, friend," said Grey. "I was remarking on it is all. I was not and am not planning on putting one foot out that door until this storm stops."

He almost added, *If it stops.*

"Bloody glad to hear it," said Looks Away. "I—."

From above came a stern call. "Are you coming or do I have to carry this son of a bitching case all by myself?"

Grey grinned. "Yeah. Quite a woman." He started toward the stairs then paused. "Looks Away—?"

"Yes?" the Sioux asked.

"I think we both know that you haven't been entirely straight with me about what's going on here."

"I haven't lied to you."

"That's not the same thing and you know it."

Looks Away said nothing, which was answer enough.

"When we get settled," said Grey, "we are going to have a full and frank discussion about this. About *all* of it, you hear me? Am I getting through to you on this?"

"You are," said the Sioux. "And . . . we will. I think it's high time for that conversation."

They exchanged a single nod, and then Grey climbed the stairs as the storm's intensity spun up again. It raged and the house creaked and Grey's heart hammered.

Chapter 27

In here," called Jenny Pearl, and Grey followed the sound of her voice down a darkened hall. It was a two-story house with a tin roof, and the rain made an awful din above his head. There were wrought iron sconces on the walls but the candles were unlit and cold. The darkened hall conjured an old memory in his mind, and he wasn't sure if it was real or something belonging to a dream.

In the memory, a much younger Grey—a boy still too young to shave—crept along a corridor like this but longer, with dusty wood paneling and the framed faces of dead relatives scowling at him from the walls. Unseen mice squeaked behind the wainscoting and their voices sounded like sly laughter. A dead cockroach lay on its back, one leg continuing to kick as if death's grip on it was tenuous. Cobwebs trembled in the corners as he reached the end of the hall and turned to follow a second and longer one. There were doors on either side. Shut and bolted. Always in his dreams those doors were locked against him. And even now, walking along Jenny Pearl's hall, he passed closed doors and felt deliberately shut out by them. Or . . . was something else shut in?

That was the secret of those old dreams. That was the thing that gnawed at him. At the self who walked through those halls. At the dreaming boy in his bed who sweated and writhed as his young limbs aped the movements of walking where he did not want to walk. And at the man he was now. Big, strong, experienced, armed, ruthless, tough by any standard. And all three of them, all three aspects of himself, were afraid. Even the gunslinger. Even the killer he was now.

Strength, he had learned through hard lessons, did not free you from fear. A life spent in combat and in small acts of violence, only proved to you how much hurt was there, how much danger. Bullets run out, muscles fail, stamina flees, and even the strongest warrior can find himself on his knees, weaponless and unable to raise his arms as his enemies close in around him.

And yet that sure knowledge, the understanding of his own mortality and his physical limits, were not the things that truly frightened him now. Here, in this strange town, with a storm raging outside that could never be called "natural," with dead men who walked and ghosts who followed him, Grey Torrance feared the things he did not understand. He was not afraid of dying. No, he'd danced with Death's cold daughter too many times to fear that. No, he was afraid of what might happen to his soul if death did not shut out all the lights and close all the doors. What then?

What then?

Grey saw a matchbox on the dresser, removed a Lucifer match, and popped it alight with his thumbnail. He forced his fingers not to tremble. He lit both candles and was relieved by the warm yellow glow. The shadows retreated to the far corners and clustered up near the high ceiling. Not gone. Waiting.

Always waiting.

The thought, as absurd as it was, sent a small chill down his spine.

Outside the thunder roared. The wind shrieked in demon voices.

The last door along the hall was ajar and light spilled out onto the floor. Grey tapped a knuckle against the frame.

"You decent?" he called.

He heard a short laugh. "I'm dressed, Mr. Torrance, but I'll never make claims about being decent."

Smiling, Grey opened the door.

Jenny stood on the far side of the room. The curtain and a mound of sopping frilly whites lay in a heap and she now wore a simple dress that hung straight enough to let him know there weren't too many slips and layers of bloomers beneath. She was buttoning the front and he caught a glimpse of soft cleavage. From her small curl of a smile it was clear she both knew he'd seen it, and that it was intended.

Watch this one, he warned himself. Grey was not afraid of facing any man with gun, blades, or fists, but he had been brought low by women more times than he could count. Samson and Achilles weren't the only men with weak spots.

Jenny nodded to the corner to Grey's left. "That's the trunk. I kept my pa's clothes."

"Can't let them go?" Grey suggested.

She shrugged. "He went missing but I never had a body to bury. It's stupid, but I . . . I suppose I keep hoping. . . . Well, you know."

"I do," he said. "And you have my condolences and my best wishes that he's out there somewhere. I guess it's fair to say that these days anything is possible."

She nodded and bent to scoop up her clothes. He knew, though, that she was hiding the flecks of tears that sparkled on her lashes.

"He must have been a good man," said Grey.

Without looking she asked, "Why do you say that?"

"Hard to imagine a bad man being loved that much."

Jenny did not answer. She picked up the clothes and

dumped them in a canvas-lined wooden washing bin. Grey busied himself with the chest. The lid was unlocked and inside the bin were five pairs of jeans, several shirts—most of them neatly mended—under drawers, socks, gloves, scarves, two light canvas jackets, and one Sunday go-to-meeting black suit. It occurred to him that if Mr. Pearl came home alive he'd need the farm clothes; if they found him dead they'd bury him in his church clothes. It was a sad thought.

He selected a pair of jeans and held them up, expected them to come up short, but after studying himself in the mirror he realized that he might have to roll the cuffs.

"How tall was your dad?"

"Six feet and four inches in his stocking feet. We used to make a joke of it and sometimes called him 'Seventy-six.'"

Grey unfolded one of the shirts. The man must have been a bull. Narrow at the hip but broad in the shoulders, with long arms and thick wrists. Grey figured they'd fit just fine.

"Thank you for the loan of these," he said. "I'll take good care of them."

She turned. "Pa was a good man. A decent man. He used be known as Lucky Bob. Survived the war down South, survived the Indian Wars and some of the Rail Wars. Lived through the Great Quake without a scratch. When things went bad out here, people looked to him. You could, you know. Look to him, I mean. He was that kind of man. Even when everything else was going all to hell, Lucky Bob kept his head and saw to others. When we lost the first of the wells, he was the one who organized the people here in town to share their water and help each other with their crops and herds. Even if he hadn't been my father I would have loved him and trusted him."

Jenny crossed to a small writing desk on which there

were several photographs in hand-carved wooden frames. She removed one and stood looking down at it, her face softened by memories. Her breasts lifted and fell as she drew in a deep breath and exhaled it in a sigh. Then she turned and held the frame out to Grey, who took it.

"This is your pa?"

"Yes. It was taken two years ago."

The man in the photo looked like a hero from some old tale. He stood with two other men, both of whom looked impressive and strong, but Lucky Bob Pearl towered over them. A big man with broad shoulders and a face that could have been chiseled out of granite. Firm chin, high cheekbones, a clear brow, and penetrating eyes that stared frankly out from beneath the flat brim of a black hat. He had an uncompromising gaze, but there was the smallest hint of a self-aware smile. That little smile was not a smirk; there was nothing mocking or condescending about it. This was a man aware of his power and faintly amused by it. Even though power and speed were promised by the lean body and the hard muscles that showed through the tension lines of his clothes, there was nothing of the bully about him. Merely confidence. Grey found that he liked the man in that photo and was damn sorry he wasn't here in Paradise Falls. As he handed the picture back he took another and more appraising look at Lucky Bob's daughter.

She had his strength. That was there in the straightness of her back, the lift of her proud chin, the clarity in her eyes. There was the same intelligence, the same confidence. And it occurred to Grey that he was probably doing a disservice to her in his mind by comparing Jenny to her father. Here was a woman who was powerful in her own way. In a way that was not—and could not be—defined by any man. They were individually powerful in a family that, for all Grey knew, could have been descended from heroes, kings, and queens. Stranger things were possibly in this world.

"He must have been quite a man," he said as he picked up the clothes again. He gestured with them. "Thanks for these."

Her eyes hardened. "You can put on my pa's things but you make sure you remember the kind of man whose clothes you're standing up in."

Grey nodded, seeing the hurt in her eyes. And the challenge. Left to burn, that challenge could turn into an unfair but entirely understandable resentment. So he decided to head it off at the pass.

"Miss Pearl, I wish I'd known your pa. I didn't, but I've known men like him. Not many, 'cause if there were more men like your dad maybe this world wouldn't be in the state it's in. That's not flattery, it's a fact. Men like me—we're tough and we're hard, and a lot of times we talk about how we're meaner than a rattlesnake and tougher than rawhide. But the plain truth is that we all want to be men like you say your dad was. It's humbling to stand here holding his clothes, and it will be an ice-cold day in Hell's backyard before I make claims to deserve to be spoken of in the same breath. I know I'm not that kind of man. I wish I was, but I'm not. You say your dad stepped up when others were hurting. That's what they call nobility. That's honor. And not half an hour ago you stood up to six armed men to draw water for the people in this town. Ever heard the expression about apples and how far they fall from trees?" He took a step toward her and lowered his voice. Jenny watched him with eyes filled with blue challenge. "You don't know the value of my word, so you can choose to accept what I say or not, but I tell you this, Jenny Pearl, that while I wear these clothes, I'll not dishonor the man who owns them."

Jenny's eyes were locked on his and for a moment

neither of them listened to the screaming wind or the pounding rain. Grey felt his heart hammering again, but this time it had nothing to do with fear or ghost rock or the risen dead. His throat went dry and he wanted to clear it, but he dared not break the spell.

The storm, however, had other plans.

There was a massive crack of thunder—many times louder than anything that had come before. It shook the whole house as if a giant had reared back and slammed both fists into it. Jenny cried out and staggered forward; Grey caught her and they ran to stand in the paltry shelter of the doorway, dreading that the whole place was coming down. The windowpanes rattled like chattering teeth. Blue lightning stabbed their eyes and not even when they squeezed their eyes shut could they hide from that glare. Grey and Jenny clung together as the fury of the storm raged and raged. They could hear the blast echoing away, rolling like a threat toward town.

And then past it.

And then off, over the cliffs and out into the ocean.

The trembling timbers stilled. The glass settled uneasily into the frames.

Slowly, slowly, the terrible tension eased. Even the howl of the demon wind and the barrage of the rain seemed to abate. Not completely, but to a much lower level than before.

Still, they stood there, wrapped in each other's arms with only her thin dress and his wet undershirt and britches between them. It wasn't much, and it soon dawned on him that if they stood there any longer it wasn't going to be enough.

He forced himself to step back and to push her gently away. And now he did clear his throat. The spell woven by high talk, closeness, shared experience, and the darker magic of the storm, finally snapped like a soap bubble. Jenny suddenly noticed an invisible wrinkle on her skirt and turned aside to smooth it out. Grey scooped up her father's fallen clothes and did his very best to stand behind them in case his interest in her showed. It occurred to him that hiding an erection behind the folded clothes of a woman's murdered father was both sick and wrong. But it was what he had.

"I'll leave you to change," said Jenny as she headed toward the door. She didn't leave at a dead run, but it was close. Grey stood there and listened to her shoes on the steps. Then he closed his eyes, bent forward, and slowly, deliberately banged his forehead on the doorframe.

Chapter 28

Grey and the other men dressed in bits and pieces of Lucky Bob Pearl's clothes. Their own wet things were draped over the backs of kitchen chairs arranged around the fat-bellied cast-iron stove. Brother Joe—who seemed quite familiar with the inside of the Pearl home—brewed coffee and began frying eggs. Jenny joined them a few minutes later and took heavy coffee mugs from a closet and began filling them.

When Grey tasted the coffee he winced and nearly spat it out, and he was a man who enjoyed his coffee strong enough to pick a fight. But this was hot tar in a cup. When he trusted himself not to actually curse the monk for being a poisoner and a blasphemer against the sanctity of the gods of coffee, he said, "You, um, make a strong cup, Padre."

Looks Away hid a grin behind his cup.

Brother Joe was unabashed, however. "We don't have much water, so we brew it strong. People drink less of it that way, and still get to enjoy the flavor."

"Is enjoy really the best word?" Looks Away wondered aloud. "Experience seems more apt."

If Brother Joe got the joke he did not show it.

The eggs were fried in bacon fat, and they tasted good enough. Grey had eaten many worse things over a life in the saddle.

"I think we should have our talk now," he said after swallowing a forkful of eggs.

"There's clearly a lot of strange things happening in this town. In your town. I'm a stranger here, so exactly what in the Sam Hill is going on? Who wants to start?"

He expected it to be Looks Away, but Brother Joe surprised him by speaking first.

"I've been living in these parts for many years. I was born near here, but then I followed a missionary down to Mexico and spent six years in a monastery. I took holy orders and came back here to build a church. My father left me some money and it was enough to buy land and materials."

"I didn't see a church," said Grey. "Not a Catholic one. Actually not any churches come to think on it."

Brother Joe shook his head. "There was one, but it's gone now. It was a lovely thing, too, though it's prideful to say so. A tall steeple and a bell so clear and true that you could hear it miles away. Enough pews for four hundred people, and for two full years we filled those pews. People came from other towns for services."

"When was this?" Grey asked, but he thought he knew the answer already.

"We opened the doors on the first day of spring 1866."

"Ah," said Grey. The Great Quake was in 1868. "I'm sorry."

"For the church? No," said Brother Joe. "Lovely as it was, it was just a building. Brick and stone, nails and paint. But remember that the Great Quake happened on a Sunday."

Grey winced.

"So many people," said Brother Joe in a voice that was raw with pain. "And they were good people, Mr. Torrance. Fine, hard-working people. Decent people who worked the land and came to their knees on a Sunday. Maybe not every Sunday, and maybe not every one was the best Christian he or she could be, but everyone sins."

No one commented on that.

"Everyone," repeated the monk. "God knows."

Grey caught a strange note, a deeper sadness in the monk's voice. He saw unshed tears glittering in the man's dark eyes.

Brother Joe took a pull on the bad coffee and seemed to steel himself before he continued. "As sinners must, I want to make a confession," he began, directing his words only to Grey. "When I said that I was not a priest, I should have said that I was—but am one no longer. Because I sinned a great sin, I lost the blessings of the church. I disgraced myself and have betrayed the love of God."

Looks Away reached across the table and patted his arm. "There, there, old chap."

"What happened?" asked Grey.

Brother Joe closed his eyes and his fingers knotted together into trembling knots.

"When the Great Quake tore these lands apart, we were in the middle of a hymn. 'Nearer My God to Thee.' Perhaps the timing was a joke of the Devil. A mockery. The first of many." He shook his head, eyes still closed. "The tremors struck so quickly. We had no warning, no clue. One moment we were all there, bathed in the shared joy of worship, and then the world split apart. The church itself split apart. All in an instant there was a sound like green wood being split and the floor itself was rent from the doors along the aisle to the transept. It broke apart the church like two halves of an eggshell. The walls leaned away from each other and great masses of the roof came plunging down. Everyone . . . everyone . . ."

"Joe," said Jenny, touching his shoulder, "you don't need to do this."

He opened his eyes but didn't look at her. Instead he stared at his interlaced hands. Tears rolled down his brown cheeks.

"The people screamed. My parishioners, my flock . . . my *friends* . . . they screamed as our church was torn apart and the pit opened beneath us. Many were . . . killed . . . when the roof fell. More died as the steeple plunged down among them. I saw a woman—a lovely young farm wife no older than Miss Pearl—torn to pieces as the stained glass window exploded. I saw her die, still clutching her child as she tried to protect him with her own body. I witnessed people burn as smoke and fire belched up from the bowels of the earth. I saw people try to hold onto the pews, the broken timbers, the floor boards to keep from falling into the inferno. I heard them all scream. I heard them call out to God and His angels to save them. I . . . I prayed, too. I prayed harder than I ever had before. But, God forgive me, I did not pray for them. I did not pray for the people in my church." Tears streamed down his face and fell onto his hands. "I prayed to God to save me. *Me*. I begged the Almighty to spare me. Not them. Not the men and women. Not the old. Not the children. I prayed that I would be spared. And I was." A sob broke in his chest. "I was saved from fiery death because the great hand-carved crucifix that hung above the altar fell down across the crack in the floor. And while everyone I loved, everyone I had sworn to guide and protect *died* I . . . I . . . crawled across the body of our Lord to escape."

He buried his face in his hands and wept. It was terrible to see. The sobs came from such a deep place that they shook his thin body, striking him like blows. Jenny got up and came around behind him, wrapping her arms around the monk's frame, and he half turned and clung to her. The way a drowning person would. The way a child would.

Grey wanted to walk out of the room. He didn't want to see this man's shame and grief and remorse, or to share in any of it. Nor did he know how this related to the matters at hand, but he did not move. Something deep inside his chest, inside his heart, told him to stay. He glanced at Looks Away and the Sioux's face was troubled and sad, so Grey sat there drinking the bitter coffee and thinking bitter thoughts as storms raged outside and inside the old house.

It took Brother Joe a long time to claw himself back from the edge of his personal abyss. Jenny eventually stepped back and reclaimed her chair. The monk wiped his streaming eyes with his sleeve. He took a sip of coffee and coughed his throat clear.

"I'm sorry," he said, but no one responded to that.

Instead Grey said, "Tell me the rest. What happened after that?"

"After that? Paradise Falls was destroyed," said Brother Joe. "Most of it, anyway. Three-quarters of the homes and buildings. Nine tenths of the people. Gone. We would learn later that this was not a judgment leveled against us but against many. Most of what had been California had been rent apart and thrown down. Like a bandage removed to reveal a terrible wound, we saw what lay beneath our land. Pits. Great caverns where the foul things of the earth long dwelt in shadows. Bottomless holes and endless caverns from which the earth exhaled a breath of brimstone and ash. Men have come to call it the Maze, but it is the landscape of Satan's burning kingdom revealed."

Jenny poured him more of the wretched coffee.

"Paradise Falls nearly died on that day. I do not know why any of it survived and I do not pretend to understand God's mysteries. Like many of the survivors did, I left. I went down to Mexico and made a confession to the Cardinal."

"What happened?" asked Grey.

Brother Joe almost smiled. A rueful, twisted little smile.

The kind never associated with a happy memory. "He spat on me."

"He *spat* on you?"

"And I do not blame him," the monk said quickly. "If he'd had a knife at hand I believe he would have plunged it into my breast, and he would have been right to do so. There are some sins that go beyond any tolerance. I had broken faith with God and with my flock, and I had crawled across my Savior to—."

"Bullshit," said Grey, and it brought Brother Joe up short. "Far as I can tell you're an ordinary human being. I'm no Catholic and I'm not much given to attending church, but I seem to remember from having been there once or twice that priests and parsons are no different than anyone else. You're flesh and bone, man. *You're* not an angel or God Himself."

Brother Joe shook his head. "No, you don't understand what it means to be a priest of the church. It was my duty to protect my flock."

"What, like Jesus protects everyone who calls themselves a Christian? No, don't look so shocked. You can't sit there and tell me that faith alone is any kind of shield. It never has been. The Romans nailed Jesus to the cross, and they whipped him bloody before they did it. And I read enough of the Bible to remember that most of the apostles and saints got themselves tortured and killed. John the Baptist lost his damn head. They crucified Peter upside down, and millions of good Christians have died since then. You want to sit there and tell me that none of them—*including* some of the saints—weren't afraid? That they didn't want to bargain their way out? You think all of them went willingly to their deaths? People think that because that's how the Bible's written, but didn't Jesus ask God to let that cup pass by?"

"He still went to the cross."

"Sure. He was Jesus. You're not. You're only a man like the rest of us. If it had been me in that church, I'd have crawled over more than a wooden cross to get out of there."

The monk kept shaking his head, and Grey let it go. He flapped a hand at Brother Joe.

"Whatever. Tell me how that walks us all the way to right now."

"Very well," said Brother Joe. "After I made my confession I was defrocked. My robes were torn, my surplice cut to pieces and my holy orders rescinded. The cardinal stopped short of excommunicating me because another priest interceded on my behalf. A good and righteous man who had been in seminary with me. He begged that I be allowed to work for my reclamation by returning as a brother of the Order of Outcasts. The order was formed after the Quake and is made up of brothers and a few priests who have each survived the destruction of their churches."

"Like I said, you're not the only one."

"I am the only coward," said Brother Joe.

"I doubt that," said Grey unkindly. Then he amended it. "I mean, I doubt you're the only one who did what he had to do to survive."

Brother Joe chose not to comment on that. Instead he picked up the thread of his narrative. "When I returned to Paradise Falls, I expected to find only scattered people. Or perhaps no one at all. Instead I found that a leader had risen among them. A good man who, though not a Catholic, was clearly doing God's work. He had gathered the survivors and organized them into work parties to search for other survivors, to gather food and water, and to begin rebuilding the town."

"You're talking about Jenny's dad," said Grey. "Lucky Bob Pearl, am I right?"

"Yes," said Brother Joe. "Bob Pearl saved this town.

He protected it the way I should have. He was a great, great man and if he is indeed dead, then I know that he sleeps in the arms of the Lord."

Jenny smiled a sad little smile.

"Brother—?" prompted Looks Away, "at the risk of being indelicate, we are straying from the point."

"No he's not," said Jenny. "This all started with the Quake, and the people here in Paradise Falls are what's left of a good town. Brother Joe may have done wrong as he sees it, but he came back. He worked right alongside my pa to rebuild. He worked hard, day and night. Since he's come back he's bled for the people here."

"Miss Pearl, please—," began the monk, flushing with embarrassment.

"Hey," said Grey, "you don't need to defend this man to me. I'm not in any position to throw stones, God knows. I have enough check marks on my own soul to buy me a front seat in Hell, and that's not a joke."

They all looked at him. The rain rattled against the windows and lightning burned the night.

"Maybe these days there's no one pure as a babe," continued Grey. "So let's not waste a lot of time on confession or absolution. Let's talk about what the hell is going on."

"What's going on, old chap," said Looks Away, "is that as soon as the dust settled from the Quake they discovered ghost rock."

Chapter 29

A h," said Grey. "Now we're getting to it."

"You know about that," said the Sioux. "Everyone does. And you know that the supplies of it are becoming scarce very quickly. Prospectors found several large pieces of it in the caves just over the cliffs from where we're sitting. Enough of it to make those gentlemen enormously wealthy. They hired other men to continue mining."

"If there was so much of the rock around then why is the town so damn poor?"

"Ah, well there's the crux of it," said Looks Away. "You see Lucky Bob and the good Brother Joe here weren't the only people offering to help out the good citizens of Paradise Falls. A certain gentleman from the East came and offered to provide start-up capital and loans for rebuilding. At a modest rate of interest, of course."

"And—?"

"And instead of being charged interest, the people here signed away their mining rights."

"Well, that was goddamn dumb."

"It was a timing issue, don't you see?" said Looks Away, looking pained. "The offer was made *before* ghost rock was discovered. Just before, in point of fact. The ink was barely dry on the loan papers when the prospectors found the first veins."

Grey leaned back in his chair. "How soon before?"

"One week," said Jenny.

"Now isn't that mighty interesting timing," said Grey.

"Isn't it just?" agreed Looks Away. "The people here had barely enough money or liquid capital to build the few homes and stores you see. Not enough for anything else."

"What makes it worse," said Jenny, "is that since the Quake the ground doesn't grow much that you'd want to eat. More than half of the crops that we can grow are either too bitter to eat or they're infested with worms or bugs or other critters. We're surrounded by ten thousand farmable acres and everyone's slowly starving to death. And forget about raising cattle. They drink from the wrong well or eat some of a strange new kind of grass that has been growing wild these last few years. The farmers try to weed it out, but it's more ornery than crabgrass and it seems to spring up overnight. Everyone has some in their fields. Any cow or sheep that eats it either keels right over or goes mad and runs off the cliffs."

"Christ," said Grey.

"Which resulted in people having to borrow more and more money and to pay for food brought in by rail from other towns," said Looks Away. "Mr. Nolan Chesterfield—of the Wasatch Railroad—controls all supplies being brought in, and he has been trying to acquire the mineral rights. Not only for the veins of gold and silver exposed by the quake, but for ghost rock. A few folks didn't sell their rights, but they're on land where no ghost rock has been found. So far Chesterfield has picked everyone's pockets but hasn't gotten much in the way of rock. Such a pity because his wife, Veronica, is quite a lovely person who has tried to help."

"Help—how?"

Brother Joe said, "She's donated money and some barrels of grain to my church."

"Why would she do that if her husband was squeezing the town?"

Grey saw the monk look down and Jenny cut a sly and mildly accusing glance at Looks Away. For his part, the Sioux wore an expression of bland and entirely artificial surprise.

"Why, I suppose," he said, "it's because she has a—oh, how should I phrase this?—a generous nature."

"Generous is right," Jenny said in a sharply disapproving tone. "Humph."

Grey grabbed the conversation and brought it back to the topic. "Chesterfield's the son of a bitch who hired those Apaches, isn't he?"

"Indeed. They were his muscle."

"Were?" asked Jenny. "Did something happen to them?"

"Someone decided to—how should I put this?—cut *short* their term of employment."

"What's that mean?"

"It means, Miss Pearl," said Grey, "that someone cut their heads off and left 'em in the desert with a sign that pretty much says 'get lost.' Words to that effect."

Brother Joe went pale, but Jenny snorted. "Good. Those men were sons of bitches and they're better off as coyote meat."

"Dear me," said Looks Away, pretending to be shocked. Then he turned to Grey and arched his eyebrows. "Would you care to venture a guess as to the name of the other party involved in our little Shakespearean drama? Namely the philanthropist who owns the bank and holds title to every viable mine where ghost rock *has* been found?"

Grey Torrance felt his lip curl. "Aleksander Deray," he said. Flat. Not a question.

"So," said Looks Away, spreading his hands, "now you see the shape of it. The townspeople are buried to their eyeteeth in debt, which ties them to the land by legal and moral obligation. Deray and Chesterfield are like a pair of vultures."

"They're worse than vultures," snapped Jenny. "They're monsters. They won't be happy until he owns us body and soul."

Brother Joe nodded. "I fear that they are both in concert with the Devil."

Grey wanted to ignore that, but the screams of the wind made it hard to easily dismiss any such comments.

"When the townsfolk had no more mining rights to sell," said Looks Away, "Deray offered new loans in exchange for their water rights. Some of those rights, by the way, had already been sold to Chesterfield to pay for seeds, medicine, and bulk goods, like dried beans and salt beef. Before you ask, no, the terms were far from equitable, but then no one here is in a position of strength when it comes to bargaining."

"Which is damned unfair," declared Jenny, "since around here water's the only thing worth as much as ghost rock."

"And both of them worth more than gold," agreed Looks Away. "Funny old world."

"So," said Grey, "while Nolan Chesterfield has been competing with Aleksander Deray to suck this town dry, Veronica Chesterfield has been trying to help? You said she gave extra food and such to the church?"

"She is a generous woman," said Brother Joe. "I think she would be even more so if she could."

"I take it her husband disapproves?"

"Her husband doesn't bloody well know about it," said Looks Away. "Veronica has to make secret arrangements to get supplies out to Brother Joe. And she risks much in doing so."

"She's afraid of her husband?"

"Very," said Looks Away. "And with good cause. No-lan Chesterfield is a fat, obnoxious, short-tempered, violent, greedy parasite."

"Don't dress it in lace, son. Tell us what you really think."

Looks Away sneered. "I can say without reservation that if he went the way of his Apaches, I would shed so very few tears."

"Please, brother," cautioned the monk. "We should not wish ill on anyone."

"Bollocks."

The sound of the rain changed and they all looked up.

"The storm's passing," said Jenny. "Thank God."

It was true. The hammering rain had diminished to a few pings and the awful screams were only whispers on the wind.

"Still might wait a piece before we go out," suggested Grey.

"Did you see any of us bolting for the door?" asked Looks Away.

"Need to find our horses."

"Mm. However horses are easier to replace than one's skin. Just a thought."

Grey nodded and sipped his coffee. "Now, that brings us around to you and your boss, Doctor Saint. If Deray owns all the mining rights, then why's Saint have a laboratory out here?"

"No, I said Deray has *almost* all the mining rights," corrected Looks Away.

"Right, but the rights he doesn't have are for land without ghost rock."

"Yes and no. You see here in the Maze there are traces of ghost rock in much of the substrata and—."

"In the what?"

"Let me back up a bit. Paradise Falls is in what was once the San Joaquin Valley. Hard to tell that anymore, but there it is. Geological explorers, like some of my teachers, believe that this whole area was once a great inland sea many, many years ago. Probably millions of years ago. Water erodes all forms of rock and mineral, and moving water tends to spread it all around, don't you know. When the mountains were formed—probably by some ancient earthquakes every bit as powerful as the Great Quake—the sediment left traces of every rock it eroded. Are you following me?"

"I think so," said Grey slowly. "So if ghost rock was already down there in the Maze, and if some of it eroded, then . . ."

"Then traces of it are everywhere," said Looks Away, nodding his approval. "Not chunks, not pieces you could easily spot."

"Then so what? How's that worth anything to anyone? I never heard of anyone panning for ghost rock and making much more than beer money off of it."

"It's not about money," said Looks Away, although from the expression on Jenny's face it was clear she didn't entirely agree. "Doctor Saint developed a process to extract trace particles of the rock from sediment. It's a time-consuming process, though, and still very much in the experimental stages."

"Again—so what?"

"So, Doctor Saint was able to process enough of it to power some of his weapons."

"Ah," said Grey, nodding.

"Ah, indeed. When he returns here, Doctor Saint will continue his extraction process, and that will give us something more than fisticuffs, harsh language, and the odd bullet or two to help us in our campaign."

"*Campaign*?" asked Jenny, Brother Joe, and Grey, all at the same time.

Looks Away's lips curled into a thoroughly devious smile. Very nearly malicious.

"Oh yes, my friends," he said. "Between Nolan Chesterfield and Aleksander Deray this little town is being squeezed dry and crushed flat. They are clearly willing to brutalize men of the cloth and innocent women to protect their property, and the property in question is water necessary for basic human survival. Is it really a debatable point that they've crossed a line in the sand? This is no longer about property. These men are trying to either drive us all out, or ensure that everyone here dies. As a Sioux, I believe I understand that kind of thinking better than anyone else at this table. Before we formed our own nation my people were being driven to the edge of extinction. We fought back. We made a stand. Not because we think we're better—though, I have my own thoughts on that subject—but because we believe that being born comes with certain rights. Your Declaration of Independence has, I believe, some verbiage to that effect. Inalienable rights. Life is notable among them. Chesterfield and Deray want to take that away from us. I do not believe *they* have that right. So, I think it is high time we stop bending our collective necks to the chopping block and make our own stand."

There was a heavy, thoughtful silence following his speech. Brother Joe was the first to break it.

"I can't agree to anything that involves killing. My vows—."

"—are all very admirable, Brother," said Looks Away. "We're not asking you to do any actual fighting. You are skilled in medicine, I believe?"

"I'm not a doctor, but I know something about herbs and healing draughts."

"Good enough. You can fix us if we get dented."

"I'll damn well fight," declared Jenny Pearl, her eyes blazing. "Those bastards took everything I have, including my pa."

They all looked at Grey.

"You already know where I stand," he said. "But before we—."

Whatever else he was going to say was cut off by a terrible high-pitched scream. It was not the spectral howl of the demon storm.

This was the scream of a child.

Human.

Close.

Screaming in fear and in pain.

Outside in the rain.

Chapter 30

Grey and Looks Away launched themselves from their chairs and ran through the house to the front door. Grey whipped it open but stinging rain struck his face, driving him back. Even though the storm had slackened, the raindrops still felt like acid.

"You can't go out there!" cried Brother Joe, pushing past him to close the door.

"The Hell I can't," snapped Grey.

"The rain will kill you."

That almost stopped Grey and in the space of one heartbeat the fear that was always simmering inside his chest nearly drowned the dented honor that used to define who he was. Maybe if it had been only Looks Away there with him he might have stayed, but Jenny looked too much like Annabelle, and he could not allow himself to be a coward in her eyes.

You're a damn fool, he told himself.

And he mentally told that part of himself to go to hell.

"Here!" yelled Jenny as she dug an oilskin poncho from the closet and threw it to Grey. He snatched it out of the air and quickly pulled it on. It must have belonged to her father because it was too big for Grey, but that was fine. Larger meant more protection.

"Do you have another?" demanded Looks Away.

"Upstairs in the trunk," said Jenny, starting for the stairs, but Looks Away dashed past her and took the steps two at a time.

A second scream tore the night. Higher and more terrible.

Without waiting for the Sioux, Grey opened the door and flung himself into the storm.

The wind was intensifying even though there was less rain. Great gusts swept up the street toward him, seeming to attack, to try and drive him away. Riding the wind came the howls of damned things. Grey bulled his way into it. Hitting the wind was like pushing against a wall, and the muddy ground tried to catch and hold his booted feet. Even with the poncho the rain found openings at wrist and ankle and below the brim of his hat and stung like a swarm of bees.

He tried to hear through the wailing wind to orient himself, but almost at once there was no need for that. A figure came racing up the street toward him. Small. A little girl of no more than seven or eight. Red hair streamed behind her like a horse's mane and her face was as pale as a corpse.

Except where it was streaked with blood.

In the flashes of ghost lightning the blood looked as black as oil, but Grey knew what it was. The girl ran as hard as she could, but she was slowing, staggering, nearly gone. She would have stopped to rest if she could except for the *thing* that followed her.

It came more slowly than she ran, loping along like some great, pale ape.

Only it wasn't an ape.

It was Deputy Jed Perkins.

He was nearly naked, his body covered only in torn streamers of what had been his clothes. His skin was white except for sunburned forearms and face. His hair hung in dripping rattails. His mouth was open, smiling. Laughing.

Laughing in all the wrong ways.

And his chest.

His chest.

The flesh of breast had been slashed to ribbons, the meat and muscle pulled back to expose his rib cage. And there, driven by some insane force into the very center of his sternum was a piece of polished stone. It was as black as the night except for a tracery of white lines that seemed to wriggle through it. The stone glowed from within but it was neither fire nor electric light. This was something far worse, something far stranger. Deep inside the chunk of ghost rock a cold, intensely bright blue light glowed with hellish ferocity. The deputy's eyes glowed with the same weird light. Too bright, as if lit from within.

Grey nearly lost himself in that moment.

He had already seen the dead walk and encountered witches and monstrous storms, but this was something else. This was sorcery. This was the kind of dark magic he'd read about in old books, the kind they sing of in songs when they are not trying to lull you to sleep. This was what evil looked like.

This was something that broke the laws of nature. Perkins had to be dead and yet he ran howling after a child, his eyes filled with starlight, his hands reaching to tear and rend.

Scared as he was, Grey's hand moved with practiced speed. The Colt seemed to appear in his hand, he saw and felt his thumb cock the hammer, felt his index finger squeeze the trigger. Heard the report. All of it happening as if he were witnessing someone else perform the familiar actions.

The *bang* jolted him.

The bullet drilled a hole through the night air, sizzled past the rain, and punched into the hard, flat muscle of Perkins's left pectoral. Just off-center of the black stone. The impact knocked a single cough from the man's lips.

Just that.

And nothing else.

It barely slowed the man.

Perkins's eyes shifted from the girl he was chasing and stared at Grey with a bottomless hatred that sent a thrill of terror through him. His teeth peeled back from his lips and he growled like a mountain cat.

He bent low and raced forward with manic speed. Straight at Grey.

This was black magic.

He fished for the word, the right word. It was down there in the bottom of his mind where he kept the things he didn't ever want to think about. Ugly things. Wrong things.

Bad things.

The word awoke in his thoughts. Like a serpent stirred to wakeful rage it hissed in his mind.

The word for what this was.

Necromancy.

The magic of the dead.

"God damn you to hell!" bellowed Grey as he fired again. And again. The bullets took Perkins in the right chest and in the stomach. They made him twitch.

But they did not stop him.

With a howl like the demon wind itself, Jed Perkins flung himself at Grey and bore him down into the mud and the burning rain.

Chapter 31

As Grey fell onto his back he brought one foot up, jammed his boot against the deputy's chest, and let the force of the roll turn them both like a wheel. With his leg as the spoke, Perkins rolled over and then backward and Grey gave him an extra kick to send the man flying. Grey had fallen so hard that he had enough momentum to roll his own body all the way over onto his knees, with one hand snapping out to steady himself.

Somehow he'd managed to keep his pistol in his other hand, and to keep the mechanism out of the mud. He pivoted on his knee and snapped off two more shots at Perkins, who had splatted down into the mud and was struggling to get up. The first bullet took Perkins in the shoulder and Grey could see a lump of meat and a chunk of bone fly into the air.

But all that did was make Perkins laugh.

Laugh.

It was a laugh as wrong as all the damage in the world. A high, cackling bray that carried no trace of the deputy's own voice. Instead this was shrill and alien. A nightmare laugh that revealed a horrible secret to Grey—that there was something *else* hiding within the man's body. And, again, Grey remembered the stories he'd read as a boy, of demons that could inhabit human flesh and wear it like armor.

The laughter was both an anticipation of its triumph

over a mortal foolish enough to do battle with something that could not be whipped, and an exultation in its freedom to wander the world of the living.

The laughter tore through the night and stuck knives in Grey's mind. The injured little girl screamed, knowing that there was no hope left.

So Grey put his next bullet into that laughing mouth. The heavy slug shattered the rows of white teeth and then blew out the back of the deputy's skull, right at the base where it attaches to the top of the spine.

There was a moment—just a flicker of time—where the demon thing still smiled, even with a mouth of shattered teeth. Then Deputy Perkins's head tilted forward, no longer supported by vertebra and the weight of it jerked the body down.

Even then the thing did not die.

It flopped in the mud and began thrashing wildly, arms and legs whipping around, feet kicking, mouth trying to bite in Grey's direction.

"God damn, why don't you die, you ugly son of a whore?" bellowed Grey and he fired the last bullet in his gun. This time he aimed for the flat plane of the deputy's forehead. The slug punched in at a bad angle and instead of bursting through the other side, it ricocheted off some angle of bone inside, and then bounced around. The deputy's head shuddered from the inner impacts.

Then all at once the blue light winked out from its eyes and Perkins fell face forward into the mud and did not move.

Grey did not believe that even now this was over. He broke open his pistol, dumped the spent brass, and hastily shoved six fresh rounds into the cylinder. As he did so he edged over to stand between the little girl—who, against all sense, had stopped running to watch the fight—and the monster. Grey snapped the cylinder into place and pointed the gun at Perkins.

The body lay still. It looked different now. Empty, somehow.

Empty of life, if life was a word that fit.

Dead.

Dead for good and all.

Dead, like the members of the posse—Riley and the others—after he'd managed to end them.

End them.

That thought stuck like an arrow in Grey's mind. How exactly *had* he ended them?

Perkins had been shot over and over again. None of those rounds had even slowed him.

Only that last bullet.

In the head.

No. In the brain.

The brain?

Why there? Why not the heart? Why not the damn spine? Either of those would have dropped even a mountain bear.

The brain.

Kill the brain and kill the . . .

The what?

As if in answer to his troubled, tumbling thoughts, a voice spoke a word that Grey did not know, not in this context.

"*Undead!*"

He turned to see Brother Joe standing ten feet away, panting, draped in curtains to fend off the rain, eyes wide with horror.

"W-what?" asked Grey numbly.

"That thing is an abomination against God. It is one of the *undead*. Dear Jesus and Mary protect us."

"What *is* it?"

"It is a corpse given a dark semblance of life—unlife," said Brother Joe, crossing himself. "It has been inhabited by a demon spirit so that it can do Satan's will on Earth."

Grey wanted to tell him that this was pure unfiltered bullshit.

Wanted to. Could not.

Jed Perkins lay at his feet and all of this had happened. Had truly happened.

Two figures came running through the dwindling rain. One wore a set of gray oilskins and the other a cloak with the hood pulled tight around a lovely face. Looks Away and Jenny. He had a pistol in his hand and she carried a single-barrel twenty-gauge shotgun. They saw Perkins and slowed, standing shocked and puzzled.

"What happened?" asked Jenny as she realized the child was there. She hurried over to the girl, shifted the shotgun to one hand and used the other to wrap her cloak around the child. "Grey—what happened here?"

Grey holstered his gun, squatted, and turned Perkins over so that the man's ruined chest was exposed. The rain gradually washed away the mud, revealing the terrible wounds. And the thing embedded in the deputy's breastbone. It no longer glowed with blue fire, but the lines of white were like threadworms in gangrenous flesh.

Brother Joe cried out. "Blasphemy! This is black magic."

"Necromancy," said Grey. "I . . . think that's what they call it. Necromancy."

Looks Away knelt next to him and very carefully touched the edges of bloodless skin around the stone. He did not touch the stone itself.

"Ghost rock," he said. "Not very pure, but definitely ghost rock."

"I don't understand," said Jenny. "What *happened*?"

It was the little girl who answered. "The monsters came in through the window."

Every eye turned toward her.

"*Monsters?*" echoed Jenny. "God . . . are there more than one?"

The night, as if listening with dark humor, once more held the answer. There was another scream. A man's this time. It rose higher and higher, losing gender and identity until it was nothing more than a shriek of unbearable agony. Then it suddenly stopped with wet finality.

The little girl screamed into the ensuing silence and broke from the shelter of Jenny Pearl.

"*Dad!*"

She ran toward the sound of certain death.

And Grey, Looks Away, and Brother Joe ran after.

Chapter 32

It was immediately apparent that it was not merely a single home that had been invaded.

The town of Paradise Falls was under siege.

Figures moved in the gloom. People, heedless of the rain, ran into the street, screaming, pleading. Some of them had weapons. A shovel, a broken table leg. One woman held a frying pan. Fewer still had guns. Mostly shotguns, fowling pieces, and one old-time muzzleloader.

However there were other shapes moving through the rain.

The other deputies.

And several men Grey had never seen.

They were all dead men. Each of them had a ruined chest in which a black stone was fixed. Blue light sparkled in the heart of each stone. Blue had always been a good color to Grey. Lucky. Happy. Summer skies and deep water. Cornflowers and a woman's eyes.

Now blue was the color of hate and hurt, of harm and horror.

Grey knew that these men were all dead. Risen dead. Torn from the earth. They laughed as they chased the fleeing townsfolk.

"No . . . ," whispered Looks Away.

There were so many of them.

Of *them*.

The word rose like bile to Grey's mouth.

"*Undead*."

Looks Away opened fire at the closest of them and Grey saw black holes appear in bloodless flesh. However the creatures kept advancing. Their wild laughter tore the air.

Grey reached out and pushed Looks Away's gun arm down, forcing the Sioux to turn his wild eyes away from the walking dead.

"What the bloody hell are you playing at?" cried Looks Away.

"The head—aim for the head. Nothing else stops them. Remember the posse? That's how we stopped them. Aim for the brain."

The memory of that terrible night was too clear to make it a chore to convince Looks Away.

"The whole sodding world is mad," the Sioux muttered as he reloaded. "Stark staring mad."

Brother Joe edged around the crowd and gathered the little girl into his arms. Then he retreated, watching the monsters as they watched him.

While Looks Away finished reloading, Grey raised his pistol in a steady two-handed grip and stepped into the path of the running corpse. They saw his gun and laughed.

Maybe they don't know, he mused, and prayed that it was true.

The closest of them was thirty feet away. It was one of the other deputies.

"Go back to Hell," said Grey Torrance as he pulled the trigger.

The bullet hit the dead deputy right above the left eyebrow and exploded the back of his head. The undead's legs kept running for three more steps before the dead, slack weight of the dying body dragged it down.

The other grinning corpse ran past.

But the ones out front were no longer laughing, and their smiles seemed frozen onto their dead faces.

They didn't know, thought Grey. *But they sure as God know now.*

The undead all froze for a moment, and a dozen pairs of burning blue eyes turned toward Grey and his friends. Grey could not tell if they hesitated because one of their own had been killed and it gave them pause, or because all of their murderous rage was suddenly now focused on the two men and one woman with the guns.

In either case Grey knew this could only end one way.

In death.

Knowing that he was being watched, he used his thumb to draw the hammer back to full cock, and narrowed his eyes to sight down the barrel at the face of the closest monster.

"Come on, you ass-ugly sons of bitches," he said. "Come and take us."

They came.

Howling with red delight, they came.

Chapter 33

Grey, Looks Away, and Jenny all fired. The bangs of their guns were simultaneous—two pistol cracks and the boom of the shotgun.

The front line of abominations tried to dodge out of the way. Grey's shot blew the jawbone off of one, but he spun away and kept upright. Still running. Looks Away put his round through the temple of a second, but the round must not have hit the right part of the brain. The creature staggered and began wandering off, as if confused.

However it was immediately clear that Jenny Pearl's shotgun wasn't packing birdshot. A big deer slug fired from the small-bore weapon smashed through the bridge of the third undead's nose and its head seemed to fly apart. The creature collapsed and two other monsters behind it tripped over it and fell.

Grey stepped forward and fired shots at both of the fallen things. Looks Away snapped off three shots and dropped two more.

Six down.

The rest of the monsters scattered. Like cockroaches fleeing the light, they fled from the firestorm of hot lead. Some raced up onto porches and hurled themselves through glass windows or kicked in doors. Screams burst from within each house. Other undead ran for any cover they could find—a side alley, behind a parked wagon, or into a darkened store.

Grey fired at them until his gun was empty, but he only killed two more. Looks Away fared less well, killing one. By the time Jenny reloaded her single barrel shotgun, there were no targets left on the streets. Nothing left to kill.

Inside the houses, though, the slaughter had begun.

"We have to do something," cried Jenny. "They'll kill everyone."

"I know, damn it," said Grey as he broke into a run. He jumped onto the closest porch, shouldered through the door and saw a walking corpse struggling with a one-legged old man. Grey kicked the monster in the ribs as hard as he could. He knew the blow wouldn't do the thing any harm, but the force of it sent the creature crashing into the wall.

Grey swung his pistol down and was a hairsbreadth from pulling the trigger when the creature spoke.

"Don't!" it begged. "Please. For the love of God, don't kill me."

The mocking smile was gone and in its place was the terrified face of a man. Still dead pale, but now there was no trace of the demonic presence that had owned this flesh seconds ago.

The old man whimpered and began crawling toward the hall, his face battered and bloody. His face was stricken as if the presence of these monsters had cracked something in his mind. Grey couldn't blame him. His own mind felt like it was hanging from one broken hinge.

"What are you?" demanded Grey as he pressed the barrel of the Colt against the dead flesh.

The creature tried to shrink back, and it was impossible for Grey to tell whether this was some kind of ploy or not. He had far too little to go on.

Behind him he heard gunshots and more screams.

"Tell me why I shouldn't send you straight to hell," he said to the thing.

A tear broke from the corner of the man's eye. Grey would not have thought that a dead thing could weep. The blue light from its eyes turned the tear into liquid sapphire.

"I am in hell," said the monster in a hoarse voice. "I—I died. I mean, I think I died. I remember falling. I remember seeing my own blood. And then . . . and then . . ."

His voice disintegrated into sobs.

Grey adjusted his hand on his pistol grip and had no idea what to do.

"Why are you attacking these people?"

The undead looked surprised. "Attacking? I didn't . . . I mean . . . I . . . I . . ."

"You ran in here and tried to kill that old man."

The thing cut a look sideways at the old man crawling along the hall toward the kitchen. A deep frown of confusion grooved his brow.

"Mr. Chalmers? Is that you? It's me. It's Bobby Sandoval. You know me. I used to work at the sawmill with Tommy. You know me. I . . . I . . . I swear it's me."

Grey glanced over at the old man to see how he was reacting.

It was the wrong thing to do.

With the speed of a snake, the monster's left hand flashed out and slapped the pistol from Grey's grip. The expression on its face changed from confusion and horror to malice in a heartbeat.

But it was a long heartbeat, and even as everything became crazy, Grey's mind pulled apart what he had just seen. The hand moved, and the thing attacked, but the face registered what looked like genuine surprise at what its body was doing. It was like a horseman who was reacting to a mount suddenly stumbling. The expression did not match. Not at once. Only after the creature reached for Grey did the confusion melt away to be replaced by that malicious leer. The undead kicked up with both feet, catching Grey in the thigh and chest and sending him staggering backward. Then the dead man—Sandoval—arched backward and reverse-jackknifed forward so that he flipped onto his feet like a circus tumbler. The azure fires in his eyes flared as he rushed Grey.

Grey hit the edge of the sofa and sat down hard, but as Sandoval threw himself at him, Grey flung himself sideways. Sandoval hit the backrest and the whole sofa rocked onto its back legs and crashed over. By the time it hit, Grey and Sandoval were already locked in a deadly struggle.

Unlike Riley Jones and the dead members of the posse, this monster was a skilled and tricky fighter. There was none of the vacuous blankness in Sandoval's eyes. There was hate, there was malice, but there was also sly cunning. And the son of a bitch could fight.

Sandoval tried to knee Grey in the crotch, head-butt him, box his ears, and bite. He fought like someone who had been in more than his fair share of big-ticket scuffles. It was like fighting three people at once. The man attacked with total commitment and ferocity.

But Grey Torrance knew a few tricks of his own.

He turned his hip inward to take the knee thrust on his thigh instead. It hurt, but not nearly as much. Grey ducked his head to take the head-butt on the forehead instead of the nose. That hurt, too, but he caught Sandoval exactly as he didn't want to be caught, and the lights momentarily flickered in the killer's eyes. That spoiled the creature's attempts to box his ears, too, and as Sandoval tried to recover and bite, Grey hit him across the chin with the heel of his palm. He put a lot of heart into the hit. A lot of muscle and fear, too. And he twisted his hip as he connected.

He got it just right and he followed through with a scream and all his rage.

Sandoval's jaw slewed sideways amid an audible

crunch of cartilage and bone. Grey pulled his hand back six inches and hit him again. Same place. Twice as hard.

The jaw lost all shape and nearly tore loose from the tendon and muscle that held it to his face. It sagged down, flopping against Sandoval's chest. Fear ignited in those strange eyes.

Grey liked to see it there.

He wanted to see more.

With a grunt, he hip-bucked and turned, throwing the man off of him. As Sandoval fell flat on his back, Grey rolled over and knelt on him, pinning one knee into the undead's crotch and bracing his other foot against the floor for stability. From that vantage point he schooled Sandoval—and the demon inside of him—about the niceties of gutter-fighting done right.

He short-punched the man in the nose, the throat, both eyes. Grey knew how to punch with snaps instead of powerhouse thrusts so that he didn't bust up his own knuckles. He grabbed the dead man's lank hair, picked his head up, and slammed it against the floorboards again and again. That knocked all of the fight out of the thing and it lay there, twitching and terrified. Grey did not understand that fear but now wasn't the moment to try and sort it out. Instead he reached into his boot, removed a short knife, held the monster's head down with a flat palm against his forehead, and drove the point of the blade deep into the thing's eye socket.

The blue light in its other eye—and the glow deep in the heart of the stone lodged in its breast—flared and then went out.

Grey sagged back, gasping.

No blood welled from the punctured eye socket, and Grey wasn't sure if he was relieved or even more disgusted. It was proof of how unnatural this truly was.

He turned to the old man. What was his name? Chalmers?

"Chalmers," he barked and the sound of his voice made the man's head snap up, "are there any more of them in here?"

"M-more—?"

"Is anyone else here?"

"No."

Grey got to his feet and picked up his gun. He immediately began reloading. "Lock yourself in a closet and don't come out until you know it's safe."

"H-how will I know?"

Grey left without answering because he had no answer to give.

He dashed outside and saw Jenny Pearl standing guard over a small knot of townsfolk. Brother Joe crouched over the huddling mass of old folks, women, and children. Jenny stood wide legged, shotgun raised, as three of the walking dead circled her. The monsters faked right and left, trying to make her spoil her next shot. If she did, they would all fall on her and the people she was trying to protect. Looks Away was nowhere in sight.

"Jenny!" he cried as he ran into the street. "On your left. Now!"

She whirled and fired at a corpse who was running in, sneaky and low, on her blindside, a pitchfork clutched in its dead hands. The thing was so close that she almost died right there. The pitchfork stabbed in at the moment she fired. The deer slug punched between the tines and caught the undead on the right cheek and blew half his face off.

Grey began firing from twenty feet away. He put three slugs each into the other two creatures. His first shot hit the chest of the closest one, which effectively jolted the creature in place. That steadied his target so he could put the next two into its brainpan. Then he whirled and repeated it with the final fiend, who had already abandoned the attack and was trying to run. The bodies crumpled to the ground and Grey turned to see Jenny use the stock of her shotgun to crush what was left of the first corpse's shattered skull.

"Reload," he ordered, and they both did. Grey realized with horror that he only had four bullets left in his belt. Four rounds and there were screams coming from everywhere in town. His heart turned to ice in his chest.

"Where's Looks Away?"

"I don't know. I think he went over to Doctor Saint's place."

"Now? What the hell good is that?"

"I don't know," she said tightly. "Wasn't really the time to chat about it, was it?"

Blue lightning flashed overhead. The storm seemed to be building again.

"Jenny—get everyone into the Chalmers place. Bar the windows and block the doors."

"What are you—?" she began, then snapped her mouth shut, gave him a terse nod, and ran to herd the people to safety.

Grey lingered for one moment, watching her. She hadn't panicked, hadn't fallen apart, and hadn't wasted time with useless questions. Lucky Bob Pearl had raised himself one hell of a daughter.

She caught his eye and damn if there wasn't a flicker of a smile on her lips.

Yeah, he thought, this Jenny Pearl is one hell of a woman.

Grinning despite everything, he turned and ran toward the sound of screams.

Chapter 34

He ran down the center of the muddy street as the rain, which had dwindled to a thin drizzle, strengthened to a steady downpour that hissed and burned like acid. It seemed to do him no real harm, though, but it hurt like the blazes. Grinding his teeth together, Grey endured it as he went hunting for monsters.

They were there. Waiting for him.

And they had grown wiser in this fight.

He felt something whip past him like an angry bee, and almost as an afterthought, heard the dull bang of a gun.

Grey flung himself down, rolled through the mud, and came up to his feet on the sheltered side of a wagon filled with empty barrels. Three more gunshots rang out. Two from the same direction and one from across the street. Two guns.

He crouched and peered around the corner of the wagon, watching for the next shot. Bang! And he saw the muzzle flash. An undead gunman stood with a Winchester snugged against his hip, firing as he came. Aiming too high, though. Hitting where a standing man's head would be. So, at least the monster wasn't a genius. Grey braced his gun hand against the curve of the wagon wheel, took careful aim, and fired.

The bullet hit the thing under the edge of his jaw and from the flip of hair on the far side of his upper scalp, it was clear that it went all the way through. The man fell like a sack of potatoes. Grey watched the Winchester spin through the air toward him and for a moment he thought the Fates would deal him a better hand of cards than the one he was playing. But the Fates, as Grey had long come to realize, were a bunch of vindictive bitches. The rifle landed barrel downward and buried itself six inches into the mud.

"Shit," he growled, then he ducked back as a hail of bullets began tearing apart the barrels and a good part of the wagon itself. Splinters filled the air and ricocheting rounds whined off into the storm. Grey tried to curl into a ball too small to be hit, but fingernails of flying wood jabbed him.

Grey flattened down under the wagon, making sure to keep his face and his gun out of the mud. He saw six of the undead walking out into the street. All of them had guns. One, though, held two big pistols and the others flanked him as if he was in charge of this mad invasion. This one was different from the others. His face was less weathered, less eroded. He was as pale as a ghost but he did not look like a rotting corpse. Instead he seemed to glow with an unnatural and savage vitality. He wore a flat-brimmed black hat, black clothes, and a white shirt that were streaked with mud. The shirt and vest were unbuttoned to reveal a ghost rock burning in his chest. It was a bigger stone than the others wore, and the light it emitted was like a beacon whose glow sparkled on the falling rain and underlit his ghostly face. He strode forward with the absolute confidence of a predator who knew that anything he encountered was his for the taking. Tall, broad-shouldered, powerful. All of the other undead, fearsome as they were, looked like pale shadows of this towering figure.

Grey's breath caught in his chest. Not because of the fearsome nature of this new threat, but because he *recognized* him. A man who everyone believed was dead.

A man who, despite his ferocious vitality, was probably dead.

The name was on his tongue, but he dared not speak it.

Then he heard an anguished voice cry out.

"*Dad!*"

Grey and the corpse turned to see Jenny Pearl standing in the middle of the street, her shotgun in her slack hands, eyes wide with a terror so great that it seemed to even quiet the raging storm. Her mouth, having shouted that word, now repeated it in soundless horror.

"Dad."

The monster that had been Lucky Bob Pearl, turned toward his daughter.

And he smiled.

He smiled as he held up a hand and the gunfire died away. Even the storm seemed to withdraw its power at his gesture, as if everything in this night bowed to a creature of such inarguable power.

Jenny Pearl sank slowly to her knees. The shotgun fell to the mud. And her proud back bent as she hunched forward over the impossible agony in her heart.

"Hello, sweetheart," the monster said in a voice that was gravel and dust and wrongness.

Then he raised both pistols toward Jenny.

Chapter 35

No!" cried Grey as he wriggled like a snake out from under the wagon. "No, goddamn it."

The faces of the undead creatures all turned toward him. Lucky Bob turned more slowly, less concerned, less impressed. His smile did not waver. He was something more. The name came unbidden to Grey's mind . . . he was dragged forth from the earth and possessed by a far greater spirit. He was *Harrowed*.

"And what are you?" he asked in his dead voice. "My daughter's suitor? Sweetheart? Her young man of favor? Or are you another hound dog come sniffing after the goods?"

Grey answered with a bullet.

But just as he fired, one of the other undead threw himself between Lucky Bob and Grey and took the round in the face. It blew out his teeth and exploded from behind his left cheekbone, but the angle was wrong for a kill shot. Even so the monster tottered backward, arms spread, using his body to protect what was clearly his master.

Lucky Bob bashed the interfering corpse aside and opened up with both guns.

Grey spun away and rolled back to shelter under the wagon as a swarm of lead tore into the place where he'd lain a moment before.

"Hide, little rabbit," mocked Lucky Bob. But to his

followers he said, "Drag that worthless piece of man flesh out here. I want to see him bleed."

"No," begged Jenny. "Pa—what are you *doing*?"

"Doing?" echoed the Harrowed. "Why I've come to bring peace to our little town. Isn't that what everyone really wants, my girl? Peace and quiet? The peace of eternity and the quiet of the grave."

The monsters laughed like a chorus of jackals.

Three of them began crawling under the wagon, reaching for Grey with worm-white fingers. Grey kicked at them and wriggled away, fighting the urge to use his last three bullets on them.

"What . . . what *happened* to you?" begged Jenny, struggling to her feet. Her dress dripped with mud and rainwater. The wind plucked her hood back from her head and the stinging rain stung her face. "Why are you doing this?"

Grey slithered out from under the far side of the wagon as Jenny asked this question and it gave him a moment's respite in which he saw the expression on the Harrowed's face. The look of evil confidence flickered for but a moment. Like a candle flame at the very edge of a draft, it trembled, and for the second time that night Grey saw a different kind of expression on the monster's face. Not the gloating monster, but an expression far more human. One that called to mind the face of the man in the photograph in Jenny's house. Jenny must have seen it, too, for she gasped as if struck.

"Pa . . . ?"

The Harrowed's mouth moved and for a moment the sounds he made were garbled, as if two people were trying to speak at once using the same tongue and lips.

"Oh . . . Jenny . . . ," whispered that mouth. "Oh, my girl. *Run!*"

But even as he finished saying those few words his

trembling lips broadened once more into that pernicious grin.

"Run," he repeated, but this time with an entirely different meaning. "Run so that my boys here can have some sport."

Lucky Bob raised his arms. Lightning glittered on the silvery filigree along the barrels of his matched Colts. He spread his arms, threw back his head, and laughed in a voice that came from no human throat. It was huge and it stole the sky from the thunder itself.

"She is yours, my brothers. *Devour her, body and soul!*"

"No . . . Pa . . . *no!*" Jenny gasped.

The swarm of walking dead howled and surged forward toward Jenny, and she was too terrified and heartbroken to move. She stood there, gaping at her father's corpse while death came to take her.

Grey instantly broke from cover and ran faster than he had ever done in his life. He hooked an arm around Jenny's waist and plucked her from the ground. Even as he did so, he pivoted and fired.

He had three bullets left but he'd be damned if he would waste them.

The closest of the fiends seemed to leap backward, his face disintegrating.

A second tried too late to dodge away and instead ducked into Grey's next round. His head snapped back so hard that the sound of his spine snapping was almost as loud as the shot that killed him.

Jenny fought against Grey, reaching backward toward her father, who was striding forward, bellowing at his followers to kill them both. Grey struggled with her as he raised his gun and aimed at the head of the man whose clothes he wore.

"*Take them!*" ordered the Harrowed.

The swarm of walking corpses passed him like river water around a rock, racing to obey their master's orders. They boiled forward, all of them laughing. All of them hungry.

Jenny bit Grey's shoulder, and when he flinched back, she broke away and ran toward her father.

"*Pa!*" she screamed.

Lucky Bob saw her and laughed with mad glee. Then he raised his gun and snapped off a single shot. Jenny cried out and staggered, her hands pressed to her chest.

"*No!*" bellowed Grey as he threw himself at the Harrowed, firing his last round in the same moment that Lucky Bob aimed his gun at him. Both pistols banged in the same instant. Lucky Bob was spun halfway around as red burst from his shoulder, and Grey felt his entire midsection explode into a fireball. The pain was impossible and he caved forward and dropped to his knees. The empty gun tumbled from his fingers and fell into the mud. Grey couldn't breathe and he waited for the blackness to take him. His eyes bulged from his head as he saw Jenny lying there, her body completely still, rain beating on her slack features.

Grey looked beyond her and he thought he saw the faces of all his ghosts watching, waiting for him to die. Waiting for him to be theirs.

He looked down at his hands, expecting to see blood pouring out, expecting to see his guts slide out into the rain.

But even though his hands were wet there was no blood.

The pain, though, it was unbearable.

He could not understand any of it.

He toppled sideways and lay helpless before the laughing corpses, and they came forward to take him.

And then a figure seemed to step out of the dark wind

and blowing rain. At first alien and misshapen, then il-
luminated in eerie detail as lightning forked through
the sky.

A man wearing a harness on his back fashioned in
some strange design. All gleaming copper and steel, with
glowing tubes of glass thrust out in all directions. Coils
of wires trailed from the center of the burning tubes to
the butt of the strangest pistol Grey had ever seen. It was
oversized, with a glass wrapped entirely around the barrel. Blue gas swirled within the bowl, and it seemed to
Grey that inside the gas tiny bolts of lightning flashed
and popped. From the center of the globe thrust the
black mouth of a barrel made from brass and wrapped
with turn upon turn of silver wire. The man wearing this
bizarre contraption wore a pair of goggles with lenses of
blood-red quartz.

"Damn you all," said Thomas Looks Away as he raised
his impossible gun.

There was a sound like a thousand snakes hissing at
once.

Grey's eyes drifted shut as a terrible light filled the
world. It stabbed at him even through his tightly shut
eyelids.

Grey heard the screams.

Terrible screams.

Awful. High-pitched.

Begging for mercy.

Crying out to whatever gods or devils there were to
save them.

Not the screams of the people of Paradise Falls.

He lay there and listened to the death screams of the
walking dead.

Somewhere, impossibly, Grey heard Jenny calling her
father's name.

And he heard another voice. An impossible voice from
long ago whispering softly in his ear.

"Go to sleep," she said. "It's over now. Go to sleep."

He tried to say her name, but it came out as a whisper. *"Annabelle . . ."*

Above him, defiant in the path of the storm, Looks Away stood there with his strange gun and fired and fired and fired.

Chapter 36

The storm winds blew long and black.

They howled like the dying and the damned.

Grey lay in the mud with his eyes shut.

And then a great silence fell like a blanket of snow.

Was this death? He did not know. He feared it, though. The ghosts would be waiting for him. Waiting to exact the revenge they had earned with their blood.

Grey waited and waited.

The downpour dwindled to a drizzle, then a few desultory drops. Then nothing.

If death was hovering nearby, it did not touch him with its cold fingers.

It took courage for Grey to open his eyes. He expected to see Looks Away dead and the gibbering dead standing in a leering ring around them, ready to play a deadly joke. Surprise, surprise, surprise.

Yet the surprise was different.

Grey was not dead.

He touched his stomach, searching for the ragged bullet hole.

Finding none.

Finding . . .

His heavy belt buckle was bent nearly in half, the crease digging into him like a knife. The bullet—Lucky Bob's bullet had—against all odds, against all sanity, hit the buckle and had not passed through.

Grey wanted to laugh. He wanted to cry.

"God," he breathed.

He raised his head and looked at the sky.

And beheld a sight that nearly drove the last shreds of sanity from his mind.

There, far above the troubled town, half obscured by the fading storm clouds, was a ship.

A ship unlike anything Grey had ever seen. Stranger than anything he had even imagined.

There were no sails, no sweeps, but it floated on the wind like something out of an opium dream. Vast and silver-gray, with massive wings that were unfurled from its side. The wings were black, the wings of some obscene bat. Thin and veined with red. As Grey watched they rose, rose, rose, then snapped down with a thunder crack, propelling the steel body of the ship deeper into the clouds. Another crack, another sound like thunder.

And then it was gone, vanishing into the darkness and distance, as if it had never existed at all. A fading fantasy of a troubled mind. A delusion of shock.

That's what Grey tried to tell himself.

A fantasy. Nothing more.

But the horrors of this night bared the lie even to his reluctant mind.

It was real, as all of this was real. Dead men walking. A fall of snakes and frogs. Storms that screamed.

All of it.

Real.

He heard a soft moan, and he turned to see Jenny Pearl sitting up, her hands pressed to her breast. Her face was slack and eyes dull. She did what he had done, looking down at the place where a bullet should have killed her. The front of her dress was torn and there was the darkness of blood, but it did not pump from her. It did not rush from her. She touched the whalebone of her bodice.

"No," she said, her voice thick and strange in her shock.

"Jenny—?" he croaked and began crawling through the mud toward her. "Jenny?"

She reached out a hand to take his. Her fingers were icy with rainwater. He pulled her to him and they clung together in a stricture of shared pain that went all the way to the bone. To the heart. To the soul.

Jenny Pearl writhed against him, in agony. Body and soul.

Ten yards from where they lay, Looks Away sat in the middle of the street, his goggles pushed up on his head, face haggard, lips slack and rubbery with exhaustion. All of the tubes on the machine he wore were dark, the glass of each cracked and smoking. The strange gun was on the ground, thin lines of steam rising from it, the metal melted.

Grey craned his neck to look for Lucky Bob and the other monsters.

Many of them lay in the mud.

Dead and still.

Dead for good and all.

Their heads were gone. Just . . . gone.

Nothing above their shoulders was there anymore. Instead the ground and even some of the faces of the buildings on either side of the street were splashed with red, with some viscous black substance that Grey figured must be the blood from their decaying veins, and gray lumps of brain tissue. In each of them the black chunk of ghost rock was shattered and smoke rose from each of them.

Grey looked and looked, but he did not see a figure dressed all in black. He did not see the torn and burned remains of a flat-brimmed hat, nor a pair of matched pistols.

"By the Queen's lacy garters," said Looks Away in a soft and distant voice. "Did you see?"

"I saw too much."

"Did you see the ship?"

"I . . . ," began Grey, then he shook his head. "I don't know what I saw."

"Ah," said the Sioux. "I fear the world is broken. Or I am. Hard to say at this particular juncture." His precise word choices were totally at odds with the moment, and Grey feared for the man's sanity. But then Looks Away shook his head as if coming awake out of a dream. He looked at Grey as if surprised to see him.

"You're alive," he said. "God rot me, but I thought I saw Lucky Bob gun you both down."

Grey showed him the dented belt buckle.

Looks Away actually laughed. "You are the luckiest man alive."

"I feel like I've been cut in half."

"At least you *can* feel."

They both turned to Jenny. She shook her head. "Don't you dare call me lucky."

"How—?" asked Looks Away, then he blinked. "Dear God, are you going to stand there and tell me that your *corset* deflected a bullet?"

Jenny kept one hand pressed to her chest. "It grazed me. Don't make anything out of it."

"Let me see," insisted Looks Away.

"No," she said. "Leave me alone." Her eyes were puffed red, tears had cut lines through the mud on her cheeks. "Pa—?"

The Sioux scientist raised his head and looked past the pile of corpses that littered the street. "He's gone."

She shuddered with relief. "Thank God."

"No," said Looks Away. "I don't think so."

Feet slapped through the mud and Grey turned to see Brother Joe hurrying over. The monk helped Jenny to her feet and then offered a hand to Grey, who took it gratefully.

Grey touched Jenny's arm with tentative fingertips.

She stepped away, shrugging off his touch. Grey sighed and slogged over to Looks Away. He offered his hand, but the Sioux knelt where he was.

"Give me a moment."

"Sure," agreed Grey, but he nodded to the machine. "What in tarnation is that contraption?"

Looks Away picked up the melted handgun, considered it, and let it fall back into a puddle.

"Long or short answer?"

"Short. One I'll understand."

"Gas expansion pistol."

Grey thought about it. "Medium answer."

A faint smile flitted over Looks Away's mouth. "A weapon, powered by *chalcanthite* and ghost rock waste gasses. Designed to focus a beam of superheated plasma that radically expands the gasses trapped within solid ghost rock resulting in an explosive chemical reaction."

"Um . . ."

"Did you get any of that?"

Grey nudged the gun with a booted toe. "That thing blew the heads off the undead?"

"It did."

"By doing something to the ghost rock inside them?"

"An oversimplification, but yes."

Looks Away sighed. "If you're still offering a hand up, my friend, I'll take it."

Grey gripped his arm and pulled him to his feet. The effort hurt both of them and they spent a good long time cursing and wheezing. Looks Away stood wide-legged and wobbly. He unbuckled the straps and let the device crash to the ground.

"Hey!" said Grey. "We might need that—."

"We probably will, but that unit is buggered." Looks Away turned around to show that the back of his shirt was singed and the skin beneath blistered. "It's a prototype. Doctor Saint scrapped it because we couldn't keep the coils from overheating."

"Ouch."

"Ouch indeed."

"Jesus. Can you fix it? Or, um, reload it?"

"I study rocks, old son. I'm not a mechanical engineer. Doctor Saint built it, and as far as I know, only he can repair it."

"Balls," said Grey. "You got it from his lab, right? Is there anything else we can use if the things come back?"

"I'm . . . not sure. I didn't have time to look."

"Then we'd better have that look." He went over to the nearest of the formerly walking dead, knelt, and began removing bullets from the man's gunbelt. He put the first six into his Colt and then slotted the rest into the loops on his own belt. Then he went to two others and took their ammunition as well. Once all the slots on his belt were filled, he dumped the rest into his pockets. The weight was comforting.

Jenny came over. She still had one hand pressed to the damaged front of her dress. She looked angry and sheepish at the same time, and she wouldn't meet Grey's eyes. But she stood foursquare in front of Looks Away.

"You tell me the truth," she demanded. "No lies. Did you try to kill my pa?"

Looks Away took a breath, and then nodded. "He ran away and took the last dozen of them with him. But, Jenny, listen to me—I do not believe that *was* your father."

"Of course it was."

"Of course it was *not*. Come on, woman," said Looks Away, "you *saw* him. He was a corpse. Withered. He's been dead for weeks. Probably ever since he went missing. Whatever that thing was, I daresay it was not Lucky Bob Pearl. It was some kind of construct, a galvanized mockery brought back to a pretense of life by the qualities of ghost rock. Ask Grey. We've both seen the dead walk. We fought them. They are not the people they were when they were alive."

"That was my pa," she insisted. "He spoke to me."

"It wasn't."

"It was, damn it. You think I don't know my own father?"

Brother Joe joined them. "Miss Pearl. That was a demon straight from Hell wearing your father's body like a suit of clothes."

"You're not helping," said Grey quietly, but Looks Away shook his head.

"No," he said, "I rather think he is correct."

"Demons now?" Grey sighed. "We have the walking dead and screaming storms, and now you want to add demons to this stew?"

Jenny punched Grey in the chest. "My father is not a demon."

"Ow! Why'd you hit me? I didn't say he was a demon. I'm on your side."

"You tried to shoot him."

"Yeah, well, okay, fair enough," said Grey quickly, "but let's count the cards on the table. He was shooting at me. And at you."

"My point exactly," said Looks Away. "Does that sound like your father?"

She glared at each of them in turn. "Then maybe he's sick or something. People rave when they have fevers and—"

Looks Away pointed at the corpse that had attacked them. "A fever? Really? Until now I've rather admired you for your practicality and clarity of vision, but you are genuinely at risk of becoming another *ordinary* hysterical fool."

"Whoa, ease up, pardner," murmured Grey.

Jenny balled her fist and looked ready to swing a roundhouse punch at the Sioux, but then she abruptly turned and walked a dozen paces away. Her body was ramrod stiff. She stopped and stared into the darkness at the edge of town.

Looks Away glanced helplessly at Grey. In a hushed voice he said, "I'm merely trying to make her see reason."

Grey shook his head. "Reason left town a long time ago, brother. She just watched her father lead an army of corpses in an attack on everyone she knows. You want to maybe give her a minute?"

The Sioux opened his mouth, thought better of it, and turned away. He tapped Brother Joe on the shoulder. "Come along. There are people who could probably use our help."

They hurried off to tend to the wounded, the shocked, and the grieving.

Hitching up his borrowed pants and all of his courage, Grey walked over to where Jenny stood. The carnage around her was horrific. There was one final rumble of thunder, far away over the ocean. Above them, though, the moonlight was scattering the last of the storm clouds. It spilled a pure white light down on everything.

It seemed odd to Grey. He'd always hated the night and the cold eye of the moon. Now it was the purest thing in his world.

For a long, long time he said nothing. He did not touch her, did not speak her name.

She stood like a statue, frozen by the impossibility of what was happening, and Grey understood that. The world was wrong. Everything was so damn wrong.

He knew that he should find Picky and get the hell out of Paradise Falls. Out of the Maze. Out of California.

Maybe go East. See if Philadelphia was still normal, still sane.

Or perhaps take a ship. He'd heard about something called the *Légion étrangère*. The French Foreign Legion. They were supposed to be a group of misfits and outcasts, and nothing seemed better suited to him than that.

He almost smiled at the thought. Putting ten thousand miles between him and this godforsaken little town. Putting an ocean between him and this whole broken country.

It was a nice thought.

The moonlight painted everything with a veneer of purity. The mud, the bloodstained buildings, the mangled dead.

The light traced a silver line along the profile of Jenny Pearl.

A pearl in pearlescent light.

A poet could make something out of that.

Very softly, Grey said the only thing that he could say that might matter to her.

He said, "I'm sorry."

It broke her.

She bent and put her face in her dirty hands and wept. It was a horrible sound. So deep. Torn from some private place.

Jenny turned and leaned against him, and then she wrapped her arms around Grey and clung to him. He hesitated for only a heartbeat, then he took her in his arms and held her as the storm and the madness of this night went away.

Chapter 37

They walked through the town together. Silent, his arm around her shoulders, her hand clutching the torn front of her dress.

The town was coming alive, but death circled like a carrion bird. People were in the street and there were torches and gas lamps lit. Three bodies lay on the back of a wagon. A young man named Huck who worked in the livery stable and an older couple—the Delgados—whose family had lived in Paradise Falls for nearly a century. More than thirty were hurt, including a twelve-year-old boy with a bad bite on his upper arm.

Looks Away and Brother Joe were tending to the wounded. It did not surprise Grey that the Sioux was skilled in medicine. The man seemed to have a remarkable depth of knowledge, especially in scientific fields. He diagnosed injuries, cleaned and dressed wounds, and mixed compounds that he said would prevent infection or ease pain. Brother Joe, on the other hand, seemed to be more shamanistic in his approach, using herbs and prayers. In both cases, though, the people seemed to respond to the treatments. It was, Grey knew, as much from the appearance of authority and knowledge as it was from what the men did.

They found the little red-haired girl sitting near Brother Joe. Grey learned that her parents had been badly injured but were expected to recover, and that the girl—whose name was Felicity—was herself unharmed. The blood on her face had not been hers.

Saying that she was uninjured and knowing it to be true, though, were different things. When Grey looked into the girl's eyes he saw that shadows had taken up residence and they would be hard to exorcise.

He carried his own shadows around, so it was something Grey knew all too well.

Thinking that made him glance toward the unlighted far end of town. It was a reflex; something he did when he felt like ghostly eyes were watching him.

There was no one there, though. No one—nothing— that he could see.

"What is it?" asked Jenny.

"Huh?" he said, jolted back to the moment.

"You look like you saw a ghost?"

He turned to her. She was trying to force a smile, but it was a ghastly attempt. It broke apart and fell away, and then she, too, was staring toward the darkness.

"Is it them? Are they back . . . ?"

"No," he said gently, making himself turn his back on the night. "It's nothing. They're gone. They won't be coming back."

"How do you know?"

"That damn contraption of Doctor Saint. The gas gun thing. Whatever it is. I think they've had enough," he said, and nearly added "*I hope.*"

Jenny nodded.

"What I don't understand," she said after a few steps, "is *who* they were. That was Jed Perkins and his men. I mean, that's who some of them were. What happened to them?"

"I'll be damned if I know."

They walked together to the well at the other end of town. There were four teenagers busy drawing bucket after bucket of water up from the shadows. The town's school marm—a hatchet-faced old buzzard named Mrs. O'Malley—stood guard with a woodsman's axe clenched in her hands. She had a fierce glare in her eyes and her dress was splashed with black blood.

While they were still out of earshot, Grey murmured, "There'll be a story behind that."

"Sure," agreed Jenny, "but I know her. She was my teacher, too. She keeps things to herself. Farthest thing on God's earth from a gossip. If there's a story there, and I have no doubt there is, she won't be the one to tell it."

Grey nodded. "That's how it often plays out."

Jenny leaned her hip against a hitching post outside of the feed store. "What do you mean?"

He took a moment before answering, but he could see that she wanted to talk. Probably to distract herself from what she *needed* to talk about but wasn't yet ready to face. So he lowered himself onto the edge of the feed store porch.

"History books and newspapers talk about battles as if they're one big event. This side and that side. They talk about the land that's being fought over, the generals or officers, maybe a hero, and they count the dead, but that's not what makes a battle. Not really." He leaned his forearms on his knees and watched the teens bring up the water. "Battles are people. Battles are small things. They're big, sure, but up close it's man against man. When it starts, okay, it's lines of men firing rifles, but then you get into it, then it's one guy shooting at another. Specifically at another, you understand?"

She nodded.

"It becomes very personal. You fix on someone and you try to kill him, and it hurts you because up close you see that it's just some fellow wearing a uniform. If your folks had moved a hundred miles away and settled on the far side of some invisible line, that might be you over there. It's kids a lot of the time. Especially if the war goes on for a while. Boys who can't shave who are being fed into a meat grinder." Grey paused, shook his head. "There are these moments in a battle. No one sees them because everyone else is having their own series of moments. But it's all about you in that moment. You. A guy comes at you and you fire your gun—and you miss, or maybe your powder's wet, or maybe it hits his buckle and wings off. Then it's you and him, up close. Hitting each other with your guns 'cause you don't have time to reload. Maybe bayonets or swords or knives. Sometimes it's just hands. And teeth. Dirty fighting. Gutter fighting. And you'll do anything to live through it. To not die."

She nodded again.

"I remember once, back when I was sixteen—no, seventeen. It was my third battle. We were down in Culpepper County in Virginia. I was with the 46th Pennsylvania Infantry. Papers called it the Battle of Cedar Mountain, though afterward most of the fellows I know called it Slaughter Mountain. Stonewall Jackson plumb beat us to death and nearly ran us all down. The battle was important, because it was the beginning of the South's Northern Virginia Campaign. But on my level, it was me and this other guy fighting in a streambed. He was twice my age and he looked like my Uncle Farley. A lot like him, which still bothers me. Anyway, we were on the fringes of our two lines and we emptied our guns at each other. I could feel his bullets whipping by my head but nothing hit me. Then for a while we were swinging our rifles back and forth like gladiators with swords. Whanging them off each other, trying to bash in each other's heads. It was right about then that the slope we were on crumbled and the two of us slid down into a stream. There we were, half drowned, no guns left, beating the pure hell out of each other. He tried to bash my head in with a hickory branch. I hit him with some stones I picked up. I'm telling you, this fight went on and on. We chased each other up and down the muddy slopes. We kicked each other in the privates. We beat on each other's faces until our hands were busted up."

"What happened?" she asked.

Grey shook his head. "He slipped on a mossy stone and fell. Hit his head on another stone and was just lying there in the water. So I . . . well, I . . ."

"What?"

He cleared his throat. "I sat on him and pushed his head down into the water and held him there for maybe ten, fifteen minutes. Long, long after he stopped moving."

The night was huge and now there were thousands of stars. The teenagers worked like machines. Lowering, filling, cranking, dumping, lowering again.

"I never told anyone about it," said Grey.

"It must have been awful," said Jenny.

"No, that's just it," he said, "it's *always* awful. It was awful for every man on that field. It's awful for everyone in every war, on both sides and for everyone who lives in the path of the armies." He pointed to the town. "This was awful for every one of them. Most of them will eat their pain and their horror. Like I did. I never told anyone because it's not something you do. Not unless you save the day and you need the applause to help you win a promotion or an election. Like generals. Like heroes. They say history is written by the winners. That's true to a point. I think what's really true is that history is written by the ambitious."

Jenny glanced over her shoulder at Mrs. O'Malley. "She's not the ambitious type."

"No."

"She wouldn't brag if she won a prize hog at a county fair."

"A lot of people are like that."

"Is it pride?" asked Jenny. "Or fear?"

"I don't know. Maybe it's just that on that level, killing is personal. It's something you own, something you have to deal with."

"Is that how you see it, Grey?" she asked.

When he didn't answer, Jenny came over and sat next to him. So close that her body touched his, and despite the wet clothes she wore, he could feel her heat.

They sat together in a silence that was at first awkward but which became gradually comfortable. Even comforting.

"Those men tonight," she began slowly.

He nodded.

"I knew most of them. Not just Perkins and the deputies, but a lot of the others as well."

Grey turned sharply toward her. "What?"

"Most of them I knew only to see. They worked for the railroad. For Nolan Chesterfield."

"Ah."

"But the others? They were from here."

"Here, meaning—?"

"Paradise Falls," she said. "They were all men from right here in town."

"Jesus."

"Aside from the deputies, the rest were men who worked in the mines."

"Mining for what?"

She looked at him. "What do you think? Ghost rock's the only thing people care about, apart from water."

"As I understand it, the mines are owned by two men. Some by Chesterfield and most of them by Aleksander Deray."

"Yes," she said. "Those men . . . some of them worked for one, and some worked for the other. But they all died. Mine collapses. Tidal surges into the caverns. And other stuff. Men gone missing and people talking about sea serpents and cave monsters. Crazy stuff."

"Crazy," he said, but it didn't sound one bit crazy to him right then. And probably not to her, from the tone of her voice.

He steeled himself to ask the next natural question.

"Jenny . . . ," he began, but she cut him off.

"I know that was my pa," she said.

He said nothing.

"He knew me, too."

Fresh tears glittered on her cheeks.

"And I know he was a monster."

"I'm so sorry . . ."

Her mouth was a hard, uncompromising line. "Somebody did that to him. You saw them. Those *things*. You saw the stones in their chests. Somebody did that to them. Which means they did it to my pa. They turned my father into a monster and they sent him to kill me." She shook her head. Two slow, decisive shakes. "I can't let that go. I never will. I need to find whoever did this—Chesterfield, Deray or someone else. I need to find them and I need to kill them. No . . . that's not right. I *will* kill them. As God is my witness—if there's even a God left in heaven—I will kill them."

Grey reached out and took her hand. He entwined his fingers with hers and pulled the back of her hand to his chest. He wanted her to feel the strong, steady beat of his heart.

"And I am going to help you put those evil sons of bitches in the ground."

Chapter 38

Even the longest of nights must end, and that night passed, too.

Grey found his horse, Mrs. Pickles, shivering under a pal.. ..ce half a mile from town. Queenie was a few hundred yards away along with a dozen other horses, cows, and sheep. Why the animals had come to this spot to stay safe was something Grey never found out. His horse nickered reprovingly at him, but when Grey produced some carrots from a pocket, Picky forgave him and even pushed against his chest with her long, soft nose.

Grey, feeling a bit like Noah leading the animals to the Ark, guided the mixed herd back to town.

It was the only pleasant moment of that night. Grimmer work lay ahead.

Those with the strongest stomachs helped gather up the ruined bodies of the attackers, and they were taken by wagon out past the edge of town to where a small cemetery lay withering. Water-parched trees leaned dolefully over cheap markers and handmade crosses. Only the older graves had proper headstones, and they seemed to mock the current poverty of the town.

Four strong men took turns digging a pit, and then the dead were laid in it, stacked like cordwood. No one threw roses. No one sang hymns. Those would be saved for the burials of three people the dead had murdered.

The burial was not without ceremony, though.

As the sun curled red fingers over the serrated teeth of the broken mountains to the east, Brother Joe came and read a prayer for the bodies of the dead monsters. It was a strange ceremony. Everyone came to it, but except for the gravediggers the townsfolk stayed outside of the low slatted rail fence that bordered the graves. The men took their hats off. The women wept. It was nearly impossible to identify any of the dead except by their clothes, but some of the families laid claim to a few of them. One mother collapsed down into a sobbing pile as the dirt was shoveled into the pit.

Grey stood with Jenny and Looks Away. They were filthy and exhausted and sick at heart. The Sioux's posture was unnaturally still because of the burns on his back, although Brother Joe had smeared a noxious mixture of chicken fat and herbs on it. He said it helped with the pain, but the rigid lines around his mouth told a different story.

Brother Joe read the burial prayer for the dead. "I am the resurrection and the life, saith the Lord; he that believeth in me, though he were dead, yet shall he live; and whosoever liveth and believeth in me shall never die."

Normally Grey was indifferent to the words, his own tethers to religion having worn thin after all he'd been through, but today those words hit him hard. They chilled him. Jenny Pearl took his hand and squeezed it hard enough to make his fingers hurt. On the other side of him Looks Away's face had turned to wood.

Yeah, Grey thought, *maybe that wasn't the right choice of prayer. Not after last night.*

The monk droned on, apparently oblivious to the possible interpretations of his words. Typical of a lot of preachers, mused Grey. They say the words, but he was pretty sure a lot of them didn't study on them in the way they were supposed to.

"I know that my Redeemer liveth, and that he shall

stand at the latter day upon the earth; and though this body be destroyed, yet shall I see God; whom I shall see for myself and mine eyes shall behold, and not as a stranger. For none of us liveth to himself, and no man dieth to himself. For if we live, we live unto the Lord; and if we die, we die unto the Lord. Whether we live, therefore, or die, we are the Lord's. Blessed are the dead who die in the Lord; even so saith the Spirit, for they rest from their labors."

Having stalled on the first part, Grey's mind became numb to the rest of it. Brother Joe's words seemed to flow past him. He glanced around and saw a variety of expressions on the faces of the crowd. Some of them held bitter resentment in the hard lines around their mouths, though whether it was directed at the monk, at the undead, or at God Himself, Grey couldn't tell. Others wore the blank masks of shock. A few looked impatient, clearly wanting to get back to the tasks of the day, even if those tasks involved burying the dead and repairing damage done by monsters. And a handful murmured the prayers, word for word, with Brother Joe.

"The Lord be with you," intoned Brother Joe. "O God, whose mercies cannot be numbered: Accept our prayers on behalf of thy servant, and grant him an entrance into the land of light and joy, in the fellowship of thy saints; through Jesus Christ thy Son our Lord, who liveth and reigneth with thee and the Holy Spirit, O God, now and forever. Amen."

Grey mouthed the word and it tasted like ashes on his tongue.

The funeral gathering broke apart. Most of the people drifted listlessly back to town; a few lingered to watch the rest of the dirt being shoveled into the pit. Grey saw Mrs. O'Malley standing with Felicity, the little red-haired girl. The teacher's eyes were hard as bullets; the girl's eyes were empty.

"She'll be okay," said Jenny, who had followed his gaze.

"Will she?" asked Grey.

Jenny, clearly unwilling to pursue the lie, squeezed his hand and led him away.

But Grey paused as they passed Brother Joe. He gestured for the monk to join them, and they all stepped aside under the shade of a juniper tree.

"Nice service," lied Grey. "I'm sure the families were comforted."

The monk wasn't fooled. "There's nothing I can say that can comfort these people."

He leaned on the word "I," taking the whole measure of blame and adding it to his stock of personal and spiritual favor. Grey would have liked to take the man off the hook, but he was too tired and this wasn't the time. Instead he nodded toward the mass grave.

"Tell me about the 'Harrowed,' " he asked, thinking of Lucky Bob. "I've heard of that, but I don't know much. I don't know enough. Tell me what you know about these Harrowed. What are they?"

"Brother Looks Away might disagree," began the monk, "since he tends to see everything in terms of science and what can be measured or labeled."

Looks Away shrugged. "After last night, dear chap, consider me open to alternative suggestions. Besides, I have some experience with the phenomenon. So, please, share what you know and I'll contribute if I can."

The monk looked around to make sure their conversation was not being overheard. "Some of this is what I have heard from others in my order. Some is from what I have learned from travelers. Do you know the word 'manitou'?"

"Sure," said Grey. "It's the Algonquin word for spirit. Like Gitchee Manitou, the great spirit. Kind of their take on God, as I understand it."

"To some, yes," said Brother Joe. "The word—or variations of it—are present in many pagan beliefs."

"Pagan? Careful where you tread, old son," warned the Sioux.

"Forgive me, brother," said the monk, placing a hand over his heart. "I meant no offense. I know that among your people, the Lakota Sioux, they call the Great Spirit *nagi tanka*. I respect that, but the manitou of which I speak are not that. They are not of God. Not of anyone's version of God. They are more like demons."

"Demons?" echoed Grey.

"Yes. Devils of the Pit. More like the *kagi* of your faith, Brother Looks Away," said Brother Joe, and the Sioux gave him a guarded nod. "The monks of my order believe that the manitou are the irredeemable souls of sinners who were cast into Hell. These tormented souls are always searching for a way to escape their punishment and return to the land of the living."

"My father was not a sinner," hissed Jenny, and Grey had to step between her and the monk to prevent violence.

"No, no, let me finish," said Brother Joe. "I need to tell you some things in order to talk about what happened last night."

Jenny wore a hostile scowl, but she nodded.

"Manitou are always trying to enter our world. Before the Great Quake it was much more difficult, but they have managed it. The Bible speaks of possession, and that is one way. It is very difficult, of course, for a manitou to enter a living body and conquer its rightful host. Exorcists of the church have fought against this for many centuries, and in some of these struggles the manitou were cast back down into the Pit."

The others said nothing.

"There are rumors—horrible rumors—that some sorcerers and devil worshippers over the years have performed rituals to invite a manitou into their body. This is done in the crazed belief that the demon will grant powers and share ownership of the flesh. But . . . manitou do not like to share."

"Egad," said Looks Away tartly. "Like a party guest who will not leave."

"Far worse than that," said Brother Joe. "In such cases the human is driven mad and frequently commits terrible acts of violence and cruelty. There is a story from Europe about a prince, Vlad of Wallachia, who performed such a ritual and the list of his crimes is legendary. Perhaps other great mass murderers and conquerors have been similarly overcome. Maybe even the Caesars of Rome and—."

"But you digress," said Looks Away quietly.

"Sorry, sorry . . ." The monk looked momentarily flustered, then he found the thread of his tale. "The second way in which the manitou try and enter our world is by invading and reviving the bodies of the dead."

Grey exchanged a quick, covert glance with Looks Away. Visions of the dead posse seemed to loom above them.

"What happens to these spirits when the body is destroyed?" asked Jenny. "Are the manitou killed, too?"

"I don't think so. The abbot of my order believes they are released back into the spirit world. Into what many call the Happy Hunting Grounds."

"'Happy' is a relative term," mused Looks Away sourly.

"There is another way in which a spirit can walk in our Earth as a person," continued the monk. "If a demon of sufficient power enters a body soon after death—and the soul inside has a strong will or something else the demon thinks makes the reward worth the risk—it can attach itself to the corpse permanently. This is what we call the 'Harrowed,' and they are far more powerful than ordinary undead. For the undead the possession, as dreadful as it must be, is fleeting. However with the Harrowed, the demon actually feeds off the holy light of the host's soul. And in exchange it exists in a parody of actual life, even to the point of healing the stolen flesh when wounded. If it was not so dreadful a thing we would praise it as miraculous."

"It sounds quite horrible," said Looks Away quietly.

"It is," said the monk, "for the soul and the invading spirit wrestle for constant control."

"*Wrestle* is a funny word," observed Grey. "Is there a chance the human soul can win?"

"Perhaps," said the monk. "I've heard it said that a strong-willed individual might win back control of the flesh. Some say that there have been times when the human soul achieves this but then uses some of the demon's supernatural abilities. Most often, though, it is the demon that is strongest and it takes dominion, suppressing the host and using the stolen flesh to cause as much strife and mischief as it can, delighting in the pain and suffering it inflicts."

"Couldn't we just put a bullet in them and end it there?" asked Grey. "Wouldn't that end the—what's the word?—*occupation*?"

"*Possession*," supplied the monk. "And it's not as simple as that."

Grey sighed. "Of course it's not."

"You see, my friends, if the host is destroyed—say by a shot to the brain or burned to ashes—the demon is slain as well. Therefore it will do absolutely anything to prevent that from happening, and you cannot even imagine the lengths to which a Harrowed will go. It would burn down Heaven if it could. My abbot was uncertain as to whether this would release the soul of the possessed or cast it into greater spiritual torment. It is because of this that the Harrowed are perhaps the greatest example of the struggle we all have with sin and temptation and—."

"Drifting, drifting . . . ," murmured Looks Away.

"No," said Brother Joe, "I am not. Tell me, gentlemen, do you know why the War Between the States ended?"

"Ceasefire," said Grey. "Everyone knows that."

Brother Joe shook his head. "No, that is the lie that everyone believes. It's what we have all been told. But the truth is that this world—our world—has been changed somehow. It has become an abode of evil."

"Oh come on now," began Looks Away, but Grey gestured for him to be quiet.

"What do you mean?" he asked.

"It began at the Battle of Gettysburg," said Brother Joe. "In that terrible, terrible place where so many died. But, God save us all, the dead did not stay dead. They rose."

Those words hung there and no one dared speak. After what he and Looks Away had seen, Grey could not call this man a liar.

"It was a slaughter," said Brother Joe, "with the dead killing the living and thereby swelling their own ranks. It forced the generals on both sides to withdraw. It happened again when the Union's Potomac Army and the Confederate Army of Northern Virginia clashed. Red slaughter and the dead walking abroad in defiance of the natural order of things. The war ground on for years, but the horrible truth of the living dead, my friends, is what eventually brought on the ceasefire."

"Those were manitou?" asked Jenny, her eyes huge.

"Yes, and with the risk that every battle would further empty the halls of Hell itself, the generals and politicians quietly ended hostilities. It was not a move toward peace and sanity but a desperate act to prevent the wholesale slaughter of everyone in North America."

"By the Queen's silken garters," breathed Looks Away.

"But a lot of people have died since then," protested Grey. "Why aren't we ass-deep in walking corpses?"

Brother Joe shook his head. "There are so many mysteries. Some believe that only those who die by violence are at risk of being resurrected in this fashion. My abbot believes that it is only those who die in war. They could both be wrong, and for my part . . . I do not know."

Grey grunted. "You know, I did hear some rumors like that. But it was from men who were being treated for war stress. In army hospitals and such."

"Or," mused Looks Away, "is that where they put the witnesses to discredit them?"

It was an ugly question.

"My point," said Brother Joe, "is that this kind of possession is the most frightening. They are the most rare of all these undead *things*, but they are also the most powerful. There are some who believe that a few of these Harrowed are still abroad in our world, hiding among us. Living in our own towns. Maybe in our own families."

"How can you hide in plain sight like that if you're dead?" asked Grey.

"What makes you think you could look at one and know?" asked Jenny.

"What do you mean?"

Her eyes were filled with pain. "If my pa had walked up to me on the street this afternoon, I wouldn't have known he was . . . different. Tonight, he sounded the same, looked the same."

"Hey," said Grey, "let's not forget that he *shot* you. It was only a lucky break that the bullet bounced off that fancy corset you're wearing. Shooting you doesn't exactly sell family unity and love to me."

"He could have shot her in the head," suggested Looks Away.

"C'mon, that was a monster out there, and—."

Jenny's face flushed with anger. "I know that, but he looked like my pa. I still can't believe it's not him."

"The demons that animate the Harrowed want to walk among others. That is where they can cause the most harm. Their wounds heal and I am told they don't look like corpses. Not like some of the other risen dead, at least. Some even say that a very strong-willed person can bring himself back from death, which is both encouraging and frightening."

"My pa had a will of iron," declared Jenny. "Sounds like he'd be the perfect candidate for these . . . things."

Grey noted that she used the past tense. *Had*. It was a sign that she was accepting certain realities, but it also broke his heart.

"He did," agreed Brother Joe, "and he was a God-fearing man. If he wasn't in church every Sunday I have no doubt he was abroad doing good in this world. He was like that. And yet the abomination we saw last night could not have been him. Not completely. The Lucky Bob I knew would never willingly do harm to innocents, nor would he consort with those who would. This is why I believe that he was murdered and that a demon has stolen his body. This is a sin against God and against the memory of a good and decent man."

The words hit Jenny like a series of blows, and her anger crumbled beneath the pummeling. She hung her head. However Grey saw that the young woman's fists were balled at her side. Overwhelmed by grief, to be certain, but ready to exact a terrible revenge.

He found it all extremely—and strangely—exciting. What a woman.

"Clarify something for me, old chap," said Looks Away, "there were quite a lot of those monsters out there. How many were Harrowed and how many were simply nimble corpses?"

"I can't say for certain," admitted the monk, "but it is

most likely that Lucky Bob was the only Harrowed. The rest were demons."

"Are the souls of the dead still in there?" asked Jenny, her eyes wide with fear.

Brother Joe shook his head. "No. For most of them . . . only the demon wears their flesh. If they speak or act like the person that they were, it's because the demon can still read the memories in their brain. Unlike the Harrowed, they are pure evil. Destroy the brain and the demon loses its hold on the flesh and they flee back to hell. The body, which was merely a disguise of flesh, merely dies."

"Well, that's something," said Grey. "It simplifies things."

"Does it?" asked Looks Away.

"No, but it felt good to say it."

The Sioux shook his head. "White men."

The monk said, "I myself have heard stories about some of these Harrowed working for the rail barons, fighting in the War Between the States, and even riding as agents for the Texas Rangers and the Pinkerton Agency. It is frightening to think that so many of them may be among us . . ."

"Hold on," said Grey, shaking his head, "none of this explains what we saw last night. What about the pieces of ghost rock in the chests of those other things, the undead slaves. I admit I don't know as much about possession as you do, Brother, but I never heard about that."

"Nor have I," admitted the monk. "I can only speculate that some dark rite was performed on this ghost rock itself. Ghost rock is the Devil's creation so it would make a fine receptacle for some unholy spell. Some even say ghost rock itself is made of damned souls. We've all heard the tormented screams that issue from it when burned and—."

Jenny swiped angrily at the fresh tears in her eyes, but she said nothing.

Looks Away pursed his lips for a moment. "I admit that after last night I'm more inclined to accept a preternatural explanation for things. For some things. However I have had some experience with ghost rock and with the reanimation of the dead. Doctor Saint and his colleague, Mr. Nobel, agreed that there was some kind of chemical reaction resulting from an explosion of the mineral that temporarily restored life to the recently dead. They reasoned that because those people had been dead for too long, with the resulting deprivation of oxygen to their brains, when they reanimated they were hysterical and mentally deranged. We did not view this as having any connection to matters of a spiritual nature."

"That was then," said Grey. "Where do you stand now?"

"Quite frankly? On very shaky ground, old chap. I wish we understood more about these blighters," said Looks Away.

"We know how to kill them," said Grey grimly. "A head shot seems to do it for the bulk of these bastards. But tell me, Joe, what about the Harrowed? How do we kill them? I mean, what happens if we shoot *them* in the head?" He was careful not to mention Lucky Bob by name, but Jenny still gave him an evil glare.

"That is the only thing the demons truly fear," said the monk. "If they enter such an individual, then they are bound to the flesh. If you kill the body by destroying the brain, the Harrowed dies, too."

"But . . . ," began Jenny, then she took a breath and asked the dreaded question, "what happens to the soul of that dead person?"

The monk shook his head. "I . . . don't know. I wish I had an answer, I wish I could speak comfort to you,

Jenny, but we do not know. And this is something the brothers of my order would dearly love to know. Because if the souls of the undead are released and allowed to fly to the arms of Jesus, then we would offer no objection at all to men like Grey and Looks Away doing whatever they had to do. Instead of breaking the commandment against murder."

"I thought all killing was anathema to you clerical blokes?" said Looks Away.

Brother Joe smiled wanly. "Have you ever read the Old Testament? Achan was put to death by Joshua because he caused the defeat of Israel's army by taking some of the plunder and hiding it in his tent. David had an Amalekite put to death because he claimed to have killed King Saul. And Solomon ordered the death of Joab. No, my brother, there is so much blood written into the pages of our holy book. But we are told by God not to commit murder—the wanton act of killing."

"Wait, wait," said Grey, "let's stick on that point for a minute. Jenny's right. If we killed the Harrowed, or even the lesser undead, are we doing some kind of spiritual harm to the possessed, or are we setting them free to go on to Jesus? Or whatever you want to call it."

"As I said," explained Brother Joe, "I simply do not know."

That stopped them all, and for several painful moments they could do nothing but look at each other and weigh the events of last night against their fears.

"You're sure my pa got away?" asked Jenny in a small, fragile voice.

"I am," Looks Away assured her.

"You wouldn't lie to me, Looksie, would you?"

"No, my dear, I would not." He bent and kissed her on the forehead. "And I thank whatever gods may be that Doctor Saint's gun burned itself out before I could take that shot. Let's call it the hand of providence for now."

Jenny kissed his cheek. "Thank you."

They began walking again.

Looks Away trailed behind them, hands clasped behind his back, head bowed, chin resting thoughtfully on his chest. Grey glanced over his shoulder at him. "You got that gun contraption from Doctor Saint's lab?"

"Mmm? Oh, yes," said Looks Away absently. "But as I said, it's ruined now and—."

"He have anything else in there?"

The Sioux stopped and sucked a tooth while he thought about it. "Quite frankly, my dear chap, I don't really have a clue what all is in there. The good doctor has most of his equipment locked up and I don't have all the keys. It's his private workshop and I was only an assistant."

"Can't we break the locks?" asked Jenny.

Looks Away shook his head. "I wouldn't dare. Doctor Saint is—."

"—not here," she interrupted. "We are."

They stopped in the street and he half-smiled. "Doctor Saint has been very generous and supportive to the people in this town," said Looks Away. "Some of what's in his lab is the result of years of his work."

Jenny pointed to the cemetery. "Then you go tell those people that we can't help because we're being too damned polite. Explain to them that good manners forbids us to check to see if there's a weapon or two in Saint's lab that might help us. Tell the parents of all those men who you killed last night—all those undead—that their sons died in vain but it's okay, they'll get to join them soon because you're too bloody British for your own good."

"Now hold on a sodding minute, Jenny," protested

Looks Away. "Don't lay this on me because I'm trying to respect the privacy of a good and decent man. And moreover, this isn't about me being British. I'm a Sioux—."

"—and the Sioux took back their nation, didn't they? Or are those the American Sioux? The ones who still have their balls?"

Grey winced.

Looks Away turned livid. "Fine! You want me to commit larceny? Absolutely. Follow me, you daft cow."

The Sioux spun on his heel and stalked angrily toward a large shuttered barn on the edge of town.

As soon as he was out of earshot, Jenny let her stern face melt away to be replaced by a bright but devious smile. "Good. That was even easier than I thought."

She set off in Looks Away's wake.

Grey lingered a moment longer. Then, grinning, he followed.

Chapter 39

Grey caught up to Jenny as she caught up to Looks Away. The Sioux was fitting a strange and elaborate key into the lock of the barn. There were signs nailed above the doors and along the sides:

PRIVATE PROPERTY

DANGER

KEEP OUT

Bolts of blue lightning radiated out from the letters. *Eloquent*, thought Grey sourly.

"Open it," urged Jenny.

"I *am* opening it," snapped Looks Away. "Give me a bleeding minute."

The lock clicked and Jenny pushed Looks Away aside and went into the darkened building. Grey paused and leaned close to the Sioux.

"Is she always like this?"

"Oh, no, not at all," said Looks Away, "sometimes she's pushy and abrasive. You caught her on one of her good days."

"Ye gods," murmured Grey as he followed her in.

Looks Away scraped a match on the sole of his shoe and lit four oil lamps, dialing up the flames so that a great mass of yellow light filled the room.

The barn was not a barn. It had once served that purpose, but builders had been hard at work converting the interior of the big structure into something else entirely. There was a large central space in which several wagons of different size were stored and strange equipment was positioned in the beds of each. The equipment was so arcane in design that Grey could not even hazard a guess as to what purpose it might serve. Around this, a series of small rooms had been built, each of them closed and secured with heavy padlocks on steel hasps. One door stood ajar and Grey could see a simple workbench beyond, covered with dozens of finely-made tools.

Overhead, hung from the beams, were strange devices that looked like suits of armor from the days of King Arthur, but these were mostly made from woven materials unknown to Grey. Many had bulbous metal heads with wire-mesh grilles over glass faceplates. And against one wall was a mass of drilling and mining equipment. Wheelbarrows were piled high with pick-axes, shovels, sledgehammers, and coils of leather hose.

Jenny stood gaping at it all, her lips parted. She turned in a slow circle like a child at the circus.

"What *is* all this stuff? I thought Doctor Saint was working on weapons."

"He's working on quite a lot of different things," said Looks Away, then he gave an officious sniff. "Percival Saint is a great man, you know. He is an important man. He will be remembered long after we three are dust."

"Sure," said Jenny. "Good for him. Where are the weapons?"

"Please understand, Doctor Saint is not primarily concerned with destroying things. Most of his work is intended for the betterment of mankind and—."

Jenny gave him a sparkling smile that went less than a millimeter deep. "I don't care if he can cure the common cold or turn chicken shit into gold. We need weapons."

"How eloquently you put it."

"Children," said Grey mildly, "don't make me cut a switch on both of you."

For that joke he received identical lethal stares that he was certain burned two full years off his life. He held up his hands and retreated.

"My point," said Looks Away with asperity, "is that not only don't we understand the nature and dangers of most of this equipment, but we also run the risk of destroying crucial experimentation that could in very real point of fact benefit all of humanity. There is, after all, a world beyond Paradise Falls."

Jenny jabbed him in the chest with a stiffened finger, emphasizing each word. "I. Don't. Care."

"Well, I bloody well do."

The ensuing argument slid down the side of a privy slope and soon the two of them were slinging words that made even Grey flinch and flush.

He tried not to listen—though he was mildly impressed that Jenny Pearl seemed to have the greater vocabulary when it came to descriptions of disgusting liaisons with livestock and mishaps of the water closet. Looks Away was losing ground very quickly and clearly hadn't brought the right bullets to this gunfight.

Grey wandered over to the mining equipment, bent over to examine the tools, and selected a straight-peen sledgehammer with a twelve-pound steel head. He nodded to himself, hefted it, found the balance point, walked over to the first locked door, and while the argument raged behind him, raised the sledge and brought it down with a savage grunt.

The padlock was undamaged but the hasp was torn from the wood with twin shrieks of protesting metal and timber. Splinters flew and the heavy padlock dropped, bounced once, and skidded to a stop by Looks Away's foot.

The argument stopped as surely as if he'd backhanded them both—which, in truth, he had considered—and they turned on him like scalded snakes.

"Enough!" he barked before they could open up on him. "Enough talk. Enough bullshit. It's been too long a night and I'm too exhausted to listen to you two squabble like cats. Looks Away, I'm sorry that we might be breaking Doctor Saint's rules, and I'm almost sorry that we may mess with some of his inventions. But there are people dying in this town, and as far as I see it that trumps everything. And don't even try to give me a speech about posterity or benefiting the future of humanity. It may be true but we don't have the luxury to care about it."

Looks Away opened his mouth, but Grey turned to Jenny.

"I don't know you very well, ma'am, but I know you well enough to know that sometimes your mouth gets ahead of your horse sense. Whatever. Stop it. We don't have time for that either."

He brandished the sledgehammer.

"I'm going to knock every damn one of these locks off. That's not an option and it's not a discussion. It's what is going to happen. Looks Away, I want you to go through every room and find whatever you can to help us. Jenny, you're going to help him."

"Who," asked Looks Away coldly, "the bloody hell put you in charge?"

Grey raised the sledgehammer and brought it whistling down so that it smashed a hole in the floor between Looks Away and Jenny. They both cried out and jumped backward.

"I did," said Grey into the silence. "Now let's get to work."

They got to work.

Grey was so deeply exhausted that every time he

swung the sledge he felt ten years older. He kept at it, though, and after only a small hesitation—perhaps for good form's sake—Looks Away began invading the rooms as they were opened.

By the time Grey had smashed all eighteen of the locks off, he was sweating and trembling. Jenny had run outside and returned with a bucket of cold well water, and she handed a full ladle to Grey.

"Thanks," he said, and dumped it over his head. Jenny gave him a refill, and this time he drank it, and two more besides. "God, that's better than any whiskey I ever swallowed."

"Costs more, too," she said. "More than the finest champagne."

"No doubt." As he drank a fourth mouthful, he considered Jenny. He knew that he was probably seeing her at both her best and her worst. This was a time when great courage was called for, and she certainly showed that, but it was also the kind of thing that can shake a person to their core. And Jenny was undoubtedly shaken. First the loss of so many friends when the town was nearly destroyed, then her way of life as the farm failed, then the loss of her father, and now the corruption of her father's memory. Even though Grey had no personal stake in this town or its people, he believed that he could sympathize with her. After all, his world had been torn apart by these events, too. Not in the same way, but in a way he knew he'd never shake off.

And, he considered, maybe he was fooling himself about not having a stake in this town. Or its people.

As Jenny took the ladle back from him her fingers accidentally brushed his.

If, indeed, it was an accident.

The look she gave him was not. Nor that knowing, secret smile that was certainly not meant for Looks Away to see.

Grey ran fingers through his hair to comb it back from his face.

This woman confused the living hell out of him. Not a handful of hours ago she'd stood in the rain while her dead father tried to gun her down. Now she was flirting and casting slanting glances at him. It made no sense. Either she was mad or . . .

Or what? Grey didn't know where else to go with that. What deepened his unease was how much this kind of whimsical play reminded him of his lost Annabelle. She was always playing saucy games no matter how proper she was on the streets or how dire the tension was.

Wrestling with these thoughts was difficult and painful. He was starting to genuinely like Jenny Pearl, but he had to wonder how much of that was old longing transferred unfairly to this troubled young woman.

"Jenny," he said softly, pitching his voice for her ears alone, "I'm sorry I yelled and—."

She touched her fingers to his lips. "You hush now. I was playing the fool and we both know it. You hadn't spoken up when you did I'd have done a nasty to Looksie. Or him to me."

He took her hand and held it for a moment. "Guess we have enough enemies without that."

The blue of her eyes was the blue of summer skies and blooming cornflowers. Her lips were without rouge but they were pink and delicious and he wanted very badly to kiss her.

"Jenny," he said, "when this is over I'd like to maybe invite you out for a carriage ride in the country."

"Well," she said, a bit breathlessly, "wouldn't that be nice?"

He wanted to kiss those lips. Her lips parted and long lashes brushed her cheeks as Jenny tilted her face up toward his. Grey was actually beginning to bend down toward her when a voice shouted, "You sodding bastard!"

Looks Away.

Yelling from inside one of the rooms.

Not directed at them, but clearly yelled for them to hear.

Jenny jerked back from him, turned, and cleared her throat. Her face was flushed. "He . . . um, must have found something."

"I guess so," said Grey. "Wish to hell I'd hit him with that damn sledgehammer."

Jenny turned and flashed the brightest smile he'd ever seen. Then she spun and dashed out to see what Looks Away had found.

Heaving a great sigh, Grey followed.

Chapter 40

They found the Sioux scientist in a large room at the very back of the barn. Inside there was a long mission table on which lay various pieces of Doctor Saint's bizarre machinery. Set haphazardly around the pieces were notebooks, loose papers filled with handwritten notes, larger sheets of drawing paper covered with complex diagrams, and even some pages produced by one of those newfangled typewriting machines. On the wall across from the door was a big and very detailed map of this part of California. It was an older map, clearly made in the days before the Great Quake, but Saint had meticulously overwritten it with a carefully measured tracery that showed the new coastline and much of the Great Maze. Grey, who had always loved maps, was drawn to it and stood studying the details. It was by far the most detailed map of the Maze he'd ever seen.

He found Paradise Falls on the map and spotted several notations made in Saint's crabbed hand. One was the location of Nolan Chesterfield's estate, situated in a green valley that had been left mostly intact by the devastation. Another was an old mining camp whose name, Dragon Wells, had been crossed out and the name DERAY written over it. The pen strokes of each letter had gouged into the thick paper. Clear evidence of Saint's dislike for the mineral tycoon.

There were other markings, too. Lots of places notated with "GR," and Grey figured these were places where ghost rock was discovered. There were at least a hundred of these spread out over an area that encompassed all of the farmland around Paradise Falls. There were twice as many with "GR-?," suggesting spots where either ghost rock was reported but not found, or where mineral scouts planned to look. And there were dozens with a slash mark through the GR. They must have been bad leads that yielded none of the ore.

One notation struck Grey. In the broken hills between Chesterfield's valley and Deray's mine, Saint had written:

HERE THERE BE DRAGONS

It was a strange thing for so practical a man to write. That was something they used to put on maps to indicate the perils at the end of the known world.

"Grey," said Looks Away, "if you please—?"

Grey turned away from the map and joined Jenny and the Sioux at the table. On the table in front of them lay something that looked like a rifle but wasn't. Or at least not any kind of rifle Grey had ever seen. Apart from having a barrel, stock, and trigger the rest was entirely alien to him.

The rifle was fashioned from highly polished steel and gleaming brass, with fittings of copper and silver. Crystals were inset into the body of the weapon and even in the bad light they seemed to glow with dark-red promise. The pistol-grip handle was wound turn and turnabout with gray silk.

"Oh, dearie-dearie me," murmured Looks Away nervously, "I hadn't realized Doctor Saint had built a prototype."

Grey bent and peered at it, but did not touch the thing. "What is it?"

"This is something very special," said Looks Away. "And something very, very dangerous."

"It's a gun, though, right?" asked Jenny.

"Oh yes, it is very definitely a gun. And, if it works the way the good doctor theorized, it will be a dreadfully powerful gun. Even a small platoon of men armed with weapons like this would triumph over an entire regiment, and probably without the loss of a single man."

"How?" gasped Jenny.

"Ghost rock."

"Oh, bullshit," said Grey. "That's tall tale stuff. Ever since they first found ghost rock people have been going on and on about stuff like this. The ultimate weapons of conquest. Weapons so powerful they would end all wars."

"You don't believe that?" asked Jenny.

"Not even a little. I mean, sure, someone will eventually create a better gun. Happens all the time. Double-action pistols trump muzzle-loaders. Flintlocks trump crossbows. Going all the way back to when someone invented the club and kicked the ass of everyone who was still using fists. The wonders of modern science. I get that," said Grey. "What I don't get is why anyone thinks that a weapon—any weapon—will end war. I mean, how the hell could a weapon end a war?"

"When you conquer your enemies," said Jenny. "That's how."

"Really? And then what? There are always more enemies. My family lines come from England and Scotland. They conquered each other lots of times, and conquered other people. That didn't end war. When white men landed at Plymouth Rock and started killing the red men, that didn't end war. Soon as they cleared out the Indians, they started killing each other. And then we fought the British, and the French and the Mexicans. Look at all the ghost rock weapons out there now. Have they stopped the Rail Wars? Has either the North or South won the damn war? Uh-uh, honey, no weapon is going to end war. Can't happen."

Looks Away sighed. "I tend to agree with you, Grey. Doctor Saint, for all of his brains and wisdom, is of a different mind, however. It's his belief that if someone developed what he called an 'ultimate' weapon, then peace could be achieved. A lasting peace, I mean."

"How?" asked Jenny. "Grey's right, people are plain contentious. They'll find some way to pick a fight, no matter what."

"Contentious, yes, but are they suicidal? What if there was a weapon so powerful that to use it would ensure the utter destruction of one's enemy? Wouldn't knowledge of such a weapon make any rational person choose to opt out of a conflict?"

Grey and Jenny considered, then they shook their heads.

"People aren't that smart," she said.

"People are plumb crazy," agreed Grey.

"Hey," said Looks Away, "don't get me wrong. I didn't say that I was sold on Doctor Saint's idea of a weapon to end all wars. I'm saying that he believes it. He is rather emphatic about it. Dare I say obsessive?"

Jenny tapped the rifle with a fingernail. "What is this and what does it do?"

"This, dear girl, is a prototype of the Kingdom Mark One air-cooled, electric reload, ten-shot infantry repeating rifle. It fires iron-core, silver-tipped forty-caliber copper-jacketed chemical bullets powered by compressed gas collected by the discharge of the process of smelting ghost rock."

The silence following that explanation was crushing.

Grey was the one to break it. "You want to take another swing at that, son? Maybe this time in English?"

Looks Away gave them a crooked smile. "The Kingdom M1 is something entirely new. There is nothing like it anywhere in the world, of that I am quite certain. You understand, I hope, the concept of an electric motor?"

"I read about it, sure," said Jenny. "Even before the big ghost rock invention craze. Something about coils and such holding lightning?"

"Not exactly," said Looks Away, "but close enough for our purposes. Doctor Saint worked with a bright young naval officer named Frank Sprague from Milford, Connecticut. Mr. Sprague is part of the American Navy's efforts to build machine-driven warships powered by ghost rock engines."

"Everybody's navy is working on that," said Grey. "Airships, too. I think Deray might have one, too. I saw something during the storm."

"As did I," said the Sioux, "but I didn't get a good look at it. That only reinforces the point that everyone seems to have a natural bent for armed conflict, even in an age of prosperity and discovery." He gestured vaguely toward the town. "And by 'prosperity' I refer to virtually anyplace that isn't Paradise Falls."

Jenny made a face.

"My point," continued Looks Away, "is that Doctor Saint was able to take some of Sprague's designs and build a very compact version of a functional electric motor. He put that inside the Kingdom M1 and discovered a process of keeping the motor working at a perpetual rate of fire by something he calls 'gas injection.'"

"But you're talking about ghost rock? How's that a gas?" asked Grey. "I thought that when they smelted it all they got was a stinky cloud that tends to scream as it comes out of the smokestacks. They got all those smelting plants in Salt Lake City and the sky's black with that smutch. People call it the 'City of Gloom' for a damn good reason."

"There are side effects, I'll grant you. But what most people dismiss as merely gaseous discharge—waste products, if you will—Doctor Saint has discovered possess certain useful attributes. One of Doctor Saint's . . . um . . . what's the word I'm fishing for here? Rival? Colleague? Something like that but I can't find the exact word. Anyway, one of the other scientists working on developing advanced military mechanics is based in Salt Lake. Dr. Darius Hellstromme. You've heard of him?"

Jenny shook her head.

Grey narrowed his eyes. "I have. Been some wild-ass tales coming out of Utah. I met a guy once who swore on his own mother's grave that he saw a machine man walking down the center of Salt Lake, big as two men and clanking like fifty headaches. Of course, that fellow was a known drunk and his mother's still alive, so who knows what he really saw."

Looks Away shrugged. "Machine men? Really? I doubt that. Though . . . I might be unfair. I suppose if machines can fly, then maybe they can be made to walk. But what concerns me, or rather what concerns Doctor Saint, is the Kingdom rifle. He explained it to me, but I'll try to put it in simpler terms for you."

"That would be nice," said Jenny. She gave Grey a knowing wink. "For the benefit of us lesser mortals."

"Hilarious," said Looks Away sourly, but he was smiling. "The whole thing involves capturing the smoky discharge from the smelting process and then compressing it into small cylinders. The more gas that can be compressed into, say, a five-inch cylinder, the better. More gas pressure creates more energy when released. You follow?"

"Like a bloodhound," said Grey.

"There is so much raw energy, even in the ghost rock smoke, that one cylinder, properly regulated, can be used for many bursts of energy. What Doctor Saint has done is connect a replaceable cylinder to the electric motor. Each time a burst of gas is discharged, it winds the copper coils of the motor at such a high rate that a strong electrical charge is created. This charge is used for two purposes. First it is injected into the brass shell casing of each bullet through a special kind of firing pin, thus triggering a blast that has far more power than black powder. The projectile flies faster, farther, and straighter. The second thing it does is activate all of the destructive properties of tiny grains of ghost rock that have been placed inside the core of the bullet. That turns what appears to be an ordinary bullet into a round that has the approximate explosive power of an explosive artillery shell. Imagine, if you will, a twenty-four-pound field gun firing canister packed with thousands of tiny iron pellets. Grey, I'm sure you've seen the effect first-hand."

"Too many times," admitted Grey. "One round can rip a whole platoon apart. But that's a big shell." He picked up one of the loose rounds and examined it. The bullet was only a little larger than a rifle round. "Even if this broke up it couldn't do that kind of damage."

"Yes," said Looks Away sadly, "it could. That bullet is not what it seems. Inside are grains of ghost rock. Not enough to be of much value for sale, but when charged during a compressed gas firing, each one of them explodes like a tiny grenade. There are fifty grains in each bullet. The effect is every bit as devastating as fifty small bombs going off in a tightly packed area."

They stared at him in horror.

"So you see what would happen if an army went into the field carrying Kingdom M1s?"

"It would be a slaughter," said Jenny, aghast. "That's terrifying."

"It is indeed. One effect is that any ghost rock used is utterly destroyed, as is any ghost rock it encounters. One of Doctor Saint's intentions was to create a weapon that would obliterate any ghost rock–powered weapon of the enemy."

"What would happen if you fired that at one of the undead?" asked Grey.

"Or a Harrowed?" added Jenny.

Looks Away shrugged. "As I said, the ghost rock is obliterated. Doctor Saint was never concerned with the spiritual aspects of his devices, but given what our friendly monk says about the manitou, I rather think they would be obliterated as well."

Grey felt that sink in. A weapon that could actually destroy a demon was so far beyond anything that he'd ever thought about that he didn't know how to think about it. He had to resist the temptation to glance at Jenny. If the Kingdom Rifle was used on her father, would it destroy the demon inside him as well as his own human soul?

So many ugly questions, and so many unbearably ugly answers.

"Now," said Looks Away, warming to his topic but apparently oblivious to its emotional implications, "here is where it gets even worse."

He led them out of the room and into the adjoining room where a dusty sheet covered what Grey took to be a lumber wagon. Looks Away took a breath, shook his head, then took a corner of the sheet and whipped it away. There, beneath the cloth, mounted on the back of a wooden delivery cart, was a huge machine.

Copper and steel and silver.

A Kingdom gun.

But this was no rifle. This gun was the size of the biggest cannon Grey had ever seen.

"Imagine what an army could do with a hundred of these," said Looks Away. "Just imagine."

Chapter 41

Jenny approached the gun cautiously, as if it could somehow come to life and devour her. The machine was impressive, but Grey did not like the sight of it. He had seen beautiful cannons before. Old time brass ones, iron monsters, and even some whose metal skin had been engraved with filigree and a tracery of wild flowers. He had never understood that, though looking at this one, he wondered if making a weapon beautiful was somehow a way for the maker to convince himself that peace—defending it or keeping it—was truly the end result of warfare.

Personally he didn't think so.

His life tended toward other interpretations. War was pain and suffering. War was loss and regret. War was innocent blood and stolen lives.

He walked past Jenny and ran his fingertips along the ribs of copper wire that encircled the middle of the weapon. Even though it was inert he could imagine the thrum of power contained in its dormant battery. Power waiting to come to unnatural and unholy life.

Grey stopped and studied that thought and the word choices that had flitted through his mind.

Unholy.

It was a strange word for him. Not one he used. Holy or unholy. Those concepts belonged to a broken part of his long ago childhood back in Philadelphia. Not to the stoic and cynical killer he'd become since going to war.

Not since he had let war and all of its ugly trappings define him.

"Impressive, is it not?" asked Looks Away.

Jenny turned to him. "It's the ugliest thing I've ever seen. This is unholy."

Grey did not comment on that.

"If one bullet from the small gun could kill a dozen men, this thing could . . . could . . ." She shuddered and hugged her arms to her body. "No, Looksie, this is wrong."

The Sioux arched an eyebrow. "Are you saying that you wouldn't use this against Deray, even if you found out that he was behind the murder of your father? Even if you found out for certain that he was responsible for the deaths of all these people and the attack on the town?"

Jenny did not answer. The inner conflict was clear on her face, though.

"It's not easy to answer, is it?" asked Looks Away gently. "And, for the record, I'm with you on this. I disagreed with Doctor Saint on many points. He is a good man, don't misunderstand me, but he actually thinks that select use of an ultimate weapon will remove from men's heart the desire for conquest."

"No," said Jenny.

"No," said Grey.

"No," agreed Looks Away, "and more's the pity." He sighed deeply and patted the barrel of the deadly cannon. "Luckily this is something we do not need to concern ourselves with at the moment. As the French are so fond of saying, we have other fish to fry."

"That's a French expression?" asked Grey.

Looks Away shrugged. "Who cares? We don't have sufficient ghost rock gas to power a weapon this large. There are magazines for the small rifle, but only two gas cartridges and nine bullets."

"That would put a dent in the monsters," observed Grey.

Jenny wheeled on him and finally spoke the thought that Grey knew had to be burning on her tongue. "Are you saying that we use it on my pa?"

He held his hands up. "Whoa, now. I'm not saying that," he lied. "I was thinking out loud. But since we're talking about it now, let's look at that. I'm not saying we use this on your dad, but I wouldn't shed too many tears if we were to thin his crowd a bit."

"Even if it means destroying a human soul along with the demon?"

"First, we don't know that it would do such a thing . . . and second . . . maybe. We might have no choice. I'd rather use that gun and destroy those . . . *things* . . . than stand unarmed and let them slaughter every *living* person in Paradise Falls. In an ideal world we'd never have to make that kind of decision, but let's face it, Jenny, we're being dealt some pretty bad cards here. We have to do what we have to do. And who knows, maybe Brother Joe can intercede with the Almighty to save those souls."

"And what if he can't?" demanded Jenny.

"Like I said, we do what we have to do. That rifle may be our only chance."

"Isn't it funny," observed Looks Away, "that we can discuss using the rifle while we all consider the cannon to be somehow obscene. Why is that?"

No one offered an answer.

"Yes . . . exactly what I thought," said the Sioux. "We're all barking mad. All of us. Every human who ever walked on dear-old planet Earth."

"I got no argument for that," said Grey.

Jenny merely sighed heavily and nodded. They went back to the room and stood looking down at the rifle. "We live in such strange times," she said. "It's like we're living in a dream. A nightmare. Those things that happened last night . . . that was wrong in so many ways. I mean . . . snakes and frogs? That's so strange. It's like something out of the Bible. Out of the Old Testament. The plagues of Egypt."

Looks Away smiled. "You think Deray conjured that like Moses to drive us from this land?"

"Maybe."

"I was joking."

"I'm not," she said. "I think everything that's happened has been part of that kind of plan. To get us off this land."

"But why?" asked Grey. "All he has to do is wait another few months. Without water no one can stay here. Shipping it in's got to be more expensive than it's worth."

"It is," said Jenny.

"Why not buy it from other towns?"

Jenny cut past him as she crossed to the big map on the wall. "Other towns? Sure. Other water sources? Absolutely. There's Branton." She slapped the map over the name of that town, which was a few miles to the north. "And St. Lopez." Slap. "And Casper's Corners." Slap. "Golden Springs." Slap. "Diego Sanchez." Slap.

"What's your point."

"They're gone," she said.

"Gone?"

"Gone. Every town for a hundred miles in any direction is gone. Dead."

"The Quake?"

"No. They're ghost towns. Chesterfield bought up most of the land south of here. Deray bought the rest. And any place too stubborn to sell out was either burned out or they had their water rights stole out from under them. You can call it legal purchase, but we all know what it really is."

Grey gaped at her. "All of them? You've got to be wrong."

"She's not, you know," said Looks Away. "If anything, Jenny's understating the problem. You're coming into this at the end of a very destructive and very thorough process. Deray and Chesterfield are like two fists and Paradise Falls is the flesh caught between the punches. Lucky Bob thought he could turn it around. He thought he could get one or the other to see reason and maybe find a compromise that would allow Paradise Falls to survive. I advised him against it. So, for the record, did Jenny. Lucky Bob was like that, though. Clever as he was, his weakness was always believing the best in people. He thought that if he could speak with them face to face that there could be some kind of opening of the heart, a meeting of the mind."

"He went to see this Deray character?" asked Grey.

"Indeed."

"And we think that Deray somehow turned him into a Harrowed? Or one of those lesser undead?"

"The man is, after all rumored to be an alchemist of some note. That certainly stands against him. And Brother Joe claims that he's a necromancer as well," said Looks Away.

"A what?" Jenny asked. "That some kind of wizard?"

"Yes," said the Sioux. "One who has power over the dead."

"That fits," Jenny said sourly. "Deray's army are all monsters."

"That's just swell," said Grey. He grunted and sucked a tooth thoughtfully for a moment. She looked at Grey. "Does that scare you?"

"Of course it does, but if you think it's going to chase me off, think again. What about Chesterfield? Is he a wizard, too?"

"No," said Looks Away. "He's an asshole."

Jenny gave a short, hard laugh.

"He doesn't have power over the dead or any of that?" asked Grey.

"No. Why?"

"Nothing . . . I'm just working it all through."

"Working what through?" asked Jenny.

"Maybe Lucky Bob had a good idea."

"But we know how that turned out," said Looks Away, shaking his head.

"Right, so I'm wondering if Jenny's pa went out to see the wrong man." He tapped the map. "Chesterfield's place is pretty close. Couple hours easy ride. If Deray is the kind of monster we all seem to think he is, then maybe Chesterfield's only a corrupt asshole."

They looked at him.

"That's almost certainly the case," said Looks Away. "However what possible leverage could we use on a rich man who is, as you so eloquently phrase it, a corrupt asshole?"

"You ever hear the expression, that the enemy of my enemy is my friend?"

"Yes. But in my experience it's almost never as simple as that."

Jenny snorted and nodded. "Chesterfield is every bit as bad."

Grey picked up the Kingdom M1. "Then I guess we'll have to be worse."

The smile that blossomed on Jenny Pearl's face was one of the most disturbing things Grey had ever seen.

"Hold on right there," he said quickly. "You are not coming along."

"The hell I'm not."

"The hell you are."

She stepped toward him. Five foot two to his six four. But her sudden anger seemed to fill the room. He'd read so many dime novels about women with fiery tempers, but not one woman in any tale could hold a candle to the swift fury of Jenny Pearl.

"And why not? I can ride and shoot as well as any man, and better than most."

"I do not doubt that," he said. "But I need you to stay here in town."

"Why?"

"Because who else is going to keep these people safe if something else happens?" he asked flatly. "Brother Joe? Mrs. O'Malley? Come on, Jenny, you're the only one around who everyone's afraid of, which means they'll listen to you."

"He's jolly well right about that," said Looks Away. "You're more valuable here in town than as another gun in what is ostensibly a diplomatic venture."

"My ass."

Neither man dared make a comment. They let their silence do their talking for them, and Grey could see Jenny work it out. Her expressions showed on her face. Every expression did. She was lovely, but she had no poker face at all. He wondered if she'd ever wanted to play cards. He'd learned a kind of poker from a frisky lass in Louisiana. Loser had to shuck a garment.

Her answer snapped him back to the moment.

"Very well, damn you both," she said.

Chapter 42

Looks Away argued that no such expedition could be undertaken in their present condition. They were dead for sleep, filthy, and hungry. So they did their best to lock up the workshop and they trudged back to Jenny Pearl's.

With the deputies all dead and the town's well free—at least for now—they were able to get enough water to take actual hot baths. Jenny heated big pots of it and corralled a couple of the town's kids to run them out back to where Looks Away and Grey sat, naked but uncaring, in a vast metal washtub. The men scrubbed and scrubbed and finally wrapped themselves in sheets and tottered inside. Jenny gave them a choice of spare bedroom or couch. Grey let Looks Away take the bedroom and he flung himself down on the couch and slept all through the day and into the night.

He'd left orders to be awakened if absolutely anything untoward happened.

However the night passed without incident.

Though, that was not entirely true. It passed without violence. It passed without trouble.

But not without incident.

Deep in the night, the moon still riding the sky and long before the first cock crow, Jenny Pearl came down the stairs in a cotton gown and nothing else. Grey heard the creak of the stairs and opened his eyes to what he thought was a spirit in a dream. Her blond hair was unpinned and fell around her shoulders and her eyes were smoky and half closed.

For a heartbreaking moment she looked less like Jenny and more like Annabelle, but Grey felt ashamed of thinking that. Annabelle was long gone now. All except for the ghost that haunted his life. She was gone and Jenny Pearl was alive.

So alive. So real.

So beautiful.

Without saying a single word she unfastened the gown and let it puddle around her ankles. Grey's heart beat wildly inside his chest as he saw her painted in silver moonlight. Slim but ripe. Full breasts with nipples the color of dusty roses. White blond hair on her head, a dark blond below. A flat stomach and lovely legs that were strong and graceful. On her sternum, between her breasts, was a dark scab left from the bullet that had nearly killed her. It was right over her heart.

She raised the corner of the blanket under which he lay and crawled onto the couch, on top of him. She wrapped her legs around his hips and even as she sat astride him she deftly guided him inside of her.

Grey began to speak, but she silenced him with a kiss.

"Please," she said in a husky whisper. It was the only word she spoke.

They made love with infinite slowness. It was a gentler encounter than he would have guessed from her fiery nature. Slow and soft, unhurried and unforced. A sweeter encounter than any in Grey's experience. And all the sweeter for that.

Neither of them rushed toward any cliffs. They discovered a rhythm that was the song of their mutual connection. And when Grey felt himself lift finally toward the inevitable, she was there with him. Even then it was not a screaming climax, but a warm release that nearly brought him to tears. It was in those moments that he realized how far his life's trail had taken him from any true understanding of what gentleness was.

He kissed her lips, her throat, her breasts, her forehead, and then held her to him, feeling the hummingbird flutter of her heart against the walls of his chest.

They fell asleep like that. As one. Safe in the moment, safe in each other's arms.

When he woke, though, she was gone.

Weak sunlight slanted through the shutters on the window and drew yellow lines on the floor.

Grey wondered if it had been a dream.

But the smell of her was there. Perfume and sweat and natural musk.

It was no dream.

For a long time he lay there and stared at the ceiling and thanked whoever was running the universe that the world was not so broken that it had run out of perfection.

Like Jenny Pearl.

Then he got up, washed, dressed, strapped on his guns, and braced himself to face whatever the new day offered.

Chapter 43

The morning was bright and cold. A wet wind whipped in off the ocean but there were no storm clouds anywhere to be seen. Grey stood on Jenny's porch with a cup of coffee in his hand and a belly-ful of eggs and grits. He watched a boy walk up the street leading Picky and Queenie. Looks Away walked with him, and he had a large canvas bag slung over his shoulder.

"Penny for your thoughts, cowboy," said a voice and he turned with a smile to see Jenny Pearl standing in the open doorway. She wore a yellow dress that was but-toned primly to her throat, and a light wool shawl that was the exact color of her blue eyes. Her hair was tied into a loose tail by a ribbon that was the same color as her shawl. She also wore a knowing smile, but almost at once her throat and cheeks flushed a brilliant scarlet.

"What I'm thinking is worth more than a penny," he said. "Maybe as much as a whole dollar." He touched her cheek with the backs of his fingers. "You're some-thing else, Miss Pearl."

The moment was sweet and they smiled at each other for the span of maybe three heartbeats before it suddenly changed, turned, became incredibly awkward. It was im-mediately clear to Grey that this kind of thing was new to Jenny. Maybe not the sex, because that was no virgin who'd swept like a ghost into his dreams, but maybe the rest of it. The tenderness after the fact. The intimacy of conversation that followed those times when the passion was right, when the connection was correct.

It had been a long time for Grey, too. He'd loved many women but had only been in love once. A sweet girl named Annabelle. She was dust and bones now. Though, sometimes at night, he feared that her ghost was part of that shambling horde that followed just beyond his line of vision. Sometimes, in his darkest moments, he caught a glimpse of her as he'd last seen her—bloody and broken—staring accusingly from the corner of his eye. One of the many people he had failed and left behind.

Now here was Jenny.

Was he in love with her?

Last night was sweet and pure in its way, but had it ignited something important in both their hearts? Could love possibly blossom that quickly? It seemed perverse that it could happen in the midst of tragedy and horror.

Or maybe that *meant* something. A thing that was important to know when all other knowledge fails or is proven false.

These thoughts tumbled like an avalanche down the slopes of Grey's mind as he stood there with her, feeling a tender moment turn sour.

"I—," he began, but she just nodded and walked past him to stand at the edge of the porch to watch Looks Away and the boy lead the horses.

He tried again. "Jenny, about last night . . ."

"Last night?" she echoed softly. "Last night was a dream. Don't you know that?"

She did not look at him as she said it, and before he could assemble a response, Jenny stepped down off the porch and went to meet Looks Away.

Grey resisted the urge to bang his head on the porch column, though it seemed like a reasonable choice. Instead he thrust his hands into his back pockets, pasted on an expression that he hoped looked entirely casual, and followed Jenny.

"I think I have everything we'll need," said Looks Away brightly. He set down the canvas sack and knelt to open it. His mouth tightened momentarily as he did so.

"How's the back?" asked Grey.

"Medium rare. Brother Joe was kind enough to give me more of his entirely offensive-smelling salve."

"Does it help?"

"Hard to say, though considering the amount of animal fat in it, I will probably attract every hopeful carrion bird in this end of the state."

"You do smell . . . interesting."

"Please go and stick your head in an ant hill."

"It's not that bad," said Jenny. "And don't worry—Brother Joe's salves and poultices do a power of good. They work like magic."

"Magic," said Looks Away, "is not a word I want to hear just now."

From the bag, Looks Away produced the Kingdom M1 rifle and its ammunition, along with a spare ghost gas cylinder. "We don't have any rounds so if we use it, we should probably keep to single shots. And . . . besides, I've never fired it so I don't know what kind of kick it has. Quite frankly the ruddy thing scares the bejeebers out of me."

"That's comforting," complained Grey.

"Then take comfort in this." Looks Away produced a conventional Winchester .30-30 and handed this to Grey. "Courtesy of Deputy Perkins. I found his horse and this was in a saddle scabbard. I doubt he'll need it henceforth."

Grey took it and checked the action. It had clearly been cleaned and oiled since the rain.

"I had the guns seen to," said Looks Away. He removed a double-barreled shotgun from the bag, too. It was a snubby little thing with both stock and barrels hewn short. It came with a modified pistol holster.

Grey smiled. "Where the hell'd you find that?"

"It was among the weapons taken from the undead. Twelve gauge with lots of shells."

"You expect me to carry that frigging thing?"

"No," said Looks Away, "I expect *me* to carry that frigging thing. You're the crack shot of this outfit. I'm okay on a good day with a stationary target, but overall I'm an indifferent shot. Scatterguns fire in a wide spray, so I'm likely to hit something useful."

"It doesn't have a stock. You can't use your body to brace for the kick. Gun like that'll knock you on your ass."

Looks Away sniffed. "Then I'll reload while sitting."

"Fair enough. What else you got in there?"

"A pair of excellent hunting knives, a compass, and lots of ammunition. Two boxes for your Colt as well."

"Nice."

They shared the supplies between them, stowing the extra boxes of shells and cartridges in their saddlebags. Jenny watched all of this without comment. She stood with her arms folded, head cocked to one side like someone at a gallery appraising art. Or, Grey thought, someone judging pigs at a county fair.

As they swung up into their saddles, she broke her self-imposed silence. "I still think I should be going with you."

Grey crossed his wrists on the saddle horn and leaned forward. "And for two pins I'd take you along."

"But . . . ," she said, glancing at the boy from the stable and then past him to the center of town.

"But," he agreed. He smiled at her, but her returning smile was filled with so many emotions that Grey couldn't catalog them all. Doubt and anger, passion and compassion. Love, too? He didn't know if he saw it or merely wished for it.

Looks Away glanced from Grey to Jenny and then down at his fingernails as if suddenly finding them deeply fascinating.

"We're burning daylight," he said quietly.

"Be off with you, then," said Jenny, stepping back. "You boys come back quick and you come back safe, you hear?"

"Yes, ma'am," said Grey, and Looks Away pretended to doff a hat that he wasn't wearing.

"As your ladyship commands," he said, "so shall it be."

They tugged the reins to turn their horses toward the road that led past the Pearl farm and out toward the east. But Jenny suddenly ran up to Picky and took the bridle, stopping the animal. Then she tugged the ribbon from her hair and tied the blue length of it to the head collar.

"For luck," she said.

Grey smiled at her. "Thank you."

"A lady's favor on the steed of a knight aboard on a mission of errantry," said Looks Away, rolling his eyes. "Good Lord save me from romantic fools."

He kicked his horse into a gallop.

Grey winked at Jenny and cantered after.

Chapter 44

They rode in silence for much of the way.

Grey pointedly ignored the occasional amused glances aimed his way by his companion. The one time Looks Away tried to open a conversation about Jenny, Grey laid his callused hand on the butt of his holstered Colt.

"Point taken," said Looks Away.

The miles fell away beneath their horses' hooves.

The land was clearly broken and in places it still looked raw. A game trail through a grove of trees would suddenly end at a jagged cliff to which the fractured trunks of dead trees still clung. Then they'd have to pick their way through boulders and rotting logs and between towers of splintered granite. At one point they crossed a gorge along a slat bridge that was so new the lumber was still green.

"Grey," said Looks Away during one of the times they had to dismount and lead the horses, "I'm sure you recognized some of those walking corpses that night."

"You mean Perkins and the deputies? Sure."

"I can't rough out any scenario where that makes sense. I mean . . . we're going on the assumption that Deray created the undead, or controlled them, with these magic bits of ghost rock. Right?"

"Yup."

"But Perkins *worked* for Deray. We saw him less than half a day before those deputies turned up dead and reanimated. What happened to them? How did they die? *Why* did they die? And why were they brought back?"

"All important questions," agreed Grey. "And my considered opinion is that it beats the shit out of me."

"Ah."

They remounted and rode along a deep cleft at the bottom of which lay the smashed remains of a farmhouse, barn, and corn silo. The bleached bones of at least a dozen cattle were scattered among the splintered wood.

Grey was about to ask if Looks Away knew if the farmer family had survived the Quake, but then they passed a line of crudely made crosses standing in a row. The paint was faded after all these years, but Grey could see that everyone buried there had the same last name. From the birth and death dates it looked like grandparents, parents and young kids. Eleven graves in all.

He wondered why any of the survivors would stay in such a place as this. Death, the wrath of an insane planet, and the villains who mingled science with sorcery. What could make someone like Lucky Bob and his daughter think this land was worth fighting for?

The nomad in Grey's soul was so practiced at riding away whenever troubles got too big that he no longer felt able to understand any other choice.

As if reading his thoughts, Looks Away said, "It's hard to walk away penniless from something you've put your whole life into."

"What?"

"Jenny. It's why she stayed after her father died. It's why most of the families here want to fight this out. If they left, where could they go? And how could they start something new without funds or resources?"

"That's not a decision, it's a trap."

"It's a choice for some," said Looks Away. "They love this land. Their family members are buried here. That ties them to the land."

"Is that Sioux wisdom?"

"It's human nature, Grey. People want to put down roots."

"Not everyone."

Looks Away nodded, but he wore a knowing smile.

A mile later Grey said, "I take it you and Chesterfield's wife—."

"Veronica."

"—Veronica, are friends?"

Their horses walked nearly a dozen paces before Looks Away answered. "There are a lot of lonely people in this world, my friend. Is it wrong to offer comfort? Is it wrong to provide a shoulder to cry upon or an ear to listen? Is that a moral crime? Is that a sin in your world?"

"You're asking the wrong fellow. I don't study on sin very much. Not anyone else's. My own sins—and they are many—provide me with enough to think about."

"So you don't judge?"

Grey sucked a tooth. "I'm not saying I can't or won't form opinions. For example I'm of the opinion that Nolan Chesterfield and Aleksander Deray would do the world a power of good if they stood in front of a fast-moving train."

"We're of a mind in that regard."

"Beyond that?" Grey shook his head. "It's a cold, hard world and if someone can find a little warmth and comfort, then good on 'em."

That seemed to satisfy Looks Away, and he said no more on the subject.

They reached the top of a series of broken foothills, and there they paused. Beyond the ridge, stretching out for miles, was a green and lovely valley. Long, broad fields of blowing grass, orderly groves of fruit trees, and a stream as blue as Jenny's ribbon wandering through it all. Beyond the stream was a dirt road that ran in a slow curve toward a mansion that would have fit better on a

Georgia peach plantation. Three stories tall, with a row of white columns along a deep porch.

"By the Queen's sacred knickers," said Looks Away, even though he had presumably visited the place before.

"Is that the Chesterfield place?" asked Grey.

"It is."

"Oh shit."

"Indeed."

It was not the obvious wealth or the ostentatious splendor that made them both stiffen in their saddles. It was not the nearness of a potential enemy that made their hands stray toward their guns.

It was the state of the place.

The trees lining the driveway were nothing but blackened stumps. Some had fallen, their trunks split by what looked like lightning strikes. Horses and cattle lay everywhere.

Dead.

All dead.

There were long, black trenches running back and forth across the grounds. They looked like the kind of mark Grey made when he scraped a match on a doorpost. Except these were a yard wide and some of them ran for a hundred feet across the lawn, through hedges, and even through parts of the house's big slope roof. Anything in the path of those burns had been incinerated.

The front of the house was blackened with soot and part of the shingled roof had collapsed inward. A thin curl of smoke rose into the wind and was dissipated into nothingness by a steady breeze blowing inland.

"What the hell could have done that?" demanded Grey.

Looks Away said nothing, but his face was pale and he stared with naked horror. He silently mouthed a word. A name.

Veronica.

Chapter 45

Looks Away started forward but Grey clapped a hand on his arm and held him in place.

"She's in there," insisted Looks Away, trying to tear his arm free.

"Okay, we'll go in and find her," said Grey as he drew his pistol. "But let's do it the smart way. Not the I-want-to-be-dead-way. You understand me? We do it smart or we go back to Jenny's place."

Looks Away glared at him, but then he snorted air out of his nostrils and nodded. "Very well, damn you."

"Good. Let's go, but keep your eyes open."

They rode down the slope into the green valley. The closer they got the worse it all was. There were huge burn spots on the grass, and most of the dead animals had been charred. Some had burst apart, or been torn asunder. Some of the trees looked like they had been torn from the ground by some force Grey could not comprehend. They lay on their sides trailing roots that snaked away into the troubled dirt.

Looks Away touched Grey's arm and nodded to something that glinted in the trampled grass.

"Shell casings," he said. "Lots of them."

"Heavy caliber. Gatling gun?"

Looks Away nodded. "Or something with a heavy rate of fire. There are two or three weapons manufacturers with newer, faster models than the Gatling. Want to guess what makes them work so fast?"

Grey sighed. "Makes me long for the old days. I mean . . . is anyone trying to use ghost rock for something other than war?"

"Of course they are, but science tends toward warfare first and humanitarian purposes later. Airships and faster trains will carry food, goods, and people as easily as guns and cannons."

"Mm. Nothing humanitarian about what happened here."

They dismounted and studied the house.

"You see any bodies?" asked Grey. "People, I mean."

"None." And under his breath the Sioux added, "Thank God."

"Under any other circumstances that could be a good thing," said Grey. "It won't be here."

"No," agreed Looks Away glumly. He slung the Kingdom rifle over his shoulder and slid the chunky sawed-off shotgun from its hip holster. They tied Picky and Queenie in the shade of one of the few remaining unburned trees, nodded to each other, and approached the house. Grey checked the loads in his Colt, and then held it down at his side as they moved in.

As they did so, Looks Away shifted off to the left of the main entrance and Grey went right, both of them moving without haste and making maximum use of cover. Aside from smoke and heat-withered grass, nothing moved at all.

Grey gestured to indicate that Looks Away should cover him as he approached the door. The Sioux ran low and fast to the front wall and knelt beneath one of the fire-blackened windows, holding the shotgun in both hands. Once he was in position Grey walked straight up to the door and only angled to one side as he got within twenty feet. The big oak doors were pocked with bullet holes and splashed with blood. Grey used the toe of his boot to ease the door open. It swung inward with sluggish reluctance.

Grey waited.

Nothing. No voices. No shots.

He nodded to Looks Away, steeled himself against whatever might be waiting, and then went in low and fast, the Colt held out in a firm two-handed grip. He immediately cut right and swept the room with the gun, his eyes tracking in concert with the barrel. Looks Away dashed in a heartbeat later and went right, the shotgun stock braced against his hip.

The entrance foyer had been smashed apart and was open to the hall on Grey's side and to a drawing room on Looks Away's left. The walls were shattered. Bricks were shattered, exposing the wooden bones of the house. The red foyer carpet was singed black by ash and a figure lay half in the hall and half in the drawing room. Perhaps it had once been human, though whether man or woman was beyond telling. It was a set of bones wreathed in crisp layers of ash. The tendons, shrunk by heat, had contracted and pulled the corpse into a fetal position. Though clearly an adult, the posture called to mind one of the cruelest aspects of death. To Grey it looked like a dead infant rather than a grown man or woman, and in his mind he imagined he saw the newborn baby, the tottering first steps, the simple joy of a toddler at play, the full potential of a life unsullied by influences, choices, or actions. Snuffed out now like a match, and discarded by whoever had done this.

Even though this was the house of a probable enemy, Grey felt a small stab of grief and another deeper one of anger.

"It's not her," said Looks Away, and the sound of his voice almost made Grey jump.

"What?"

"That body—I think it was a woman named Anna Maria. See the right foot? It's clubbed. Anna Maria Ramirez had a club foot."

"Was she another friend of yours?"

"Anna Maria was a shit," said Looks Away. "Nolan hired her as a maid, but she was really there to spy on his wife. Veronica was a virtual prisoner in this place."

"Are there places Veronica could have hidden during all of this?"

"God, I hope so. But, Grey, there's something else. Anna Maria is the first body we've seen. Don't you find that strange? I mean, there are forty people working for Chesterfield. House staff and hired guns. More if you count the wranglers and yard servants. But, there's clearly been a war here, and except for livestock this is the first body we've found. Human body, I mean. I dare say that Chesterfield lost this particular engagement. Do you agree?"

"It's a goddamn slaughter. But . . . you're right, where are the other bodies?"

Looks Away crossed to the doorway to the connecting room. "No one here, either. Should we search the whole place?"

"I think we have to at this point."

They were talking in hushed voices, and in the same hushed tone he added, "Shall we do this stealthily or like bravados?" His smile was small and wicked.

"Much as I'd love to kick doors and take names, friend, until we know who—or what—did all this, I think we should creep around like mice. Then we find Veronica and get the hell out of here. How's that for a plan?"

"Jolly good, actually."

So, they went with only as much speed as caution would allow.

They took turns entering rooms with one or the other providing cover. They found more devastation. The place was decorated in the very height of style, with imported

French furniture, paintings from Italy, a library with every English classic ever written and thousands of volumes of poetry and history, Turkish rugs, and curios from China and Japan. All of this magnificence was ruined, though; stained with soot, splashed with blood, torn by some savage claw, or holed by ordinary lead bullets. In the upstairs master bedroom, Looks Away knelt at the edge of a Persian rug that Grey was sure cost more than the entire value of the town of Paradise Falls. The embroidery within the rug showed a series of episodes from the life of Sinbad.

Grey began to leave the bedroom but stopped when he realized that Looks Away wasn't following.

"What is it?" he asked.

The Sioux nodded. "Come over here for a minute. Tell me what you see."

He came and stood next to him and studied the carpet. It took him only a moment to catch what Looks Away had already seen.

There was considerable debris strewn across the floor as well as some ash residue that covered everything. However in the center of the carpet was an outline. It was large and probably male. But there was no body.

"They took the body?" Grey wondered. "Why would they do that?"

However Looks Away shook his head. "I don't think that's what happened. See . . . ? There's the outline of where a man fell. But what I don't quite get is that it looks like he stood up again and walked off. See there? That's a handprint like a man might make if he was leaning on the floor to push himself up to his feet. And there, those are his footprints."

"So he fell down and then got up again. I'm not sure why this is so fascinating."

"You're not reading it the right way," said Looks Away.

"I may not have spent much of my adult life among my people, but from the time I could walk I was taught how to track, to read sign."

Grey nodded. It had been clear from their trip from Nevada that the Sioux was far more skilled than he was at tracking. Grey could follow a horse through a forest, but Looks Away seemed able to follow a rabbit over hard rock. It was an enviable talent, and in the presence of that level of ability it wasn't worth arguing.

"Tell me what you see," he suggested.

"I think the man was shot over there, by the dresser. There's some blood drops on the top and down the side of the drawers. Not much on the carpet, though, which is why I believe the shot was a fatal one."

"A dead heart stops pumping blood. Dead men don't bleed unless the wound is pointed toward the floor, and then it merely leaks out. It won't pump out of a dead man."

Grey nodded, unnerved but impressed.

"There are no marks to indicate that anyone came to help him up," continued Looks Away. "Which begs the question of how a man with a fatal gunshot wound gets up and walks away."

He straightened and they stood there, looking at the outline of ash and debris.

"Pretty sure we're both thinking the same word," said Grey.

"Does it start with a *u* by any chance? As in 'undead'?"

"It does."

"Then bloody hell."

"Yup," agreed Grey. He considered. "Not sure how much else you can read into this, but do you think this dead man was Nolan Chesterfield?"

Looks Away shook his head. "It's his room, but that body shape is from someone tall and thin. Chesterfield was heavyset."

They searched the rest of the upstairs but found no bodies. However, they looked for and found several places where bodies had fallen, and some of these were clearly not easy deaths. In one room there was a massive pool of blood, suggesting someone bled out there. In another they found long streaks of arterial droplets running up the wall to the ceiling.

No bodies, though.

They found bloody footprints, but that was all.

Even though Grey understood that this was now part of the world, that through some process the dead were able to rise again, it was still deeply unnerving. Knowing something isn't always a pathway to accepting it. Each time they found fresh evidence of the returning dead Grey felt more frightened and less certain that they were going to figure a way out of this.

They reached the far end of the top floor and found a set of stairs that led from the servants' quarters down to the kitchen and pantry. And it was there that they found something that changed the whole complexion and direction of their day.

It changed everything.

In the pantry there were a row of cupboards. Most of them had been shattered and they sagged from the walls, their contents spilled out onto the floor in a profusion of powders, grain, rice, beans, bottles, and cans. The air was rich with the scent of a hundred exotic spices. But stronger than the crushed herbs and seasonings was a foul and fetid stench that swirled out of the shadows between a wooden frame and a hidden door.

The door now stood ajar. The concealed handle and the jamb were smeared with bright red blood. Beyond them, revealed in the gap, was a set of stone stairs cut into the living bedrock. They circled around and vanished into shadows that were as black as the pit.

The aroma that rose from below carried with it the

fresh-sheared copper smell of blood and the rotting fish stink of something alien and grotesque.

All of the footprints the two men had found led them to this pantry, this doorway, and those steps.

Thomas Looks Away pulled the door open and stared down into the darkness.

Beside him, Grey Torrance stood with his gun in a tight fist and cold sweat running in lines down his face. He cleared his throat and spoke in a hushed whisper.

"We have to go down there."

"God help us."

Grey shook his head. "I don't think God lives down there."

Chapter 46

They were both brave men, tough men, experienced men who had seen violence more times than most. However, going down those stairs took more courage than either of them believed they possessed. Going into battle was always terrifying, and Grey knew for sure that any man who said otherwise was a damn liar. He'd done it time and again since his teenage years, but in each of those cases he knew essentially what he was facing. Men with guns and knives.

Not monsters.

Not the walking dead.

Not the unknown.

Not something that might do worse than kill him. Something that could steal his flesh and wear it like a suit of clothes. Something that could possibly rend his soul. Something that could turn him into a monster.

The gun in his hand felt small and inadequate. He did not want to go down there. It was foolish and mad and probably suicidal.

He went down anyway.

Chapter 47

Looks Away found an oil lantern in a closet by the front door and lit it. He held it out before him with one hand and clutched his shotgun with the other.

The stairs wound around and around, and as they descended, the light pushed back the shadows.

No, that was not right. That wasn't how it looked or felt to Grey. It seemed as if the shadows crept backward from the light, always retreating to just around the turn in the spiral staircase. Not gone, not banished. Waiting. Drawing the two of them down, down, down.

They came to the bottom and stood in a wide circular stone chamber. There was another expensive rug on the floor and the walls were hung with heavy tapestries. The images on these tapestries were strange, though, and completely at odds with the ones upstairs. There, Chesterfield had tended toward scenes from myth and magic. Not only Sinbad, but King Arthur and Tam Lin and Hercules.

Down here the subjects took a darker turn.

At first glance the nearest tapestry seemed to show naked nymphs in a grove standing around a fire. But as Grey bent to study it, he saw that they weren't nymphs at all. They were naked women bound to stakes about to be burned.

He said, "Shit . . ."

"Look at this one," said Looks Away.

The second one had a scene of a woman—also naked—strapped to a chair that was being lowered backward into a stream of running water. The delicate embroidery caught every line of tension in her screaming mouth. Beside the stream a group of men in Puritan clothes stood by. Most were scowling, but the man controlling the pulley was laughing.

"Jesus," muttered Grey.

They went from one tapestry to the next. In each a naked woman or women was being tortured, beheaded, enclosed in a spiked box, impaled, or otherwise abused. In each of the images the woman was still alive and whoever had made these tapestries seemed to want to capture that exact moment between the terror of anticipation and the moment of destruction.

"I sense a certain misogynistic theme here," said Looks Away dryly.

"A what?"

"The man hates women."

"Chesterfield? He's married, isn't he?"

"And how does that change things? Haven't you ever met a married man who despises women?"

"Yeah, damn it."

They looked around the chamber but there seemed to be no exit.

"Strange," remarked Looks Away.

"Lower the light for a minute," said Grey as he knelt. "Down here."

The Sioux set the lantern on the floor and from that angle the shadows changed. Small lines appeared on the cold stone. Looks Away bent and studied them, then turned and slowly extended a finger to a tapestry across the chamber.

"The footprints are nearly gone, but it looks like they went that way."

The tapestry over there was of a young and very

buxom blond woman screeching as she was about to be torn apart by four horses. It sickened Grey to look at it, and for a bent copper penny he'd have torn them all down and tossed a match onto the pile.

Now wasn't the time.

Instead he and Looks Away approached the tapestry from either side. Grey touched the center of the big fabric and it yielded as if there was nothing behind it.

With a nod to his companion, Grey took a fistful of the brocade edge of the tapestry and gave it a mighty downward jerk. The rings stretched and popped and the material fell heavily to the floor, revealing a short passage behind it. At the end of which was a door made from heavy oak timbers and banded with iron-riveted metal bands.

The door stood slightly open and the light from a lantern glimmered within.

Together, they crept down the hall and on a signal from Grey, Looks Away kicked open the door. They rushed in together, fanning right and left.

There was no one to shoot.

There was nothing alive in that room.

But they both stopped and gaped at what was there.

The room was much bigger than the chamber outside, with walls that stretched back farther than even the light of two lanterns could reach, and rows of stout pillars supporting the roof. Along all of the walls were sturdy pallets made from rough-cut oak, and on these were stacked pieces of metal. Each piece was about seven inches long, not quite four inches wide, and one-and-three-quarter inches thick. Each pallet was piled to shoulder height.

The men stood stunned, utterly unable to speak.

Looks Away finally managed to take a few steps forward, but his feet were clumsy and he staggered, falling against one stack. He set his shotgun down and picked up a single gleaming bar. It was the color of hot honey and it was improbably heavy.

"By the Queen's lacy garters," he breathed as he hefted it in his hand. "This is . . . this is . . ."

Words failed him and he was unable to finish the sentence.

Grey staggered over to another pile and lifted a plate whose argent sheen was like metal moonlight. "Is this silver?"

"No," said Looks Away as he picked up a second gold bar, "that's platinum. As are the next—what is it? Ten? A round dozen?—stacks. I believe the silver is over there."

"Looks like," said Grey in a hollow voice, "there has to be a couple of tons of this stuff."

The Sioux set the heavy bars down with a dull clang and picked up the lantern. He and Grey walked along the rows. Looks Away stopped at a series of pallets of metals Grey did not recognize.

"This is palladium or I'm a Chickasaw." He moved to another. "And this is ruthenium. They only discovered this in '44. I met the man who wrote a paper on it. A Baltic German—Karl Ernst Claus. Doctor Saint bought some because of its usefulness in electrical conductivity. And this . . . God, Grey, this is an entire mound of rhodium. It's corrosion resistant, but I've only ever seen it in small quantities. And there, that bluish metal? That's osmium. Heaviest damn stuff you'll ever find, and God save me, but that is iridium over there. A ton of it at least."

He stepped away to the center of the room and turned in a wide circle.

"By the Queen's several birthmarks, Grey, this is not merely a fortune—this is perhaps the greatest single fortune I've ever even heard of. Millions of dollars. Maybe thousands of millions. Good lord, man, just one wagonload of these bars—any of these bars—and a man could buy himself his own country."

"So what the hell is it all doing down here?" asked Grey, astounded at what he was seeing and hearing. "I mean, first off, how the hell did Chesterfield acquire all this? What was he going to do with it? And . . ." He stopped and shook his head. "No, I got nothing. My brain is spinning."

"Mine, too." Looks Away came over and touched Grey's arm. "Listen to me. This isn't what we came for, but let's face it, old chap, this is better than anything we could have hoped for. Clearly Chesterfield and his family are dead. Everyone in this damned house is dead."

"So what?"

"So what is that we have a much simpler solution to our fight with Aleksander Deray than we thought. Look around you. All we have to do is get some of this out of here. Not all. We don't need to be greedy, but a wagonload or two."

"And what? I'm not interested in buying myself my own country."

"That's not what I'm saying. We can take this back to Paradise Falls and distribute it evenly between the remaining residents. Don't you see, Grey? We can make them all rich. But we give it to them on the condition that they move the hell away from here. Let Deray have the damned land. It's falling apart anyway and who wants to stay and fight someone who can raise the sodding dead? No, let's make everyone rich on the condition that they bugger off out of here. Sound like a plan to you?"

Grey holstered his gun and rubbed a hand over his jaw. The mountains of metal gleamed in the lantern light.

"Or," said Grey, "we could use this money to hire us a private army and go and reclaim this land from Deray. Walking dead or not, he can't stop an entire army, and we can hire ten thousand men—and pay them well enough to guarantee their loyalty."

The Sioux smirked at him. "And that would allow Jenny Pearl to keep her farm and earn you her undying gratitude and affection."

"You say it like it's a bad thing."

They grinned at each other.

"Either way," began Looks Away, but his words were instantly cut short by a terrible high-pitched scream of unbearable horror.

Not a child's scream this time.

The shriek that rang through the underground trea-sure chamber was torn from a woman's throat.

Chapter 48

V eronica!" cried Looks Away.

A second scream tore the air.

"Maybe it's not her," growled Grey as they snatched up their weapons and each took a lantern.

"Dear God let it not be so," said the Sioux as he broke into a run.

Grey was right on his heels.

The path between the stacks of precious metals was narrow and long.

The scream faded to a harsh silence as they ran and thereafter all Grey could hear was the slap of shoe leather and the pants and grunts of their breathing. The rows of precious metals gave out and the walls were bare. The light from their lanterns rolled before them and it seemed as if the long dark of that place was endless. Then they saw the rear wall. It was set with a single iron door and, as before, the door stood partly open. At first Grey saw what he thought was some thick, pale snake lying across the open threshold, but as they drew near he saw that it was an arm.

A man's arm.

They slowed to a careful walk.

The arm reached out from the other room, fingers splayed, muscles slack.

They moved cautiously now, angling to let their light spill inside while staying outside of the line of any ambush gunplay. As they shifted, Grey saw that the arm was thick and flabby, without apparent muscle and the hand bore no trace of the calluses of manual labor. There was a large emerald ring in a gold setting on the index finger.

"Is that Chesterfield?" he asked quietly.

"No. That was his foreman. I recognize the ring."

In the lantern light the arm gleamed like a fat slug.

Grey pushed the door open the rest of the way, looking for the owner of that limb. However the arm was all there was. The other end was a ragged stump that lay in a small puddle of blood. It was immediately clear that no blade that had cut the arm from its owner. The wound was savage, raw.

"Something tore it off," said Looks Away.

"Something like what?"

The Sioux had no answer.

They stepped inside, guns up and out, ready to fight, to kill.

The room beyond was another of the circular chambers and there was a second set of spiral stone steps. There, sitting on the third step down, was a woman.

Middle-aged, lovely in a faded way, with masses of dark hair pinned up in a bun, and a sheer dressing gown that offered very little concealment to her ample curves. However the gossamer was stained with blood and soot, and that handsome face was white with shock and blood loss.

She sat in a pool of blood.

It ran over the edge of the step and down to the next and the next. She held a broken silver letter opener in one hand, the blade stained with gore. Her other hand was clamped against a dreadful slash that had opened her from breastbone to hip. Bubbles of red expanded from between her lips, swelled and burst, misting her face with tiny dots of crimson.

"Dear God," said Looks Away as he rushed over. "Veronica!"

The woman's eyelids were closed but opened at the sound of her name. Her eyes were a dark green, but they were unfocused and glassy with shock and pain.

Looks Away set his lantern down and laid the shotgun on the top step. Then he knelt and very gently brushed a few wisps of dark hair from her brow.

"Oh, Veronica," he murmured, "what have you gotten yourself into?"

His voice was soft, his tone familiar, his touch intimate. It made Grey sad because the wound the woman was trying to stanch was horrific. Muscle and bone were torn, and through the gaping slash he could see the bulge of a purple coil of intestine.

"Thomas . . . oh, my sweet Thomas. My sweet man . . ."

"My dear," said the Sioux, "who did this to you?"

She mouthed some words and they both bent to hear. "The chickens got out."

"The what? What do you mean?"

"Isn't it . . . strange? I thought they were . . . chickens."

She coughed and fresh blood leaked from the corners of her mouth.

"Grey—?" asked Looks Away, his fingers pressing over hers to try and seal what could not be mended. "Grey, we need to do something."

Grey did not move. There was nothing either of them could do.

Veronica Chesterfield raised her eyes and looked into Looks Away's face. "I'm sorry, Thomas . . . ," she said.

"No, no, no," he said quickly and softly. "No, it'll be fine, lass. We'll sort this out and—."

"Mrs. Chesterfield," said Grey, "who did this? What happened?"

"Damn it, Grey, not now," snapped Looks Away, but

Veronica smiled at him. There was blood on her lips, but she managed a faint smile.

"I . . . came down here to hide," she said in a faint voice. "Isn't that funny? Me thinking that it was safe down here?"

"What do you mean? Who did this?"

"Aleksander was very upset with Nolan. So . . . upset." Her eyes sharpened for a moment.

"He came for us, Looks. He sent them for us. From the sky . . . from the shadows. From everywhere."

"Why?" begged Looks Away.

"It was because of Nolan," she said in a faint voice. "Nolan has been naughty. He thought Aleksander would not know . . . but the devil always knows."

"What happened, Mrs. Chesterfield?" asked Grey. "Help us understand exactly what happened here."

"Don't you know?" Her green eyes shifted toward him. "They opened the doorway to Hell and all the chickens got out . . ."

The words chilled Grey to the marrow.

Veronica coughed and the wound tried to gape wider. Looks Away uttered a small cry and clamped both hands over it. Tears boiled into the corners of his eyes.

"Grey," he begged, "please . . ."

Grey came and sat down on the step next to his friend. He placed one hand on the Sioux's shoulder and the other over the hands trying to hold back the inevitable. It was all he could do in an impossible situation.

"He . . . ," began Veronica and her voice was noticeably weaker, "Nolan made a deal with the Devil. He did. Everyone thought . . . they were enemies . . . that they were at war . . . with each other. Then he broke his deal . . . broke his word . . . and the Devil came for him. With a ship that sails through the sky . . . with soldiers and their clockwork guns . . . with other things . . ."

She shuddered and coughed and blood bubbled from between her lips.

Grey plucked a handkerchief from his pocket and handed it to Looks Away, who dabbed at the blood on Veronica's mouth.

Even then, even dying, she favored him with a smile and a courteous little nod. It was so genteel a thing that it touched Grey's heart. He suddenly found that he liked this woman.

"When you say he made a deal with the Devil, ma'am," he said, "do you mean with Aleksander Deray?"

"Yes," she said. "With him. With . . . the Devil."

"What was the deal?" asked Looks Away.

"They . . . wanted . . . it all . . ."

"All of what?" asked Grey. "The mineral rights? The water? The ghost rock?"

"No," she said weakly. She was fading and it was a terrible thing to witness. It was almost like the soul of the woman stood behind a faded portrait of what she had looked like in life, and with each moment the soul took another step backward. Withdrawing life from the image. Going away.

The tears burned their way down Looks Away's face.

"No," repeated Veronica, "my husband and . . . that monster . . . they wanted it all."

"All of what, sweetheart," said Looks Away, and his voice cracked as he spoke.

"All . . . ," she said. "It's all . . . down there, Thomas. Down . . . there . . . When they came for Nolan, I ran down here to hide."

"Where's Nolan," asked Looks Away. "Where's your husband? Did they kill him, too? Did they turn him into one of those things?"

It seemed to cost Veronica a lot to answer. "The Devil . . . took . . . him . . . down to . . . hell . . ."

That last word stretched and stretched until it became clear it was riding a long, soft, terminal exhalation.

Her body settled against the steps and the confusion and pain drained away from her face, leaving behind only her beauty, cast now in cold serenity. Looks Away bent forward and kissed her lips, and then touched his forehead to hers. He sat that way for a long time.

Grey withdrew his hand and stood, then sagged back against the far wall. He stared down into the darkness below them. He fancied that he heard a ghostly voice whisper his name. Not down there, but somewhere behind him. Was it the voice of his sergeant, Harrison? Was it Corporal Elgin? Was it the whisper of the woman he'd loved and lost so many years ago? Was it Annabelle's voice calling him as she walked along with the others he'd failed and abandoned?

"I'm sorry," he murmured. "I am so sorry."

For a moment, for a splinter of time, he felt a shift in the world. In his world. As if that apology, given here in this blighted place, meant with a heavy heart, had caused his legion of ghosts to falter, to miss a single shambling step.

But that was absurd. Of course it was. The ghosts were nothing more than the shadows of a guilty conscience and nothing more.

Then, like a whisper inside his mind he heard the voice of the witch Mircalla.

The dead follow you everywhere you go.

"I'm sorry," he said again. Very quietly. So quietly only a dead ear could hear him.

That was when he saw the marks on the stone steps.

They were tracks half hidden by the shadows. Small, splay-toed. There were many of them, and their paths crisscrossed in and out of the lines of blood that had run down the steps. Grey frowned and squatted to study them.

What had the poor woman said?

They opened the doorway to Hell and all the chickens got out.

Yes. That's what she said.

The tracks on the steps were not made by a human foot. Not even the risen dead. These were much smaller and stranger.

Chicken tracks?

No.

They were a little too big and they were . . .

Strange was the only word that would fit into his mind.

So strange.

Little birdlike feet running through blood down into darkness.

Chickens had four toes.

These prints had two, and both toes had wicked claws.

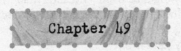

Chapter 49

Looks Away climbed heavily to his feet, pawing at the tears on his face.

"I didn't realize you two were this close," said Grey awkwardly.

The Sioux gazed down at the dead woman and then at Grey.

"The thing is . . . we weren't," he said softly. "We were lovers, but that was mostly intrigue. An escape for her and some compassion on my part. It was fun to make a fool of her husband and make fanciful plans about a future neither of us thought we'd ever share. But . . ."

Grey waited.

"But," continued Looks Away sadly, "how close do two people really need to be before it's appropriate to grieve for them? She was a good person who deserved better than this."

"Yes," Grey agreed.

"Her husband can rot for all of me, but Veronica . . . she was truly an innocent in this. Her only crime was trying to help and wanting to be free of domestic oppression." He sniffed again, then his sharp eye caught the footprints. "What the bloody hell is that?"

"Veronica said something about chickens . . ."

"Those aren't chicken tracks. A blind man could see that."

"I know," said Grey, "so what are they?"

"I'll be buggered if I know. They're as big as an ostrich, but it's not one of those either."

"What's an ostrich?"

"A bloody big bird from Africa. Ugly as sin and cranky as a—. Hello! What's that?" He jogged down five steps and bent to retrieve an object Grey hadn't even seen. Looks Away held it out.

It was a feather. Long and stiff, colored a dark orange with a band of black.

"Do you recognize it?" asked Grey.

"No . . . I don't, and that's rather an odd thing. I'm no ornithologist, but I know my local birds, and I've never seen these markings. And certainly nothing similar on any bird that could have left tracks that big. Those prints look almost reptilian."

"Can't be. They're in sets of two. No lizard I ever saw walks on two legs. And no bird I can think of could slash a person up like it did to your lady friend."

Looks Away said nothing, but he let the feather drop from his hand and went back up the stairs to retrieve his shotgun.

They stood for a moment, glancing back the way they had come and then down into shadows.

"We came out here to try and talk sense to Nolan Chesterfield," said Looks Away.

"Yup."

"Not to go searching through catacombs."

"Nope."

"Our moral responsibility would be to return to town; organize a wagon train; take as much of the gold, silver, and platinum as we can carry; and brush the dust of this town off our feet."

"That's smart thinking," said Grey, nodding.

"There is no sane or intelligent reason to go down these stairs."

"None that I can think of."
They stood there.
"Shite," said Looks Away.
"Shit," agreed Grey.
Guns in hand, they started down the stairs.

Chapter 50

It was a long way down.

The stone steps curved around and around, and soon Grey lost all track of how far they'd descended. At one point Looks Away stopped and bent with his lantern to inspect the steps.

"These are new," he said.

"New?"

"I think they were made since the Quake."

"How can you tell? The house might have been built over one of those old Spanish missions. Those guys used to build all kinds of cellars and sub-cellars."

"No, that's not what this is," said Looks Away. "I know my geology and I've been to enough ruins to know one style of stonework from another. The Spanish used broader, flatter stairs. These are narrow and a bit steeper. Much more in the style of French or English castle architecture."

"If you say so."

"I do, and I find it rather curious. Chesterfield's family is from England, and they were rich going back to the time of the Plantagenets. So, while I can see Chesterfield using the building style he's familiar with, I can't quite suss out why he cut a staircase so deep into the earth. It must have cost a fortune to do this much excavation through solid rock."

"He could afford it."

"Okay, fair enough," said Looks Away, "but why

spend that money on this? What the hell is down here that's worth all of this effort to conceal it from the world?"

They had no answers.

Until they reached the bottom of the stairs.

The steps ended in another circular chamber. Once more there was a single doorway. Once more it was open.

More than open.

The door had been torn from its heavy iron hinges and smashed to kindling. Pieces of it were scattered all around. There was blood on the floor and walls, and the scuff patterns told of a battle between two men wearing ordinary boots and things that made impressions even Looks Away could not read. Much of the bloody spill was smeared as if someone had dragged something long and heavy from inside the room, through that destroyed door, and then back in again. The small two-toed prints were everywhere, but nothing with feet that small could have torn that door down. The timbers of the door had to be half a foot thick.

"I'm having some serious second thoughts about coming down here," said Grey quietly.

"I'm having third thoughts," said Looks Away. "And if we don't find something useful soon I'm all for getting our bums back up those stairs."

They approached the open doorway and held their lanterns up to reveal what was inside.

There were three metal carts of the kind miners used. They squatted on wheels, however, not rails. Two of them were piled high with chunks of rock cut unevenly from the ground. The third cart had been knocked over; its contents spilling outward like guts. Grey felt his mouth go dry. The rocks littered the floor. They were mostly crude, a mix of sandstone, volcanic rock, and variegated sedimentary stone. However each piece also contained

fragments of a black stone that was streaked with wavering lines of white.

"By the Queens' lacy . . . ," began Looks Away, but he couldn't finish.

Grey estimated that each of the carts could hold a full ton of broken rock. If even after smelting the total yield of all three carts was only a hundredweight of that which was the white-veined black rock, then there was a fortune here to rival two full pallets of gold bars.

"Ghost rock," he whispered.

And ghost rock it was.

"This is what Chesterfield was hiding," said Looks Away. "I think he was mining ghost rock and selling it. He was making himself insanely rich."

"Not sure that makes enough sense for me," said Grey. "Doesn't explain why Deray attacked this place. If it was to get the gold and the rock, then why leave it here?"

Suddenly they froze and it took Grey a moment for his mind to catch up with what his senses had recorded.

There it was again.

A sound.

A scuff of a stealthy foot.

Grey raised his lantern and held it so they could see the rest of this chamber.

"Look!" cried Looks Away in a choked voice. "Dear God what is that thing?"

Twenty feet away, caught in the spill of lamplight, stood a creature unlike anything Grey had ever seen. It was nearly as tall as a man, but it was no man. It stood on two impossibly muscular legs, and each foot had two splayed toes. The creature had a third toe, however, and this one was raised on both feet. It was longer than the others and where they had claws, the third toes curved out with a talon as long and sharp as a dagger. But the strangeness did not end there. The thing had a birdlike body, much like a condor, but larger and more massive.

And instead of arms or wings it had something that was akin to both. Short, sharp-clawed arms pawed the air and these were completely covered by smoky gray feathers. The rest of the body was covered by feathers that were a rusty orange banded with black. A crest of red feathers ran backward from the center of its skull, however the face was not birdlike at all. It had a protruding muzzle like a lizard, but its mouth was large enough to bite through a grown man's leg. As it stood there, the thing opened its mouth to display rows of curved, needle-sharp teeth. It glared at the men with eyes that were black and bottomless.

The creature was like nothing Grey had ever seen before. However Looks Away breathed a word, a name, and it rang a faint bell in Grey's mind.

"Dinosaur . . ."

"What?"

"By the Queen's garters that is a bloody dinosaur."

"What the hell's a—?"

"Something that can't be here. It's impossible."

The thing snarled at them and took a threatening step forward into the light and in doing so became more impossible still. Now they could see that many of the feathers were bent and broken or missing entirely, and through those gaps they could see that the flesh was strange. Unnaturally pale and withered, like that of some dead thing that had lain rotting in the dark. Maggots wriggled through flaps of torn skin and from many open wounds wafted the dead meat stink of advanced rot.

"Jesus Christ," breathed Grey. "That stench . . ."

Looks Away gagged. "Dear God, that thing's . . . *dead*."

"No," said Grey, pointing. "It's worse than dead."

In the center of the creature's chest, amid the feathers, gleamed a multi-faceted piece of black rock that was shot through with white lines.

Ghost rock. In the chest of an undead monster.

The creature threw wide its mouth and screamed at them as if defying any classification of either dead or alive. The men raised their weapons in trembling hands, ready to fight, ready to kill this monstrosity.

But far away, deeper in the large underground chamber, came the answering cry of other monsters just like this one.

They cried in rage and hate.

And those cries were coming.

Straight for Grey and Looks Away.

Chapter 51

"Christ—watch out!" bellowed Grey as he shoved Looks Away to the side as the first of the monsters rushed them. The creature raced toward them and then leaped into the air. Grey saw the third and terrible claw on its foot snap forward and he tried to twist out of the way. The claw hooked into the pocket of his jeans and tore it open as if it was tissue paper. Coins flew across the room and bounced off the metal carts.

The first of the undead dinosaurs was too close for Grey to get a clear shot at without hitting Looks Away, so instead he clubbed at the thing with the butt of his Colt. The monster shrieked in pain, but instead of shrinking back from its much bigger opponent, it hissed and leaped again, slashing this time at Grey's groin.

He flung himself backward and the claw missed him by half an inch. He landed on his back and used the momentum to roll up onto his shoulders so he could kick out with both heels. He caught it square in the chest and sent it flying backward into the side of a metal cart. It struck with a ringing thud and fell dazed to the floor.

Grey scrambled back to his feet.

"Move—move!" shouted Looks Away as he surged forward and shouldered him out of the way. The Sioux braced the stock of the shotgun against his hip and fired. Grey twisted around to see the buckshot catch another of the dinosaurs full in the chest just as it launched itself to slash. The blast punched a huge red hole in the center of the thing's chest, obliterating the ghost rock implant and tearing off its feathered arms and screeching head. Thick, black blood splashed the men, the cart, and the faces of half a dozen more of the monsters.

Before the echo of the blast could begin to fade, Grey whirled and shot the first creature in the head as it fought to get back to its feet. It flopped back and lay absolutely still.

"How is this even possible?" demanded Grey as he hastily reloaded.

Looks Away shook his head, but then said, "Deray is a necromancer. That means he has power over the dead. It looks like he's discovered some alchemical process for raising the dead and suborning them to his will. Like those creatures who accompanied Lucky Bob. He was a Harrowed but the others were something else. Mindless dead."

"Mindless?" said Grey, pointing with the barrel of his gun. "Maybe they can't think, but that look in their eyes says that they *feel* something, and it's not anything good. We need to get the hell out of here." The death of two of the beasts had momentarily stalled the charge of the others. They stared as if in shock. Then all of the strange, feathered and rotting heads turned slowly toward Grey and Looks Away. Those faces may not have been human, but their expressions were easy to read.

Hate.

Rage.

Hunger.

"Oh . . . shit," said Grey and Looks Away at the same moment.

The monsters surged forward.

Both men stumbled backward but they opened fire at the same time. Grey emptied his gun into them. The Sioux fired his last shell. The fusillade of pellets and bullets hit the attacking wave like a storm. Three of the monsters went down into red ruin. A fourth staggered sideways, one eye blown away and blood dark as ink poured from a dozen pellet wounds.

The remaining two did not pause this time. One jumped at Looks Away, slashing at his belly with its terrible claws. The other did its best to rip open the arteries on the inside of Grey's thigh.

Grey felt a line of white-hot fire explode along his hip. He cried out in pain and swung the pistol again and again, clubbing the scything foot, battering at the bizarre creature's head and chest. It snapped at the gun and caught the barrel between its jagged teeth. If there had been one more round Grey could have blown out the back of its head. Instead as the dinosaur gave a mighty pull on the trapped barrel, Grey released it and emphasized it with a kick to its gut. The monster staggered backward and Grey immediately whipped out his hunting knife. Now he had his own claw.

"Come on, you undead little bastard," he growled, baring his teeth at it. He could hear Looks Away and the other monster fighting somewhere behind him, but he didn't dare turn and look.

The dinosaur spat out the useless pistol and lowered its head as it prepared to charge. The big claws on each foot tapped downward onto the floor. The thing's long tail stuck straight out behind it, counterbalancing its weight and twitching with pure rage.

Then it launched itself at its prey.

Grey expected it to be fast, but it was so much faster. It became a blur of feathers, scales, teeth, and claws as it leaped into the air, slashing with those claws.

It was faster than he was.

He, however, was smarter.

As soon as it launched itself into the air, Grey dodged to one side and then twisted, pulling his body out of the path of the claws. He did not stab at it. Stabbing is a fool's way to fight with a knife. Grey whipped his arm in a tight arc that slapped the edge of the blade across the throat of the dinosaur. The combined speed of its leap and Grey's own speed made the blade bite deep. A black spray burst from the throat, but Grey did not want to make any assumptions about how tough the monster was or if blood loss could ever kill it. He jumped at it as the thing landed, clubbing it with one balled fist and slashing again and again with the blade.

Feathers flew. Blood erupted. Tissue parted.

It fell forward onto its wing-like arms, but immediately tried to rise. With a savage howl, Grey raised his foot and began stomping on its head. Once, twice, again and again until the bones shattered and his heel mashed the shards into the creature's brain. All at once it sagged down into death.

Grey staggered back from it, then turned as he heard a series of heavy thuds.

It was Looks Away pounding at the head of the last of the reanimated dinosaurs. Or at the pulpy mess that had been a head. But Looks Away kept hammering and his face was a mask of fear that hovered near the flame of madness.

"Looks," said Grey. "Whoa, now . . . it's done. You killed it. Ease back now."

The Sioux froze with the bloody shotgun raised for another strike. His wild eyes looked at Grey, at the dead creatures that lay everywhere, and then down at the mess beneath him. He lowered the shotgun and sagged back onto his heels.

"God save the Queen," he breathed. The mad light faded from his eyes, replaced by shock.

There was a squeak and they both whipped around to see the dinosaur with the gunshot wound to the eye staggering slowly away. Black ichor ran sluggishly from its nostrils. It was clearly dying and it left a trail of splay-toed prints identical to the ones that had been on the stairs.

Looks Away got up, cracked open the shotgun, and dumped the spent shells, fitted two new ones in, and walked up behind the dinosaur. It turned to look up at him with its one remaining eye. It tried to hiss. It tried to slash at him. But it was too far gone.

"No," said Looks Away as he placed the barrel against its head.

The blast was huge and wet and it echoed off of the darkened walls.

Chapter 52

The last of the booming echoes disintegrated into the sober silence of death. Gun smoke hovered like a chorus of phantoms in the still air.

His face turned to emotionless wood, Looks Away replaced the spent shell, pulled a handkerchief from his pocket, and began methodically wiping the blood of monsters from his shotgun. Grey said nothing. He limped over to retrieve his Colt, checked that it was undamaged, and reloaded it.

Then he addressed his wounds. The creatures had done their best to eviscerate him. Only the toughness of his jeans and the leather of his gun belt had saved his life. Even so, there was a bad gash on his hip and it bled freely. The pain was searing and he clamped his jaw shut as he used strips torn from his shirt to compress and bind the wound. It was a sloppy job, but it would serve. Luckily the talon had torn only skin and not the muscle beneath. He could still move easily and he set his teeth against limping. That would wear him out too quickly and besides, it was only pain. Grey had maintained a long and passionate affair with pain. He knew all her secrets.

Once he was finished he wiped his bloody fingers on his thighs and waited for Looks Away to speak.

When he did, the Sioux's voice was filled with both stress and wonder. "These are—or, at least *were*— dinosaurs."

"Yeah, you said that, but I don't know what that means. They're animals, right? From where? They from Africa or—?"

"They're extinct," said Looks Away. "All we've ever seen are bones and paintings done to try and reconstruct what they might have looked like. Dinosaur. It means 'terrible lizard.'"

"Fair enough as something to call them," muttered Grey. "Ugly sonsabitches works for me, too."

"The term was coined by Sir Richard Owen. I met him twice—when our show played in Lancaster, and then again in London. He was a surly, contentious old git who thought Charles Darwin was completely wrong about his theories of evolution."

"Darwin? I read about him. A lot of folks said he was trying to say God didn't make the world."

"That's not precisely what he said. Darwin believed that our world is much older than suggested by the ages of the people named in the Bible, and that long before humans came along there were ages and ages of natural development. The animals and plants that we know today are there because they were the ones best able to survive those long millennia of growth. He also believed that before there were the animals we know about, there were others before them. This was about the only point he and Owen agreed upon, though Owen tended to think that Darwin simplified the process too much."

"Did he?"

Looks Away shrugged. "I studied rocks, not animals. I'm not qualified to judge."

He squatted down and studied one of the dead creatures. Grey joined him.

"So, what are you getting at? Were these things the ancestors of alligators and horny toads?"

"Maybe. I've heard arguments to that effect, and I've heard arguments that they evolved into birds."

Grey ran his fingers along the feathers. "Seems pretty likely. But if they're the ancestors of birds and such, why the hell are they here? How did Deray get his hands on them?"

"That is a very, very good question, old chap," said Looks Away. "I have a theory, or part of one at least."

"Oh, I can't wait to hear it."

"Well, look around," said Looks Away. "Ever since the Great Quake all sorts of strange things have been happening. Reports of flying lizards and sea serpents. These things are strange, I'll grant you, but surely they're not the strangest things that have been said to come out of the Maze. Not if even a tenth of the reports are true."

Grey grunted. "Before I came out here I was of the mind that all of those stories started at the bottom of a whiskey glass. Now . . . well, I mean, does something really actually need to bite you on the ass before you take it as Gospel fact?"

"For my part, my friend, I shall henceforth endeavor to keep a very open mind."

Looks Away grabbed the shoulder of the creature and rolled it onto its back. The chunk of ghost rock embedded in its chest was small, about the size of a grape. The white lines seemed to shift and flow like restless worms, though Grey told himself that it was just the flickering lantern light or his own imagination. "I think that maybe these creatures were trapped down here. See how pale their flesh is? That suggests a life lived away from the sun. When Deray came down here he must have encountered all sorts of strange creatures. Encountered them, slaughtered them, used his sorcery to bring them back to life, and then found a way to enslave them with ghost rock."

"I didn't think ghost rock could do that."

Looks Away shrugged. "It can't, as far as I know. As I said, this is as much alchemy as it is ghost rock science.

Maybe more so." He shook his head. "And God only knows what else Deray has waiting for us. If he can command the dead . . . the possibilities are staggering."

Grey rubbed his jaw and looked back the way they came. "There's always a war going on somewhere. Countries fighting, land wars, rail wars. Lots of dead people to be had. If you're thinking what I'm thinking, then we are in deep, deep shit."

"My friend," said Looks Away as he reloaded, "I believe that without a doubt we are in very deep shit indeed."

"Deray," muttered Grey. "More and more I'm getting the feeling that I need to park a bullet in his brainpan."

"You, my dear chap," said Looks Away, "will have to stand in line."

Grey knelt beside one of the monsters and plucked a feather out, sniffed it, winced, and tossed it away. Then he peered at the chunk of ghost rock. "I thought there was some kind of rules to this ghost rock business. Same with the Harrowed. The way Brother Joe put it, this was ghost rock or some demons or whatever taking over corpses. That's what we saw in Nevada, and it's what you told me happened when that factory blew up in Europe. If that's the way it's supposed to work, then how do you explain extinct dinosaurs with ghost rocks in their chests? I mean . . . give me a place to stand so I can think about that the right way."

"I'm afraid I can't offer you such a refuge, Grey," said Looks Away. "I am in totally unknown territory here. You know as much as I do."

"Which means we don't know enough."

Grey began to reach out and touch the stone, but Looks Away shook his head. "Not with your bare hand."

"Why? Does it do something?"

"I have no idea," admitted Looks Away, "but we can surmise that the chunks of ghost rock he's implanted in the chests of his victims—human and animal—allow him some measure of control. They're clearly his slaves."

Grey drew his knife and used the point to touch the stone. It made a dull metallic *tink* sound. Nothing else happened. "So he took something that was already dangerous as hell and used black magic to make it worse?"

"Yes. We've only begun to understand the nature and properties of ghost rock. Dr. Saint is exploring new scientific directions, and now we have proof that Deray's necromancy has taken him in even more obscure and frightening directions. It's so much to consider, but for now we'd best leave it be. We have a job of work ahead of us."

"Work?" asked Grey. "As in getting the hell out of here?"

Looks Away shook his head. "I don't think I can do that, Grey. Not at this point. Not after all that we've seen. I think we have to gird our loins and enter the belly of the beast."

"Meaning what?"

Looks Away stood and picked up one of the lanterns. "Didn't you see this?"

"See what?" asked Grey as he rose.

"I saw it just as those beasties rushed us."

The Sioux walked a couple of paces toward the back of the room and the spill of light revealed a sight Grey had not noticed before. The rear wall of the chamber was in ruins. The naked stone had been shattered, pushed outward by some titanic force, and lay in heaps of rubble. Beyond the debris was a gaping maw of a hole that yawned like the mouth of some fabled dragon.

"I think that is where our monsters came from," said Looks Away. "And if my guess is correct that tunnel will lead us to the answers we seek."

Grey Torrance closed his eyes for a moment, and in the brief silence he could once more hear the muffled footsteps of the ghosts who haunted him. They were behind him and darkness opened before him.

"Damn it," he breathed. Then he opened his eyes and nodded. "Let's go."

Chapter 53

Grey didn't know exactly what "girding one's loins" meant, but he squared his shoulders and set his jaw as they moved toward the gaping hole. Looks Away padded along beside him, his face grim and determined.

As they approached the hole it became apparent that the destruction had not been accomplished by anything like dynamite. The whole wall had been pushed into the chamber. They stopped at the entrance and held out their lanterns.

"Jesus Christ," said Grey.

Beyond the hole was a tunnel. Roughly round and crudely made, it curled around down into the bowels of the earth. The sides of it glistened and when Looks Away reached to touch it he quickly withdrew his hand. His fingers were wet and sticky and they smelled like rotting fish.

"What the hell is that?" asked Grey.

"I have no idea," said the Sioux as he rubbed his fingers together under his nose. "It's disturbingly like the secretions a worm makes. But God—the smell."

The odor wafting up from the tunnel was clearly the source of the stench they'd smelled earlier. Here, though, it hadn't been diluted by distance. The stink was almost palpable.

Looks Away drew a breath and raised his leg to step over the fractured rim.

"You'll die in there," said a voice behind them.

They both whirled, bringing their guns to bear.

A figure stood at the far end of the chamber, surrounded by the corpses of the reanimated dinosaurs. It was a woman who wore the shredded remnants of a sheer dressing gown. Her hair was up in a loose bun, her eyes were filled with dark mystery. A dreadful wound had been opened in her side through which they could see purple coils of her intestines. She seemed to be bathed in the glow of a pale blue-white light, but she cast no shadow.

Beside him, Grey heard Looks Away utter a low cry of bottomless pain and endless fear.

It was Veronica Chesterfield.

And she was dead.

Chapter 54

The dead woman spoke in a voice that was as cold and alien as a cemetery wind.

"Thomas," she said. "My sweet man."

Looks Away would have fallen to his knees if Grey hadn't dropped his lantern and caught him. The lantern fell over and burning oil spilled out. The flames cast wild shadows onto the walls, though none were stranger than the dead thing that stood before them.

"What . . . ," began Looks Away in a strained choke, "what *are* you?"

She held her arms wide. The gesture pulled the bloody gossamer tight across her ample breasts, and the wisps of cloth seemed to float around her as if stirred by a wind that neither man could feel. Grey realized that the blue-white light did not fall upon her but was instead *part* of her, as if she were alight within. It was beautiful in its way, but in this moment and in this place there was nothing in Grey's heart but terror.

"Don't you know?" she asked. "Don't you recognize me? Don't you know your own loving Veronica?"

"God rot you," snarled Looks Away, "you are *not* her. Damn you to Hell!"

"To Hell?" mused Veronica, letting her arms drop. "No, my love. That's not where I belong. Nor do I belong among the living. I walk now between those worlds."

"I don't . . . I don't . . ."

She smiled sadly. "Such a brave man. You've faced

such horrors already. Will you shrink in fear from a help-less spirit?"

"Spirit? You're a . . . a ghost?" breathed the Sioux.

"Though I've only been dead for a short time I feel as if I've lived forever here in the world of spirits. Ghost? That is so impure a word, and so shallow. Call me that if it helps, but know that it does not truly tell you what I've become."

"You can't be here. It's wrong . . . it's a lie. What are you that you are so cruel?"

For a moment the she-thing before them seemed to waver, her face twisted into doubt. "I don't mean to be cruel," she said in a voice that was filled with sadness. "Truly I do not."

"Then why do this?" demanded Looks Away. "You have no right to use Veronica's body like this. It's un-holy."

"*Unholy?* That's a strange word for you to use, Thomas. I thought you didn't believe in God. Or the Devil. Or any-thing. Isn't that what you told me? Or, isn't that what you told her? That you were a man of science, not of ancient superstitions."

Grey saw his friend stiffen. "How could you know what I said to her?"

"Because I am her. When she died, I rose from the flesh, but all that she was I am except that flesh. Please, Thomas, try and understand."

"Don't call me that. Only she was allowed to call me that. You don't have the right."

The ghost considered, then nodded. "Then I will call you Looks Away. Great Sioux warrior. Noted scientist. May I address that man rather than the lover of the woman who died?"

"This is insane," Grey said sharply.

Veronica turned to him. "Ah . . . Greyson Torrance," she said slowly, a half-smile on her lips. "The haunted man. Oh yes, don't look so surprised. In the worlds beyond the flesh there is much we spirits know. Much we can see. And do you want to know what I see when I look at you?"

Looks Away frowned as he studied Grey. "What is she talking about?"

"Nothing," said Grey. "This thing just wants to mess with our heads."

"Oh no," said the ghost. "I can see a tarot card burning in the air above your head. The martyr's card. It is your sigil now. You are the haunted man who walks one step ahead of the tireless dead."

"Grey—?" murmured Looks Away.

"She's lying."

"Am I?" asked the ghost. "Did Carmilla not read your fortune?"

"I don't know anyone named—."

"Mircalla then. She spoke prophecy to you and its truth burns within you. I can see the flame. Be careful, Grey Torrance, or it will consume you."

"I don't give a mule's hairy balls about prophecy or card tricks or any of that guff. You want to know the future? Sure—it's me putting a hot lead bullet through the brain of that twisted bastard Aleksander Deray."

Veronica's smile faded from her pale lips. "Then listen to me, both of you. And you, Looks Away, most of all," she said softly. "I will tell you now what I was too afraid to say while I lived. "Nolan was nothing but a pawn of Deray. My husband was little more than a slave. He worshipped Deray like a god. He crawled on his belly before the necromancer. They conspired together to destroy this town because the Maze here is ripe with wealth. Gold and precious metals. You've seen it, you know. The great Gold Rush was nothing compared to the veins of ore that were exposed after the Quake. Nolan discovered the vast riches here, and he knew how to find the ore. He knew how to smelt it and extract the purest metals. And he knew where to find ghost rock."

"If you're Veronica, then why didn't you tell me this before," demanded Looks Away.

"Because, no matter what else, Nolan was still my husband and I swore to keep his secrets. That oath perished with my vows." She smiled again, and it was ghoulish and cold. "The vow was 'til death do us part, and we are surely parted now. I am beyond the bindings of my wedding vow and beyond the cruel force of his hand. There is nothing Nolan can do to me anymore. But I fear Deray, because he has mastery over the dead. He could raise my body as one of his undead slaves. He is worse than a murderer, worse than a monster. He is evil incarnate. Even the dead and the damned fear him."

"So what?" asked Grey. "We already know he's a miserable blood-sucking bastard. That's why I want to park a bullet between his eyes. And we pretty much figured Nolan was his lackey."

"Nolan was all that, but the presence of all that gold and ghost rock here in his basement weighed on him. It was not his—he was merely the treasurer for Deray. He coveted it, though. It ate at his mind and gnawed even at his devotion to Deray. He came to worship a different god—that of his own greed. And so he rebelled. He used the gold to buy the loyalty of many of Deray's men. The deputies in the town, some of the hired gunmen. With enough gold you can buy any mortal man's soul."

Looks Away said, "You're speaking about Chesterfield in the past-tense. Is he dead?"

"Not yet," said the manitou. "Every man, woman, and child on this estate has either been killed, captured, or given over to the undead summoned by Deray. A few yet live. Nolan himself still lives, but his hours are numbered. As for the rest? Most of them have been raised through the black magic of Deray's necromancy and bound to his will by the ghost rock he has fused into their flesh."

"Good lord," said Looks Away faintly, "that's quite . . . horrible."

Veronica nodded. "For love of you, my dear Thomas, I have come to you to tell you this. I came freely and willingly, even though I know I am abhorrent to your eyes. You look at me and you see only a wretched ghost. But hear me, I beg."

"We're listening," said Grey thickly, and he did not correct her on the use of his given name.

"Deray has Harrowed in his service, and a legion of the undead. This is the army he will use to realize his mad dreams."

"What dreams? He's already richer than God," snapped Grey. "What the hell else does he want?"

"He wants to conquer."

"Conquer what?"

She shook her head. "I . . . do not know. His mind is closed to me as it is closed to all lesser spirits. What I know for certain is that if he is unchecked all will suffer. Your kind and perhaps even mine. Necromancy is an abomination that threatens the living and the dead in equal measures."

Chapter 55

That's impossible," said Grey. "I admit that I'm not much for church and all that Bible stuff, but I'm pretty sure I read somewhere that souls are immortal. Eternal. How can he do you any further harm?"

"Oh, my love there is so much you don't know, so much you can't know until death opens your eyes. Magic is not merely a tool, it is a doorway. With necromancy, Deray can enslave the souls of the dead. He could take me and *use* me in ways the living could never imagine—not in your wildest nightmares. I have an eternity to suffer, and Deray has the power to turn forever into Hell itself. Haven't you heard of banshees wailing or ghosts moaning? Suffering does not end when the heart becomes still and the flesh cools. Believe me, it does not."

"By the Queen's garters," breathed Looks Away.

"What is it you expect us to do?" asked Grey.

"You need to stop Aleksander Deray," said Veronica, "by any means necessary."

"How?" demanded Looks Away. "If he's that powerful, if he's able to force ghosts and demons and every damned hobgoblin that goes bump in the night to his will, then what chance do we have?"

"Almost none," she said sadly.

"Well that's encouraging as hell," said Grey. "Thanks so much. Maybe we should take the gold, gather everyone in town and move to—oh, I don't know—anywhere else."

She shook her head. "You cannot escape what is coming."

"I can give it one hell of a try."

"If you run all will be lost. Deray is not doing all of this just to conquer the town of Paradise Falls. He cares nothing for this place. Surely you can see that."

Grey said nothing.

"The future is not a window but a house of mirrors reflecting ten thousand possibilities. Worlds will turn on the wink of your eye," said Veronica, repeating what Mircalla had said. "Worlds will fall in the light of your smile."

Grey felt his mouth go dry as dust.

"What does she mean?" asked Looks Away, frowning at him.

Grey said nothing.

"Not all who walk in shadows are evil," continued the ghost. "Not all of the lonely spirits of the dead wish you harm."

And with those words she turned and walked away. The firelight danced along the swirling folds of her gossamer nightgown. Then she vanished into the distance and the darkness.

Looks Away took a single, uncertain step as if to follow, then he stopped and sagged back in grief and defeat. Finally he turned to Grey.

"We are already in Hell," he said. "So I guess we must play our parts like good puppets."

He walked past Grey and stepped through the ragged hole in the wall. Grey lingered for a long moment, feeling an icy chill on his spine and a fiery burn in his gut. Then he, too, turned, stepped through the destroyed wall and began his journey into darkness.

Chapter 56

Grey caught up with Looks Away, who had walked fifty feet along the slime-covered corridor. The Sioux stood without a lantern, awash in shadows. Grey carried the only remaining light and as before it cast capering shadows onto the walls.

"This is madness," said Looks Away without preamble.

"This is not normal," agreed Grey with a tone that was ten tons lighter than the weight on his heart.

"What are we doing? After all, we don't even know if this tunnel will lead us to Deray."

Grey looked at him. "Sure we do. Where else would it lead?"

"Bedlam?"

"Where?"

"Oh, never mind," groused Looks Away. Then he cut a sharp look at Grey. "What was all that about Mircalla? You dodged me before when I asked."

Grey did not want to tell him because it would open the door to more questions and to things he never wanted to share with anyone. However, that kind of privacy no longer seemed to matter. He began walking and Looks Away fell into step beside him. Their path sloped down and curved away into unknown territory.

As they walked, Grey told him about what had happened at the brothel and his dream about that tarot card reading by Mircalla.

"The martyr card?" mused Looks Away. "Hardly what I'd call an apt description."

"Why not? I'm down here risking my ass, aren't I?"

"Sure but—."

"And don't think it's just because you hired me. Give me a little more credit than that."

"I do, actually," said Looks Away, looking amused. "And I wasn't casting aspersions on your valor, old chap. It's just that martyrs sacrifice themselves and you're a fighter, Grey. I believe you'd fight them all the way to the bitter end."

Grey thought about it, and shrugged. "Guess I don't have a whole lot of 'give up' in me. If I did you'd be down here alone."

Looks Away nodded, his face serious. "I wonder if maybe I should be down here alone. After all this isn't really your fight."

"You're paying me to make it my fight."

"Oh, come now, old chap, I hardly think my offer of employment extends to fighting demons in an underground anteroom to Hell itself."

"I still took your coin."

"It was a token. You can give it back and no hard feelings."

Grey dug into his pocket and realized that it was the one that had been torn by the dinosaur's claw. "I guess I can't."

"But—"

"So I guess you're stuck with me."

The Sioux shook his head. "I don't know which of us is more daft."

"You're doing this for love and I'm doing it for—."

"Love?" asked Looks Away. "No, don't try and look so innocent. Do you think I did not hear you two downstairs?"

Grey said nothing and he felt his face burn.

"Jenny's a fine and decent woman," he said.

"Yes," Looks Away agreed, "she is. As was Veronica Chesterfield. They are the ladies of our heroic little tale and I suppose that makes us the knights errant."

"Oh, please."

"Who knows . . . maybe we'll even get to slay a dragon."

Grey shook his head. "You need to shut the fuck up."

They kept going, deeper and deeper into the belly of the beast.

Chapter 57

They walked for miles down there in the dark.

For the first hour the tunnel was featureless except for the dripping slime on the walls and strange footprints that fit no creature they had ever seen. Several times Grey caught Looks Away pausing to study those walls.

"You seeing something I should know about?"

The Sioux nodded, looking worried.

"There are certain kinds of worms that secrete acids through their skin that allow them to essentially burn their way through the soil. Mind you, we're talking about tiny creatures. Two or three inches long."

"So?" began Grey, then he stopped and reappraised the slick, unnaturally smooth walls. "Oh . . . shit."

"Yes," agreed Looks Away.

"Is that even possible? Something this big?"

Looks Away turned and gave him a withering stare. "After all that's happened you can ask that question with a straight face?"

Grey sighed. "I guess I keep hoping we've seen the worst of what Deray has up his sleeve."

"I wish," muttered the Sioux.

They pressed on, and soon turned a sharper corner and found themselves in a vast cavern. They stood gaping in wonder at the things they saw.

The cavern stretched out in all directions and gnarled pillars of sandstone rose to support a roof that was lost in the darkness far above. They did not need the lantern to see because there was a light that seemed to come from blue fungi that clung to all the walls. The ground was broken, but there were pathways formed of natural sand runoff. Water dripped from the points of massive spears of quartz crystal that had been thrust outward from the walls by some titanic force. They looked too old to have been the result of the Great Quake, and Grey decided that this cavern, unlike the slimy tunnel they had just traversed, had been here for maybe a million years and only opened by the quake. Fantastic mushrooms sprouted from the ground to their right and rose in staggered ranks to cover one entire wall. The stems were as big around as oak trees and the caps of even the smallest would have covered an entire stagecoach. Bats clustered beneath the hoods, wriggling in their leathery thousands, and below them, insects writhed through the piles of guano. The stink of ammonia rolled at them in waves, but to their left was a different sight, and it brought with it a different and more powerful smell. The landscape sloped downward toward the rock-strewn shore of an underground sea. Waves broke upon the shore and cast broken shells and bizarre bones onto the sand. With each breaking wave a fresh stench of spoiled fish assaulted them.

The sea stretched on for miles, the wave tops glimmering with more of the eerie blue luminescence, but in the misty distance it faded into a uniform blackness.

Looks Away softly murmured some lines of poetry, "In Xanadu did Kubla Khan a stately pleasure-dome decree, where Alph, the sacred river, ran through caverns measureless to man, down to a sunless sea."

Grey gave him a sharp look. "Wait, you know this place?"

"No, old boy," said Looks Away, his eyes alight with wonder, "that is an old poem. Coleridge, and it was written about a mythical place far, far away. It's just that it seems to fit, does it not?"

"I guess . . . but I wish it had stayed in a poem."

Looks Away walked over to the closest rock pillar and bent to peer at the glowing fungi. He sniffed at it. "Grey . . . come here and see this."

With great reluctance, Grey joined him. The fungi looked like tiny cabbage leaves, but it rippled like sea anemones.

"This is so strange," said Looks Away. "This is some form of *panellus stipticus*—what most people call 'bitter oyster.' But bioluminescent fungi emit a green light. This is blue."

"And it's a pretty damn familiar blue," said Grey.

"Indeed it is. The fungi must pick up trace amounts of ghost rock. Not enough to react to the flame of our lanterns, but enough to change the color of the bioluminescent glow."

"That's not much of a comfort. And, damn, but it's hot as hell in here," said Grey. "Could there be a volcano down here?"

"Anything's possible in the Maze," said Looks Away. "Whatever it is, there's some form of geothermal activity. You can smell the sulfur in the air."

"All I smell is batshit and dead fish."

"No, there's more. That rotten egg smell. That's sulfur."

Grey sniffed. "Oh, right."

They looked around. Far off in the distance and up near the inky darkness of the roof, they could see small birds flapping or drifting on thermal currents.

"This is all so—" began Looks Away, but a sudden sound jolted them to silence. They raised their weapons as something seemed to detach itself from the stem of one of the gigantic mushrooms. At first it looked like part of the stalk was sliding off, then with a thrill of mingled terror and disgust Grey saw that it was something far worse. The thing—for thing was the only word his mind could conjure—was as long as an alligator but it was no reptile. It had a narrow body that seemed composed of hundreds of banded segments, and from the sides of each of these segments sprouted a pair of jointed legs. The shell was the same dead-white color as the mushrooms, but the legs were black; and the whole thing glistened wetly.

"Dear . . . God!" cried Looks Away. "Are you seeing this?"

"I wish to Christ I wasn't."

The creature crawled out onto the floor of the cavern and began moving toward them on a thousand feet, and it uttered a weird, high-pitched, chittering sound.

"Is that . . . is that a . . . ?" Grey began but couldn't finish.

"It's a whacking great centipede," said Looks Away.

Grey shoved the lantern into his hand, took his pistol in a steady two-hand grip, and fired three spaced shots into its head. The impact of the hot lead punched through the chitinous shell and exploded the first three segments. However the body kept moving forward.

"Shite!" yelped Looks Away. He quickly set the lantern down and took aim with his shotgun.

The blast was enormous and it rang through the cavern. Masses of bats broke in panic from beneath the mushrooms, and the air was filled with the thunder of ten thousand leathery wings. All around them came the cries and chirps and clicks of creatures seen and unseen, and Grey knew that they were surrounded by more things than they could possibly fight.

What was left of the centipede twisted and thrashed on the ground like a worm on a hot rock. Even with three bullets and a round of buckshot the thing was somehow still alive.

"Is that thing one of those undead sonsabitches?" demanded Grey.

"No. I don't think so," said Looks Away uncertainly. "There's no ghost rock implant. I think this is something that was always down here. Maybe no one would ever have seen something like this had it not been for the Great Quake."

"I wish I'd never seen it."

"I tend to agree, old chap," said Looks Away. He was sweating badly and his hands trembled with fear and disgust.

"Tell you what, Looks," said Grey as they crouched beneath the storm of hysterical bats, "I'm having some serious second thoughts about this. Maybe we should fall back, regroup, get drunk, and talk ourselves out of this."

"I'm inclined to agree," muttered Looks Away. "We may need different equipment for this kind of expedition."

"Fifty armed men as backup, a Gatling gun, and a shitload of dynamite would be at the top of my shopping list."

They rose slowly and began edging back toward the door when they heard another sound. A sharp, piercing cry that echoed through the caverns and stabbed painfully into their eardrums. It came from above, but it was neither a bat nor a bird.

They looked up and once more terror filled Grey's heart. Above them the small birds were swooping down, but Grey immediately realized how wrong he had been. They were not small at all. They were merely very far away.

Now they were getting closer and with each fragment of a second they grew larger, and larger.

And larger.

"What the hell are they?" cried Grey, raising his gun.

"By the Queen's garters!" whispered Looks Away. "I read a paper on these things not five years ago. They were just discovered in Kansas by Sam Wilson."

"What *are* they?" growled Grey as the creatures swooped lower and lower. Just as the dinosaurs they'd fought had been covered with feathers, these birdlike monsters were scaled like reptiles. They had vast leathery wings that stretched twenty feet across, long spike-like beaks and sickle-shaped crests protruding from the backs of their skulls. Even at that distance Grey could smell the dead-flesh stink of them. Unlike the centipedes and bats, they were reanimated corpses. Their cries threatened to crack Grey's head apart.

Just as the two men broke and ran, he heard Looks Away speak a word he had never heard before. "*Pteranodon!*"

"Terra-what?"

"Never mind . . . just kill the bastards."

Grey fired three shots at the closest one, but he had no idea if he hit it. At that range there was no certainty of a head shot. He whirled, bolted, and ran toward the tunnel.

But he instantly skidded to a stop as two of the monsters swept down and cut him off. Looks Away fired his shotgun, but the distance was against him. The pellets peppered the monsters, and they screamed more in rage than pain. Maybe they couldn't even feel pain. Grey grabbed his shoulder, spun him around, and shoved Looks Away in the opposite direction.

"Run!"

Chapter 58

They ran.

The living dead pteranodons flocked after them, screaming for a meal of living flesh. The beat of their wings was like thunder, and all the bats whirled away and vanished under the mushrooms once more. Grey thought that was a smart damn idea, so he dragged Looks Away toward the forest of towering fungi. A gust of wind buffeted him from behind and he staggered down to one knee just as something snapped the air where his head had been a moment ago. Grey rolled to one side to see one of the monsters sweep past, its beak empty but not for lack of trying. Grey's gun was empty, so he shoved it into his holster, scrambled to his feet, and raced on as another of the monsters snapped at the ground on which he'd been lying.

"They're too big to fly under the caps," yelled Looks Away, who was now ten yards ahead, picking his way through the forest. Grey raced to catch up. They crunched ankle deep through pools of bat droppings and insects, and then squeezed between two mushrooms that had become twisted together as they'd grown between spears of crystal.

"Reload," ordered Grey. "Reload."

They reloaded as the pteranodons flapped over the mushrooms, shrieking in fury. The cap above them suddenly tilted and groaned and Grey realized that one of the beasts had landed atop it. He saw the rest of the flock

rise and arc away into the shadowy sky, then wheel and come rushing back.

Several of them landed in the clearing beyond where the two men huddled. They looked so alien, like nothing that should ever have been allowed to trouble the world of living men. On stubby legs and clawed hands attached to their wings they crept forward, searching for a way in to get at their feast.

"They're coming," breathed Looks Away. "Christ!"

Four more of the pteranodons dropped to the ground and began approaching on different sides of their narrow haven. A huge one landed on the spear of quartz above them and stabbed downward through a narrow gap, trying to spear them with its beak. Grey hammered the side of the beak with his fist and then fired past it, trying to hit the monster's eye in hopes of punching through to the brain. The angle was bad and the bullet merely scored a deep groove on the top of its skull. Even so the impact knocked the creature backward.

Grey pivoted and fired four shots at the approaching pteranodons, the rounds punching through folded wings and hitting one in the chest. The creature roared and reared up, then staggered against another monster. Wounded or dying, Grey couldn't tell.

"What about that damn fancy rifle of yours?" he gasped. "Seems like a good goddam time for it, don't you think?"

"Shite!" cried Looks Away. "I'm a bloody fool. I've been carrying it all this time and forgot about it."

Looks Away slid the loaded shotgun into its holster and jerked the strap to swing the Kingdom M1 rifle from his back and into his hands. He began fumbling with small brass and crystal switches and dials.

"Do you even know how to work that thing?" demanded Grey.

"In theory, in theory . . . ," muttered Looks Away under

his breath. A series of small green lights sparkled to life along the gun's sides and Grey could hear a low hum as the rifle began to vibrate.

"Should it be doing that?"

"Probably not," said Looks Away nervously. "But we have to try. I just hope the bloody thing doesn't blow up in my hands."

"Is that likely?"

Looks Away answered with a sour grunt.

"How many rounds do you have?"

"Two magazines. One full one, which has five rounds; and one with only four. Plus two gas canisters. That should be enough to fire what we have."

One of the pteranodons began chopping at the mushroom caps in order to get at them. Two of the others watched for a moment, and then they joined it. Their sharp beaks tore at the spongy fungus.

"Will it stop them?" Grey said, backing away.

Looks Away shook his head. "I have never used it before. I'm not one hundred percent certain it will work at all."

Pieces of the mushroom cap began to rain down on them as the monstrous pterosaurs hammered away. Grey could already see the faces of the monsters. Their eyes glittered with hunger and bloodlust.

"Come on, damn it . . . we're out of time!"

Looks Away was still fiddling with the dials and controls. "I don't know where to set the gas pressure," he said between gritted teeth.

"Then take a wild goddamn guess and—oh, shit."

Grey shoved Looks Away to one side as a huge beak stabbed down through the ragged gap. It speared the air a scant inch from the Sioux's unprotected back. The gun fell and slithered halfway out of their niche. Looks Away dove for it, scrabbling with fingernails as the stock slid away. He caught the very end of the brass butt-plate, but then he snatched his hand back as a savage beak snapped at him.

Grey grabbed his collar and hauled him back to safety as the beak of one of the monsters locked its powerful jaws around the stock of the Kingdom rifle. It lifted the gun up, and with a mighty jerk of its head flipped it into its mouth and tried to eat it.

"Grey!" cried Looks Away.

"I know," he snapped. He leaned halfway out of their niche, dug the barrel of the Colt into the throat of the pteranodon, and fired. Deathless monster or not, the bullet tore a big red hole in the leathery flesh and exited at a sharp right angle, sure evidence that it had ricocheted off of heavy bone. The pteranodon's head suddenly canted sideways and flopped onto the creature's upper wing, and Grey knew which bone his bullet had struck. With a broken neck and two bloody holes in its throat, the giant creature toppled slowly sideways. The other pterosaurs sent up an ululating cry of indignation and fury.

"Did you see that?" yelled Looks Away. "A head shot *and* trauma to the spinal cord will do for those buggers."

"Great, we'll throw a party later. You lost your damn gun."

As the dying beast struck the ground the Kingdom rifle fell from the yawning beak and landed hard. The rows of little lights flickered, flickered, flickered . . . but then they steadied.

The rifle lay ten feet outside of their niche.

"Oh . . ."

Above them the two mushroom caps that formed their ceiling were falling to pieces beneath the renewed assault of the pteranodons.

"They're going to get us," cried Looks Away, fumbling for his shotgun. His hands were shaking badly, and Grey could not blame him. His own trembled with the palsy of genuine terror.

"We need that gun," he growled.

As if in conscious defiance of their needs, one of the pteranodons placed a foot over the weapon. Grey knew that it couldn't be more than happenstance, but it felt like a statement to them.

You are our meat.

It terrified him.

It infuriated him.

As he reloaded he thought about what Mircalla had said about his life. He thought about what Veronica had said. The martyr.

Martyr.

The gun lay there, ten feet away. He could reach it. If he could get it away from the monster then maybe he could throw it to Looks Away before the pteranodons killed them both. They would kill him, of that there was no doubt.

No doubt.

Was this it? Was this the moment predicted by the witch and the manitou? Was he destined to sacrifice himself and to die here in the fetid darkness, the meal of monsters? Was that a tragedy or would it redeem him in the eyes of the universe? And what then? Would he join the band of wandering vengeance ghosts and drift along the fringes of the living world until the sun burned itself out and time ran down to its last few ticks?

Those thoughts flashed through his mind even as he felt his body moving.

Moving.

Rushing toward the cleft, toward the gun.

This is a better death than I deserve, he thought.

And then he was falling sideways.

Something buffeted him and sent him crashing against the tree-like stem of a giant mushroom. He fell hard and saw Looks Away throw him a madman's grin as he dove through the cleft.

Chapter 59

"No!" cried Grey as he struggled back to his feet.

When Looks Away had shoved him out of the way, Grey had dropped his gun. He scooped it up now and prayed that the barrel was not clogged.

It all happened fast.

So fast.

Looks Away had his shotgun in his hands and as he dove he fired both barrels into the face of the towering pterosaur. The creature towered ten feet above him, but the spray from the sawed-off barrels spread wide, and the entire flight of pellets struck beak and eyes and throat and head, and all of it exploded into a cloud of pink mist. The recoil from the poorly braced weapon hit Looks Away in the center of the chest and sent him into an awkward, crashing fall. He landed hard and his head banged against the ground as the headless pteranodon toppled the other way, slamming into two others and dragging them down.

There was one single moment of absolute stillness.

The Kingdom rifle was five feet from where Looks Away lay, but he lay there, shaking his head, dazed, hovering on the edge of blacking out.

"Looks!" shouted Grey as he flung himself out the niche just as three huge beaks stabbed down. He opened up with the Colt and fired at the pteranodons who were recovering from their shock to realize that fresh and helpless meat lay there for the taking.

Grey scooped up the rifle and thrust it at Looks Away, who had managed to prop himself up on one elbow. His nose was bleeding and he was wheezing like a dying trout.

"Here, damn it!"

Grey fired his six rounds, unable to miss at that range. Beyond the closest pteranodons there were more.

So many more.

At least fifty of the living dead things were crawling through the forest or perched atop the mushroom caps. More circled in the humid air, jealous of their brothers who were close enough to join the impending feast. The stench of their rotting flesh was stifling, overwhelming.

Grey fumbled at his belt for fresh cartridges, knowing that there was no time left. This was it. All of his roads had led here and this was where he was going to die. Consumed and forgotten.

"God damn you all to—!"

That was as far as he got and the world seemed to explode.

The four closest pteranodons flew apart as if they were straw dolls in a tornado wind. Blood and leather flew everywhere, slapping the other creatures in the faces, painting the mushroom caps with red, and filling the air with the smell of strange blood. A boom, like the echo of a great thunderclap rolled outward toward the sunless sea, and once more the frightened bats fled their refuge and fled like a dark cloud toward the fungi-covered columns.

The force of the explosion drove Grey to his knees and knocked the gun from his hand. He clapped his hands to his ears and wheeled around, staring at the figure that stood behind him.

Thomas Looks Away, covered in bat guano and lichen, blood streaming from his nose, teeth bared, eyes wild, stood wide-legged with the Kingdom rifle in his hands. Then he whirled around, raised the weapon again, and fired at the pteranodons atop the mushroom caps that had formed their refuge. The round hit the closest of the beasts, and there was another shocking boom of thunder, and a shockwave picked both men up and flung them against another of the towering mushrooms.

The pterosaur that had been hit and both of the other monsters were shredded as the compressed ghost-gas bullets detonated into a blinding series of miniature explosions. The bursts followed one another almost too fast to hear—first the explosion of the rifle shells and then the howling scream as the ghost rocks embedded in the dead flesh of each animal burst apart. That, and the screams of the undead things, shook the entire cavern. Chunks of sandstone cracked off and plummeted from the ceiling, smashing down on the pteranodons, crippling some, killing many. Grey grabbed Looks Away by the arm and they scrambled under the hood of another giant mushroom. The massive cap quivered and a jagged crack appeared in the stem above their heads. They cried out and rolled over against the base just as the stem cracked like a tree in a hurricane wind and a ton of mottled fungus canted over and crashed down inches from where they lay.

The ground shook again and bloody rain fell all around them.

They dared not move.

The whole world shook and trembled around them. The pterosaurs screamed.

And then there was a new sound, that of many leathery wings flapping as all of the surviving creatures flung themselves into the air in a colliding, wild attempt to flee.

Silence settled very, very slowly.

The two men lay there, half buried under the shattered

mushroom cap, half deafened by the thunder of the Kingdom rifle, half mad with terror.

Then, finally, Grey began to crawl out. After a moment Looks Away followed. They climbed to their feet and stood there, swaying and drunk with fatigue. Around them lay the shredded remains of a half dozen of the pteranodons. A few crippled ones were dragging themselves away from what had been their intended dinner. These monsters had been torn by flying shrapnel from the mushrooms, from rocks, and from flying bits of bone, but they hadn't been caught in the blast radius of the exploded ghost rock and so they had not exploded, too. Even so, they were torn to rags.

Looks Away wiped a nervous hand across his mouth as he watched them shudder along and tried to make a joke. "A clear case of the biter bit, what?"

The quip came out crooked and landed flat.

Grey picked up the Kingdom rifle from where it had fallen when they'd been thrown backward. The little lights were still glowing bright even though it was covered with drops of blood. He held it up and thought about the cannon-sized one at Doctor Saint's lab.

"God Almighty," he whispered.

Chapter 60

They picked up their other weapons: the ordinary Colt and shotgun that now seemed both childish and somehow more wholesome than the gleaming Kingdom M1.

"Do you think that gun destroyed the demons in those flying lizards?"

"Reptiles," corrected Looks Away, "and I don't know. Actually, old chap, we don't even know if they were the same kind of undead as Lucky Bob's crew or simply bodies he raised using alchemy. Add that to our list of mysteries."

"It would be nice," groused Grey, "to get to the point where the answers outnumber the dad-blasted questions."

"I don't know that any results we get on prehistoric monsters are going to be reliable in terms of what the Kingdom rifle might or might not do to undead gunslingers. Or to a Harrowed like Lucky Bob. We have to be careful there, old boy. I think it's fair to say that Jenny would prefer we did not destroy her father's eternal soul."

"Yeah, well, there's that . . ."

They reloaded and did an ammunition check.

"I have fourteen shells left," said Looks Away, closing the shotgun breech with a snap. "You?"

Grey had removed all of the rounds from his belt and put them in his one remaining trouser pocket. They were much easier to grab. "Thirty-one rounds."

In any normal circumstance it was a lot of ammunition. This was a million miles from normal.

Above them the roof of the cavern was free of any undead flying reptiles, while the bats had once more gone back to hide in the mushroom forest. Even the insects, large and small, seemed to shun them. Grey could almost understand it. Even though they had done what was necessary to survive an impossible attack, using that gun made him feel strangely unclean. Like it was emblematic of a line in the sand that they should not have crossed.

Grey said none of this to Looks Away. After all, it was his mentor, Doctor Saint, who had created the gun, and the cannon. It was Looks Away who had used that other strange weapon to stop the reanimated army from slaughtering the town. In both cases those weapons had been the deciding factor in keeping them alive.

So why did it feel wrong? Why did Grey feel dirty?

He shook his head, unable to sort it through.

Looks Away took a sip from his canteen and handed it over. Grey sipped and gave it back.

"You know, I grew up way back east in Philadelphia," said Grey. "I wanted to be a lawyer or someone like that. I was good in school, always read, got top grades."

"So—?"

"So what the fuck am I doing in this hellhole?"

They both laughed. The sound echoed badly and it hushed them again.

With infinite care they left the scene of carnage and searched for a path through the cavern. Even though neither of them possessed certain knowledge that this cavern actually led to the necromancer's residence, each of them felt it in their guts. If Veronica was right and Chesterfield had betrayed Deray, inviting dire retaliation, then the tunnel that brought the attackers—however it was made—had to come from somewhere.

But where? And how far was it? Grey had no way of knowing.

Just as he had no way of knowing what new horrors stood between them and the answers.

Looks Away carried the lantern and walked bent over, frowning at the ground, making soft grunting noises to himself to confirm or reject possible trails. Then he found it. On the far side of a cracked ridge of lichen-covered rock there was a distinctive line of glistening slime. They both agreed it was the same as the trail of whatever had bored through the tunnel into the basement of Chesterfield's mansion. Moving as quickly as caution allowed, they followed the trail down the slope and along the night-dark sea.

The sand crunched softly under their feet, and in places felt dangerously soft, as if some trap or pocket might open up beneath them. Tendrils of colorless seaweed lay rotting on the shores, moved now and again by desultory waves. The bioluminescence in the seawater made the waves glimmer, but not in any way Grey thought was attractive. The water itself seemed to be rank with the odor of decay.

The light from their lantern and the glow from the fungi allowed them to see much more of the underground waters than they wanted to. Dark shapes moved in the waves, crashing through the rollers, pale and unnatural. Misshapen bodies that did not look like fish rolled to show mottled gray-white bellies. Fins as tall as the sails of fishing boats sliced along and once they saw a huge mouth rise up and swallow a foundering creature that was as large as a circus elephant. Then a moment later a tentacle thicker than a maple tree rose dripping from the water, wrapped around the monstrous shark, and dragged it thrashing down into the depths. Blood as black as oil bubbled up.

"This must be what Hell looks like," gasped Grey,

recoiling from the chunks of half-eaten meat that washed up onto the sand.

"I've heard Hell is much pleasanter," quipped Looks Away, though there was no humor in his expression.

Their words sounded too loud, even with the thunder of the surf, and they fell into a desperate hush as they hurried along.

The beach stretched on and on, and the slimy trail ran along it, smearing the sand to a glistening paste. It occurred to Grey that anything massive and powerful enough to have gnawed a tunnel from this cavern all the way into the cellars of Chesterfield's house would be far beyond their skill to defeat. Maybe even beyond the soul-destroying power of the Kingdom rifle. Following the creature was one thing, encountering it would be something to avoid at all costs.

A cry made them stop and look up and there, circling at the very edge of the upsweep of light, was a pterosaur. Another joined it. Then another.

"They're getting over their fear," said Grey, laying his hand on the butt of his pistol.

"I'm bloody well not," Looks Away assured him.

The pteranodons continued to circle but did not, at least for the moment, draw closer. Grey wanted to take that as a hopeful sign, but he found that nothing down here reassured him.

The trail abruptly swerved away from the midnight sea and they followed it through an archway of smoky quartz spears, some of which were as massive as redwoods. The spears were interlaced like the steepled fingers of some sleeping giant and they crept beneath them. Grey nudged Looks Away to direct his attention to the deep cracks and fissures in some of the overhead shafts, and from the look of sick fear on his friend's face, he wished he hadn't. They quickened their pace.

Then they came to a break in the ground. A chasm a

dozen feet across that dropped down into inky blackness far beyond the reach of their lantern. The cleft seemed to run on for miles in either direction, and yet the slimy trail continued on the other side as if the thing they pursued was so massive that it could thrust itself across the divide without tumbling into it.

"That's done it then," said Looks Away. "We should have brought a coil of rope."

"We should have brought an army and some dynamite, too," said Grey. "But we didn't. We either solve it or go back."

The cry of a hungry pteranodon behind them seemed to cancel out the latter suggestion.

The alternative was daunting. There was a broken crystal shaft above them that leaned out over the chasm. The jagged point reached almost to the other side, but fell short by six feet. It was not a tremendous jump in regular circumstances, but to manage it here they would have to climb onto the shaft and run along it to get up enough momentum to carry them over.

When Grey explained this to Looks Away, the Sioux stared at him with frank astonishment. "You have clearly gone 'round the bend, haven't you? You're barking mad."

"It's not the ideal plan . . . ," Grey admitted.

"It's suicide."

"Then we go back and deal with those birds."

"Pteranodons are not birds."

"Who cares? Pick a card here."

The choice, however, was made for them.

A scraping sound made them spin and look back the way they'd come, and there, filling the mouth of the tunnel of quartz spears, was a gigantic cat. It had massive shoulders and huge paws from which claws like baling hooks dug into the ground. Massive oversized fangs dropped like daggers from its upper jaw, and embedded in its chest was a large black stone laced with white. And everywhere were signs of advanced decay. Rotting flesh, open sores, bloated pustules, and masses of wriggling maggots. It reeked of its own decay.

The saber-toothed cat wrinkled its face in a silent snarl of pure animal hate, and yet its eyes held a darker and more complex expression than should be evident in a simple beast. A cruel, calculating intelligence glimmered in those eyes.

They were trapped with a bottomless pit behind them and a monster before them.

Looks Away whipped the Kingdom rifle around, staring with wild eyes that were filled with the dangerous lights of panic. He uttered a cry of sick fear and began raising it to his shoulder, but Grey leaped at him and pushed it down.

"Stop, you damn fool!" he snapped. "You'll bring the whole ceiling down on us."

Above and around them the crystal spears—clear or blue or smoky gray—were shot through with cracks.

The wild look in Looks Away's eyes turned to panic. "We have to do something."

"Yes we damn well do," Grey said, "but I don't want to die trying. Give me your shotgun."

The undead saber-toothed cat took another step forward. Its eyes narrowed as it read the scene. It crept forward, one deliberate step at a time.

"Give me the damn shotgun," said Grey in a fierce whisper.

Looks Away clutched the Kingdom rifle and sought to raise it against the downward force of Grey's restraining hand. "Let me go, damn your eyes, I can kill it—."

"Sure, and kill us both at the same time," said Grey. "Snap out of it, man. We need a bang—just not the voice of goddamn thunder."

With a dubious nod, Looks Away drew the weapon and extended it stock-first to Grey. "I hope you know what you're doing."

"Me, too," said Grey quietly.

The big cat kept coming. It was now only forty feet away, but as it approached one section of the tunnel, it paused. There were two crystal spikes laid like crossed swords above the narrow walkway. Grey and Looks Away had needed to crouch to pass beneath them, but the cat was so massive that it would have to crawl on its belly to pass beneath. The narrow bottleneck was the only reason it hadn't charged them, and Grey knew it even if his companion was too frightened to grasp it.

Even with the shotgun Grey doubted he could drop so monstrous a creature with a couple of shots. And driving it mad with the pain of buckshot did not seem like the smartest of plans in so tight a spot.

"Looks," snapped Grey, "see that arch? You're the rock expert, tell me the best place to hit it."

Looks Away began to argue, but then he abruptly seemed to come back to himself. He studied the fragile crystalline structure and nodded.

The living-dead cat flattened out and began crawling through the arch. Grey could swear there was a dark humor interwoven with the hunger and hatred on its face. It *knew* it was going to win. The very fact of its obvious confidence made Grey tremble.

"Talk to me," he said in a quiet voice that was at odds with every screaming nerve in his body and mind.

"There," said Looks Away, pointing, only to immediately change his mind and point to a different spot. "No— *there*!"

"Make up your damn mind . . ."

"That spot. See that dark smudge inside? It's a fracture point . . ."

The cat was more than halfway through. Already the muscles in its haunches were bunching in anticipation of slaughter.

God, the thing was huge. It was as massive as a full-grown bull and infinitely more dangerous.

"There," insisted Looks Away, stabbing the air with his finger. "Shoot—shoot!"

With a scream louder than thunder, the saber-toothed cat began its killing leap. And Grey took three fast steps forward and fired. One barrel. Then the other.

Boom.

Boom.

The concentrated buckshot hit the flaw in the smoky quartz pillar.

Chunks of crystal exploded outward, scything through the air. The whole structure of the arch groaned and shook. The cat screeched in fury and fear. A shudder rippled along the corridor of spears. The echo of the shots made stalactites shiver on the ceiling and snap off to drop down like falling daggers. They struck the archway, cracking every single spike of crystal so that the whole world seemed to splinter and shatter. The crossed-sword arch trembled.

Trembled.

The cat squirmed forward to free itself before the crushing weight of a hundred tons smashed it to pulp. Deep cracks spider-webbed out from the impact points, and smaller patterns of lace spread from where the pellets on the edges of the spray had struck. The air was filled with a sound like breaking ice.

The huge cat froze, its massive muscles quivering with tension.

Looks Away and Grey stood stock-still. Smoke curled from the barrels of the shotgun. They all looked up at the archway. The cracks ran on and on, deepening, widening, and the predatory gleam in the saber-toothed monster's eyes quickly changed to a fatalistic dread. Even the animal knew what was happening.

Snapping sounds filled the air all around them.

Grey felt a triumphant smile begin to take shape on his mouth.

"Kiss my ass, you overgrown house cat," mocked Looks Away as a massive chunk of the crystal leaned out and fell. It smashed down onto the causeway and shattered into ten thousand glittering pieces.

But that was it.

The rumble stopped.

Just like that.

The cracks seemed to freeze as if they had always been there. The crystal arch did not fall.

The last trembles shivered through the crystal tunnel and then there was a deep silence that was heavy with all of the wrong implications. The saber-toothed cat looked up at the archway, then down at the broken chunks, then up at the two men who still crouched, hiding behind the now empty shotgun. The fatalistic gloom on the cat's face vanished and triumph blossomed on its hideous face as the grins drained from Looks Away and Grey like blood from a corpse.

Looks Away said, "Oh . . ."

And Grey said, ". . . *shit*."

The monster cat bared its teeth and sprang.

Chapter 61

They both wanted to scream.

They did not have the time for it.

Looks Away flung the lantern at the monster as it broke free of the tight crossed-swords arch. It struck hard and burning oil splashed the thing. Instead of stopping the beast, the fire and pain galvanized it. The monstrous cat threw its massive weight against the structure and they could see its muscles rolling and bunching as it simply tore itself from the narrow passageway.

Grey thrust the shotgun back to Looks Away and drew his Colt and snapped off three quick shots. The fire hit the impact points, but that did not seem to matter. The creature was not even slowed. It was what Grey feared. A handgun was not an elephant rifle and this brute had to have bones as thick as marble slabs.

For a fraction of a second he thought about the Kingdom rifle but he was still convinced that it would bring down the whole ceiling. Grey did not want to die down here, buried under ten billion tons of rock.

However there were few choices left and none of them good. All of them were insane. Most were suicidal. Only one offered a chance. A slim, knife edge of a chance. It was something only a complete madman would consider.

So he spun, grabbed Looks Away's shoulder, and shoved him toward one of the broken spears of rock that leaned out over the chasm.

"Go!" he bellowed. "It's our only chance."

Looks Away staggered to the edge, then half turned. "You're insane!"

Before Grey could answer, the cat screamed again. And they saw it break free of the tunnel. The creature's head and shoulders were ablaze, the hairs withering to black wires, the skin retracting to pull its lips back into a permanent scream.

Perhaps the fire would ultimately kill or cripple it, but the beast was determined to take them first. It came forward, slowly at first and then, driven by rage and pain, faster and faster.

"Go—go—go!" shouted Grey as he gave Looks Away another shove.

The Sioux leaped up onto the broken shaft, staggered for a moment with flailing arms, steadied himself and ran.

The cat jumped into the air, slashing toward them with the massive claws on its front paws.

Grey flung himself sideways. As he fell, he saw Looks Away race along the length of the spear and then leap high into the air, his legs continuing to pump as if he was trying to run across the air itself. His arms reached toward the far side of the chasm, fingers clawing. He hit the edge and bounced backward.

And down.

Down, down, down.

Into darkness.

"Nooooo!" cried Grey, but then the cat swiped at him and he had to dive away to save his face from being torn away. He landed hard and rolled badly, then frog-hopped forward to evade a second slash. The whole back of his vest tore away and he felt the tips of two claws trace burning lines across the skin over his kidneys.

He flattened out and rolled sideways like a log until he was under the broken crystal shaft that leaned over the drop-off. The cat reached after him, slashing at the ground, shredding the last of Grey's vest and tearing away most of his shirt. But Grey kept rolling until he was on the other side of the spear. Then he was up onto fingers and toes, running like a dog for ten feet until he could get to his feet again.

He looked wildly around, but there was still no other choice. The only possible way out was the same suicidal route that had claimed Looks Away. Either he got to the other side of the chasm, or he died right there and then.

The cat was still trying to find him under the spear and Grey knew that as soon as it realized that its prey was not there, the cat would simply climb over and that would be it.

Grey steeled himself and scrambled up the side of the spike. The smell of burning cat filled his nostrils. He marveled that it could still come after him even as the burning oil was consuming its flesh.

Then he remembered the chunk of ghost rock imbedded in its skin. Could that be driving it? Was that why there was such a dangerous intelligence in the monster's eyes? Grey was certain of it.

He got to his feet and, as Looks Away had only seconds ago, he had to fight for balance. The top was not a flat walkway but rather a lumpy, cracked and distressingly rounded surface. The cat either heard or sensed that its prey was about to escape. It pulled sharply back from the spear and raised its burning head. For a moment it stared through flames right into Grey's eyes.

That's when he heard the sound. Not the scream of the cat, but a scream nonetheless.

It was the ghost rock.

It was burning.

And the demons within it were screaming.

Screaming.

Screaming.

The sound tore at Grey's mind.

Then he was running along the shaft. His path to safety ended too soon. With a howl of desperation, Grey Torrance flung himself toward the far side of hope. And, like Looks Away had before him, Grey hit the edge of the cliff. And, like Looks Away, he fell.

Down.

Into darkness.

Chapter 62

He slid down the side of the chasm.

Down and down. He scrabbled for purchase and found none. He kicked at the sheer wall and could find not the slightest toehold. Grey went down deeper and deeper, and in his panic he thought he could hear a chorus of ghostly voices crying his name. Even as he fell he knew that this was no fantasy. He knew that the ghosts who followed him saw him about to escape into an ignoble death in a forgotten hole, and they cried out in joy.

Was Annabelle's voice among them? Would she—even she—delight at the thought of his bones lying here at the bottom of the Maze for all eternity? Could his betrayal of her have truly turned her to such cruelty? The mind is quick and ruthless at such times. Grey thought he could see her there, at the top of the chasm, leaning over to stare down at him as he fell.

And he did fall.

Down, down, down.

But . . .

But not . . .

But not faster and faster.

His gunbelt and hands scraped down the side of the cleft as he dropped, but he felt his body slowing.

Slowing.

Then the toes of his boot met a new angle of the wall and he felt his legs moving outward. Then his whole body bent backward until it was his belly and then his chest that was pressed hardest against the wall. He slowed more and more . . . until he stopped.

Just like that.

The world and all of its madness spun down like a windup toy that had clicked on its last cog. Grey lay facedown on a curved slope of rock. Panting, sweating. Bleeding. Nearly weeping.

Alive.

Far, far above him the screams of the living dead saber tooth were changing. He heard the hiss of frustration turn into a long wail of agony. He listened to it. He heard the demon inside the cat's shrieks.

He heard them both die.

Or, maybe it was only the cat that died. Maybe the demon was cast back into Hell.

Grey had no idea which fate was worse. Burning to death or living to burn.

It took a long time to realize what had happened.

The chasm was not a sheer drop after all. Its sides were sloped like the inside of a bowl and the deeper he went the more the bowl curved inward.

His heart lurched as he realized that had he not leaped all the way to the edge of the bowl, then he would have plummeted straight down. Providence turned a failed escape into the only possible pathway to survival.

Grey lay there and pressed his forehead against the ground, closed his eyes, and thanked whatever gods there might be for dealing him a lucky card.

Lucky.

Looks Away.

Oh God.

"Are you dead, white man?" asked a familiar voice.

Chapter 63

Grey rolled over. Slowly, painfully.

He saw Looks Away sitting with his back to a boulder. The bioluminescent fungi burned on the walls all around him and the eerie glow made him appear like a ghost from some ancient tale. Jagged lines of fresh blood were painted blackly against the Sioux's skin.

"Jesus Christ," breathed Grey.

"Not even close."

He extended a hand and pulled Grey up as far as a hunched sitting position. It was the best they could each manage. Grey craned his neck to see if a ghost-pale face still looked down at him, but all there was at the top of the chasm was the dying flicker of fire from the burning monster. He hung his head and put his face in his palms.

"Well," said Looks Away with weary sarcasm, "aren't we a pair?"

"We're alive," said Grey.

"Oh, jolly good, then. All's right with the world and we can skip tra-la."

"Fuck you."

"Well, there's that. And a cogent argument you make."

Grey scrubbed his face with his callused hands, and then got to his feet. His whole body trembled from exertion and injury. The slash on his hip felt like a hot poker driven all the way to the bone. His hands, toes, belly, and chest tingled with friction burns. And he doubted that, even should they escape from this hellhole, he would ever sleep soundly again.

"We have to find a way back up," he said.

"Thank you for that shockingly obvious observation."

Looks Away also got up, looking every bit as bad as Grey felt. They turned and studied their surroundings. The walls of the chasm rose steeply on either side, and even though there was a slope to each, it would be impossible to climb up the way they'd come down. The sides were far too smooth. No handholds, nothing to give them a chance of getting out. The bottom of the chasm was narrow but mostly flat, and it stretched away to either side of them. The left-hand path wended its way through chunks of fallen quartz and stone. The blue fungi allowed them to see everything as clearly as if a full winter moon hung over them.

"Which direction?" asked Looks Away.

"Hell if I know," said Grey. "Pick one."

"Well, I think we more or less came from that way," said Looks Away, nodding to their right. "Maybe if we make our way along the bottom we'll find a way up. Not a good plan, I grant you, but it's—."

"—better than no plan," finished Grey. They took a moment to check their weapons. Grey reloaded his Colt and Looks Away slapped his pockets for more shells. And slapped and slapped.

"Oh, bugger that," he growled as he found a ragged hole in his trousers. "I've lost the bleeding shells."

They did a quick search of the debris at the bottom of the drop and only found one cartridge, but it was crushed and the buckshot spilled out as Looks Away picked it up. There were no other shells in sight. Looks Away considered the shotgun, sighed, and slid it back into its holster. "I feel like tossing this thing as far as I can, but it's been useful and we might get lucky."

Grey wasn't sure what kind of luck his friend was

referring to. The only other shells for the weapon were in Queenie's saddlebags, but he made no comment. It was easier to find ammunition than it was to acquire a new gun.

"What about the doohickey?" he said, nodding to the Kingdom rifle.

After a quick examination, Looks Away nodded. "Seems sound. A trifle dented but the mechanism works and we still have a few rounds left. Let's hope we don't need them, what?"

"Sure," said Grey, "let's hope."

"I have a bit of a concern about using it down here, though."

"Why?"

"Well, the explosive force released when it obliterates the ghost rock it encounters is rather dramatic and we are, after all, in a cavern formed by an earthquake. I don't know how much we can trust to the stability of the ceiling. A blast of unexpected size in the wrong part of this place could bring the roof down and bury all of us under a billion tons of rock."

"Jesus. And *now* you tell me?" demanded Grey.

"Be fair, old boy. It's not like I had any experience with this, and I'm sure Doctor Saint never tested it under these conditions."

"So, we can't use our best weapon, is that it?"

"I didn't say that. It's just that we should exercise prudence."

Grey closed his eyes. "Jesus H. Christ, Esquire."

With their expectations running low and their fears bubbling over, they set off along the path, but after three hundred yards of twists and turns the way became impassible. A massive tumble of granite and marble had toppled from the upper walls of the cleft and filled the entire chasm to a height of eighty or ninety feet.

"Maybe we can climb it," said Grey, stepping back to

look upward. The rocks were haphazardly stacked but there were many obvious hand- and footholds.

However Looks Away shook his head. "Not a chance, old sport. See there? And there? Those rocks are held in place by loose dirt and some quartz splinters. It's all as fragile as a house of cards." To emphasize his point he picked up a fist-sized rock and walked backward, guiding Grey with him by an outstretched arm. "Stand back."

He tossed the rock to a midpoint on the pile. He didn't throw it very hard, but the rock struck one of the crystal splinters and suddenly the whole wall began to vibrate. Chunks of broken stone ground together and a dozen boulders as big as cooking pots bounced down toward them. Both men dove for cover as the whole gully shook and grumbled. Dust belched out from between clefts in the stone. They waited until it subsided before they stood up again.

"Damn," murmured Grey. "You've got a good eye."

"For rocks, at least," said Looks Away with a shrug. He turned away from the blocked trail and looked back the way they had come. "Well . . . there's nothing for it. Come on, dear fellow, quick march."

With that he set off down the left-hand trail. Grey followed. They reached the point where they'd fallen and Grey glanced covertly up, still looking for that pale face. Now, though, even the firelight was gone. He wasn't sure if that was a comfort or not.

The left-hand trail wormed its way through the shattered landscape for miles. Grey figured they walked two or maybe three miles down there in the fractured gully. He was exhausted and the walk seemed to be draining what little reserves he had left. There was almost nothing left in the canteen, and neither man wanted to drink from the infrequent lines of water running down through mossy cracks in the wall. The water smelled of rot and sickness.

Then, with a start, Grey realized that one of the reasons the journey seemed so tiring is that they were no longer walking along a flat bottom. The ground had begun to tilt upward. Looks Away nodded when Grey pointed this out, clearly having reached that conclusion already.

Within minutes the incline became more pronounced and within another quarter mile was rising sharply. It was slow and ponderous work to climb that hill, and they had to press their palms against the nearly smooth sides of the cliff to steady themselves and push their weary bodies upward.

Time seemed to lose all meaning.

The blue fungi grew thicker and its light intensified until it was as bright as a cloudy afternoon. Grey could have read by that glow. It made it easier to pick out their trail and to find what few handholds were available, but Grey was sure he would have preferred less light. The glow revealed one of the terrible secrets of this cavern.

The path was littered with bones. Many of them. Some were clearly ancient and had withered to dry, cracked relics; others were far too fresh for comfort and still glistened with scraps of meat and strings of tendon. Some of the bones were those of animals. Grey saw fish skeletons and the skull of a horse. They walked between the curved ribs of some vast thing that must have been as tall as a house and as long as a locomotive.

"What the hell is this?" he demanded, slapping his hand against one of the huge ribs. "I've seen elephants and this is ten times bigger."

Looks Away shook his head. "I've seen drawings of bones like these," he said, "but I don't recall the name. Look, see there? That line of vertebrae? Lord above, what a neck it had. And there, the skull? How delicate for so ponderous a beast."

Grey saw where he was pointing and shook his head. "No way a brute like that had a head this small."

But the skull lay there as if to mock him, positioned in perfect alignment to the remnants of its spine. Worse still were the marks on both skull and neck bones. Deep grooves that could only have come from some savage claw. Not even the hulking saber tooth could have made cuts that deep.

Clutching their weapons, they hurried on. Then the path whipsawed through a series of switchbacks, and in the third section there were many small boulders that had tumbled down from some quake. They appeared haphazard at first, but as the men approached it became immediately obvious that this was far from the case.

"Look," whispered Grey, "those are stairs."

Stairs they were indeed.

Although rough-hewn and covered with moss, they were far too orderly to have been the work of anything but a deliberate hand. The steps led upward for a hundred feet and then vanished around a sharp turn.

"You're a rock expert," whispered Grey, bending to examine the rocks, "how old are these stairs? Is this some ancient passage, maybe cut by Spanish missionaries or—?"

"No," said Looks Away decisively. He ran his fingers along one edge and the moss peeled off easily. "Not a bit of it. This is mostly marble and it's cut from the living rock. See there? The chisel marks haven't had time to completely oxidize. No, old boy, I'd say these steps are less than ten years old."

"Ten years, eh," mused Grey. "And how long has it been since Aleksander Deray and Nolan Chesterfield set up shop hereabouts?"

Looks Away grunted, and then grinned. "Eleven years," he said. "Give or take."

"Give or take."

They straightened and Grey put a booted foot on the bottom step. "Don't know if you're a gambling man, Looks, but I'll give you twenty-to-one odds that I know who lives at the top of these steps."

"That, my friend, is what I believe they call a sucker's bet."

"It is."

They smiled at each other.

"Shall we pay our respects?" asked the Sioux.

"I believe we should," agreed Grey. "It would be the neighborly thing to do."

Without a further word they began climbing the stairs.

PART THREE

A Man of Wealth and Taste

———◆———

Fear not death for the sooner we die,
the longer we shall be immortal.

—BENJAMIN FRANKLIN

Chapter 64

They went slowly, taking time because neither of them wanted to arrive at Deray's door out of breath and unable to fight.

But the steps did not lead directly to a door.

It led instead to a gate.

They emerged from the stairway on a flat plane that Grey presumed was on the same level as the underground sea. The roof here was not as high, however, suggesting that they had reached one end of the massive cavern. The stalactites reached down like fangs above their heads, and stalagmites rose around them to complete the disturbing illusion. There was a rough natural wall of some dark stone that ran all the way across this end of the cavern, broken only in one spot. This gap, clearly the result of the same earthquake that had destroyed most of California, was bridged by a stout wall of blocks fitted neatly together and fixed with lines of cement. In the middle of the blocks a gate made from tall crystal spikes stood on end and was bound, turn and turn around, by massive iron bands set with huge rivets.

A set of new-looking steel railroad tracks ran past the gates and then curved away to run along the distant underground sea, heading opposite to where Chesterfield's house lay. Halfway to the black waters sat a still and silent locomotive to which was coupled ten hopper cars laden with some cargo they could not identify and then twenty empty flatbed cars. No steam rose from the train's smokestack.

Grey ducked down behind a boulder and pulled Looks Away into the shadows beside him.

The crystal gates stood open.

But the gateway itself was not empty.

A line of men were walking in orderly lines from beyond the gate. Dozens and dozens of them.

No. Hundreds.

"Who are they?" whispered Looks Away.

Grey shook his head because the men were too far away to see clearly. He gestured to a spill of rocks to their right, and they moved off, keeping low and being careful to make no sound. The rocks were the debris from a fallen natural pillar, and they offered excellent cover as the two men drew close. Then Grey pulled his companion down again as the first rank of marching men went past them at no more than a stone's easy throw away.

The men wore uniforms. They were soldiers. That much had been clear from a distance. But up close it was evident that they were not Americans.

The men in the front ranks wore dark blue jackets set with red trim and brass buttons. Dark trousers were tucked into gleaming black boots, and on their heads they wore tapered leather helmets topped with spikes.

Looks Away grunted in surprise, then very quietly observed, "*Dunkelblau waffenrock*."

"What?"

"Those are the uniforms of Prussian infantry."

"But . . . ," Grey let the rest hang as more of the soldiers passed by. He estimated that there were at least a hundred of the Prussians. Behind them came other soldiers, and as they passed, Looks Away identified them.

"Polish . . . French . . . Italian . . . Swedish . . ."

The men marched in precise lines, with resplendent officers riding horses and sergeants barking out commands. On the chest of each officer were medals and ribbons from the many wars of their several nations. Grey had seen pictures of some, but most were unknown to him.

When the foreign soldiers had all marched out, a different group followed them. They were hard-faced men dressed in a uniform unlike any Grey had ever seen. Black trousers and jackets, with blood-red sashes embroidered with some kind of strange magical symbols— swirling stars and planets, mathematical notations, and the stylized gears like those inside a clock. Deray's bodyguard, perhaps, mused Grey. Or . . . his private army?

Most had Winchester '73s laid against their shoulders. The sergeants, however, carried guns of a kind Grey had only recently come to know. Weapons he did not expect to encounter down here. These were exotic-looking long guns with wide-barrels made from brass and mirrored steel, with gemstones set into frameworks from which coils of copper seemed to loop and feed back into themselves. Strange guns.

And strangely familiar.

Grey turned to face Looks Away, to accuse him, to demand answers, but from the look of shocked horror on Looks Away's face it was evident that his friend was as startled as he was.

"Those are . . . ," began Looks Away, then tripped over the words. "Those are . . . Kingdom rifles."

Grey nodded, feeling a hollow space open up in his chest. He grabbed a fistful of Looks Away's shirt and pulled him close. In a fierce, tight whisper he hissed, "How?"

But all Looks Away could do was shake his head.

They crouched there and watched as the soldiers marched past. The strange blue light of the fungi gleamed on the polished brass and rare jewels of those deadly guns.

Then Grey noticed something and he looked closer still. The guns were very similar to the Kingdom Rifles, but they were not exactly the same. He glanced back and forth from them to the weapon slung over his companion's shoulder. The same materials and a decidedly familiar design. And yet . . . the gun designed by Doctor Saint had a cylinder for the compressed ghost rock gas and a magazine for the oversized bullets, but the guns carried by the sergeants did not. Instead they had ratcheted dials on the sides of slightly longer magazines. And the glowing jewels set into the frames were of different sizes and cuts.

Grey bent close and said all this to Looks Away, and somehow that helped the Sioux shake off his shock. He narrowed his eyes and bent closer to study the weapons as Grey had.

"Are they Doctor Saint's stolen weapons?"

"No. There are too many of them. And I've never seen this design. There's no gas capsule. Besides, it would make no sense for Deray to arm his people with weapons that could destroy the souls of his own undead servants. Mind you, he may have used ghost rock's energetic properties for some other purpose, perhaps to increase rate of fire or perhaps to achieve greater range but—"

He didn't finish because a sound made them both start and then turn.

It was the cry of a man in terror.

Not one man.

Many. A dozen at least.

They came running and staggering through the gates, their hands bound before them, their shirts torn away to reveal bodies crisscrossed by the red marks of the whip. The men stumbled into each other, they fell and staggered, and crawled away from the gate, fleeing in mad, blind terror.

As they ran onto the broad plain, the ranks of soldiers—Confederate and foreign—split apart and at the bellowed orders of sergeants, they trotted left and right to form a large ring around the prisoners. In perfect unison the soldiers drew bayonets and fitted them to the ends of their rifles and within minutes had formed a ring of needlepoint blades and the black mouths of gun barrels. The prisoners wailed and collapsed into a huddle, most of them begging and weeping. One man buried his face in the dirt and cried out for his mother to come and rescue him.

The soldiers stood their line, faces hard, mouths hard, eyes harder yet. Even from a distance Grey could tell that there was no trace of mercy on the face of any man holding a gun.

Not a trace.

Then there was a great rumbling and for a moment Grey thought that he was hearing the sound of a locomotive. But it was something far stranger. From the shadows beyond the gate came a machine that Grey had once seen demonstrated on a military base in upstate New York. It was a carriage made entirely of metal but it was not pulled by horses, nor did it have wheels. Instead it rumbled forward on bands of linked metal plates that squeaked and clanked. Steam rose from twin pipes mounted aft of a kind of crow's nest, and from the center of this structure sprouted a long cannon barrel.

It was what his old commanders had called a "tank," and it thundered across the plain. Grey saw that the flag of Prussia was painted on the side of the cannon turret.

A second machine followed that one out through the gates, this one marked with the flag of Denmark. A third came. A fourth. For each ground of foreign military there was one of these monstrous tanks. The stink of their engines filled the air and beneath the weight of their clanking treads and grinding gears Grey could hear the tormented shriek of ghost rock.

"Are you seeing this?" whispered Looks Away.

"Yes," answered Grey.

"Deray is arming them for war. Good lord, Grey, Deray isn't merely experimenting with these forces, he's selling his goods to the madmen of this world. He's an arms dealer on a level I've never seen before."

When the last of the tanks was in position, a sergeant in the livery of Deray's private army raised his saber, let it stand glittering above him, and then swept it down. The engine roars and their accompanying screams died away.

Then the sergeant nodded to his colleagues among the various armies, and the foot soldiers stepped forward and raised their rifles to their shoulders, all barrels facing the prisoners.

Looks Away muttered, "Damn poor positioning for a firing squad. They'll bloody well shoot each other."

But Grey shook his head. "No . . . I think they're going to—."

His theory died on his tongue as another sound made them turn once more toward the gate.

A man walked slowly out of the shadows, and his feet made no sound. However behind him, still cloaked in darkness, something else moved. There was the hiss of a steam engine and the clank of metal, but whatever it was did not yet follow the man out onto the plain.

The man was very tall and very thin. He wore a suit of the finest cut and quality. Black pants and a jacket of such a dark purple that the color could only be seen in the bulges of creases as he walked. His waistcoat was gray with moon-colored silver traceries embroidered onto it. The stitchery flowed in the same pattern of planets, mathematical symbols, and gears as on the sashes of his troops. In another place, on another man, Grey would have thought it too posh and even silly. Not, however, on this man.

No, there was nothing silly about this one.

He wore a low top hat with a silk band that matched his waistcoat. His shoes were polished to a gleaming finish.

The man walked with a decided limp, though somehow this infirmity did not suggest weakness. Rather it seemed to mark him as one who had been through Hell and walked out, likely alone. He leaned on a slender walking stick whose copper head was fashioned into the snarling face of a kraken—a creature Grey had seen in his books. The tentacles of the beast curled downward and wrapped around the shaft of the stick.

Grey did not need Looks Away to tell him who this was. Who it had to be.

His mouth formed the name but he did not dare speak it aloud.

Aleksander Deray.

A hush fell over the entire plain and the mechanical sound from within the gates likewise ceased. Even the weeping prisoners held their pleas.

Except for the man who still cried for his mother.

The weeping man was fat and lacked muscle; his blubbery skin was covered with coarse hair but his flesh was pale and unhealthy. He clawed at the ground and banged his forehead on it until his skin broke and blood fell like tears.

Looks Away suddenly gasped.

"What is it?" demanded Grey.

"By the Queen's garters—that's Nolan Chesterfield."

Deray approached the circle of soldiers and they parted without hesitation to let him through.

As Deray entered the circle the soldiers closed ranks once more.

The prisoners recoiled from Deray and tried to back away, to flee, but no matter where they turned they encountered a wall of bayonets in the hands of merciless soldiers. In helpless defeat they stopped and stood their ground, chests heaving, faces streaked with tears, eyes empty of all hope.

Deray walked in a slow circle around the men, and they cowered back from him, clustering into a tight knot, their eyes following every movement, every step. The man's path took him to within a dozen feet of where Grey and Looks Away crouched, and it gave Grey his first chance to study their enemy.

And *enemy* seemed to be a perfect word for him.

Aleksander Deray had a thin, aquiline face, with the full lips of a sensualist but the narrow nose and hooded eyes of an ascetic. He could have been a monk from some remote monastery, or a composer of dark and dangerous music. His hands were large, the fingers long and white. Grey noted that he wore a star sapphire ring on the index finger of his right hand and an emerald on the other. Both stones were as large as robins' eggs.

The expression of his face was not haughty or arrogant, which Grey expected to see on so powerful a man. Instead he appeared to be calm, introspective. His eyes roved over the prisoners without apparent animosity, his lips did not curl into a sneer. They were before him and he observed them, nothing more.

Somehow that chilled Grey all the more. For someone to command such power and to have both science and sorcery at his fingertips it would have been more comforting to see the gleam of madness. Instead Grey saw intelligence and insight. This was not a man who could be provoked into some foolish action. Here was a man who calculated the odds and took chances only when the cards were falling his way. Grey had played poker and faro with such men, and he invariably lost.

"Where is he from?" asked Grey, who doubted the man was American.

However Looks Away shook his head. "He claims to be a descendant of Egyptian pharaohs, which I very much doubt. Doctor Saint thought he might be a bastard son of Italian nobility, or maybe a legitimate nobleman who fell out of favor and changed his name. There are a hundred stories about him, and all of them contradict."

"Not an American putting on an act?"

"Not a chance."

Deray walked past where they hid and stopped in front of Nolan Chesterfield.

"Look at me," he said in a cultured voice and Grey could hear the cultured European accent. It didn't sound Italian, though. More like someone from Eastern Europe. Grey had met a Balkan once. Similar accent, similar cold and imperious bearing.

The quivering man did not respond to Deray's command.

"Nolan!" said Deray sharply. "Do as I say. Look at me."

Chesterfield flinched back from the sound of his name. Sobs racked his body, shuddering through his pale skin. He did not raise his head.

With a sigh of disappointment, Deray turned away and looked around him. The officers attached to each foreign army bowed to him from the saddles of their horses. Mounted, they towered above him but everyone there knew that it was he who was the giant here. Everyone was tense, waiting, watching, listening.

"My friends," said Deray, pitching his voice to address the crowd but not shouting. The spectators who could not hear leaned forward. The effort was theirs to do, not Deray's. Another sign of the man's subtle power. "The land that was once America was not born on a quiet bed. It was born in fire and blood. As all great nations are."

The officers nodded. The soldiers remained stock-still.

"When war split this nation, first in half and then into many parts, the weak were consumed while the strong were forged in those fires. Those who rule earn that right. It was true of Alexander and Genghis Khan. It was true of Alaric the Visigoth and Attila the Hun. Greatness is earned through conquest. Hannibal knew this as did Scipio Africanus. Read the histories of Cyrus the Great and Sun Tzu, of Julius Caesar and Thutmose III."

The officers kept nodding. These were clearly the saints of their church. The warlords and conquerors.

"And for our generation? How many of us here will write our histories in the blood of those we conquer? Who among us has that greatness burning in their hearts? Who here will ascend to their throne on a stairway of corpses? Tell me, my brothers, who?"

A dozen swords instantly flashed from scabbards as every officer cried out his own name, bellowing loud enough to imprint their arrogance like a tattoo on the flesh of destiny. Every soldier echoed the name of his general. They crashed their rifle butts onto the hard ground and they all spoke with the thunderous voice of conquest.

Deray let it go on and on until fragments of crystal and rock fell like rain from the ceiling. Then he raised his hand. A simple gesture, palm out, at shoulder height. Silence crashed down around them.

Grey heard Looks Away very softly say, "By the Queen's perfumed knickers."

The silence held for ten long seconds before Deray broke it.

"Ghost rock," he said, putting the words onto the humid air. They seemed to hang there, burning. "Earth herself tore open her flesh and vomited it into our world. A stone, ugly and useless to the unenlightened. But to those with vision, to those who *dare*—?" He paused so that his next word would eclipse what he had already said. A simple word, filled with so much meaning. "Power."

On the ground, Nolan Chesterfield whimpered.

"Since it was discovered, the wisest, the most devious of our engineers and scientists have labored to unlock its secrets, and much have they discovered. Much have we been able to accomplish. Weapons capable of mass destruction. Machines that will work day and night, and at speeds never before imagined. Warships that can sink any wooden fleet without risking the lives of their own crews. Mechanical wagons with cannons that can chase down mounted cavalry and grind them into the dirt." He paused and repeated the word. "Power."

He began walking again, circling the prisoners without looking at them.

"My brothers," he continued, "you have come thousands of miles and traveled deep beneath the earth to join me on this propitious day. You have already seen many of the weapons that I am willing to share with you. The new generation of small arms that will let a few conquer many. As you travel home with your purchases, I will watch the news with interest as the houses of the weak fall to the guns of the mighty."

Once more the generals and their soldiers bellowed, and once more the cavern shook.

And once more Deray held up his hand for the silence that fell immediately.

"Now I want to show you more. So. Much. More." He spaced the words out. "Now I will show you the new age of warfare." He held a hand theatrically to his ear. "Listen. Can you hear the future coming? Can you hear the gears of this world grind into a different gear? Can you hear it?"

They could all hear it.

Everyone there could hear it.

From beyond the gates came the machine sound Grey had heard earlier, and in the shadow he could see something move.

Some.

Thing.

It walked like a man.

Tall, on long legs, with its head held high.

But it was not a man.

No.

With clanking footsteps that struck the stone like artillery shells, it strode out from between the gates. The generals' mouths dropped open as something came out through those crystal gates. This was not a soldier, nor was it one of the ghost rock-suborned dinosaurs or pterosaurs, nor even one of the undead or a Harrowed. This was something much bigger, vastly more frightening. Thirty feet high. Gleaming. Steel and copper, bronze and platinum. Jewels the size of Grey's fists were set into its metal skin. Thick bundles of armored wire ran along its flanks and up into sockets on its neck. A massive chunk of ghost rock was half buried in its chest, and the stone seemed to throb, the white lines writhed and twisted. And the eyes . . .

Those terrible eyes.

They glowed with fire. Actual fire. Its head was a furnace for burning ghost rock, and when it threw wide its jaws, the screams of the tormented damned shook the pillars of Hell.

The generals—even those men who had witnessed the horrors of Deray's caverns—recoiled in abject horror as the metal giant raised his fists and clenched them together. The squeal of steel cut through the air.

The giant walked boldly forward and the soldiers broke ranks and fled. The bravest formed defensive groups around their officers. The brute clanked all the way across the field, and the prisoners fled in all directions and would have escaped had a few of Deray's own men not beat them back.

Aleksander Deray raised one thin hand, and the giant stopped.

Just like that. He stood behind Deray and slowly, slowly closed his mouth so that the screams of the damned inside the burning ghost rock were muted. Not gone, but quieter, as if even those in Hell hung on whatever the necromancer would do or say next.

Deray smiled. His lips peeled back from white teeth that looked too straight and too sharp to Grey.

"This," he said softly, "is power."

Chapter 65

Grey leaned close and whispered in Looks Away's ear. "We have to get out of here right goddamn now."

"And do *what*?"

"Warn people," said Grey.

"Who?" retorted the Sioux. "The law in Lost Angels? They're every bit as corrupt as these bastards."

"No," said Grey, "I was thinking of warning people that could do something about this. The U.S. Army, for one. And maybe your people, too. You think Deray would hesitate for one second to march across the borders of the Sioux Nation?"

Looks Away chewed his lip and did not immediately answer.

On the plain, a general in the uniform of the Dutch army cleared his throat and nudged his horse a few steps forward. His men clustered around him, guns pointing at the metal man.

"My lord," said the general, addressing Deray, "I have heard rumors of some fantastical constructs but never believed that they were real. Even with all of the wonders we have seen since the discovery of ghost rock. But . . . tell me, you have sold us many millions in weapons and equipment and now you show us this. What are we to think? Have you saved the best for last, or have you kept the best for yourself?"

Deray smiled. "A bit of both," he said as he walked

over and patted the steel giant on the shin, "and neither. Samson here is not for sale. Not yet, at least. He is a prototype. A one of a kind, the poor fellow. Quite alone in the world."

"Then this is—what? An entertainment?"

"No, my friend," said Deray. "Samson is a glimpse into the future. It will take years for me to build a legion of brothers for him. Years. During that time you and your fellow generals will conquer your lands. That will take time, even with my rifles and tanks." He gave an elaborate shrug. "Let it take time. Revel in it. Bathe yourself in the blood of those too weak to defy you. Cleanse your lands of all who do not bend their knee to your will. If that takes years, then so be it. How much grander will be the stories that history will tell?"

The generals exchanged looks with each other. There were doubts there, and suspicion, Grey could see that, but after a few moments they all nodded. After all, they had their guns and their tanks.

"And when the wars are over?" asked an Italian general.

Deray smiled at him. It was not a nice smile. "Then, my brothers, you will need to defend what you have taken. And that is where Samson comes in. He and his brothers. They will be the police who will guard your borders and crush any who raise voices against you. By the time you have conquered your lands, the Iron Legion will be there to maintain control."

The generals looked at the giant. Doubt was still written on their faces.

The Russian general said, "Show us. He is impressive, yes, but he is large. He is an easy target."

"Is he?" asked Deray casually. "Is he indeed?"

He turned to his sergeant and snapped his fingers. The man hurried over and snapped off as crisp and professional a salute as Grey had ever seen. "Sir!"

"Arm the prisoners. Give them each a rifle. Make sure the guns are loaded."

The sergeant saluted again and called for their corporals, who were apparently prepared for this. The foreign soldiers buzzed and shifted, their guns tracking the prisoners, while the prisoners looked confused and frightened.

Deray addressed them. "Listen to me," he said in a loud, clear voice, "you are all in the employ of Nolan Chesterfield. Or you were. Some of you took my coin and yet answered to him, and for that I should feed you to the creatures in this cavern."

The men trembled as the corporals handed them their rifles. Most of the men held the weapons away from themselves as if trying to gain distance from whatever was about to happen. One man refused to take a rifle and the sergeant drew a wooden truncheon and began beating the man, shouting at him to take the gun. Bleeding and on his knees, the wretch took it and clutched it to his chest, weeping over it.

"You each deserve to die, you know that," continued Deray as if the beating had not happened. "And yet I will give you a single chance to live."

The prisoners looked sharply at him now.

"Take those weapons. They are real and they are loaded. No tricks. Take them and use those guns to kill me. Do that and I promise you—I give you my word of honor—that you will be set free with no further harm and enough gold so that you can live like kings."

The men stared at him, and then down at the guns in their hands.

"It's not a trick, I assure you," said Deray as he raised his arms to the side so that he stood cruciform before them. "Kill me and earn your freedom. Kill me and live out your lives in luxury and excess with all the whores and whiskey that money will buy. Kill me and you are free. Do it. Do it now."

Most of the men were too frightened to move. The gathered soldiers and their officers were clearly alarmed by this.

"Don't be a fool, man," cried one of the generals.

But in that moment a single prisoner raised his rifle and fired. He was forty feet from Aleksander Deray, and he snapped off four lightning quick shots.

There was a blur and a fragment of a scream and then the air was filled with a red mist and pieces of torn flesh flew everywhere. The man with the rifle was gone. And in the spot where he stood was the clenched fist of Samson.

It had been that fast.

Too fast.

Inhuman, supernaturally fast. Nothing on earth could move that fast. It had to be a trick.

Had to be.

The other prisoners stared in abject, uncomprehending horror. Their faces and bodies were painted with blood and dripping bits of meat.

The generals stared slack-jawed, as horrified in their way as the prisoners were. The soldiers cried out and fell back.

Then Samson was among the prisoners.

He moved like greased lightning, swinging his fists, stamping with gigantic feet. The men fired at him and the bullets whanged off and whined high into the distance. One ricochet hit a Prussian soldier in the thigh and his comrades gunned the prisoner down.

That was the only man the giant did not kill.

One intrepid man dove away and tried to fire from the hip as he came out of a roll. The bullet missed Deray and punched a hole in the air above the place where Grey and Looks Away hid. A heartbeat later the man was gone, replaced by a crimson smear on the ground.

And then it was over.

All of the prisoners were dead.

Only one was whole—the one who had been shot. The others were pulped into red ruin.

Leaving a stunned audience.

And Nolan Chesterfield.

The man knelt there, drenched in the blood of the men he had hired, his eyes wild, screams piercing. He beat insanely at his own face, his mind broken.

The giant turned slightly toward Deray, but the necromancer shook his head. Instead he used two fingers to pluck a silver whistle from his waistcoat pocket. He put it between his lips and blew. The sound was all too familiar, and a moment later it was answered by a screech from above. Then all of the soldiers fell back in fear as a pteranodon swooped down out of the darkness and plucked Chesterfield away.

Not all of him.

Just his head.

The fat body knelt for a moment longer, blood geysering from the ragged stump of his neck. Then it fell slowly over, twitched once, and lay still.

Silence, profound and massive, dropped over the plain.

Then someone began clapping. It was the Prussian. He stood up in the stirrups and began pounding his hands together.

After a moment the other generals joined in.

The soldiers hooted and shouted.

Deray, his arms still held out to his sides, turned in a slow circle as everyone applauded. The cheers rose above the plain and threatened to tear down the heavens.

Chapter 66

The demonstration of Deray's power seemed to be at an end. Grey and Looks Away ducked even lower as the generals dismounted and went over to shake hands with Deray. Servants in white brought trays of glasses and there were many toasts to conquest and success.

"That's our cue to get the hell out of here," said Grey. "Let them get drunk."

Looks Away nodded and began leading the way along the ragged line of boulders. When they were a hundred yards from the scene of slaughter, they paused. The last rock in the line was big enough to hide them both, and they could see a clear path that led down to the shoreline. If they could reach it, then they could try and make their way back to Chesterfield's basement.

The only problem was that between their rock and the safety of the distant shoreline was an open space of nearly five hundred yards. Crossing that without being seen was virtually impossible. The soldiers were at ease and still milling around. Some admiring their new tanks, others staring in wondrous appreciation at the gleaming hulk of Samson. Grey noted that no one looked at the smears of red. Was it cold dismissal? Indifference? Or were they afraid to see what these new machines could do to bodies as frail as their own?

Grey had to believe it was the latter more than anything.

He was a soldier, too. Maybe he no longer wore the uniform, but his life had been defined by warfare. He'd grown up during the age when machines were replacing men. There were factories in Chicago, Detroit, and Philadelphia where machines clanked along day and night while the former factory workers starved. Metal warships were fast replacing wood and sailcloth. And now this. Horseless carriages that could bring cannons right up to the enemy's gates, and metal monsters who could slaughter ordinary flesh-and-blood soldiers with impunity. It was ghastly.

Some of this was the result of ghost rock and the scientific leaps that had occurred since its discovery. Some—perhaps much—was simply that the world had changed. It was no longer the one he'd been born into thirty-three years ago.

"We have to warn people," he said again.

Looks Away nodded. "If it's not too late."

The gap between shelter and escape seemed to stretch for a million miles.

"I, um . . . ," began Looks Away nervously, "could cause a distraction. You could slip away . . ."

"Nice gesture, but no. We *both* get out."

"How?"

"I—," Grey was about to answer when he saw a familiar figure walk out from between the gates. Tall, dressed in black, wearing a gun slung low on his hip. He walked with a pantherish grace and came to stand with Deray and the generals. Looks Away saw him at the same moment and seized Grey's wrist in a crushing grab.

"Look!" he cried. "That's—."

"Lucky Bob Pearl," finished Grey. The Harrowed accepted a glass of wine and sipped it, his dark eyes roving over the faces of the generals. Then they all laughed at something Deray said. Lucky Bob's laugh looked and sounded genuine, but Grey wasn't fooled. Those eyes were the eyes of the dead.

They were demon eyes, and he could only imagine what things a manitou would find amusing. Certainly not a conversational witticism.

Deray separated himself from his guests and stood apart with Lucky Bob, their heads bent together in private conversation. Grey and Looks Away were too far away to hear a word of it.

"Well, they certainly seem chummy," observed Looks Away.

"Whatever they're talking about, I don't much like it."

They crouched there, tense and uncertain, for nearly half an hour. Then fortune dealt another card.

It was one of the soldiers who spotted her. An Italian, who was standing atop the tank his general had bought. He happened to peer off toward the path that led down to the chasm. He frowned, cupped his hands around his eyes, and stiffened. He pointed and rattled off something in Italian. Other men turned. And eventually, so did Aleksander Deray and Lucky Bob Pearl.

They all turned as a slim figure in sheer gossamer walked with languorous slowness toward them. Her body was ripe, her hair a mass of black curls, her eyes as dark as a midnight sky.

Although they did not look it from that distance, Grey knew those eyes were green.

The woman called out a name. "*Deray!*"

The necromancer stiffened, and beside him Lucky Bob went for his gun, but Deray stayed him with a gesture. He shook his head and a dark smile blossomed on his face.

Grey heard Looks Away utter a low moan of sick despair.

His friend spoke her name.

"*Veronica.*"

The dead woman walked toward the gathered men who stood waiting for her as if this were all part of some prearranged drama. It was not, of course, and Grey found himself frightened by what Deray might do to the woman who wore the skin of the woman his friend had loved.

"What's she *doing*?" demanded Looks Away in a strangled whisper.

Veronica did not walk directly to where Deray stood, but instead angled over to stand in front of the silent giant, Samson. All eyes were on her.

"I think . . . I think she's giving us a chance," said Grey.

To do what—?"

"To live," said Grey, then he amended it. "To get out of here alive."

"But why? That's not even Veronica. It's a mockery of her. A ghost or whatever damned thing she's become. She's in league with those sods. She's come to tell them we're here and—"

"No," said Grey, touching his companion's arm. "I don't think so. Whatever else she is, that woman is no friend to Deray, which means Veronica's on *our* side."

"Impossible. Veronica is dead. Lost."

Grey glanced at him. The tone of Looks Away's words was harsh and bitter, but the look on his face told a different story. There was a complexity of emotions warring on the Sioux's features. Anger and grief, pain . . . and something else.

Love?

Grey did not know what his friend truly felt for the dead woman, but he suspected that Looks Away had been greatly underplaying his affection for Veronica. That made this all so much more terrible.

Everyone on the plain had turned to stare. Veronica had become the center of all attention. Of course she was. Tall and beautiful, with a voluptuous body clearly

visible through the sheer fabric and each curve accentu-
ated by the blue-white light that burned within. Grey
imagined that many of the soldiers would be afraid of
her, repelled by her, but nevertheless enthralled. He
hadn't known the woman in life, but in death she was
magnificent.

Aleksander Deray, flanked by Lucky Bob Pearl and
the cluster of generals, approached her but they did so
without haste and perhaps with a bit of understandable
caution.

For the generals, Grey assumed it was fear and caution. For Deray? Probably curiosity and maybe some appreciation for whatever was about to happen. He had
that kind of look on his ascetic face.

Lucky Bob was smiling a cold, cold smile as he followed his master.

So many smiles. As if this was something wonderful,
as if it was something unlooked-for but delightful. Like
an improbable meeting of old friends on some unlikely
street.

He took his companion's arm and began pulling him
toward the open space they needed to cross.

"We have to go."

"I can't leave her there," said Looks Away, tugging his
arm free.

"We have to."

On the field Veronica and Deray now stood a dozen
paces away. Grey could hear a faint murmur of their
conversation, but he couldn't make out a single word.

"Looks—come *on*," snapped Grey.

"No! They'll kill her."

Grey grabbed his shoulder and turned him around
roughly, then he bent close. "They already *have*. Don't
you get that? They murdered Veronica and now whatever of her is left of her is trying to save us."

Looks Away stared at him. Conflicted and appalled.

"It's not her," said Grey in a kinder tone than he'd used a moment before. "Listen to me, brother, she's gone. Veronica's gone. Now her ghost is giving us a chance . . ."

Looks Away still didn't move. Grey tightened his grip on the other man's shoulder. "Do you want Veronica's death to mean nothing? Do you want Deray to get away with this?"

"No . . ." was Looks Away's almost soundless reply.

"Then we need to get more men and more weapons. We can't win this fight. We can't even *fight* this fight. Not now. Smart soldiers know when to retreat from the battle so they can re-engage when they have better odds."

"I'm no damn soldier," said the Sioux, slapping Grey's hand away.

"Yeah . . . you are. We both are. We're at war with Aleksander Deray," said Grey. "We have to make a choice. Fight now and almost certainly lose. Or fight later when we have a plan and a chance, and maybe actually kill that evil son of a bitch."

Looks Away unslung the Kingdom rifle. "I could kill him now."

"From this distance? Not a chance."

"If we got closer—."

"They see us coming and wipe us out. Don't be crazy."

The Sioux chewed his lip. "What about a chain reaction? If I shot the nearest undead, the ghost rock bullet would explode the rock in him, and perhaps that would cause a chain reaction."

"Would that even work?"

"I don't know, but it's worth a try."

Grey thought about it, then he shook his head. "No. It's too risky."

"God rot you, we have to do *something*. Don't be a coward."

Grey turned to him. "Easy now, my friend," he said coldly. "I know you're upset seeing Veronica and all, but try to use your brain for a minute. If you set off a chain reaction, you might kill half his army—and that's great—but Deray's so far away, and the men closest to him look like ordinary soldiers. They don't have ghost rock implants and they won't explode. If anything, their bodies would shield him and the bastard would slip away. That would leave us with no ammunition left and the *rest* of the army, and all of Deray's allies, coming down on us like the wrath of God. And that's even *if* the explosion doesn't bring down the fucking ceiling. No . . . much as I wish we could, I don't think we can guarantee that Deray would die. Anything less than that would be us throwing our lives away and failing everyone in Paradise Falls. Think it through, man, and you'll see that I'm right."

Down on the plain Veronica said something that made Deray clap his hands and laugh out loud. It was not a pleasant laugh.

The Sioux shook his head and fingered the outside of the copper trigger guard. Then he turned his face to a mask of stone, reslung the rifle, and nodded.

"I *will* kill him," he said. "You hear me, white man? His life is *mine*. And I'll kill anyone who gets in my way."

Grey nodded. "Fair enough. Now let's go."

Like silent ghosts they crept from behind their shelter and began moving across the plain toward the sea. They stayed low and moved with many small light, quick steps instead of at a full run. That kept their bodies and equipment from jiggling and making unwanted noise.

Deray's laughter seemed to pursue them.

It drove knives into them.

And it threw fuel on the furnaces of hate that burned in their hearts.

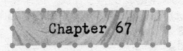

Chapter 67

Their path to freedom took them past the railroad tracks and the massive train. They went to the far side of it and ran along the row of empty flatbeds, and then reached the first of the hoppers.

What they saw in the shadows of the hoppers stopped them dead in their tracks.

They hadn't seen this side of the train from their earlier hiding place, but now they could see everything. Too much.

Laid along the ground, one between each of the endless rows of wooden ties, were corpses. They were soldiers.

Some were dressed in the smoke grey or butternut brown of the Confederacy. Others were dressed in Yankee blue. Hundreds of them. All dead.

The stench from their rotting flesh was appalling.

The bodies were clearly battlefield dead. Every man carried evidence of the wounds that had killed them. Black bullet holes. Ghastly shrapnel wounds. Knife slashes. They lay there, face up, their uniform blouses torn open to expose their bloodless chests.

"What *is* this?" said Looks Away, recoiling from the stench and the gruesome violence.

Grey could not answer the question. Instead he stood there, not looking at the bodies on the ground but instead staring in abject horror at the mound of cargo on the nearest hopper.

He had originally thought it might be coal or raw ore heading for the ghost rock smelting fires.

He wished that was true.

What he saw was far, far worse.

The hopper was piled high with more bodies.

Hundreds of them.

Thousands.

Every hopper was full. Mountains of the dead were crammed into the cars. The corpses had been dumped in with no thought to the people they'd once been. They were—what?

Surely Deray had not brought them to bury them.

Then what?

Even as he asked himself the question, he realized that he already knew the answer.

And it was a terrible answer.

"Grey—?" asked Looks Away softly.

Grey didn't answer. Couldn't.

"Grey, do you understand what this is?"

He nodded.

He had thought he'd seen the depth of horror, that he knew its outer boundaries. That he was aware of its rules.

All of that was wrong.

Deray had no rules, no limits.

Grey dragged his wrist across his mouth.

"How many?" he murmured.

Looks Away glanced up at the hopper, then at the others, then down at the corpses laid in a long row here. "Two thousand? Three? Maybe more."

Grey shook his head. "I think it's a lot more."

A gleaming black beetle crawled across the face of the nearest corpse. The soldier was from the South. A boy, no more than sixteen. He had a bullet hole in his abdomen and the crust of dried blood. A gut shot and proof that he hadn't died right away. Dead men don't bleed.

Bullet wounds to the stomach kill slowly and the pain is enormous. This boy had fought for his flag and probably died screaming and alone. Probably called for his mother rather than God in those last hours. Men do that. They know their mothers will mourn them; God seems to enjoy the slaughter.

Looks Away moved down the line of hoppers and then Grey saw him stagger as if struck. He hurried over.

"What's wrong?"

All the Sioux could do was point. The side door of the last hopper was open and a mass of bodies had fallen out to form a ragdoll mound that spilled across the rail bed. These were not soldiers. Instead of blue or grey, they wore buckskins and breechcloths. Their ruddy skin was now pale from loss of blood. Their hair was black and much of it was caked with dried blood.

They were Sioux.

All of them.

With a trembling hand, Looks Away reached for the nearest corpse and saw the distinctive body painting of the Sioux. However there were a few dots of black paint on the left side of the man's face.

"See those marks? They were with the border patrols," he said.

Behind them, on the far side of the train and across the plain, Deray laughed again.

"This is madness," growled Looks Away. "Madness."

Madness it might be, but Grey thought he understood the genius buried within the madness. All of these cars were heaped with rotting corpses from the War Between the States, and the border conflicts with the Sioux Nation. Maybe even some from the Rail Wars. A few of the corpses on this car wore dusters. Deray was clearly having bodies shipped to him here in this forgotten, hidden place. He had his dark magicks, and he clearly had his dreams of conquest. He had the weapons and a vast supply of ghost rock.

He wasn't just supplying the armies of the world. He was building his *own* army.

An army of the dead.

For the third time Grey said, "We have to warn people."

Looks Away nodded. "I have a terrible feeling we are too sodding late."

"We have to try."

They looked at each other for a long moment. "Yes," said Looks Away. "We bloody well do."

They turned and fled. But as they ran, Grey thought he saw movement off in the shadows, back near the rocks that had served as their hiding place. He fancied he saw a group of people there. Not trying to hide, but apparently not being seen. They looked like figures seen through a fog. Hazy, indistinct, nearly featureless. Except for one. A woman. Not Veronica, but like her she was someone lost to violence.

Annabelle.

Grey swore that he saw her standing there with the others.

With the ghosts.

But for once—for this one moment—they were not looking at him.

Each ghostly face was turned toward the spirit of Veronica and the necromancer.

Then Grey and Looks Away passed behind a row of stalagmites and when they emerged from the other side the ghosts were nowhere to be seen.

If, indeed, they had been there at all.

Deeply troubled, Grey ran faster, desperate now to find the tunnel, the basement, the house, and then the world. He needed to feel sunlight on his face before he lost all hope that he would ever see daylight again.

Chapter 68

It took them hours to find their way out.

Care and caution take time and they could not risk being found out. Apart from the simple truth that they were ill prepared to fight an army of men and machines, they did not want Deray to know that they had witnessed anything. There was no way of telling how that madman would react to the threat of having his plans—his alliances—discovered.

Grey was certain that the necromancer would leave the earth scorched and barren where Paradise Falls now stood.

They did not speak of this. They said nothing at all until they reached the tunnel that had been burrowed through the bedrock into Chesterfield's basement. Only then did they pause. Looks Away touched the slimy walls and shook his head.

"As a geologist I've come in contact with some of the world's strangest creatures," he said. "Those dinosaurs and pteranodons and all that—frightening as they are, they belong to some part of the natural world. Things that once lived and were believed to be extinct. But this . . ." He shook his head again. "I don't know what could have done this. If this were something tiny, a little hole, I would speculate that it was some kind of worm with highly acidic secretive glands, but . . . no worm ever lived that could make a tunnel this size and cut it through solid rock."

Grey nodded. He didn't touch the walls and didn't want any of that slime on his skin.

They looked back the way they'd come and for a moment Grey felt a deep sadness sweep through him. It was a stew made of equal parts dread and acceptance. Deray was coming, that much was clear. He had the weapons, the numbers, the science, and the bloodlust.

What did Paradise Falls have?

A few hundred farmers. Most of them old people and children. Some men who could probably handle a gun. Some women, too.

And what else? What did they really have that could be used to mount a defense against Deray? What was there in town that could stop one of those tanks? What could even hope to stop the metal giant, Samson?

And even if the impossible could be managed, there were still whatever that flying machine had been that Grey had seen during the storm, the soldiers, the dinosaurs.

The undead. The Harrowed Lucky Bob.

Any of these would, alone, probably be enough to destroy the town.

Together? Grey doubted even a nation could stand against a surge of power like that.

Get out, whispered the part of his mind that had kept him on the road since the deaths of his men and Annabelle. Get out while you can.

Grey thought of the ghosts of his abandoned friends, and of the way Jenny Pearl looked in the sunlight this morning before they'd ridden away from her place. He thought of the pain in Brother Joe's eyes and how that man had come back from the brink of personal hell to stand with the people of his town. He thought of that good man, Lucky Bob, and how he had been turned into a monster.

He thought about the deep pain in Looks Away's voice

and in his eyes when they'd found Veronica dying on the stairs.

Get out?

"Go to hell," he murmured.

If Looks Away heard him he made no comment.

Together they went into the basement.

PART FOUR

What We Die For

When your time comes to die, be not like those whose hearts are filled with fear of death, so that when their time comes they weep and pray for a little more time to live their lives over again in a different way. Sing your death song, and die like a hero going home.

—TECUMSEH

Chapter 69

They met no resistance in the house.

No gunmen, no foreign soldiers. No ghosts. No dinosaurs.

Nothing.

Everyone and everything was dead.

They climbed the stairs and paused briefly at the place where Veronica had died. Her blood was still there, pooled, drying but not dry. Looks Away bent and touched two fingers into the center of the pool, then used them to draw parallel lines on his cheeks.

"War paint?" asked Grey.

The Sioux straightened and wiped his fingers on his trousers. "Call it a promise."

Grey didn't ask what that meant. He knew.

They shared a nod and moved on.

Before they left the house they paused in the treasure room. They exchanged a brief, wordless look as they began stuffing their pockets.

While they were loading it, Looks Away said, "I wonder why they left all this here. I mean, they took the time to wipe Chesterfield out, why not plunder his treasure trove?"

Grey shrugged. "Why hurry? As far as Deray knows this is all here safe and sound, ready for when he needs it. Or maybe he's going to have his troops haul it out of here after his foreign guests have left. Might not be the sort of thing he wants to let them see. Either way, I don't think Deray frets all that much about anyone from Paradise Falls taking it."

Looks Away sucked a tooth as he weighed a bar of gold in his hand. "I wish we could scarper with all of it and leave something clever and obscene written on the wall."

"Yeah, well I forgot to pack an entire wagon train in my saddlebag."

"Pity."

They stole as much as they could carry.

When they finally stepped out into the fresh air they were shocked to see that it was nighttime. The sun was down and the moon rode naked across the sky.

"Must be nearly three in the morning," said Grey. "Can you find our way back in the dark?"

Looks Away snorted and they went to find their horses. They had to feed and water them first, and both animals stamped in irritation at having been abandoned for so long.

"Stop complaining," Grey said to Picky. "Let's all be happy we came back at all."

They mounted and rode off.

Dawn found them with miles still to go. While Looks Away could find the path, navigating it in the dark was another matter. Very often they had to walk single file, leading the nervous horses through the landscape torn by the Great Quake. Finally, as the red eye of morning began peering suspiciously at them over the eastern mountains, they saw the road that led through the last of the town's working farms. Paradise Falls was a tiny smudge in the heat shimmer on the horizon.

They mounted and began riding again.

As they did, Looks Away kept glancing at Grey.

"What?" Grey asked. "What's wrong?"

"I was about to ask you the same thing, old chap," said Looks Away. "For the last two miles you've done nothing but frown, nod to yourself, and grunt. If you're having so thorough a conversation with yourself, then please invite me in."

"Oh . . . yeah . . . I've been thinking about our boy Deray. I guess there are a few things that sort of bother me."

"A few things about Deray that bother you," echoed Looks Away. "Imagine that. And, pray tell me what in particular?"

"Well . . . for one thing, I'm not sure if I buy that whole business about helping those generals start wars."

"Why not? Deray has a reputation as a weapons merchant."

"Right, I get that part, but he's going about it in a strange way," said Grey. "It's a little too . . ." He fished for the word. "Obvious."

"Obvious? How so?"

"Looking at him, at the way he acts, it's like he sees himself as something more than a guy who peddles guns."

"He is."

"No, you're missing my point. You saw how he was treating those generals? They weren't just customers. You don't put on shows like that for people you've already sold your wares to." Grey fished for some beef jerky from his saddlebag and shared it with Looks Away. "Deray held himself above them. Like he was something bigger and more important than any general. Like it was expected of those generals to hang on his every word. Like it was expected that they would cheer him. I never met one, but I imagine that's how a king would act."

"A king? Interesting."

"You don't see it?"

"Yes," said Looks Away slowly, "I think I'm beginning to. But what of it? Deray is a famous megalomaniac."

"A what?"

"Someone who thinks too bloody highly of himself."

Grey grunted. "Tell you the truth, friend, I'm not so sure this is a matter of someone putting on airs. I think he is setting himself up as an actual king."

"What? Because he has a kingdom of dinosaurs and undead soldiers? That's hardly—."

"No, because I think he's planning on doing a lot more than helping to start a bunch of wars. Those hopper cars filled with bodies gave me a very bad idea. He's building an army of the living dead and—."

"We already know that."

But Grey shook his head. "Let me finish. His army is going to be made up of the dead. Of people who were killed in wars. Right now it's the wars here in America. But what happens when he starts raising everybody's dead?"

The Sioux stared at him in shocked silence.

Grey nodded. "Yeah. So he sells the kinds of weapons that will allow those generals to wage wholesale slaughter. Those tanks and such? They'll kill hundreds of thousands. Maybe millions."

"And then Aleksander Deray will come along and raise all those dead . . ." Looks Away's voice was hollow.

"He'll have the biggest army anyone's ever seen," said Grey. "And with those metal giants like Samson as backup—or maybe to keep his own troops in line . . . he'll be able to conquer the whole damn world."

"Dear God in heaven I hope you're wrong about this."

Grey nodded. He hoped he was wrong, too. But he was one hundred percent certain that he was right.

Chapter 70

Neither of them knew they were in danger until one of the arms of a nearby saguaro cactus suddenly tore off and went spinning into the dust.

They stared at it for a blank moment, and then like a returning memory, they heard the distant echo of the shot.

"Down!" cried Grey as he flattened out along Picky's withers. A split second later a black eye seemed to open in the barrel of the big cactus. The report followed a full two seconds later. A big gun, Grey guessed. Heavy caliber, fired from a long distance. Two hundred yards? Three?

Whoever was firing knew his business.

Grey kicked his horse's flanks and held on tight as the mare sprang forward, all weariness forgotten, as she ran flat out in the opposite direction. Queenie was right there with her, like they were the only two runners racing toward a finish line. Looks Away had slid sideways on his mount, hanging down like a saddle blanket, the way Grey had seen other Indian riders do, using the horse's body as a shield. Around them—and even ahead of them—bullets pocked the cacti or buzzed past them like angry bees.

There was a rise ahead of them and although for a split second they would be silhouetted against the sky, beyond it the land itself would offer safety. They raced for it and nose-to-nose the horses leaped over the crest and plunged down the other side. Bullets chipped the ridge and showered them with dirt.

Grey slid immediately out of the saddle, slid his Winchester from its scabbard, and crawled up the slope. Looks Away was right behind him except that he had the Kingdom rifle. The distance was too great for the shotgun to be of any use. Handguns would be equally useless.

"Who's hunting us?" asked Looks Away. "Can you see anyone?"

Grey squinted along the barrel, but all he could see was desert, rock, and cactus.

"I can't see a damned thing."

The gunfire had stopped as soon as they cleared the ridge, and now the vista was silent and still as the sluggish desert wind allowed.

"What do you figure," asked Looks Away, "a Sharps fifty?"

"Or something. Big slugs from the way it hit the cactus."

"Luckily he wasn't a better shot."

Grey began to nod, but stopped. There was something wrong about that statement.

Those shots had all come close. Very close. Some had missed them by inches. What were the odds of someone firing six or eight shots at ultra-long range and grouping the shots within an area no wider than twenty feet but missing two men and two horses?

There was luck, sure, though Grey didn't think today was anyone's idea of a lucky day for them. Even poor marksmanship had some odds in its favor.

"I don't think he's trying to hit us," said Grey.

A bullet hit the dirt between them, chasing them back down the slope.

"Jesus!" gasped Looks Away as he spat dirt from his mouth. "Not trying? Not bloody trying?"

Grey shook his head. "No . . . he's good, that one. He could have taken our heads off right there."

"He seems to be giving it the old club try . . ."

"No," insisted Grey. "Which makes me wonder why he's missing."

They considered it, then without comment they split apart and crawled up to peer over different sections of the ridge, far from where they had been.

A bullet struck the sand five inches from Looks Away's ear.

A moment later a second one shattered a creosote bush next to Grey.

"Bloody bastard," complained Looks Away. When there were no more shots, he wormed his way over to Grey. "I think I know why he's doing this."

"Yeah," said Grey. "Me, too. He wants to keep us here."

"Indeed. But for what?"

Neither of them really wanted an answer.

They got one anyway.

It began as a rumble, like distant thunder. Both men glanced at the sky, but the dawn was cloudless. There weren't even birds up there.

Another rumble. This time they could feel it in their bones.

Beneath them the sand began to shiver. Grey placed his palm against the ground and heard it. A groan from within the earth. A moan of protest as the land itself began to move.

"Earthquake!" he cried.

But Looks Away shook his head and placed his ear to the ground, eyes closed, listening to the noise. The rumbling was continuous now.

And it was growing. Grey could see the plants and cacti around them trembling. Lizards flashed through the dry grass. A tarantula hurried past, then stopped and hunkered down, clearly too frightened and confused to move further. Grey could understand. He wanted to run.

But how do you outrun the earth itself?

"Look!" gasped his companion, pointing to where a crack suddenly gaped open, belching dust and gas into the air.

"What the hell is that?"

"I don't know," yelled Looks Away as he staggered to his feet and began backing away. Grey flinched, expecting his friend to take a bullet, but there were no new shots.

However, the land itself seemed to be assaulting them. The crack yawned wider, sending tear lines running in all directions. A Joshua tree broke from its roots with a sound like a pistol shot, and then the trunk fell over sideways. A line of saguaro cactus leaped into the air as the ground exploded beneath them. More gas shot upward in scalding jets, withering the cacti even as they flew through the air. The horses reared and screamed, but they were too frightened to know where to run.

"We have to get out of here before this whole thing—," Looks Away's words were cut off as something exploded upward from beneath the earth. It shot a mass of dirt, sand, and pulverized rock a hundred feet into the air, and then it emerged.

It.

That was the only way Grey's mind could label the thing.

Massive.

Bigger than anything Grey had ever seen. A body so vast that it would have burst the walls of a barn, and as pale as dead skin. Wrinkled, segmented, impossible. It rose like some obscene finger from the hole in the ground. Yard by yard it rose above the desert floor. Glistening and featureless, like some foul intestine of one of the ancient Greek Titans.

Grey and Looks Away stood there in its shadow, showered by falling debris, mouths agape, watching with eyes unable to blink, as the monster rose and rose and rose. And then, at the apex of its rise, it trembled with an odd and disturbing delicacy, as if its massive flesh was sensitive to even the hesitant touches of the desert breeze. It wavered there, indomitable against the morning sky, taller than the mast of the tallest ship, with some foul-smelling gelatinous goo running in thick lines from pores that opened and closed all along its body.

Now they knew what had burrowed those mighty holes through the bedrock. Now they knew what had left a trail of slime along the shores of that forgotten ocean. Now they knew, without doubt, that the earth held within its bowels greater horrors than man, even in the depths of opium dreams, had ever conjured. Here was Leviathan. Here was the finger of Satan.

It was a worm.

Towering a hundred feet into the desert air, with God only knew how much of its foul length still buried in the soil.

A worm.

Blind and colorless. A thousand tons of glistening flesh.

And it had come for them.

Chapter 71

There was nowhere to run, no way to escape so monstrous a thing.

Grey felt his heart sink down in his chest, falling to some low place where he could no longer feel its warmth. Several times over the last few days he had felt that he stood on the edge of life and felt himself leaning into the abyss. Each time he had been able to do something to pull himself back from that brink.

Now . . . ?

The worm trembled and shook, and he could see its muscles twitching and contracting as it fought the pull of gravity.

And yet . . . it did not fall.

It could have crushed them more easily and thoroughly than Samson had smashed Deray's prisoners. It could have wiped them off the face of the world and never felt their deaths. They were fleas, it was a giant.

And yet it still did not fall.

"What is this?" demanded Grey. "Is this another of your prehistoric animals?"

The Sioux shook his head. "I . . . don't know what this is. I've never even heard of a monster like this. Maybe it's something Deray conjured with his black magic."

"I don't see a ghost rock implant . . ."

"No. Perhaps he controls it through sorcery. This is beyond me, Grey."

"The rifle," hissed Grey, whispering as if the thing could hear and understand. "The Kingdom rifle! . . ."

The Sioux nodded numbly and brought the weapon up. They had one round left, but he hesitated, apparently mesmerized by the brute. Or, worried Grey, simply overwhelmed by it. They had seen so much today. Perhaps for Looks Away it was *too* much.

"It's too . . . ," murmured Looks Away, ". . . it's too . . . too . . ."

Despite the clear hopelessness on his face, Looks Away raised the rifle. There was no clear target. No chest in which a heart might beat. No torso where lungs or liver might fall to a blast from the Kingdom rifle. There was only flesh. Acres of it, it seemed.

"Shoot and then we'll run," murmured Grey, beginning to edge backward. Sweat ran down his face and gathered inside his clothes. "Shoot and . . ."

"And nothing, son," said a voice.

Both men whirled to see a figure standing on the crest of the ridge. He was tall, with narrow hips and broad shoulders, and he held a Sharps .50 in his pale hands, the barrel pointed at Grey's chest. He smiled at them, and though the morning light twinkled in his eyes, there was nothing at all comforting in that grin.

"You boys are going to drop the hardware," he said. "Nice and slow. And then we're all going to go back downstairs to have ourselves a nice chat with my master, Lord Deray."

Looks Away licked his lips. "You don't have to do this . . ."

The morning light sparkled on the ghost rock embedded in the man's sternum.

"Yeah," said Lucky Bob Pearl as he shifted the rifle to point at the Sioux's face, "I kind of think I do."

Chapter 72

Lucky Bob's smile was as false as an alligator's, and there was the Devil himself laughing in his eyes. Grey wondered how that worked. If Jenny's dad was the kind of man everyone said he was, then did this mean that the manitou inside of him had complete control? That seemed at odds with the facts, because Lucky Bob clearly knew Looks Away, just as he had known his daughter even though he'd tried to kill her. How could the demon speak and even to a degree act like the man who had once owned that flesh, and still be able to perpetrate such evil?

"Listen to me, Bob," said Looks Away desperately, "you don't have to do anything."

"I always figured you for a smart fellow, Looksie," said Lucky Bob. "But I reckon you plum don't understand the way the world works."

"I know more than you think."

"Why? 'Cause you were down in the dark and you think you saw something?"

"For a start, yes," said Looks Away. "You're working with Deray and—."

"Hey now, you'll show some respect or I'll blow a hole in you big enough to stand in. It's *Lord* Deray, you red heathen bastard."

"A racial invective? From you?" Looks Away seemed almost amused. "My, you have changed."

"More than you can understand."

"Oh? You think I don't know what you are? Or what's inside of you? Or has the manitou made you stupid?"

The smile on Lucky Bob's face flickered. Clearly he did not expect that kind of response. He adjusted his hands on his rifle and there was a nervous flush on his pale face.

Interesting, thought Grey. If Lucky Bob could blush then he still had blood in his veins. That squared with what Brother Joe had told them. He wasn't just a walking corpse after all. An idea, perhaps the seed of a plan, began to take root in his mind.

Grey still had his Winchester in his hand and he knew he was a good shot. He was more than half sure he could dodge left and fire from the hip with a reasonable chance of killing this monster with a head shot. And if all he did was wound him with a body shot, the skill Grey had learned on a dozen battlefields ensured that he could work the lever and put a second round through the Harrowed's dead face.

Could he do it, though, without getting Looks Away shot?

Maybe.

Could he do it, knowing that it would break Jenny's heart?

Not a chance in hell.

Behind him globs of slime dropped from the giant worm and splashed heavily onto the torn desert floor.

"Enough jibber-jabber," said Lucky Bob. "You boys drop your guns and then we'll all go down to the Lord of the Dark."

"Whoa," said Looks Away, raising one hand, palm outward, "let's pause on that for a moment. 'Lord of the Dark'? Seriously? We're going to call your master the Lord of the effing Dark? Isn't that a bit, oh I don't know . . ."

"Theatrical?" supplied Grey.

"Silly," decided Looks Away. "I mean . . . come on, Bob. I worked in the shallowest possible end of the theater when I was with the Wild West Show, and even we couldn't have come up with something as downright absurd as—."

Lucky Bob fired a shot and put a bullet into the dirt exactly between Looks Away's feet. The Sioux jumped a foot in the air and nearly dropped the Kingdom rifle.

And that's when Grey made his move. He dropped into a low squat, pivoted, buried the stock against his hip, and fired. He aimed with all of his skill and he aimed with his heart. The bullet took Lucky Bob in the stomach. Not the head. From that distance the shot was like getting hit by a mule. The Harrowed staggered backward, and he reflexively threw up his hands. The Sharps spun upward, pinwheeled, and then struck the ground barrel-first, burying itself six inches into the torn sand. Lucky Bob tried to stagger sideways to catch his balance, but instead he collapsed backward.

Above them, the worm roared.

Roared.

Grey had not seen a mouth on it. He had never imagined that a worm had the capacity for sound. But this was a monster from somewhere deep in the earth where nothing natural lives. It had a mouth high, high up on its head, and as the Harrowed fell it let loose with a howl so loud that blood burst from Grey's ears and nose. Lightning crackled along its trembling length. The whole landscape shuddered.

Grey was already running.

Running.

Looks Away was already outpacing him, and they were both chasing their panic-stricken horses.

Great fissures split on the desert floor as more and more of the monstrous worm smashed upward from below. The echo of that terrible scream seemed to chase them like a storm wind. They ran beyond the confines of its shadow, but immediately the shadows seemed to flow after them. Grey knew that the thing was coming.

"Picky—goddamn it wait!" he bellowed. If he could get onto the damn horse then maybe he could outrun the creature.

Ripples of force whipped along beneath the ground, lifting both men, throwing them like unimportant debris. They landed hard. Grey's rifle was jerked from his hands on impact, but Looks Away somehow kept hold of the Kingdom rifle.

"Shoot the fucking thing!" bellowed Grey, and the Sioux glanced down at the weapon he carried as though he was surprised to see it. He scrambled to his feet, turned, raised the rifle, and fired.

There was no need to aim. The worm was everywhere. It was so vast that it seemed to blot out the rising sun. The gun bucked in Looks Away's hand as the compressed gas fired the deadly round. Their last round.

The bullet struck the rippling flesh and exploded, bursting outward with each tiny fragment of processed ghost rock. When exposed to the air, the pellets detonated, tearing great masses of the alien flesh apart and sending it flying through the air in clouds of bloody mist. The blast tore a gaping hole in the monster and tons of gore and shredded flesh flopped out onto the ground. The monster let loose another of its dreadful shrieks and the sky itself seemed ready to rip itself apart.

Grey and Looks Away stood transfixed, watching as the monster thrashed and twisted in agony. They braced themselves for the earthquake that would surely follow as it fell.

They waited, too shocked to move. Needing this abomination to die, willing it to die.

The tremors went on and on . . .

And then gradually subsided.

The godlike worm writhed before them, its pale flesh pulsing with pain, oozing with red ichor. But it did not fall. It did not die, confirming that it had not been one of Deray's undead slaves. There was no ghost rock in it to maximize the effect of the Kingdom rifle, and despite the damage that single round had inflicted, it was not going to be enough. As they watched, the wound filled with the clear slime that ran from its pores; and though this substance seemed able to burn through the very bones of the earth, it filled the wound and sealed it as surely as a bandage. The blood stopped flowing. The wound was now plugged.

The worm lived.

And it was *furious*.

It shuddered with rage that rippled up through the ground as if emanating from the mind of Deray himself. As he thought that, Grey realized that it was probably the truth. Grey knew that Looks Away had been right—the monster was connected to the necromancer by some dark sorcery, and it came hunting for them, herding them, working with the Harrowed to trap them. Now it was wounded. Now it had felt the power of the Kingdom rifle—a weapon that could possibly rival the infernal devices of Deray himself. That knowledge, that dread of opposition, was probably echoing down into the caverns. Deray had sent this thing, commanded it, and now it shared terrible and dangerous knowledge with him.

Grey knew this as surely as if it had been written in the sky by a flaming hand.

Using the Kingdom rifle had been a mistake. Very likely the last mistake they would ever make.

On the ground, wounded and possibly dying, Lucky Bob Pearl was laughing. Blood flecked his lips and misted the air, but he was laughing. "Now you boys have gone and done it," he wheezed. "Now you've pissed in your own graves."

The worm burst the ground apart as it rose and rose. Grey felt his mind tumbling, fracturing, disassembling. He was unable to process the size of this thing. It was taller than any building he had ever seen. Taller than the redwoods up north. Grey backed away from it, but with each step he could feel his sanity fragment. The worm seemed to draw back, to tense as if ready to smash itself down and shatter the world. There, inside its shadow once more, the two men stopped trying to run away from something that could not be escaped. The monster blotted out the sun and darkened the sky. All they could hear was the lunatic laughter of Lucky Bob Pearl as the worm from the heart of the earth . . . *exploded*.

Chapter 73

Grey felt himself falling.

Except that he was falling the wrong way. His body was in the air, moving fast, propelled by a force like a hurricane wind. However the landscape was not rushing up to meet him. It blew past him. At the same moment that his dazed brain was able to grasp that he was flying sideways, hurled by the explosion of the giant worm, gravity played her card. His lateral flight turned into an arc. And then he was falling. The ground seemed too far away for anything but a crippling impact.

He closed his eyes.

He hit the ground. But there was still so much force pushing him sideways that he hit at an angle and went slipping across the desert floor like a skipping stone. When his body finally came to rest, he was half buried in a nest of loose sand and dirt, twigs, pinecones, cactus, and sagebrush. The tumble had twisted him around so that he was looking back the way he'd come. He saw the worm.

What was left of the worm. Forty feet of it still protruded rudely from the ground. The rest, though, had been torn apart. Massive chunks of it were scattered across the landscape. Smaller red pieces continued to fall for a long time, and a thin red rain fell across everything as the last of the monster's blood fell down to paint the place where it had died.

Grey could not understand what had just happened.

The shot Looks Away fired had done damage, but not enough. What, then, could have done this? It made no sense to his shocked and battered brain.

Then he saw someone. A man. A stranger. A black man of about sixty, with a grizzled white goatee and sideburns. He was short, round but not fat, dressed in brown tweed despite the heat, wearing a tan top hat and leather gloves. Instead of spectacles, the man wore a leather band set with wide, flat lenses that were tinted the same eerie blue as the lightning Grey had seen when he first met Looks Away. The man approached him in a series of quick, nervous steps. When he was ten feet away, he asked the very same question Looks Away had asked him back in Nevada.

"Have I killed you, white man?"

Grey tried to say something. Anything. He felt the moment needed some kind of commentary, something to anchor it to common sense and ordinary understanding.

What he said was, "Uhhh."

Then he felt himself falling again. Into darkness this time.

He never felt himself land.

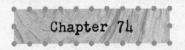

Chapter 74

He was awake before he opened his eyes.

Grey accepted that he had been unconscious. Not just asleep, but totally out of it. Why, and for how long, were mysteries. Where he currently was provided another mystery.

In a bed, though. He could feel a mattress under him. A pillow supporting his aching head. A sheet over him.

He couldn't feel his clothes.

I'm naked, he thought, and even though he knew that this was an accurate assessment, it felt strange to think it. Then he realized that he was focusing on that more than on the fact that he was alive.

Alive.

He didn't want to move until he was sure he was somewhere safe. Once, when he had been briefly captured by Confederate soldiers in the last days of the war, he had feigned being unconscious while he assessed his situation. He did that now.

If he was naked then he did not have his weapons.

On the other hand he was in a bed rather than in shackles.

He focused his senses on his chest, searching for any ache or strangeness that might indicate that he had been taken by Deray and turned into a mindless walking corpse. Or one of the more conscious but no less dead Harrowed. But there was nothing that hinted at the presence of a ghost rock implant.

Which meant that he was alive and he was himself. So where was he?

There were no sounds. But there were . . . smells. He realized with a start that he was smelling coffee. Biscuits. And bacon.

Grey opened his eyes just a fraction and immediately knew that he was not alone at all.

She sat there.

Lovely. Her blond hair pinned up, a smoke-colored shawl around her shoulders, her eyes filled with questions and concern. And in the slanting light of late afternoon, she looked so much like that other woman. The lost one. The one he'd failed.

Like Annabelle.

She even sat like her, the same posture and angle. The same depth of thought in those beautiful blue eyes. The impression was so powerful, so intense that Grey began to doubt whether it was her. Had everything else been a dream? The years on the road, the battles, the endless lonely nights? Was meeting Looks Away part of that dream? Was Paradise Falls and Deray and all of this madness nothing more than the product of some fevered dream? Grey had been helpless once in Annabelle's house. Recovering from a bullet wound to the chest, he had lingered in a fevered haze for weeks while she tended him. He remembered that morning, waking up after the fever broke, seeing her sitting there, exactly as she was now.

As Jenny Pearl was.

If it was Jenny at all.

If anything was real at all.

He tried to pull himself back from the edge of dreams, of fantasies. He made himself say the right name.

He said, "Jenny . . . ?"

But her face clouded with doubt, and like an after-echo Grey realized that, despite all of his determination, he'd spoken the wrong name.

He'd said, "Annabelle . . ."

He closed his eyes. "I'm sorry."

Then he felt soft lips kiss his closed eyelids. Then his forehead. Then his lips. "No," she breathed, "don't be sorry."

"I—."

"Did you love her?" asked Jenny.

Grey was not a man much given to tears but he felt them burn his eyes beneath his lids. He wanted to turn away from Jenny, to push her back, to flee this moment. He could feel her breath on his skin. It was strangely hot.

"Tell me," she asked, her voice soft but insistent. "Did you love your Annabelle?"

He winced. "Yes," he whispered. "I loved her and . . . I . . ."

There was a sharp knock on the door, and Jenny jerked backward. Grey opened his eyes and turned as Looks Away and the black man entered without invitation. Looks Away had a bandage wrapped around his forehead and another around his right arm. He was dressed in clean clothes, though. More of Lucky Bob's castoffs.

"Ah," he said brightly, "you're alive. Jolly good."

He hooked a wooden chair with his foot and dragged it over, sat down and waved the older man to a rocker in the corner. Grey nearly whipped the sheet away and stood up, but remembered that he was naked. Instead he pushed himself to a sitting position as Jenny stood up and went over to stand by the foot of the bed. The Sioux seemed to be excited to the point of enthusiasm. He leaned his forearms on his knees and grinned. "Now we have a real chance at this, eh, old boy?"

"Chance at what? What are you talking about?" demanded Grey.

The smile flickered. "Why, at fighting Deray, what else?"

"What are you talking about? We barely got out of there with our heads attached. If you hadn't shot that worm we'd be dead."

"Me? Ha! You saw what happened when I shot the beast. It barely twitched."

"Then . . . ?"

"The victory," said Looks Away, "belongs to the good doctor."

He gestured to the older man. Which is when Grey's bruised brain put two and two together. He pointed at the stranger in the tweed suit.

"You're Doctor Saint!"

The man smiled and bowed his head. "I am indeed. Percival Saint at your service, sir."

Saint had a deep, cultured voice that still carried soft undertones of the deep South of his youth. He leaned forward and offered his hand, which Grey shook.

"I hear you've had quite the series of adventures, Mr. Torrance," said Saint. "Looks has told me the whole story, and anything he might have overlooked was filled in by Brother Joe and Miss Pearl. I'm sorry that you've become embroiled in our little war out here in what's left of California. That said, I'm sure we're all glad to have a capable gunhand on our side."

"Thanks, and I'm glad they filled you in," said Grey, "but how about you folks filling me in on what the hell's going on? The last thing I remember is that worm exploding. If Looks didn't kill it, who did? Was that you? If so, how?"

Saint nodded and leaned back. He fished a pipe from his jacket pocket and filled the bowl with tobacco, then leaned forward as Looks Away struck a match and held it out for him. The scientist puffed for a few moments, taking his time before launching into his tale.

"Looks Away told you that I have been doing some consulting for the Confederate States of America."

"Yes."

"You look surprised."

Grey shrugged. "You escaped from the South."

"It was a different South back then," said Saint. "And I was a child. The world, as has been noted by philosophers, has moved on since then. America is no longer the emerging, young nation it was when I was a lad. Now it is a fractured and troubled place. There are grave threats to this great land. Some from without—because there are many countries who would love to conquer the New World, England among them. Germany is on the rise. Russia would like to build a new global Empire. And we need to be cautious of Spain ever since they began building their new Conquistador Fleet with ghost rock engines." He shook his head. "The Great Quake may have changed America, but as a result ghost rock is changing the world. We are poised on the brink of the greatest industrial revolution since the invention of steel. Maybe even since the invention of the wheel." He shook his head. "You look skeptical . . ."

"Actually I'm not. I saw enough down in those caverns to make a believer out of me," said Grey. "What bothers me is what we can do about it. Deray has an army. We don't."

Saint's reply was a smile. He had heavily lidded eyes and they were useful, it seemed to Grey, for the scientist to keep his thoughts to himself. He was a hard man to read.

Grey turned to Looks Away. "Tell me about—," he began, then snapped his mouth shut. He had almost asked what had happened to Lucky Bob Pearl. But, Jenny was right there. Instead, Grey said, "Tell me about the worm."

"That was all Doctor Saint," said Looks Away. "Look, I have to back up a little. After we left town yesterday morning, we missed Doctor Saint's return by less than two hours."

"Unfortunate timing," said Saint, nodding.

"I wanted to ride after you," said Jenny. "But—."

"But I convinced her to stay here in town," said Saint. "Once she explained what was happening I realized that we needed to step up our preparations for what was inevitably going to happen. She told me about the undead attacking the town."

"Did she tell you about the flying machine?" asked Grey.

Jenny blinked. "Flying . . . ?"

Grey explained what he'd seen, though his description was sparse. Looks Away nodded, and added, "I think it might have had a gas-envelope and motors to drive it. I only saw it for a few moments, but that was my impression. The body was like a frigate, but it had a balloon instead of sails."

"A frigate of the clouds," mused Saint. "How elegant."

"It scared the hell out of me," said Grey. "It's unnatural."

"Unnatural? No. Only primitive minds regard science as something to be feared. Surely, Mr. Torrance, you are not so dim as that. This is an age of invention. What you saw was a lighter-than-airship. There's no magic to it. There are several already in use around the world. Lovely things. Like whales in the air."

"Not sure 'lovely' is a word I'd paint on the side of what I saw," said Grey.

"I expect not," agreed Saint. "If I were to encounter one over a battlefield, I suppose I would use a completely different set of adjectives. However my comment stands. The designs for such machines are elegant. It's something that has been in trial-and-error stages for centuries. Da Vinci, bless his heart, designed one, although it was unworkable. Nice thought, though. I have my own sketches somewhere . . ."

"Doctor," said Looks Away gently.

"Ah, yes, yes, my boy," said Saint with a grandfatherly chuckle. "The airship you saw was very likely the command vessel used by Deray. From what I've been told, the storm seemed to accompany the attack, correct?"

Grey nodded. "It was a weird storm. Like the undead were using it as some kind of camouflage."

"Very likely they were. There have been a number of very interesting papers on using the properties of ghost rock to seed the clouds, and there is sufficient energetic discharge to initiate lightning." He stopped and smiled self-consciously. "I do go on, don't I?"

"Short version of that," said Grey, "is that Deray can control storms, raise the dead, and fly through the air."

"Well . . . that's oversimplified, but . . ."

"But yes," said Jenny.

"Yes," agreed Looks Away.

"And he has those mechanical carriages. Tanks, he calls them," said Grey. "And rifles a lot like your Kingdom guns."

"That's very disturbing," murmured Doctor Saint. "Making the weapons is not complicated, not for a scientist. Mass-producing the ammunition for it . . . well, that's the thing. Either Deray has found a limitless supply of ghost rock, or his research is driving his designs in the same direction as what I came up with."

The room fell into silence.

Then Jenny said, "And that metal man? Samson?"

"Yes," said Saint, "please tell me about that again. Describe it in as much detail as possible."

They did, with Grey and Looks Away taking turns to fill in what little they knew. Saint did not look happy.

"That is most troubling. A mechanical soldier powered by the rock would be a formidable thing."

"You don't say," murmured Grey.

"No, what I mean is that building such a thing is difficult enough. Many engineers and scientists have tried. The Wasatch Railroad has been using mechanical workers for years so they can keep pace with the vertical expansion of cities like New York and Chicago. With land acreage at a premium, everyone knows that we have to build up in order to grow. Steelworkers who are themselves made of steel would be invaluable. Metal men make for a new kind of slave labor force that never complain and no one will ever go to war to free them. Why should they? They're steam and iron and gears. But, Grey, those machines are crude and even clumsy in comparison to this. Samson is beyond anything I've ever even heard about. Something like that could not possibly have been built simply for labor."

"No argument. I don't think Deray is trying to build affordable office space," said Grey sourly. "Samson is a killer."

"I agree," said Saint, "and that's what is so troubling. One of the problems we've faced when considering either mechanical armor or independently operating machine men is the speed. They are simply not fast enough to be of use in combat because a field piece—a howitzer, say—could take them down."

"Samson was faster than goddamn lightning," said Grey.

"Right. That is the key. Deray has discovered a way to make his machines move at great speed. That is a truly, truly frightening thought." Saint puffed his pipe and for a moment he did nothing more than stare at the smoke.

Grey said, "You still haven't told me about the worm."

"Ah," said Looks Away with a grin. "Remember that Kingdom cannon I showed you at the doctor's shop?"

"Oh," said Grey. "How'd you—?"

"It took twenty men and a lot of sweat to put that son of a whore on the back of my best wagon," said Jenny. "And then it took us all damn night to drive out there. We got halfway to Chesterfield's spread by dawn."

"What made you risk it?" asked Grey, alarmed. "That road is treacherous."

"This young lady," said Saint, "has eyes like a cat. She can see better in the dark than I ever could. She found paths that a goat wouldn't take. I must admit that I was sweating lead ingots all the way."

Jenny gave him a small enigmatic smile and glanced down at her hands for a moment. "I'm a lot like my pa," she said. "He was always a good night hunter, too."

"You brought the Kingdom cannon out there, and you shot the worm?"

"Yes," said Saint, "and yes."

"And not before time, either," said Looks Away. "I thought we'd bloody well had it."

"We should have had it," said Grey. "We've been coasting on borrowed luck since the attack on the town."

Again Jenny looked down at her hands. Again there was that small half-smile. Grey wondered what it meant.

"If we have the Kingdom cannon," said Grey after giving it all some thought, "doesn't that mean we stand a chance? Even against Samson?"

"A chance?" mused Doctor Saint slowly, tasting that concept. "A small chance, perhaps. The Kingdom cannon is a prototype. I have enough ghost rock for maybe five rounds—and even then it's likely the internal works will overheat after the second or third shot. It's also an unwieldy thing. We would need to direct Samson into its direct line of fire."

"Damn. What about the Kingdom rifle? That thing was pretty handy."

"Yes, and the fact that it did not overheat is encouraging," said Saint. "It's never been fired that many times before."

"Not to bring us all down," said Looks Away, "but there was a considerable span of time between most of its uses. I don't know what would have happened if I'd fired shot upon shot."

"Damn," repeated Grey. "How many of those guns do you have?"

"Including the one you 'borrowed'?" asked Saint.

"Yes."

"Two. The other needs some work, but I think I can get it operational in under an hour."

"Good, that's better than—"

"That is not the issue," said Saint. "I have a number of other weapons in various stages of assembly and function. Even a handgun that you might find quite comfortable."

"Still sounds good to me."

"However we don't have enough ammunition," said Saint. "More precisely, I don't have enough ghost rock to make the guns work."

For the first time since he'd awakened, Grey smiled. "Tell me, Doc," he said quietly, "have you looked in my saddlebag?"

Chapter 75

Jenny took Saint outside to where Picky and Queenie were being groomed. Grey said he'd join them as soon as he was dressed. He asked Looks Away to stay behind for a moment.

"There are some big gaps in my memory," Grey admitted as he pulled on the clothes Jenny had laid out for him. "And there's also some gaps in your side of the story."

"Ah," said Looks Away, nodding. "You're wondering why I didn't mention Lucky Bob."

"No, I pretty much get why you didn't mention him. What I want to know is what happened to him?"

But the Sioux shook his head. "You were knocked out," he said. "I wasn't. After Doctor Saint killed the worm, I went looking for Lucky Bob. I was hoping to find him alive but injured. I thought it might be useful for us to interrogate one of the more powerful undead. Or, maybe drag him back to see if Brother Joe could work some kind of white man religious mojo on him. Exorcise his demons, so to speak."

"And—?"

"And he was gone. I found blood but no body."

Grey began buttoning his shirt. "Shit."

"I know. If Brother Joe is correct, then Lucky Bob's body was possessed at the point of death. The body is apparently able to heal itself."

Grey shook his head. "This is all so damn complicated. A week ago dead was dead, now there's all kinds of different death? Corpses that try to eat you. Demons stealing bodies. Why can't the world be the world again?"

The Sioux's face was sad. "Believe me, old chap, I dearly wish we could roll back the clock to the way things were. You'd like to roll it back a week. My people would like to roll it back four hundred years."

"Ouch," said Grey, wincing as if actually punched. Looks Away spread his hands.

"However the world is the world, old fellow," he said. "If it's moved on, then surely we need to dig in with our spurs and ride to catch up."

"A cowboy metaphor," said Grey. "Nice."

"Apt, though."

"I guess." He sat on the edge of the bed and pulled on his boots. They had been brushed, but there were lingering stains on them. The blood of monsters. He paused, holding the second boot between his fingers and letting it dangle. "I should tell Jenny about her dad."

"It'll hurt her. He seems to have embraced his new nature. Maybe all that was Lucky Bob is gone now and only the manitou remains. Either way . . ."

"I know, but it doesn't feel right to lie to her. Even lying by omission."

Looks Away cocked his head and appraised Grey. "You're a strange man, my friend."

Grey said nothing.

"Down in the cavern, Veronica said some things . . ."

"I know," said Grey as he pulled on the second boot. He stood up. "I don't want to talk about it."

But Looks Away shifted to stand in front of the door. "I rather think the time is past to be coy. If we have to accept that we're in a world where demons and monsters are a fact of life, then I suppose we need to be open to other possibilities. Prophecies come to mind. Mircalla and then Veronica. What is it exactly that they are talking about?"

Grey sighed and turned away. "It's nothing. Ghost stories and bullshit. Let it go."

"Really?" Looks Away said, stretching the word out. "A vampire-witch and a ghost take the time to make cryptic pronouncements about you and I'm supposed to dismiss it out of hand? Sorry, old chap, but we've come too far together for that to be possible anymore. The woman I loved was killed. The woman you seem to be falling for was very nearly killed. We're preparing to go into battle against a necromancer who can raise the dead and arm them with the world's most advanced weaponry. You—or perhaps your 'destiny'—seems to be tied to all this. So, no, I will not let it go. Bollocks to that. There's not one chance in ten trillion that I am going to let it go."

"We don't have time for—."

The Sioux scientist leaned back against the closed door. "Make time."

Grey sighed and sat back down. For nearly a full minute he said nothing, but instead stared mutely at his callused hands, watching his fingers knot and unknot. Finally he sighed out the ball of tension that had formed in his chest.

"It was the Battle of Ballard Creek. No, don't worry, you won't have heard of it. No one has. It wasn't what historians would call an 'important' battle. It wasn't even an important massacre." Grey shook his head. "Except to me. It's real damn important to me. You see I was leading a platoon of Union soldiers on a reconnaissance mission in Mississippi. We'd had intelligence reports that Confederate troops were building some kind of super cannon. It was supposed to be able to fire shells twice as far as anything we had in the north. The brass in Washington were afraid that it was something that could change the course of the war. My platoon was one of a dozen that were sent to find the testing ground."

"Ah. I heard those rumors, too. It was a lie, as I understand."

"Sure. It was a deliberate leak. The CSA intelligence division leaked a dozen different versions of the story and then monitored who reacted and how. It was all a pretty sophisticated plan to identify double-agents in their own network and to ferret out our spies. They put a lot of scalps on the walls with it, too."

"So, what was Ballard Creek?"

"We were following one of the leads, but because of some local flooding we took a different route than the one I'd been ordered to take. That meant that we slipped past the ambush that was waiting for us without ever knowing we were stepping out of the trap."

"Lucky break," said Looks Away.

Grey gave a sour grunt. "That's what we all thought. The Rebs knew they'd missed one of the teams—my team—and they put a lot of men in the field looking for us. My commanding officer managed to get word to me and told me to get my platoon the hell out of there. Easier said than done, though. The wood and swamps were alive with search parties. So, I decided it was safer to go to ground. By that point in the war there were a lot of abandoned and burned out farms. We found one way back in the bayous and we moved in. We were very careful to hide all traces. Wiped out our footprints with leafy branches, ate everything cold so there was no cooking smoke. We did it all the right way. We hunkered down and waited. And waited. I sent scouts out every couple of days. Two came back, two didn't. When our supplies started getting low, I decided to see if I could finagle something. We were all in civilian clothes, and I can do as good a New Orleans accent as you'd want to

hear. So I went riding to a local town to buy some supplies. My men had enough food for two weeks, and I
hoped to be back with a wagonload of supplies in ten
days at the most. I wore an eye patch and kept one arm
in a sling, and I was able to spin a good story about being with one of the CSA divisions that had been nearly
wiped out a few years back. It was convincing enough
because there are a lot of wounded soldiers around and
I fit right in." He paused and sighed. "And that's when
things started going too well. I met a widow woman, a
beautiful young lady who was running the general store
in a small town near Ballard Creek. I had to play my
role, so I acted the part of a battle-weary officer. All
courtly manners. Understand, I needed to win her confidence because I wanted to buy supplies in bulk, and I
couldn't risk too many questions. She was such a lovely
person. Gentle and beautiful and sad. Her father and
two brothers had been killed in battle. Her husband had
died at Manassas, and their only child, a little girl,
had died of a fever. She was all alone in the world. Her
name was Annabelle Sampson."

"Ah. What happened?"

"Ah, what do you think happened? We became close.
We, um . . ."

"You fell in love with her?"

Grey sighed. "I don't think I realized until then how
lonely I was. There had been girls here and there, but
there was never time for anything that mattered. Nothing deep. And she'd lost so much . . ."

"I'm not judging you, Grey. I can't think of a more
perfect formula for love. Loss and hurt, loneliness and
an uncertain future. That's fertile ground for passion."

"It went deeper than passion, Looks. I loved her. Really. Like they talk about in books. You can mock but it
was real."

Looks Away's eyes were filled with ghosts. "I will never mock love, my friend. I may be many things, but a fool is not one of them."

"Thanks for that," said Grey.

"How did you lose her?"

"I lost her because I'm a goddamn fool," admitted Grey. "I stayed in town for every one of the ten days that I told my men it would take me to get the supplies and get back. On the eighth night with Annabelle I told her the truth. By then we were already living together. It was like that. Fast for both of us, but right for both of us."

Looks Away nodded.

"I expected her to be shocked, but she confessed that she knew it almost from the start. She said that there were little things. That was pretty damned disturbing, as you might expect, but Annabelle said that she was sure no one else knew or even suspected. Even so, it brought me to my senses. I realized that I was wasting time in that town when I had hungry soldiers waiting on me to get back. So that night we packed up her wagon and I set out at first light. I promised to come back for her as soon as I'd gotten my men out of the area. I swore to her that I'd be back."

Out in the yard he heard a dog barking. It was so normal a sound for a day and a place that would never be normal again.

"It all went wrong from there," said Grey. "I was still two miles from the abandoned farmhouse when I saw the smoke and heard the gunshots."

"God."

"I had my own horse trailing the wagon, and I left the supplies and rode hard for the farm. When I got there, though, the place was on fire and there had to be two hundred Confederate soldiers in the woods. My men were putting up a fight, but they had no chance. They even had a white flag hung out of the front window. A sheet tied to a musket. They were trying to surrender."

"Were they taken?"

"No," said Grey, "they were slaughtered. The soldiers kept firing and firing. I wanted to help them, but there were so many of them. I could hear my men screaming inside the house. Screaming and begging and praying to God. I heard them calling my name, too. Shouting it out and damning me. If I'd gotten back sooner I might have saved them. We might have gotten out and gotten away. Instead, I watched them die. I watched from some coward's hole in the ground and saw those soldiers drag the last of my men out and cut them to pieces. They heaped the bodies in the yard and some of the soldiers pissed on them. They didn't even bury the dead. They left them all to rot. And it's all my fault, because I didn't get back in time."

"No," said Looks Away. "If you'd gotten back sooner you'd have died with them."

"You don't know that. They were my men, damn it. They counted on me, relied on me. Instead of bringing them back the supplies they needed, I was dallying with a woman. I let what I wanted be more important than what they needed. That makes me a disgrace as an officer and a failure as a man. Don't try to tell me I'm wrong."

Silence washed back and forth between them.

"What about the woman?" asked Looks Away after a time. "What about Annabelle?"

Grey had a hard time answering that. "I . . . I . . . ah . . . God."

Looks Away came over and sat down on the bed next to him. He placed his hand on Grey's back. "She died?"

Grey nodded. "The people in town . . . they figured it out. With Union soldiers hiding out in the bayou and a stranger in town to buy supplies . . . they figured it out. I thought I was being so clever, but I was just a clumsy, arrogant fool."

"What happened?"

"They came for her the next day. They dragged her out of her house. A dozen men." He wiped at his eyes. "You know what they did. You know what men do."

They sat together as the sunlight burned through the windows and threw their shadows on the wall.

"I found her after. After . . ." Grey sniffed and hung his head. "Since then I've felt them. Following me. Hunting me."

"Who? The soldiers?"

"No—my soldiers. My men. And . . . Annabelle."

"*Following* you?"

"Haunting me. That's why I left. That's why I keep moving. They're always there on my backtrail. At first I thought it was just me being crazy, that I'd lost my mind when I found her that day. But then we met Mircalla."

"And Veronica."

"And Veronica."

"I read enough books about spirits and hauntings since then," said Grey. "I'm being followed by what they call 'vengeance ghosts.' They want revenge for what I did to them."

"Dear lord," breathed Looks Away. "But, wait, that's not all Veronica's spirit said to you, old chap. She said that 'not all who walk in shadows are evil.' That 'not all of the lonely spirits of the dead wish you harm.'"

"Don't ask me what she meant by that," said Grey bitterly. "I know that I'm doomed and probably damned. If I wasn't such a coward I'd have stopped and let them catch up to me."

"You're no coward, Grey."

"Really? Tell that to Annabelle and my men."

"You could be wrong about why they're following you."

"I'm not." Grey stood up. "Come on, Jenny and Doctor Saint are waiting for us. We have a war to fight."

"You don't have to fight," said Looks Away, glancing up at him. "You've done your part. You saved lives here in town. You saved Jenny a couple of times. Let that be enough."

"Meaning what?"

"If you're afraid of ghosts, old boy, then bugger off. Ride away. Put half a world between you and the dead. Go."

Grey picked up his gunbelt and strapped it on. "No," he said heavily. "I'm done running."

"But—."

"A man can only be afraid for so long," said Grey. "A man can only be ashamed so much and then he hits a point. I'm there. If it's my destiny to die and let my ghosts drag me down to hell, then so be it. If it helps them, if that's what will give them rest, then okay. I want them to rest. I can't be the cause of their pain anymore."

He crossed to the door and stood with his hand on the knob, then turned to Looks Away.

"We probably can't win this fight," he said quietly. "You know that, right?"

Looks Away sighed and nodded.

"But I promise you this . . . I won't die easy and I won't die alone. If we're all going to hell, then let's take as many of these bastards with us as possible."

The Sioux stood up. "Just remember that Deray is mine."

Grey smiled. "No promises."

"As long as he dies," said Looks Away.

"As long as he dies," agreed Grey.

They shook hands and went out to prepare for war.

Chapter 76

They all met in the barn Percival Saint used for a lab.

Grey was surprised to find that Brother Joe had joined Jenny and Saint, but not surprised to find that the monk was haranguing them about the possibility of violence.

"We need to find another way," implored the monk.

Doctor Saint wore a kindly smile and he patted Brother Joe's shoulder in a tolerant way. "I appreciate and even respect your compassion, my friend. I admire you for it, and believe me when I tell you that if there was any other way to resolve this, I would be the first to volunteer to lead a peace delegation. But Lord Deray is not a reasonable person. He is not offering or asking for terms. He is a conqueror. He is very possibly a madman. And he is, by any practical definition of the word, evil."

"Even so, we must practice tolerance and—."

"And what, padre?" asked Grey as he and Looks Away walked over to where the others stood around a big table. "And martyrdom? Sorry, but as noble as that seems when saints do it, none of us here are saints. And I don't recall a single case, even in the Bible, where martyrdom stopped a war from happening. Can't recall when it saved innocent lives."

"Jesus Christ gave his life for—."

"Let me stop you right there, padre," said Grey. "You can preach about turning the other cheek until you're blue in the face, but in this instance you are *not* preaching to the choir. We're going to war. We're here in this room to talk about going to war. We are going to talk about how we're going to try our absolute damnedest to kill Aleksander Deray. That's what we're going to do. If you don't want to hear that conversation, there's the door. If you want to help us, then by all means go and pray. We could use the help, although at the risk of getting another black mark on my soul, I got to tell you that I haven't seen much of what you'd call divine protection. Not feeling the love of God right now. So, either help us or hush up."

If Grey had slapped the monk he could not have shut him up more completely or put a deeper hurt into the man's eyes. Brother Joe backed away from Grey as if he was a leper, but the monk lingered at the doorway and drew the sign of the cross in the air between them. Whether it was a blessing or if he was warding off the darkness inside Grey was up for interpretation. The monk turned and banged the door shut behind him.

Grey turned to the others. "Anyone want to fry my grits for being too hard on him?"

"He's a good man," said Jenny, "but I was about a half step away from punching his lights out."

Saint nodded. "I quite like the fellow. Always have. But . . ." He shrugged and spread his hands. "We don't share the same views on what you might call a cosmological level."

"And I'm a red heathen," said Looks Away dryly. "He's been trying in vain to save my soul for years."

Grey stepped up to the table. It was covered with several machines, some of which he recognized as guns. Two Kingdom rifles and parts that looked like they might be assembled into a third. Near them was a pair of devices that were about the same weight and general shape as his Colt, but like the Kingdom guns, these weapons were made from a blend of metals—steel and silver, copper and bronze. The grips were the same smoky quartz they'd seen in quantity down in the cavern. The cylinder was encased in a metal shell that was studded with tiny garnets.

"Those look interesting," said Grey. "What are they?"

"Those," said Looks Away, "are Lazarus pistols."

"Ah," said Grey, bending over to peer at them. The weapons were beautifully made, with golden tracery along the sides and barrel.

"Pick one up," suggested Saint. "Feel the weight."

Grey did and immediately grunted in surprise. "It's light. I expected it to be heavier than a regular gun."

"The frame is made from a special alloy I developed with Mr. Nobel. Forty percent lighter than steel but eighty-two percent stronger. Dreadfully expensive, though, which makes it impractical as a building material. Ah well."

Grey moved the gun from hand to hand, then rolled the trigger guard around his finger. He generally did not do tricks with handguns, but he wanted to get a feel for the balance. The gun was a marvel. He removed his Colt and placed it on the table, then tried the Lazarus pistol in its place. It fit very well. It flowed as he moved it between his hands and then in and out of his holster. With the reduced weight he found he could draw much faster. He nodded, reversed the gun in his hand, and offered it handle first to Saint, but the scientist shook his head.

"You're the gunhand, Mr. Torrance. For now I think we're better served with it in your possession. Just a loan, mind you, I'll want it back."

Grey almost made a joke about Saint having to pry it from his cold, dead fingers, but that was too close to a prophecy. He merely nodded.

"Ammunition?"

"Ah," said Saint, "that's where I think Brother Joe's

providence may actually have smiled on us. The ghost rock you brought back from Mr. Chesterfield's house was of excellent quality. It's already been processed, which makes it far more pure than anything I've dug up myself. Given time, I can make several hundred rounds for the Lazarus pistols and perhaps two dozen for the Kingdom rifles."

"That's not a lot if we're about to have a war," said Jenny.

"It's what we have," said Saint. "And it uses about one-eighth of the ghost rock these gentlemen brought back. Would that they had left the gold and platinum behind and brought only the rock . . . but, oh well."

"Seemed like the thing to do at the time," said Looks Away. "We wanted to have something to use to convince the townsfolk that it was time to pull up stakes."

Saint shrugged that away. "Too late now anyway," he said.

"What about the rest of the ghost rock?" asked Grey. "Can't you make more bullets out of that?"

"I could, of course, but I have other plans for it," said the scientist. "I'll need a considerable amount of it for the Kingdom cannon. And if there's any left, I want to see about getting some of my other little toys ready for our guests."

"What other toys?" asked Jenny.

"Well," said Saint, "I have prototypes of plasma mines, seismic webs, the Celestial Choirbox, a few rattlesnake bombs and—."

"Stop," said Grey. "None of that makes sense."

"What are all those things?" asked Jenny.

"Oh, I'm sure it wouldn't make sense to you, my dear. It's all very technical." The little scientist chuckled. He seemed amused by how confused he was making them, and was clearly content to be the smartest man in the room. Even Looks Away seemed mildly at sea. Grey found that he did not entirely like Doctor Saint. Not that he thought the man was corrupt or untrustworthy—just a bit of a pompous ass.

Jenny reached for the second Lazarus pistol but Saint moved to block her hand. "Oh, don't touch that. It's not really a woman's weapon."

Grey expected Jenny to fry him for that comment, but instead she pushed his hand aside and picked up the pistol. She weighed it in her hand. "I'll bet I could do pretty well with this."

Saint looked alarmed, but Looks Away was amused. "I have no doubts at all."

Jenny held it with two hands and at arm's length, sighting along the barrel, then turned slowly, aiming at various targets in the room. When the barrel swung toward the scientist, Saint uttered a small cry and scuttled sideways. "Question is what should I shoot?"

"Miss Pearl, please," insisted Saint. "That's too much gun for a—."

"For a woman?" Jenny finished, then she repeated, almost move for move, the tricky gun handling Grey had done a minute ago. The weapon seemed to melt into liquid metal as it moved through her hands. Saint stared in frank astonishment. Jenny stopped the gun on a dime, the handle pointed toward the scientist. "You're right, Doc, maybe it's way too much gun for a woman."

"Okay, Jenny," said Grey mildly, taking the pistol from her and laying it on the table, "he gets the point."

"Dear lord," said Saint as he plucked a handkerchief from his pocket and mopped his brow. "I had no idea. How did you . . . ? I mean, where did you . . . ?"

"My father taught me," Jenny said darkly. "He believed that a woman should know how to defend herself."

"You don't say," murmured Looks Away dryly. He had clearly enjoyed the demonstration. He cleared his throat and turned to Grey. "You were closer than me when the worm blew up. You were unconscious almost the whole day. Are you sure you're up for a fight?"

"Yes, I damn well am," said Grey. "But there are four of us. Fancy weapons or not, that's not a lot to throw at Deray."

"We have more than that," said Looks Away. He removed a piece of paper from his pocket and spread it out on the table. "While you were, um, recovering, I asked dear Mrs. O'Malley to make some useful lists. We have sixty-two people able and willing to fight. That includes everyone we could pull in from the farms. Just about everyone has a gun and ammunition."

"I've seen some of those guns. Squirrel rifles and muzzle loaders."

"My pa had a bunch of guns from back when we had a real farm," said Jenny. "Seven good rifles and a dozen handguns."

"And the weapons we took from the undead," said Looks Away. "Another twenty-six guns—handguns and long-arms. A few of the farmers have shotguns."

"Doc," said Grey, "will your gadgets be enough to make up the difference?"

Saint pursed his lips. "I don't know. If I had another week, maybe two . . . I could do better."

"We may not have that time," said Grey.

"We don't," said Jenny with certainty. When Grey glanced up he saw that her expression had changed again. The cocksure smile was gone and in its place was a far more serious expression. It was not the first time he'd seen that shift. Something about it worried him. It made him wonder if these events were pushing her over some kind of mental edge. When she spoke, even her voice was slightly different. Softer. "Deray is coming," she said. "Make no mistake. He is coming for us all."

All three men looked at her, and from the expressions

on their faces it was clear they were as startled as he was by her change of mood.

"What . . . makes you so sure, Jenny?" asked Looks Away.

Her response was delayed as if she didn't hear at first. Then she walked over to the window and looked out into the empty barnyard. "He's coming," she repeated.

Then as if a shadow that had been blocking the sun moved off to another part of her internal sky, she straightened and turned, and her devilish smile was back. "And let the bastard come, too."

No one spoke for a moment. Looks Away cleared his throat.

Grey nodded and walked over to study the big map on the wall. Every detail of the landscape was carefully marked in Saint's careful hand.

"We are substantially short on manpower, firepower, and resources," said Doctor Saint. "If we are going to survive this, we need a plan."

"All right," said Grey without turning. "Let's make one."

"You have something in mind, old boy?" asked Looks Away.

Grey turned. "Yeah, I do. It's risky, it's crazy, it'll probably get us all killed, and I can guarantee you're not going to like it."

"Now there's a sales pitch for you," said the Sioux.

"Tell us," said Jenny.

He did.

It was risky and crazy. And they didn't like it.

But they all agreed that it was their best—and perhaps *only*—chance.

Chapter 77

They worked all through the last hours of that day and into the night. Jenny got the blacksmith and a tinker to act as apprentices to Doctor Saint, while Looks Away and Grey oversaw the building of barriers and defenses.

At one point, well after midnight, as Grey was directing men to stack flour sacks filled with sand along the road into town, Looks Away asked, "You're sure this Deray will come to us?"

"Yeah," said Grey. "We killed his worm."

"That's hardly enough. It's unlikely he's all that sentimental about his pets."

"Of course not, but think about it. You think it was just coincidence that Lucky Bob and that worm were waiting for us? Deray had to have found out that we were down there. Hell, we left enough corpses behind. Those big lizard birds—."

"Pteranodons."

"Whatever. That cat with the big fangs."

"Smilodon."

"And those chicken lizards."

"Velociraptors."

"Looks—I swear to God you are the most pedantic son of a bitch I ever met."

"Benefits of a classical education," said the Sioux.

They grinned at each other.

Grey hefted another sandbag and thumped it down

chest high on the barrier. "Besides, Lucky Bob may not be as dead as we'd like him to be. I kind of think he picked himself back up and scampered off to tell his master about Doctor Saint's big ol' cannon. So—do I think they're coming? Sure. I'm just surprised they're not here already."

Everyone worked until they were ready to drop.

Grey finally staggered back to Jenny's place in the black hour before dawn. He washed in the kitchen washtub and shambled off to find the couch. However there was no blanket or pillow. Instead there was a folded piece of paper lying on the center of the cushion. He picked it up, opened it, and read the single word written in a flowing feminine hand.

Upstairs

Grey smiled and put the note into his shirt pocket.

Then, still smiling, he climbed the stairs.

Her door was ajar and the soft yellow glow of a single candle showed him the way. He went inside very quietly.

Jenny stood with her back to him, looking out at the last of the night's stars. The pale silver light shone through her nightgown, revealing curves and planes and ripeness.

"Jenny—?" he said quietly, but she shook her head.

"The night is almost over," she murmured. Her voice was so soft, so distant. Cold and sad and filled with pain.

Unsure of what to do, Grey stood there, not fully inside the room.

"Grey—?" she murmured. "If I ask you something, will you tell me the truth?"

"Yes," he said immediately, and he found that he meant it even though there were things he never wanted to talk about.

"Annabelle," she said.

"Yes."

"Do you still love her?"

He closed his eyes and swallowed. "Yes."

She nodded and turned slightly so that her profile was etched in silver fire. "You're a good man for admitting that," she said. "She was lucky to have you."

"She died because I wasn't good enough as a man."

He thought he saw her mouth curl softly. A ghost of a ghost of a smile. Then she reached up and unfastened her gown and let it fall. It drifted like snow around her ankles.

"Jenny," he began, "you should—."

"No," she said in a whisper. "No more words. I'm so cold. Make me warm."

And he came to her and carried her to the bed. Around them the night was vast and tomorrow was a threat. But he held her close and for a while—just a while—the night and all its terrors went away.

Chapter 78

Morning dawned cold and bright, but there were storm clouds on the horizon. To Grey it looked like the gods of war were sending a message that lacked all subtlety. The distant thunderheads were thick and bruise-colored and far above them dark birds drifted in slow circles. They might have been vultures but Grey had his doubts. They could have been pterosaurs, which meant Deray was definitely coming.

Grey stood on Jenny's porch, watching the birds and the clouds and trying not to be afraid of what was coming. He wore two gun belts strapped low across his lean hips. His Colt was on his left side with the handle reversed so he could snatch it with a fast cross-draw; and on his right hip was the Lazarus pistol. It was fully loaded with a ten-shot barrel magazine, and extra magazines were clipped to the belt. Grey felt awkward carrying the thing because it neither looked nor felt like a real gun, but if it was anything like the Kingdom rifle, then looks were truly deceiving.

The door opened and Looks Away came out holding two steaming cups of coffee. He handed one to Grey and they stood for a moment looking out at the clouds. It was going to turn dark soon and Grey hoped they'd all live to see the bright sunshine again.

"An east wind is coming," observed Looks Away, intruding into Grey's morose thoughts as the Sioux nodded toward the storm. "Poetic, if a trifle obvious."

Grey answered with a sour grunt.

"You're certainly cheerful," said Looks Away. "Not enough sleep?"

"We should have packed all these people up and gotten the hell out of here while we had the chance."

"If you want to play that game, old chap, then I should have stayed in London. There's far less ghost rock over there and, last time I checked, no living-dead dinosaurs or metal giants and only one quite foul necromancer that I know of. But, alas, I'm not in sodding England and we didn't sodding well leave town, so . . ."

"Just saying," muttered Grey.

They sipped their coffee.

"How do you think they'll come at us?" asked Looks Away.

"He'll have to bring his main forces across the bridge. But he has that airship, and those flying reptiles and maybe more of those worms, so he could come at us from a lot of different directions." Grey sucked a tooth. "I'm betting it'll be the bridge, though."

"Betting or hoping?"

Grey shrugged.

Inside the house they heard a sound that made them both turn. It was a lovely voice lifted in song. Jenny Pearl, singing a sad old ballad.

"'She Moved through the Fair,'" murmured the Sioux.

"Don't know it."

"It's about a man whose love is murdered before their wedding, then comes to him as a ghost on what would have been their wedding night. It's as morose a tune as any I've heard. You're a sourpuss this morning, so it should suit you."

Grey sipped the coffee and didn't comment. Last night had been so strange. Jenny had been so passionate, so intense, but after their brief exchange of words she hadn't spoken at all. Not even in the heat of climax, and not at all this morning. Now she sang tragic songs as the drums of war rumbled behind storm clouds.

"Hello the house!" called a voice and they turned to see Doctor Saint come hurrying up the side street. He wore another tweed suit—this one charcoal, perhaps in keeping with the mood of the day—and a top hat that looked freshly waxed and polished. Beneath his coat he had a gun belt strapped to his thick waist and the weapon in the holster was another of his odd copper-and-silver handguns, though this was a design Grey hadn't seen the night before. Behind him was a pair of strong young lads pushing a wooden cart with a canvas tarp tied down over its bulging contents. Another pair of boys pushed a second cart, equally laden. Doctor Saint directed them to position the carts in front of the porch steps.

Grey looked past the scientist to see that most of the townsfolk were heading their way. They were grim-faced and stern, though there was as much fear in their eyes as determination. Scared as they were, they wanted to make a fight of it. This was their town and Deray had already hurt them badly. Each of them carried a weapon of some kind—firearms and axes and a variety of farm tools.

Not enough, thought Grey. *It's not going to be nearly enough.*

Brother Joe was with them, his Bible clutched to his chest, eyes filled with anticipated pain. Grey set his cup on the rail and extended his hand as Saint joined him on the porch. The inventor nodded at the Lazarus pistol on Grey's hip.

"Are you sure you're comfortable using that, son?" he asked.

Grey shrugged. "Guess we'll find out."

"Oh dear me, yes," agreed Looks Away, "we will certainly find that out. Deray is not coming for tea and scones."

"Fine day for it, though," said the scientist with unexpected cheerfulness. A cold, damp wind was blowing through the town, sweeping up dried leaves and pieces of old newspaper.

"Is it?" asked Looks Away.

"It is indeed," said Saint. He moistened a finger and held it up, then nodded to himself. "The storm is in the east but the wind is coming in from the ocean. That's good, my boys, that's very good."

"In what way, exactly?" asked Grey.

"I'm delighted that you asked." The scientist chuckled as if this was all great fun. He turned and jogged back to the steps, crossed to one of the two carts and began untying the ropes that held the tarp in place. Grey leaned close to Looks Away.

"Does he actually have a plan, or is he just crazy as a barn owl?"

The Sioux frowned. "I'll give you even odds either way."

Saint called out to them as he held the corner of the tarp in one small, brown hand. When he spoke, he pitched his voice loud enough for the crowd to hear.

"You all know what's coming," he said. "You've been told about Aleksander Deray and his machines. You've seen the walking dead. You know that we are facing an army of considerable size and power."

The crowd stared at him in silent anticipation. The fear was now etched far more heavily on their faces than a moment ago.

Grey murmured, "Jesus. Some opener to a rousing call to arms."

Looks Away said, "I suppose it's better than 'we who are about to die salute you.'"

"Not much."

The scientist did not hear this quiet exchange. Still smiling, he pointed to the sky above them all. "This is the modern age. We are already taking the first steps out of the darkness of the nineteenth century and into the world of wonder that is the twentieth." He paused for effect, though Grey was certain that no one in the crowd was enthused by the march of scientific progress. "Thousands of years ago wars were fought hand to hand. Then the sword was invented, and those who wielded them triumphed over those who used clubs or fists. Then came the bow and arrow, then the crossbow, the cannon, the rifle. With each advancement in the science of warfare we see that the wise, the evolved triumph over the brutish. Not even the strongest and most skilled swordsman in the world can stand against a bullet, even if that bullet is fired from a gun in the hands of a weak man, a woman, or even a child."

The crowd was listening now, and their eyes flicked now and again to whatever was under the tarps. Even Grey found himself interested.

"Aleksander Deray has his weapons," continued Saint, "and I will grant you that they are formidable. In any ordinary battle he would sweep through a town like ours with impunity, with arrogance, and with certain knowledge of his superiority."

"Wait for it," said Looks Away, leaning forward over the rail, eyes alight.

"But what he does not know, my friends," said Saint, "is that Paradise Falls is not his for the taking. We are not debris to be swept aside. We are not inconveniences to be disposed of. Oh no, that is not the case. I submit to you that we are not to be dismissed so readily. When Deray's minions bring their war to us, it is war they will find. We will not fall. I tell you now that when the storm breaks upon us, Deray will find that Paradise rises!"

With that he whipped back the tarp to reveal a cargo of hundreds of brightly colored rubber balloons. Each was filled with gas, and as the tarp fell away, they stirred and lifted and rose quickly into the air. Reds and blues, greens and yellows, oranges and purples and a few that were as white as snow. They drifted upward and were caught by the freshening breeze, then scattered and blown high above the town.

The crowd gasped at first, and here and there were small cheers. But these faded as the people understood what they were seeing. The big reveal, the scientist's secret weapon, were mere balloons.

One by one the looks of wonder changed to confusion and then to doubt. Finally they lowered their heads and glared at the scientist.

"That's it?" cried Mrs. O'Malley. "That's our secret weapon? Land's sakes, Doctor Saint, you're as mad as the moon. I do believe you've killed us all."

The crowd became angry and hard words filled the air.

"Oh boy," said Grey, and when he glanced at his friend he saw only confusion and embarrassment on the Sioux's face.

"No! No, wait," yelled Saint, holding his hands up, "you don't understand . . ."

"We're all gonna die," said one of the farmers, throwing down his pitch fork. "Lord a'mighty we're gonna die."

The crowd surged around Saint, yelling at him, cursing him to hell, calling him names. Mothers pulled their children to them and wept openly. And all the time the doctor tried to calm them, tried to explain.

"I'd better do something," said Looks Away as he leaped from the porch and waded through the crowd. He grabbed Saint by the shoulder and half pulled, half carried him through the press and pushed him roughly up onto the porch. Some of the people swung at the scientist, needing to hit something in order to vent their frustration.

"No!" pleaded Saint. "You must listen. You must!"

"Get him inside," warned Grey as he shifted to block the stairs. He pushed a few people back, and though they were angry, he was bigger and stronger.

Finally Saint tore free of Looks Away, shoved the Sioux away from him, whipped the strange pistol from its holster, and wheeled on the crowd. "Shut up!" he roared.

Grey had his hand on his Colt in an instant. "Whoa! Whoa now, Doc."

"No," snapped Saint, "I want you and everyone to listen to me."

The crowd fell into an uneasy silence, everyone casting glances at the gun clutched in Doctor Saint's hand.

"Now you people listen to me," he growled. "I bring you hope and you turn on me? You ungrateful—."

"Careful now, Doc," warned Grey. "If you have something to say, then say it."

Doctor Saint gave him a withering stare, but then nodded. Holding the gun in his right hand, he dug something out of one of the voluminous pockets of his topcoat. He held out his hand to show a small metal box not much larger than a pack of playing cards. It was gold and had a black dial mounted on the top and several buttons along the side. He turned the dial with his thumb and then pressed a button. Nothing appeared to happen, but then a shadow moved across his face and everyone looked up to see one of the balloons—a bright blue one—come drifting back down. It stopped ten feet above the scientist and despite the wind it did not blow away. That's when Grey saw that there was a tiny box attached to its base, and on the box were two sets of little blades that spun like windmills during a hurricane.

"Do you fools think I came out here to play with children's toys?" said Saint, and the scolding tone in his voice was reflected in the looks of doubt that now clouded the faces of the crowd. "I'm not a toymaker . . .

I am a maker of weapons, and these are something I designed for warfare. Modern warfare. Behold the Little Disaster. Do you even know what that word means? Disaster? It's a Greek word that means 'bad star.' A pejorative, I'll admit, but in this case the ill fortune it carries is meant for our enemies. Watch and learn what I have made for you, for this fight."

With another turn of the dial, Saint made the balloon move away. It rose to the very top of the house and then wafted over toward an old cottonwood tree that had died from lack of water. The Disaster entered the network of withered branches and then stopped again. Grey could not guess what the little maniac was up to with all this.

Then Doctor Saint raised the control box and pushed a different button.

Bang!

The balloon exploded into a fireball of painfully intense blue-white light. Electricity writhed like snakes in the air. The tree flew apart, showering the crowd and the street and everything around it with splinters that burned to ash before they landed. The shock wave knocked fifty people flat on their backs and broke the windows of every house for half a block.

Grey and Looks Away were plucked off their feet and slammed against the side of the house, and even Saint was sent sprawling. The echo of that blast knocked all other sound out of the world and left the entire crowd dazed.

It took a long time for Grey to make sense of who he was and what had happened. The blast had been that intense. He sat down hard with his back to the wall, legs splayed, mouth opening and closing, eyes blinking, ears ringing.

He watched Doctor Saint get back to his feet. The little scientist was chuckling even though he had a small cut over his eye that ran with blood. Beyond him, fixed hard against the storm clouds, the other balloons seemed frozen into the moment.

Disasters, waiting to happen.

One by one the townspeople climbed back to their feet. Shocked and wide-eyed, they picked up their weapons and stared with a mix of shock and wonder at Doctor Saint.

"Lord a'mighty," repeated the farmer who had been complaining a minute before.

The scientist held the control box out. "I have spent many years attempting to rediscover the secret of Greek fire—that most elusive of the weapons of war. The incendiary that struck terror into the hearts of anyone who dared attack the Byzantine Empire. I have long suspected that the ancient Greeks found some substance similar to ghost rock and employed it as a weapon of war. I have done the same. Each of my Little Disasters is filled with ghost rock fumes and balanced with other chemical combinations of my own devising. I made fifty of them," he said, then with asperity added, "It is unfortunate that you made me waste one to prove that you should trust what I say. Let's all hope we won't have needed that last one."

As if in response to those words, thunder boomed on the edge of town. Lightning forked the sky, silhouetting the ugly shapes of flying creatures that were larger and more terrible than any birds. Legions of them were coming. And behind them, a ship rose in the east, seeming to come from nowhere, rising up between the peaks of two broken mountains. It was like a frigate from a painting of old pirates, with a deep keel and a fanlike rudder. Instead of sails, a vast envelope of silk and canvas, distended with gas and painted with the hideous face of Medusa the Gorgon. A thousand serpents writhed around her image.

On the plains below the ship, a line of machines rolled on clanking metal treads. And lines of armed men marched in squadrons, each of them carrying a strange rifle. Grey could not tell if Deray was supported by the foreign generals or if these were his own men. Not that it mattered—there were hundreds of them. Scores of living men, and hundreds upon hundreds of the walking dead. All of the corpses they'd seen heaped in the train cars. Soldiers from all over the divided country, including dead Sioux. Behind the column of tanks strode the metal giant, Samson, legs sweeping, arms swinging, lightning striking fire from its chest.

Grey got to his feet and turned to see the looks on the faces of the people of Paradise Falls. Even with the remaining Little Disasters hanging in the sky, even with the promise of the Lazarus pistols and Kingdom guns. Even with their own determination, they were few and marching toward them was an army the likes of which had never before been seen on Mother Earth. An army of science and magic, an army of flesh and steel, an army of the living and the dead.

"By the Queen's . . . ," began Looks Away, but words failed him and he simply stared.

"Good God," whispered Grey. He glanced around at his friends, at the town, and then at the approaching army. This was going to be a slaughter. Everyone knew it. Jenny Pearl came out onto the porch and stood next to Grey. She slipped her cool hand into his and interlaced their fingers.

"Don't worry," she said softly. So softly that only he could hear her. "Death isn't the end."

The storm growled and the winds howled with the voices of the damned.

Chapter 79

Grey forced himself to shake off his shock and despair. He let go of Jenny's hand and slapped his hand hard on the rail. It sounded like a gunshot and people jumped.

"They're coming," he barked. "You see it, I see it, we all do. They're coming. This is happening. You wanted to stay here and make a fight of it. Then by God that's what we're going to do. As of now, you've all seen what we're facing. You're shocked. Okay." He paused and in a harsh, cold voice said, "Now get over it."

The crowd stared at him.

"We know what they have to throw against us," he continued. "They don't know what we have. Doctor Saint's gadgets. Our unity. The fortifications. And . . . something else I have cooked up. We're done being helpless. This is a war, God damn it, so let's stop gaping and go fight it."

It wasn't a great speech, Grey knew that, but it broke the spell. He saw eyes harden and jaws grow firm. He would like to have seen heroic resolve and confidence, but that was too much to ask. Too much. People began moving away. First walking and then running to take up their positions. Finally the whole crowd scattered like leaves. Some few were even laughing with some strange kind of mad battle glee as they ran off.

Jenny and Looks Away came down to stand with Grey; and after a moment, so did Doctor Saint.

"Well," said Looks Away, "that wasn't Henry at Agincourt, but it got them moving."

"Going to be a long day," said Doctor Saint. He cut a look at the others. "Should be fun, though."

"Fun?" echoed Jenny.

"Sure. This is how history is made. A bold few standing against many."

"We happy few," said Looks Away. "We band of brothers. Let's just hope its closer to Henry V than to Leonidas at the Hot Gates."

He tipped an imaginary hat to Jenny, punched Grey lightly on the arm, nodded to Saint, then walked off to take up his post.

"Once more into the breach," said Saint, still smiling. He nodded to the waiting boys to bring his second wagon. They headed off toward one of the sandbag barriers. The cloud of brightly colored Little Disasters followed in their wake.

That left Jenny and Grey standing alone for a moment. He wanted to say something to her. The atmosphere of the day seemed to require it, but no poetic words occurred to him. Not even lines from Shakespeare. Instead he took her in his arms and kissed her. It was a long, slow, sweet kiss.

"Jenny, I—," he began, but she stopped his words with a second kiss.

"Whatever you have to say," she murmured, "tell me after this is all over."

"What if there's no chance to tell you? What if—?"

"No," she said. "Find me and tell me. No matter what happens, I'll be waiting for you."

She released him, picked up the gun belt that lay on the porch rocker, examined the Lazarus pistol, snugged it back into its holster, nodded to herself, and strapped it on. She paused for a moment, looking back at him with those blue eyes.

Thunder rumbled again and a cold rain began to fall.

"Be careful," he said.

Jenny nodded slowly. The rain looked like tears on her cheeks.

"It's been a long, strange road since Ballard Creek," she said, and her words stabbed him.

"How did you—? Oh . . . you talked to Looks Away, didn't you?"

"War is a hungry, hungry monster, Grey. It feeds on life and love."

With that she turned away and walked into the swirling rain, leaving Grey standing there. He was more profoundly confused than he had ever been.

"This is all a goddamn nightmare," he told the storm. The cry of a pteranodon far above him seemed to agree.

"Madness," said Grey as he drew his gun and went to find someone or something to kill.

Chapter 80

Grey took up position at the main barrier on the desert side of town. He had forty of the town's hardiest fighters with him, and a solid wall of sandbags. Less able townsfolk huddled behind the row of shooters, ready with ammunition, water, and bandages. The women among them also carried knives hidden in their skirts. It would be up to them to cut the throats of any enemy wounded. Taking prisoners was not part of the plan.

Brother Joe and a few of his most devoted followers—those whose beliefs would not permit them to fight—were ready to tend the town's wounded.

Deray halted his advance a quarter mile beyond the edge of town. His troops stood in ordered lines, indifferent to the rain. The tanks formed in a half circle on the far side of Icarus Bridge. and Grey could see two small figures creeping along the structure, bent close to study it. Engineers, he judged, deciding if the bridge would bear the weight of the war machines.

Grey fetched his field glasses from Picky's saddlebag and studied the opposition. A closer look did nothing to increase his confidence. Grey searched the sky for Deray's sky frigate, and saw it fading like a ghost ship into the storm clouds. He caught one brief glimpse of the necromancer, standing at the forward rail of the airship with a heavy cloak pulled around him and a wide-brimmed hat to shield his eyes from the rain. Deray

raised a cup of coffee to his smiling mouth, then paused and raised his cup in mock salute. Although the distance was too great for Deray to see him, Grey swore that the man had directed that gesture directly to him.

And for some reason he could never thereafter explain to himself, Grey nodded and touched a finger to the brim of his hat.

Perhaps it was some kind of salute between enemies. Maybe it was two of the damned acknowledging each other from opposite sides of the Pit. Grey didn't know and suddenly there was no time to think about it.

With howls of predatory glee, the swarm of pteranodons came hurtling down from the clouds.

"Guns up!" bellowed Grey, and a line of rifles, muskets and shotguns rose toward the oncoming flock of monsters. "Kill the bastards!"

They fired, throwing their own thunder against the storm.

The pterosaurs were in full dive, spiking downward at full speed and there was no chance to avoid the volley. Three of them suddenly twisted in midair, blood bursting from chests and heads. They twisted artlessly into screaming deadfalls, slamming into others of their kind, bringing two more down.

The rest kept coming.

"Fire!" yelled Grey. He squeezed off a shot with the Lazarus pistol and the round struck one of the monsters and exploded with enough force to tear the wings from three others. The men at the barricade fired again, and those with repeating rifles got off a third round before the flying monsters crashed into them. The lead pteranodon opened its beak and with a snap took the head off of the man at the end of the barricade. It swept past his corpse as a jet of blood shot upward from a severed neck. Five others hit the line of fighters even as the guns fired, and there was a confusion of screams and blood and falling bodies.

The defenders panicked and scattered as more and more of the pterosaurs struck them. A few huddled down behind the sandbags, firing as quickly as they could. Grey fired shot after shot, and the Lazarus bullets detonated in balls of blue fire that burst flesh and vaporized bone. The pterosaurs flew apart into ragged chunks.

Seven of his people were down, leaving twenty to fight a remaining dozen of the flying reptiles. Panic was in full fury, though, and most of the people were unable to cope with the terror of what they were facing. Grey pushed off from the sandbag wall and waded among the melee. He fired and fired and fired. The blue explosions rocked the street, knocking the fighters onto their backs, bursting the sandbags, but doing worse damage to the monsters.

One pteranodon landed atop the makeshift barrier and stabbed at him with its beak, and when Grey twisted away, it grabbed his gun arm with the bony fingers that sprouted from its leathery wing. The grip was extraordinary and Grey cried out. The Lazarus pistol fell from his hand. With a cry of pain and anger, Grey used his left hand to tear his Bowie knife from its sheath and he slashed with the heavy blade, cutting through tendon and bone. Then he was free, the alien hand still locked around his wrist but no longer attached to the beast. The pterosaur screeched in pain as blood pumped from the wound. Grey slashed at it again, but it leaped into the air to evade the blade. However the leap turned into a tumble as the mangled wing buckled. The monster thumped down onto the dirt. Grey dove atop it, smashed the beak aside with a powerful blow with the side of his right fist, and slashed the thing across the throat with the knife. It gurgled as its scream of pain was drowned in a tide of blood.

Grey shook the dead hand from his wrist and then

dove to the ground as another pterosaur swooped low to try to decapitate him. He flattened out in the mud as the thing passed only inches above him. His Lazarus pistol was five feet away, lying on the wet ground as rain pounded on it. He wormed his way toward it, snatched it up, rolled over onto his back, and brought it up, all the time praying that water and mud would not do to it what they would to an ordinary pistol. The pterosaur swung around and dove at him again, and Grey fired, praying he wouldn't blow his own hand off.

Little red lights made the garnets pulse with light as the pistol bucked in his hand.

The pteranodon exploded above him, showering him with bloody debris.

He rolled sideways and got to his knees, spitting gore from his mouth.

Around him the fight was going badly. Only a dozen of his people were still fighting, and the last five of the pterosaurs were swirling and swooping. The animals were learning from the deaths of their fellows; they watched for the rise of barrels, then they wheeled in the air to avoid the shots.

"Defensive circle!" cried Grey, rising and firing at one of them. He missed as the monster tilted to let the storm wind shove it out of the way of the shot.

The people were too mad with fear to listen. Grey slammed the Bowie knife into its sheath and got to his feet, firing again and clipping a wing. Then he was among the survivors, yelling at them and shoving them toward the barricade.

"Huddle up! Guns out. Don't let them get behind you. Protect the man to your right. No, damn it, your *other* right. That's it. Fire. Fire."

Two of the pterosaurs fell as the men, now in a circle, fired at Grey's direction. The animals still darted out of the way, but Grey saw a way to use that. He waited for the volley to fire and then aimed his shot to the natural escape angle and as a pteranodon veered to avoid the bullets Grey destroyed it with the Lazarus handgun.

Again.

And again.

As each monster fell, the people at the barricade became more confident. Their aim improved, although some still shot wild and too soon. The next monster fell to a hail of bullets, and the last one, realizing that it was alone, attempted to fly between two buildings, but that was a mistake. Everyone fired.

Every bullet hit it and tore it to rags.

The men burst into cheers.

But Grey looked around. There had been twenty-seven fighters with him at the barricade, and now there were eleven.

Sixteen dead.

The cheers of the survivors died away as this truth sank like poison into their stomachs.

This was not a victory. It was a slaughter.

And all they had so far fought were Deray's monster pets. The army, the machines, the metal giant, and the undead still waited.

As Grey stared over the wall and across the Icarus Bridge he felt his heart sink.

We're all going to die here, he thought. And he believed it, too.

A voice—screaming his name—tore through the air, and he whirled and ran.

Chapter 81

The cry had come from Jenny. Terror and desperation mixed in equal parts.

Grey raced down the street toward the far end of town; back to the place where he had first met her. The well.

He saw her there. She was backing away from the well. Two of the townspeople lay sprawled and bloody in the rain, their bodies strangely swollen and discolored. Both corpses had deep punctures on their faces. Jenny had the Lazarus pistol in her hand, held out straight as she fired at something that came crawling over the edge. The thing was long and low, and as it moved the lightning flashed on each of its black, chitinous segments. A thousand hairy legs carried it up and over the lip of the well. Antennae whipped back and forth and a hundred tiny eyes gleamed like specks of polished coal. It was a centipede. Thirty feet long if it was an inch, and it flowed out of the depths and moved toward Jenny.

On the ground between it and Jenny were two more of its kind, their bodies blasted to fragments, steam rising as rain struck the exposed guts. Their pincers glistened with a purple venom. Another giant insect emerged from the well. And another.

"Grey!" screamed Jenny as she fired. Instead of a deafening blast, there was a hollow click. She cursed and squeezed the trigger again and again; each time yielded nothing but that empty and impotent noise. Then on her fourth pull the weapon fired. But it was already too late. The centipede was nearly upon her. Grey fired as he ran. Not a perfect shot, but it scored, and the insect was buffeted sideways as a yard-long section of its side erupted in flame. The blast threw Jenny backward, and Grey caught her with his free arm, steadying her.

"The damn gun doesn't work!" she snapped, squeezing the trigger again and getting only the empty click.

"Stay back," he warned, and pulled her clear as the injured centipede lashed at her. There was a barb on its tail as long and sharp as a pirate's cutlass. Grey crouched and steadied his gun for a careful shot and blew the monster's head off. It flopped backward, but immediately the other two crawled over it. Grey fired again and this time Jenny's gun fired, too. One of the creatures was killed outright, its head and first ten segments bursting into balls of blue fire. The second was mortally wounded and staggered off, half its legs crippled and many of its segments ruptured. Grey holstered his pistol, grabbed the heavy wooden bucket from beside the well, and swung it up and over and down onto the monster's head. The bucket shattered, but the impact smashed the centipede's head to bits of shell and green blood.

He turned to Jenny. "Are you okay?"

She looked past him and shuddered. "God, are those things *bugs*?"

"Looks and I saw their little brothers yesterday," said Grey, nodding. "These are even bigger."

"Are they undead, like the dinosaurs?"

"No. I think Deray used some hocus-pocus to drive them up here."

She shuddered. "This is what's living down in those caves?"

"This and worse," he answered, but was immediately sorry he said it. Her face, already pale, fell into sickness.

"We can't fight this," she said in a hushed whisper. "We can't win."

It was too close to what Grey had thought after the fight with the pterosaurs. It was probably true, but focusing on that would almost certainly guarantee their defeat. Believing in the possibility of victory, however unlikely, was the only way to keep despair from overwhelming them all.

"They're ugly bastards and they're scary," he said, "but they're alive and that means they can die like anything else."

"They die when your gun shoots," she snapped. "Mine keeps jamming."

"Take my Colt," he said, reaching for the gunbelt that was crossed under the Lazarus pistol belt. However Jenny shook her head.

"Maybe Doctor Saint can fix mine. In the meantime I'll get my shotgun. I trust that."

She ran off before he could say another word. Once again she seemed to have shifted inside her skin. The dreamy-eyed woman he'd made love to last night was not evident. This morning she had been thoughtful and enigmatic, now she was the fiery farm woman again.

Grey peered over the edge of the well and saw nothing but shadows down there. No other monsters came climbing out of the water, but that was hardly reassuring. Who knew how many more of them Deray had to send. A party of armed men was hurrying down the street, drawn to the commotion but too late to be of immediate use. When they saw the dead insects they slowed and then stopped to gape.

"You two," said Grey, gesturing to two men with big fowling pieces, "watch this damn well. If anything tries to crawl up you send it back to hell. Got it?"

They were scared, but they nodded and took up

stations on either side of the well, barrels laid on the edge and angled down.

A burst of thunder made Grey spin around and he saw bright blue fire swirling amid the storm winds. Not thunder, after all. No—it was one of Saint's balloon bombs. His Little Disasters. His bad stars filled with ghost rock smoke and his own version of Greek fire.

One of them had exploded above the sandbag barrier on the east side of town.

Grey took a breath, checked the rounds in his guns, and ran off that way.

Chapter 82

As he approached the eastern barrier, he saw that there was a real fight in progress, so he poured it on. The men along the sandbag wall were firing as flaming debris drifted down from the sky and dark shapes flitted and dodged all around. At first Grey thought that a swarm of birds, driven wild by the storm, had flocked in panic toward the waiting men. But that wasn't it at all.

Instead he saw that there were dozens of small things—not true birds but some kind of clockwork devices made to look like birds—swarming down from a dark cloud. Then he realized that it wasn't a cloud at all. With a sudden surge the great sky frigate smashed through the wall of clouds. Men lined the rails of the airship now, and they trained rifles down at the town and fired, fired, fired. The plunging fire was deadly and defender after defender went spinning backward from the wall, trailing lines of bright blood.

Grey expected to see gun ports open and cannons roll out, but either great guns were too heavy for the lighter-than-air craft, or Deray was saving them for later. Either way, it was rifle fire for now, and that was deadly enough.

More of the small mechanical birds swarmed over the rails and flew toward the defenders. Grey couldn't understand what their purpose was. They were too small to carry any useful amounts of explosive. Then, as the first wave of them approached, he saw something that chilled him to the bone. The birds darted high, then snapped down into steep diving attacks and as they fell their wings folded back, their tiny mouths gaped wide and slender steel needles thrust outward. Some dark chemical was smeared on each needle.

"'Ware!" cried Saint. "'Ware the birds. Don't let them—."

The birds slammed into the sandbags and into the men behind them. The needles stabbed through jackets and shirts and deep into muscle tissue. Men swatted at them, and one man even laughed as he plucked the tiny needle from the bulk of his massive shoulder.

A split second later the man cried out and staggered, his eyes going wide, mouth open, skin turning bright red. He took three clumsy steps backward and then fell onto his knees as blood erupted from eyes, ears, nose, and his open mouth. He flopped onto his face, his entire body shuddering.

Five others went down the same way, bleeding and convulsing.

Doctor Saint sent another of the Little Disasters up into the path of the second wave of birds and pressed the button. The explosion threw everyone flat and painted the sky and the landscape in azure light that was so bright it seemed to stab all the way into the mind. Grey flung an arm across his face to protect his eyes from the flaming debris. When he risked a look he saw that the sky was empty of the needle-birds. However, Deray's sharpshooters were preparing a fresh volley. Before Grey could shout a warning they fired, and bullets punched into many of the dazed survivors.

Grey drew his Lazarus pistol and returned fire, but the range was too long for a handgun to be of any use.

"Don't waste your ammunition," said Saint, waving him off.

"Then you do something, God damn it!"

"I am, dear boy," rasped the scientist, fiddling with the controls on his little metal box. Two more of the Little Disasters came hurrying out of the rain and soared upward. The gunfire above changed as Deray ordered his men to target the balloons. The doctor's bombs were forty feet away when the first one popped as bullets pierced it. The mechanism and its explosives dropped harmlessly down into a puddle of rainwater. The second was nicked and gas began hissing out of it, but the impellor motor kept pushing it upward.

"*Do it now!*" cried Grey, and Saint pressed the button.

The Little Disaster was still twenty feet from the side of the frigate, but the blast swept the rail with brilliant blue fire. Men screamed and fell back, some of them ablaze, others beating at flames on their coats. How the chemicals Saint devised were able to burn in the wind and rain was beyond Grey, but it worked. The only thing that mattered was that it worked.

Deray, unharmed but furious, roared to his pilot and pointed wildly toward the south. Clearly he did not want to face those bombs.

"He's running," said one of the wounded men at the barrier.

"I think his balloon is filled with hydrogen," said Saint. "Mmm. Stupid choice. Highly flammable."

"Hit 'em again," Grey pleaded. "See if you can blow that bastard out of the sky. Maybe his troops will give it up if he's dead."

"Worth a try, my boy, worth a try." He sent two more of the balloons after the ship. The frigate was turning, though, moving quickly away to try and find shelter within the darkness of the storm clouds. Grey heard Saint muttering, "Come on . . . come on . . ."

The frigate slipped into the cloud bank seconds ahead of the Little Disaster.

"I can't see it," complained Saint. "Damn it."

"Blow it anyway," snapped Grey. "Don't let it get away."

The scientist pressed the button and the entire cloud bank seemed to transform into a burning sapphire. Incandescent blue light lit the clouds from within, and Grey watched in awe as ghostly lightning throbbed like veins across the flesh of the storm. Then it was gone and the clouds roiled with black fury. The wind intensified and rain fell in sheets, hammering the town. The survivors at the barrier gasped for air in the downpour. Some sat and wept, holding their dead friends in their arms, or clutching wounds whose redness seemed to be the only color left in the world.

A smiling Saint slapped Grey on the shoulder. "I think we got him."

But Grey was far less certain about that and said as much to Saint. He watched the smile drain away from the man's dark face.

"At least we've hurt him," he said.

"Hurt him maybe," said Grey grudgingly, "but mostly I think we've helped him get a good damn idea of how tough we aren't."

"What do you mean?"

"Think about it. He's hit us three times now with half-assed attacks," he said, and briefly explained about the other two attempts: the pterosaurs and the centipedes.

"None of these are full-bore."

"You think he's testing our defenses?" asked the scientist.

"Don't you?"

"Sadly, I do," agreed the scientist. "Which begs the question of where and when he will launch his full assault."

"It almost doesn't matter. If he's been paying attention, he's got to see that even though we have some muscle—thanks to your gadgets—we don't have the numbers to play this out. He can either keep chipping away at us, or he can hit us with a tidal wave and just wipe us all the hell off the board."

"At the bridge, you mean?"

"Of course. It's the only way to move big enough numbers into the town."

Brother Joe and his assistants came running to help with the wounded. Grey and Saint ran off to check the various barriers. They found Jenny at the southern barrier closest to the Icarus Bridge. Beyond the bridge the tanks were rumbling slowly forward, though none of them had yet rolled onto the bridge itself. Above them, the sky frigate hung like a promise.

"Ah . . . damn the man," muttered Saint. "I thought I had him."

"You hurt him, though," said Grey, pointing.

It was true. Although the frigate still floated above the army, the airship had clearly failed to escape the Little Disaster Saint had sent into the clouds. It had a visible list to port, and all along the starboard side the rail and decking had been blasted away. The gaping damage exposed the gears of complex machinery inside. Oily black smoke drifted from the ports and mingled with the dark clouds, and there were long streaks of red running down the sides of the shattered wood. Even though Deray had escaped destruction, he had paid with the blood of his men.

He wondered if the necromancer even counted that cost or if the lives of his own people meant as little to him as the lives of the people here in Paradise Falls.

Probably.

He wished he could get up close to the man and look him in the eye. He had met killers, criminals, and bad men before, but he had never looked into the eyes of someone who was willing to spill an ocean of blood to achieve his own goals. He had never faced down a would-be conqueror. And he dearly wanted to have that confrontation with Deray. He wanted to ask him by what right he made war on his fellow men. By what right did he cultivate war on a global scale. By what right did he set himself above all laws and all codes of ethics and morality.

He wanted those answers and then he wanted to put a hot bullet into that cold heart.

Chapter 83

They're coming!"

The cry went up from the barrier and blazed like wildfire through the town.

Grey and Saint ran to the sandbag wall and stared at the line of undead troops that had begun to pass between the gates of the Icarus Bridge. The first undead soldier to step onto the bridge did so tentatively. He tugged on the ropes, jerking hard to see if they'd part before he put his weight on the boards.

The ropes held.

"Come on you bastard," murmured Grey. "Come on."

The corpse turned and waved to his companions and Grey saw him give a thumbs up. Then the soldier turned back and put a foot on the first of the boards. It was too far away for Grey to hear the wood creak, but he remembered the sound and could imagine it now. Old wood that complained under any burden. The undead held onto the ropes as he eased his weight onto one foot and then both. Above him, Aleksander Deray leaned over the damaged rail of his ship and growled at the dead men. Grey couldn't hear the words but it did not appear as if the necromancer was offering compassion and support. His face seemed as filled with storms as the sky above him.

The dead man took another step. And another. The bridge swayed but the boards held. The ropes held.

The bridge held. When he was halfway across the gorge, the undead stopped and actually jumped up and down on the bridge, testing its integrity and strength.

Can they feel fear, Grey wondered. If so, why? It couldn't be anything to do with physical pain, their bodies were stolen. And it certainly couldn't be concerns about their mortality because they were demons. If their bodies died they'd simply go back to hell.

Was it a fear of torment in the Pit? Grey doubted it. More likely, he mused, it was a red delight in all of the terrible things they could do with those stolen bodies. If they were as evil as Brother Joe said, then they would crave pain and slaughter the way an opium eater craved the pipe. An addiction of malice. His gut told him that he'd hit on it.

But that meant that he could not bargain with them. Could not really threaten them. It would be like trying to reason with a swarm of locusts or a raging forest fire.

The corpse turned and waved. First to Deray and then to the other undead. He yelled so loud that his words drifted all the way through the wind and rain to Grey.

"It's safe! The fools have cut their own throats. Come, my brothers! Come!"

And they came.

With a howl like a pack of hellish jackals, the grinning horde drew their guns and raced forward onto the bridge. Hundreds of them. Staggering corpses whose gray and rotted flesh were a horror to behold, and they sent up a continuous moan of unbearable hunger as they stumbled forward, hands reaching toward the promise of warm human flesh. Behind the legions of the dead were the living soldiers in the employ of the mad conqueror. Deray's men wore uniforms of gray and black and purple, and each carried a rifle made from copper and steel and set with burning jewels. Across the Icarus Bridge came the armies of the underworld. Across the chasm, far above the thrashing water, came the exterminators who would slaughter and consume.

Behind the sandbag barrier, the defenders of Paradise Falls crouched with wild eyes and sweating hands gripping their meager weapons.

"God," cried one of the men at the barrier. "Look how many there are."

Grey heard weeping among the gathered fighters behind the sandbags.

"They're almost across!" shouted someone else. And it was true, the army of the damned were three quarters of the way across the creaking bridge. With every step they moved faster as their careful walk gave way to a fast walk and finally, with a howl that shook the skies, a full-out run.

The chasm was two hundred and seven feet wide. That's what Jenny and Looks Away told Grey. The bridge was made of wooden slats and miles of rope. It swayed under the weight of hundreds of running feet.

"Guess it's time," said Grey. "Be ready."

He placed two hands on the sandbag wall and swung his body over, landed with a *thump* on the hard-packed dirt, and then jogged down the slope to the mouth of the ridge, reaching it while the undead were still a dozen yards away. He stood between the bridge posts and raised both his hands. The racing dead suddenly slowed, and as the leading edge of the charge stopped, the others collided with them. In the air the sky frigate turned hard aport to give Deray a better look as Grey stood in a posture of obvious surrender.

The oncoming tide of killers stopped, but three hundred gun barrels swung toward him, and then—as Grey had hoped—a tall figure pushed through the crowd, shoving the other walking dead aside as he moved to the front of the army. Grey felt his heart sink. He knew the clothes, that hat, the guns, that face. Lucky Bob Pearl came smiling to within twenty feet of where Grey waited.

"You are one persistent fellow," said the Harrowed.

"Been called that," admitted Grey.

"And you're a right pain in my ass."

"Been called that, too. And worse."

"I have no doubt."

"You're a bit persistent your ownself," said Grey. "Every time people think you're dead you pop right back up like a prairie dog."

"More like a bad penny, wouldn't you say?" suggested Lucky Bob.

"Fair enough."

"What's your name, son?"

"Grey Torrance, and I'm the sheriff 'round these parts."

"Really? Since when?"

Grey laughed. "I'm lying. I read that line in so many dime novels I just had to say it. Sounds just as stupid out loud, doesn't it?"

A smile flickered on the Harrowed's face. Behind him some of the others were smiling, too. Grey doubted they appreciated the little joke. No, their grins were in anticipation of slaughter and feasting.

"Kill 'im, brother," said one of them, but Lucky Bob shook his head.

"No," he said loud enough for them all to hear, "let's have the niceties. After all, these people used to be my friends. It's only neighborly to have a chat before we commence with the butchery."

Grey kept his smile on his face, but it felt like it was hammered there with rusty nails.

"So," said Lucky Bob as he took a casual step forward, "what's a couple of bad pennies like us doing here, Mr. Torrance?"

"Call me Grey."

"Fine. What's the game, Grey? You have your hands up like you want to surrender."

Grey lowered his arms slowly. "Not really. More of an attention-getter. Actually I wanted to have a chat."

"A chat, is it? You want to beg Lord Deray for mercy? Do you want to offer terms for your surrender? Do you want to lay at his feet and—."

"Actually, sport," said Grey, "I don't really have much to say to your lord and master that don't involve four-letter words. I got no use for him. I wouldn't buy water from him if I was on fire. I wouldn't waste water to spit on him."

Now no one on the bridge was smiling. A cold and dangerous light ignited in Lucky Bob's dark eyes. "You want to watch that mouth of yours, boy."

"Or what? You'll kill me? I kind of think you're already playing that card faceup on the table."

"There are worse things than death."

"Yeah," said Grey. "I know. I'm looking at that right now."

"I think I'll let the dead eat you last," said Lucky Bob. "After you've watched us kill every last person in town."

"Maybe that's how it'll work out," said Grey. "But before we get to that, I want to speak to you. To the manitou and to the human soul of Bob Pearl that I know is still in there. I want you both to hear what I say. Just you two. As for the rest . . . ? Well, you'd know better than me, but I'm pretty sure they're not the reasonable type."

"Not much, no." Lucky Bob cocked his head to one side. "But before you waste your last breath on an impassioned plea, son, understand that there's nothing you can say to make this easier on you. There's only one way this is going to end and we both know it."

"Maybe," said Grey. "And then again maybe not."

"Don't die a fool, boy. And don't embarrass yourself by begging for mercy."

"Nope, not about that. This isn't about you sparing me or the people here. You're going to try to kill us and maybe you will. Before you do, though, you need to know what you're going to risk. Not your troops, but you. The manitou inside and the man. You both need to hear this."

Above them a voice bellowed. "No!"

They looked up to see Deray grasping the shattered rail of the frigate. It descended through the rain and then stopped forty feet above the bridge. Close enough for a rifle shot, thought Grey. Tough height and angle for a pistol shot, especially in this weather. Might be worth trying, though. If he thought he could kill the man with absolute certainty, he might have gone for it. Even with all those guns pointed at him. It might end the war right here.

As if reading his mind, Deray barked an order. "Pearl—kill him now. He is nothing. His words are nothing but lies."

"My, my, my," said Grey. "He almost sounds scared. Makes me wonder if he's afraid of what I'm going to say."

Lucky Bob narrowed his eyes. For a moment the evil intensity of his expression wavered. He glanced up at Deray. "My lord," he said, placing his free hand over the ghost rock chunk buried in his chest, "give me a minute or two with this fool. He felt it was important to come out here like this, maybe he has something worth hearing."

Deray clearly did not like it, but he also clearly did not want to appear weak or nervous in front of his troops. He gave a terse wave of his hand. "Make it quick, then, and afterward bring me his head."

"That's the plan, my lord," said Lucky Bob. He turned,

thumbed the hammer back on his big pistol, and nodded to Grey. "Speak your piece."

"Okay, then here it is," said Grey, pitching his voice loud enough for them all to hear. "We know who and what you are, Bob. We know about the manitou inside you. We know that the manitou and the human being are wrestling each other for control. Right now it looks like the manitou has been winning hands down, but we both know that's not set in stone. It never will be. I never met Lucky Bob, but from what everybody's been telling me he was one tough son of a bitch. Brave, forthright, strong-willed, maybe even noble. He died trying to save this town. We know this."

Grey saw how his words hit the Harrowed. He licked his withered lips and said nothing.

Behind him the undead were growing impatient and kept looking past Lucky Bob to their prey hiding behind the sandbag barrier.

"And just as we know about you, Bob," continued Grey, "we know what will happen if you die."

"So what?" asked Lucky Bob. "You killed me already yesterday and here I stand, right as this rain." With his free hand he snatched a few raindrops out of the air and then flung the water at Grey.

"Yeah, well," said Grey, "that's because I didn't kill you the right way, did I?"

Lucky Bob said nothing.

"That's because I didn't put a bullet in your brain," said Grey. "Yeah, that's got your attention. If your brain is destroyed, it won't send you back to Hell. It'll destroy you for good and all. For all time. Forever." He pointed to the row of rifles that pointed from atop the sandbags. "Every man and woman in Paradise Falls knows that they can kill your immortal soul."

The silence was immense. Even Deray's yells had dwindled down to nothing.

"Now listen to me and listen to me good," said Grey. "We don't want to do that to you. Not even to you. Far as we're all concerned, you're a victim a couple of times over. First you were murdered. I suspect that Chesterfield's men gunned you down, didn't they, Lucky Bob?"

The Harrowed said nothing.

"Then Aleksander Deray put that ghost rock in your chest and he made you his slave. Maybe he invoked the manitou and sent it to take you over, or maybe he grabbed you once that happened. Don't know and don't really care. I'll bet the manitou inside of you isn't happy about being a slave to Deray. I know Lucky Bob Pearl isn't. That chunk of ghost rock in your chest is the same as having an iron collar around your neck. Magic or chains, it all comes out the same. As long as it's there, you'll never be free of Deray. You'll never be really alive. That means you traded one hell for another."

"His words are meaningless," yelled Deray. "Don't listen to him. Kill him. I command you!"

"You're talking a lot, boy," said Lucky Bob, "but are you getting anywhere with this?"

"I am. I'm here to give you a chance, Lucky Bob."

"A chance at what?"

"At being free."

They stared at him. Waiting. Waiting.

"Stand with us," said Grey, lowering his tone so that only Lucky Bob could hear him, "and you get to live. Doctor Saint will even find some way of removing that damn rock. Stand with us, with your daughter, and save the town you love. The town you *died* trying to protect."

Lucky Bob seemed to waver, and Grey prayed that he had reached the man—that good man—inside.

"I . . . ," began the Harrowed, but he stopped and shook his head.

"Defy me and I will burn you," said Deray.

Something caught Grey's eye and it very nearly made

him falter. Forty feet away from where he stood, gathered together beneath the leafless boughs of a dead cottonwood, he saw a dozen figures. All men except for one young woman. Every face was familiar. Every face was as pale as death. Dark eyes, hard mouths.

The ghosts. *His* ghosts.

They had caught up to him at last. They were here.

Grey knew that this was all going to end in darkness. In pain.

In damnation.

But he still wanted to save Lucky Bob if he could. For Jenny. For the sake of the people they were. For his own soul.

"Please," he said, though he spoke as much to the waiting ghosts as to the undead here on the bridge.

"I can't do that," said Lucky Bob softly and with his free hand he lightly touched the ghost rock buried in his chest. "Lord Deray's cast a spell over the rock. Dark, dark magic. So . . . powerful. You can't imagine. If I tried to take it out, I'd burn. Do you understand? I'd burn to ashes, flesh and bone . . . and brain. I'd be every bit as dead. What you're offering me is nothing, boy. I've already lost. I've got no hope at all."

"Listen to me," Grey said urgently, talking now directly to Lucky Bob. "Your daughter is in this town. If you cross this bridge she'll die. Think about what Deray will do to her."

Lucky Bob shook his head and despite everything there were tears in his eyes. "No . . . Jenny's already dead. I killed her myself the other night. Shot her through the heart."

"You're wrong," Grey insisted. "The bullet ricocheted off the whalebone in her corset. It saved her the same as my silver belt buckle saved me. She's alive. Jenny is alive."

The Harrowed kept shaking his head. "You're a hopeful fool, boy. Whalebone can't deflect a bullet."

"You're wrong," repeated Grey. "Jenny is alive and you didn't murder her. You can still come back from the edge of this, man. But she's here in town and she's going to fight whoever crosses this bridge. You know how that fight will end. You know that she'll die and that she'll become a slave to Deray. Is that what you want? Is that what you—Lucky Bob Pearl, the man who saved this town—want for her and everything she stands for? Isn't there anything left of the good man who everyone in Paradise Falls loved? Listen to me, man. This is the truth."

"Don't believe his lies, Pearl," shouted Deray. "He is trying to sow seeds of doubt."

Lucky Bob walked forward until he stood face to face with Grey. Tears burned silver lines down his face. "My daughter is dead and I am in hell," he said. "There is no escape. Lord Deray will conquer this world and it will become an abode of demons who are his slaves. That is the truth. This town will fall and it's going to light a fire that will burn down the whole world. There's nothing I can do to stop it. There's nothing you can do. There's nothing that anyone can do. You want to threaten me? You want to shoot me in the head? Go on and do it. It would be a mercy because I am a monster, and I am already in hell."

Once more Deray's mad laughter filled the skies.

He's enjoying this, Grey realized. *He's letting us have this conversation because he wants to prove me wrong in front of all of his men.*

"Goddamn it, I don't want to kill you," Grey said to Pearl, then he spoke to the other leering dead. "I don't want to kill anyone except that prick up in that ship. He's the monster. I want to help you. I want you to help us. Stand with us. Fight Deray. Be free."

"He'll burn us."

Grey sighed. "So will I. If I have to."

Lucky Bob blinked. "What?"

Grey growled, "You have one chance, Bob. Get off this bridge right now . . ."

"Or what?" demanded the Harrowed.

"Or I'll kill you. Right here. Right now."

"Ha!" cried Deray. "Bold words but an empty threat. These people are sheep to be herded. They are nothing. They can do nothing. They—."

Thomas Looks Away stepped out from the old bridge-keepers' shack. He had his Kingdom Rifle raised, but the barrel was pointed not at the undead horde or even at Deray, but at the bridge on which they stood.

Exactly as planned.

They'd discussed this very moment back in Saint's barn. What to do. How to fight. Killing Deray was a priority, but Looks Away, Jenny and Saint all feared that taking out the necromancer would not stop the slaughter and sack of the town. No, the fight had to be won at the bridge.

Grey pointed down at the boards beneath his feet. "We have it rigged to blow. And before you think that we've planted ordinary dynamite, think again. Every inch of this bridge is mined with ghost rock powder and canisters of compressed gas from the smelting factories in Salt Lake. When it blows it will vaporize everything. Every bit of wood and rope and flesh. That gun fires a special round that reacts with ghost rock." He tapped the stone in Lucky Bob's chest. "*All* ghost rock. One shot and poof! You'll all die. Now and forever. Me, too, but my soul, at least, won't die with me. Maybe I'll go to heaven. Maybe I'll go to hell." He winked at them. "It's an even bet either way and I'm willing to take my chances, Bob." He paused. "Are you?"

Above them, Deray's frigate was abruptly rising, moving away from the bridge. Grey saw it. So did all the walking dead.

"Your lord and master believes me," said Grey. "And look at him . . . running to save his own ass while his slaves burn." He shook his head. "So tell me, friend, what's it going to be, Bob? Do you stand with us, or do we all go down together?"

"You wouldn't dare," said Lucky Bob. "You know what will happen if you destroy this bridge. You won't just kill us, you doom everyone in town. You'd be trapped here. You'd all starve."

"Yup, I reckon so. Actually, I figure we're dead no matter what happens. Either you kill us and maybe turn us into monsters, or we starve to death. You're not giving us any cards to play but this."

"Who knows?" called Looks Away. "We might not starve. We might get rescued. The telegraph still works and we sent a pretty emphatic series of messages. Oh . . . and we told them about Deray's plans, too. And about the foreign powers. All of it. Took forever and I fancy the telegrapher's hand is rather worn out."

"Nobody will come," called Deray. His sky ship was probably beyond the reach of fire and debris should the bridge explode, but he was well within earshot from his safe distance. He bellowed down at them in a mocking voice. "Nobody will believe you."

"Maybe not," said Grey. "Or maybe they won't have a choice. Maybe they're going to have to send someone out to check. Just in case. I expect the Sioux will. They'll want to know about all those dead red men. And the Rail Barons. The governments of the United States and the CSA. They'll have to check because, again, you're not leaving them a choice. And that, you incredible freak, is your problem. You think people will just bend over and take it. You must think everyone is as weak as Chesterfield. You have no faith in people. You don't understand people at all. And that's why we're going to take you down."

"If I fall," mocked Deray, "it will be long after you are dead and gone."

"Maybe. I don't expect to make it out of this alive. No sir, I expect I've just about played my last good card. But I can guarantee, Deray, that you won't find this country easy to conquer. People will stand up to you. They'll fight."

"People are sheep."

"Think so? Look at this, look at us here in Paradise Falls. We're ready to blow up our bridge and die to stop you. That's just a handful of people. Good luck trying to conquer a world."

Deray's answer was a mocking laugh that twisted inside the screech of the wind and seemed to shake the pillars of heaven.

In a quiet voice Grey said, "You didn't kill Jenny. She's alive. I love her and she's alive. Let her live, Bob. Be her father one more time."

Lucky Bob met his eyes, and for a long moment, as Deray's laughter shook the world, they just stood there. "You don't understand. He's . . . too powerful. He owns us. We belong to him . . . heart and soul."

"Heart maybe," said Grey. "But not soul."

With that he moved faster than he had ever moved in his life. He slapped the pistol aside with his left hand, and in the same instant, reached across his body and drew his Colt. It all happened inside of a fragmenting moment. Lucky Bob's gun fired. Grey felt the burn in his side as the bullet ripped a trench in his flesh. Then he jammed his own gun barrel against the chunk of ghost rock over Lucky Bob's heart and fired.

Lucky Bob Pearl staggered backward two awkward steps. His gun fell from his grip, struck the bridge and bounced over the edge. For some reason nearly everyone watched it fall. Even the living dead. As if the fall of that gun meant something. Lucky Bob, though, did not watch his pistol fall into the thrashing water below. Instead he stared down at the black hole in the center of his chest. Smoke curled up from it, and fragments of the shattered ghost rock still clung to the ravaged flesh. His mouth opened and closed several times as if he wanted to speak, or wanted to scream, and could not determine which. If he felt pain there was none of it on his face. His expression was not one of fear or anger. It was one of wonder. Of awe. His face wore the half-smiling mask of someone who had heard the whisper of some great mystery and wanted to hear more. To know the secret.

Lightning flashed and thunder erupted like a full broadside from a warship. The shock sent everyone staggering, and then a voice boomed like the voice of some dark god.

"*Kill them all!*" roared Aleksander Deray.

The horde of the living dead surged forward like a tide.

Chapter 84

Grey whirled and raised his Lazarus pistol toward the sinister figure leering out over the rail of his sky ship. The craft was just beyond pistol shot, but it was close enough to see the madman's face. There was such bottomless contempt there that it made Grey feel like an inconsequential bug. This man, hovering safely above the battlefield below, looked down on them all—the townsfolk and even his own people—with a comprehensive and uniform contempt. They were all nothing to him. A means to an end or a nuisance to be crushed underfoot.

Behind Grey, on the bridge, he heard the sound of a body falling to the wooden boards. Lucky Bob. Dying. Free from the ghost rock, but with a bullet punched through his heart. From behind the barriers, Grey heard a voice rise in a banshee wail of horror and grief.

Jenny.

"Jenny," her father said in a whisper of grief. "I'm so sorry . . ."

"*Kill them or burn!*" bellowed Deray. Grey could hear the deaders behind him begin to move. The seconds of the hourglass had all run out now.

With a snarl of inarticulate rage he fired at Deray.

The walking dead on the bridge fired their guns. Some fired bullets. Others had the necromancer's version of Kingdom rifles, but instead of ghost rock bullets they fired red flame in long, sizzling bursts.

Everyone on the barricade fired. Everybody was firing, firing, firing. The world seemed to explode in burning gunpowder and hot lead.

"Looks!" screamed Grey. "Now!"

Chapter 85

It all went wrong.

It all went to hell.

In the seconds before Looks Away's blast detonated the ghost rock explosives, the undead swarmed toward the mouth of the bridge. Scores of them thundered over the creaking boards and flooded through the gates of Paradise Falls. Grey landed hard on the edge of the drop-off as the killers swept past and over him. He curled into a fetal ball as booted feet trampled him. His Colt went spinning from his hand and he saw feet step on it and push it down into the mud.

Through the protective cage of his arms, Grey saw the destruction of the bridge. The middle of the span changed in the blink of an eye from wood and rope to a new sun that was born into searing brightness in the middle of the storm. Except instead of yellow, this sun burned with sizzling blue light that roared and crackled and vaporized everything it touched. Grey saw undead bodies light up like candles and then fly apart like piñatas. He saw bodies and parts of bodies fly high into the storm, burning despite the rain, then fall like dying embers into the chasm.

He saw the bridge itself burst apart. Torn ropes twisted like snakes of fire. Boards tumbled upward, spinning even as they became wreathed in flame. Then the whole mass of it plunged downward toward the spikes of rocks, and the unforgiving alien river that flowed outward from the depths of hell.

Hundreds of the undead vanished inside a sheet of flame. Their bodies fell twisting and burning into the chasm. Hundreds of the uniformed human soldiers fell with them. They screamed despite the fire in their mouths, their lungs. They tried to hold on to the bridge, on to life, but there was no hope for any of them. The force of the explosion flashed outward with titanic force, slamming into the cliffs on either side of the chasm like the fists of the god of fire. The sandstone rocks of the cliff walls, already weakened, collapsed at once, dragging down four of the tanks and hundreds more of the waiting army of the mad necromancer. Screaming men and screaming manitou tumbled toward their doom with half a million tons of rock and the weight of those machines pushing them to destruction.

The ground beneath Grey began to crumble, too, and he began to crawl, then to claw at the mud as it tried to fall away and send him to his death as well. He got to his hands and knees and crawled like a beaten dog, and then there was a hand under his armpit, pulling him up.

Looks Away.

They staggered together away from the collapsing cliff, and when they felt solid ground beneath their feet they ran.

God did they run.

"Jesus Christ . . . ," gasped Grey as they reached completely solid ground. Grey dropped to his knees again, gasping. He could feel blood running down his face and his whole body screamed in pain from all the feet that had kicked and stepped on him.

"I know," said Looks Away grimly. "How are you? Can you walk? Can you fight?"

In the turbulent air, the necromancer's frigate sailed toward Paradise Falls. Undead crouched behind the remnants of the shattered rails and fired rifles that shot streaks of red fire. Explosions rocked the town. Buildings went up in pillars of fire.

Directly ahead of Grey and Looks Away, the undead swarmed over the sandbag wall. Through the sounds of shouting and gunfire they heard a woman's scream. Jenny or someone else. A young voice filled with terror.

Grey hauled himself back to his feet and spat mud and blood into the wind. He tore the Lazarus pistol from its holster. He saw movement and turned to see people standing in the shadows beneath a withered cottonwood tree. Men whose faces he knew. And a woman whose face he had dreamed about every night since he'd left her to die.

"Annabelle . . ." he murmured.

They were right here. His ghosts had caught up to him at last.

"I tried," he told her. "I tried to save him. I tried."

Annabelle said nothing. Her face shone as if she stood in bright moonlight.

"Let me try to save the people here in town. Give me that. Let me do that much before you take me."

The ghosts of his men and the ghost of his lover said nothing. The rain slanted through the empty branches of the trees. It passed through the specters and struck the ground at their feet.

"Grey—?" asked Looks Away. He stood beside Grey and followed the line of his friend's gaze.

"Please," begged Grey. "Give me that much, and then you can drag me down to hell."

"Grey," repeated Looks Away. "Who *are* they?"

The question jolted Grey. "You can see them?"

"Yes . . . but I don't . . ."

Then Looks Away stiffened and it was clear that he understood. "Oh . . . my God . . . your men. And . . . and . . . dear god in heaven."

The ghosts held their ground. The two men held theirs. Screams and gunfire filled the air.

"Please . . . ," whispered Grey once more.

Then Annabelle nodded. Once. A small thing. Despite the rain and clouds, the day seemed strangely bright. He could feel a snarl etch itself onto his mouth. He raised his gun and touched the barrel to the brim of his hat. A salute. An acceptance. He said nothing. There was nothing more that needed to be said. Together, brothers in arms, they ran toward the fight. Both of them knowing, deep in their hearts, that they were going to die. Neither of them cared. All that mattered was taking as many of their enemies with them as they could. This fight was no longer about winning.

Now it was all about slaughter.

Chapter 86

The fight was brutal.

Nearly two hundred of the undead had made it off the bridge before it blew. They ran howling at the barricade, straight into a hail of bullets. They fell by the dozen, some with wounds that their demons' spirits would heal given time; others dropped back with head wounds that doomed them to nothingness.

Grey saw Jenny Pearl standing with a foot braced on the pile of sandbags, her face set into a mask of mingled hatred and acceptance as she fired her Lazarus pistol into the heart of the swarm. The gun seemed to be functioning perfectly now, and one after another of the dead men exploded as the compressed gas inside the ghost rock bullets blew them to red pieces.

Looks Away and Grey opened up as they caught up to the invading horde. The Lazarus bullets killed every undead they struck, no matter where they hit. Even a wound to a leg or arm set off a chain reaction with the fragment of ghost rock in their chests. Undead died screaming.

The Kingdom rifle did far more damage, though. When one of its rounds struck, the resulting blast consumed everything inside a twenty-foot radius. Souls flickered to the wind and then were torn to emptiness as brains exploded from the monstrous pressure. It took the walking dead in the middle of the swarm only moments to realize that death chased them even as they sought to overwhelm the barricade. They laughed in the face of it, though. The red madness of slaughter was all they cared about.

Other townsfolk deserted the other barriers and dashed through the ever-thickening rain to join the melee. Grey saw Mrs. O'Malley holding a musket by the barrel and laying about her like a warrior queen from some ancient legend. Old though she was, she put real power into her swings, and a heap of undead with shattered skulls attested to her ferocity.

Grey fired his gun dry and paused to reload. He had already used half of his ammunition. One of the living dead rushed him before he could finish slapping the new cylinder in place. Grey pivoted and stamped hard on its knee with the flat of his boot. Bones snapped like dry sticks and the monster fell flat on its face, and even as it landed Grey stomped down with his heel, catching the thing behind the ear. The skull shattered and the neck canted inward. The creature stopped moving. Grey slapped the new cylinder into place and ran over the corpse to rejoin the fight.

A series of explosions tore through the air and Grey wheeled around to see several of the Little Disasters—blue, yellow, pink, and purple—explode in the thick of the enemy.

A split second later, a cry went up, and to his horror, Grey saw Doctor Saint fall as a line of red energy pulses punched downward from the railing of the sky frigate. Whether the scientist was dead or crippled was impossible to determine as the tide of battle swept over him, and he was lost to Grey's sight.

Grey fought his way to the outer edge of the barricade and launched himself into the thick of a battle between two youngsters—a boy and a girl of about seventeen who looked like twins—and five of the undead. The boy was on his knees, hands pressed to a savage wound in his stomach while the girl stood her ground and fired a

Winchester, working the lever with fevered determination, hitting the enemy because at that distance there was no room to miss. One of the walking dead grabbed the smoking barrel of her gun and tore it from her hands and the creature behind him flung himself atop the girl, bearing her to the ground.

Grey shot the dead man who had taken the Winchester, but he dared not shoot the one atop the girl. Instead he kicked it in the ribs with all of his strength, flipping it off of her and onto its back. The girl whipped a knife from her belt, rolled onto her knees and drove the point of the blade into the monster's eye socket. The creature twitched once and then collapsed back, dead.

Grey flashed her a wild grin. If life was kinder and if he had any chance at a future—which he knew he did not—he would want a girl like this as his daughter.

The other three undead rushed forward, but Grey pivoted in the mud and killed them with three fast shots from the Lazarus gun. They exploded in blue fire and red blood.

"Get him to safety," Grey said, pointing to the girl's wounded twin.

But she shook her head and foraged among the dead for a new gun. "Safety?" she barked, then followed it with a mad laugh. "Where's that?"

"Grey!"

He turned at the sound of his name and saw Jenny there. Right there.

She was streaked with mud, blood, and rainwater, her hair was in rattails and her dress was torn, but she was more beautiful in that moment than ever before. She had her Lazarus pistol in one hand and a big Remington army pistol. The barrel of the Lazarus gun was pointed down, but the big, black mouth of the Remington was pointed at his heart.

"You killed him," she said.

"Jenny—?"

"You killed my pa."

"I . . . I tried to save him," said Grey. "I begged him to stand down. I wanted him to tear the rock from his chest so that he didn't have to die."

There were tears in her eyes. "You shot him in the chest."

"I—."

"Not the head," said Jenny. "You didn't shoot him in the head."

"Jenny, please . . ."

"You killed him," she repeated. Then she said, "You saved him."

Grey held his breath, frozen into the moment.

"You saved his soul," said Jenny in a voice that was strange and distant.

"This wasn't his fault," he said simply. "He didn't deserve this."

She looked down at the dead men whose bodies lay in pieces. "But you killed him."

"What choice did I have?"

Jenny shook her head, then stared up at the frigate. "Deray is a monster," she said. "He is the Beast of the Apocalypse made flesh. He turns flesh against flesh and hearts against hearts. He is the defiler."

Her voice was so strange now. Not like Jenny's voice.

"Jenny—?"

She lowered the pistol and began to turn away. Then she paused and turned her head, looking over her shoulder at him.

"We love you, Grey," she said. "We both love you."

Then she raised both guns and rushed back into the fight.

We both love you.

A sick wave of horror washed through Grey's soul.

"No . . . ," he said aloud.

No, he screamed in the empty halls of his breaking heart. He heard a chorus of despairing cries rise up from the defenders and he turned to look. What he saw nearly crushed him. The sky frigate had moved back across the chasm, past the blackened ruin of the bridge, to the far side. The undead aboard the frigate had cast down a dozen ropes, and the remaining soldiers on the far side of the gorge were lashing them to the arms of the metal giant. Then the ship rose again and bore Samson into the air.

Across the chasm.

Toward Paradise Falls.

Samson. An invulnerable engine of destruction. Coming. Not to join the fight, but to end it. To exterminate. To prove that the beast that was Deray was truly the conqueror that would crush the world under foot.

If there had been any part of Grey that was still sane, still undamaged by all that had happened over the last few days, then it broke in that moment. Understanding is a fist, a hammer, a bullet, and it smashed through him.

We both love you.

We.

With a scream so loud it tore blood from his throat, Grey followed her into the fight.

Chapter 87

If war is hell, and if wars are fought on Earth, then Earth itself is hell. At least it is when the flames of war burn hottest. Grey felt his humanity drain away as he fought. Fatigue and pain went with it, leaving behind something else. A construct as cold and inhuman as Samson, who now hung suspended from the airship. Grey saw Deray at the rail, a sword in his hand and a demonic smile on his face.

"Do it, you bastard," whispered Grey. As if he could hear those words, Deray turned and slashed at the ropes that held Samson. The giant seemed to hang for a moment longer than he should, like a fist poised to deliver a death blow.

Then it fell.

Fell.

Like a comet.

Like the hammer of some ancient god.

Like the footfall of the antichrist.

It fell.

Tons of gleaming metal dropped through the swirling rain directly down toward the barricade. Undead and humans screamed and scattered, falling back as the colossus streaked downward.

Only Grey stood his ground, his Lazarus pistol raised. He had one shot left. One.

He pointed it at the giant and fired.

Knowing that it could do no good, but needing to try

anyway. Needing to. The ghost rock bullet struck the bottom of the giant's foot.

And then . . .

There was a sound, like a hammer striking a great gong. A ringing, crushing noise that sent Grey flying through the air once more. Flung again like debris.

The sound was accompanied by a flash of blue.

Massive.

Incredible. Greater than anything Grey had ever seen. Bigger than the blast out in Nevada that had torn apart the hills. Bigger than the thunderbolt that had destroyed the great worm in the desert.

Brighter than the sun. The blue fireball seemed to open like a mouth and then clamp its jaws around the giant in the instant before it would have crushed the sandbag barrier. Then, like the fist of God, it punched Samson away. Far away. Away from the barrier. Out toward the chasm in an arc that trailed azure flames. Samson, a crumpled, blackened, twisted parody of the invincible giant it had been, fell into the cleft and vanished from sight. Everyone stood or sprawled in stunned silence. In this moment the world made no sense at all. Not to the living or the dead.

Above them, the sky frigate tilted into the wind, its great balloon ruptured, the hull cracked and splintered. It slid lower in the sky, trailing smoke and gas as it dropped down, yard by yard until its keel bumped against the roof of a big barn that stood on the edge of town. The barn that held the late Doctor Saint's laboratory.

Grey Torrance climbed to his feet, unaware of the blood that ran from a dozen cuts, some of them deep, crisscrossing his frame. He had no weapon now, and his clothes hung in rags.

Everyone else got slowly to their feet. Undead and townsfolk. One by one they turned toward the town, staring at the thing that loomed there in the middle of the rainswept main street.

A wagon.

Ordinary in most ways. Two mules stood trembling in the traces, their ears back and teeth bared in terror.

On the wagon, looking like something from a nightmare invention from the mind of some fevered tinkerer, sat the massive shape of the Kingdom cannon. Blue smoke leaked from its barrel. Leaning against it, small, round, dripping blood, was Percival Saint.

He smiled weakly at the sea of faces. Then his eyes rolled up in his head and he pitched backward off the cart to land bonelessly in the mud. He did not even try to break his fall.

"No!" cried a voice, and Thomas Looks Away staggered from the press of the crowd and took a tentative step toward the fallen scientist. Then he stopped and hung his head. He turned slowly back to the barricade and raised his Kingdom rifle. Grey had no idea if the Sioux had any rounds left, but there was pain and murder in his friend's eyes.

None of the undead moved. There were still nearly two hundred of them. There were fewer of the townsfolk. Maybe a hundred left. Corpses were everywhere. The rain mixed the blood with the soil and mud. Grey saw movement on the sky frigate. Aleksander Deray was still alive. He had a bag of tools slung over his shoulder and was climbing a section of netting to reach the tear in the gas envelope.

"No," said Grey. "No goddamn way."

He took a step toward the barn and nearly fell. There was something wrong with his leg and pain exploded upward into his back. He didn't care. He ate the pain and let it feed his desire to reach Deray. He needed to grasp a throat in his hands, to feel its structure crumble, to hear the rattle of a last breath. He forced himself on.

First in a staggering walk, then as he feasted on his own pain, he broke into a run. Behind him, the battle—stalled by shock—began again.

He heard gunfire and screams.

As he ran he saw the ghosts again. No longer under the dead cottonwood. Now they stood in the road that led up to the barn. All of his men, everyone who had died at Bailey Creek. His sergeant, the corporals. All of his friends. Everyone who had trusted him.

And Annabelle.

Of all of them, she was the least substantial. Her shade was like something painted on glass. He could see through her. Her eyes, though, they were intense. Grey braced himself, thinking that they had come to intercept him, but as he ran toward the barn they stepped back to let him pass. The dead giving license to the doomed to fight the damned. He almost laughed. It was comedy. The kind the gods would enjoy. They were perverse enough to find all of this to their liking.

The barn door was closed but Grey launched himself at it and kicked it inward. It flew backward and he landed hard and stumbled inside. The stairs were in the far corner, and Grey ran past the tables filled with strange devices designed by Doctor Saint. He had no idea what any of them were. There were no Kingdom rifles, no Lazarus pistols. Nothing that he could use. All he had left were the Bowie knife on his belt and his fists.

That would have to be enough. If not, then he really would use his bare hands. Or his teeth, if it came to that.

He heard a dull *thump* as the frigate bumped once more against the roof. *Still there,* he thought. *Good.*

"I'm coming," he said as he climbed the stairs.

At the top of the second flight there was a ladder that stretched up to a trapdoor. Grey pulled it down, took a breath, and then climbed. The trapdoor had a simple slide bolt, which he shot as quietly as he could, then he raised the door an inch. The pitched roof of the barn, with its rows of black tarpaper shingles, stretched all the way to the edge thirty feet away. The frigate bobbed in the rain just beyond it, turned stern-on to the barn. All of the windows in the stern gallery had been smashed out, and Grey could see the wreckage of what had been an elegantly furnished captain's cabin. The oak and teak from which the ship was built was ruined now—cracked and warped, singed and fractured. He saw dead men slumped over debris. Instead of a suit of sails, the ship had its big gas envelope, and Deray clung to the nettings and used what looked like a mop to smear some glistening goo along the edges of the tear. Every few seconds he paused, held the swab in one hand, and used the other to press torn sections of the canvas envelope into place. The substance he was applying must have been some kind of glue, because the fabric stuck fast. There was very little of the rupture left, though gas poured out of the diminishing hole with great force. Grey marveled at the strength of the man as he forced the pieces into place against that pressure. Deray must be fantastically strong.

Grey raised the trapdoor all the way and climbed out. There was a single beam running the length of the barn, with the rest of the roof sloping sharply down on either side. The beam was ten inches wide. One slip and he would plummet from the barn.

"So, don't slip," he muttered in a voice too quiet for anyone but himself to hear.

He stood up, and despite his confident words his body swayed with fatigue and injury. Even so, he drew his Bowie knife and stepped onto the beam. It wasn't quite like walking a tightrope, but with the wind and rain it was a foolish and dangerous thing to do. He did it anyway.

Below the barn, the fight raged. He could see Jenny and Looks Away leading the fight, but it was impossible to tell who was winning. Or if "victory" was even possible with so many people already dead.

Deray had his back to him and he was nearly finished repairing the damage from the Kingdom cannon. The necromancer had a thin saber strapped to his waist but no gun. Grey saw only a few of the undead aboard. One lay on the deck, eyes glazed as he stared at the ragged red stumps where his legs had been. A second felt his way blindly along the rail; his face was a charred mask without eyes, lips, or nose.

Only the third was whole and seemed in command of himself. He stood at the wheel of the big frigate, wrestling with it to keep the ship steady in the storm winds.

"That's done it!" cried Deray as he flung down the mop. "Hard to starboard. Bring her up and around. We'll land on the far side, load as many troops as we can, and then bring them over here to finish this."

"Aye aye," said the dead man as he threw his weight against the wheel.

Neither of the men saw Grey coming. Neither heard him until he leaped from the end of the beam, across the shattered rail and landed with a *thump* on the deck. Then they both whirled.

The helmsman was closest, so Grey jumped at him and buried the point of the Bowie knife deep into his chest. The point struck the chunk of ghost rock and burst it into fragments of glittering black. There was a screeching sound from the stone and a louder scream from the undead as he staggered backward. As he fell, Grey tore the knife free and faced Deray.

The necromancer stood there, remarkably calm despite this invasion.

"Who *are* you?" he demanded. "Who are you to come aboard my ship? Who are you to try and turn my own servant against me? Who are you to stand in the way of the natural order of things?"

"Natural?" said Grey. "Now that's a funny damn word coming from you."

The frigate began to move sideways, shoved by the hands of the storm winds. The sudden shift of the deck forced both men to take steps to keep their balance.

"Who are you?" repeated Deray. "Are you one of Saint's colleagues? Are you a government agent?"

"Me?" said Grey with a smile, "I'm nobody at all."

Rain dripped from the brim of Deray's hat and ran down the length of his sheathed sword. The necromancer studied him with cold and calculating eyes. "Then what is any of this to you? Are you a mercenary? Is that it? Did these pathetic fools hire you? Did Saint or his pet savage hire you?"

"If you mean Thomas Looks Away, then yes. I work for him. He hired me to help protect this town from you and Nolan Chesterfield."

Deray snorted. "You're not very good at your job, are you?"

"No? Ask those poor sons of bitches who were on the bridge."

Deray began pacing across the deck, his head turned so that he watched Grey out of the corner of his eyes. He was a handsome man with intelligent eyes and a smile that was almost charming. In another time and place Grey would have guessed that he was a doctor. Or maybe a stage actor. Even a politician. He had presence and charm, despite the harshness of his words.

"What is your name?" asked the necromancer.

"Grey Torrance. You won't have heard of me."

"No, and nor will anyone hereafter. History will not record your name either."

Grey shrugged and turned in place so that he continued to face the man even as Deray walked in a wide circle around him. The ship shifted around now, orienting itself so that the bow pointed away from the wind. The heavy gusts pushed it toward the chasm and the rest of Deray's army. Below the keel, the sounds of screams and gunfire continued unabated. Deray waved an arm toward the rail, indicating the battle.

"Listen to them," he said. "Your employer, his friends, the rest of the town . . . it's all going to perish. Soon this town will not even be a footnote in anyone's register. There will be no trace of it on any map because I will redraw the maps of this world. I will wash it clean of *people* like this." He spat the word "people" as if it was bile on his tongue. "This world has become chaotic and disordered. It no longer makes sense and at the rate it is going it will tear itself apart. When I look into the future I see more and greater wars. Not of conquest, not wars to build something that will last. Petty wars without purpose. Wars that do nothing but leave scars upon the earth and empower fools. This country—just look at what has happened to your America. After it broke away from England it showed such promise. It could have become a superior power, it should have become a new empire. One greater than Britain, greater even than Rome. And now it is fractured and divided and everyone here has gone mad." Deray shook his head. "That is such a waste. I will create a new world and a new world order. Something nobler, better. Something—"

Grey held up a hand. "Listen, Mr. Deray, I'm sure you have a whole soliloquy rehearsed for moments like this. Shakespeare would be jealous, I have no doubt. But can we skip the rest? I don't give a hairy rat's ass about your plans. I don't care why you want to conquer the world or why you think you're entitled. On the way up here I thought I wanted to ask you those questions, but now that we're up to it, I just want to slit your goddamn throat."

The necromancer stopped pacing, and in a much less

pretentious tone said, "You are no fun at all, are you? You have no sense of drama, no appreciation for the importance of a moment like this."

"No, I don't. As you said, I'm a nobody." Grey raised the knife and showed it to Deray. The blade was still slick with the dark blood of the dead man he'd stabbed. "All I care about is what happens next."

"Very well," said Deray, and with a movement faster than the eye could see, he drew his sword. "Then let us proceed from conversation to murder."

Chapter 88

The necromancer was fast.

So damned fast. He lunged forward with a thrust that drove straight toward Grey's heart. It was a beautifully timed movement, expertly delivered, and executed with power and speed. But Grey was waiting for it. He saw the shift of weight, the telltale alignment of posture and movement. Grey believed what he'd said when he told Deray that he was a nobody, but there was a lie even in his own admission.

He was somebody. He was a soldier. A fighter.

A warrior.

He had spent a life in combat and the slanting deck of this airship was not his first battlefield. Not even his hundredth. Grey twisted nimbly away as the saber's tip sheared through the air where his heart had been. Grey turned his left side along the blade, feeling the cold edge of it trace a burning line along his arm and back as he turned. But at the end of the turn he swung the Bowie knife around in a terrible arc and slashed the blade across Aleksander Deray's chest.

He had aimed for Deray's throat, but the man had grasped his own error and tried to evade the counterattack. The Bowie knife sliced through shirt and vest and cut into the man's skin. A line of red droplets flew into the air and was whipped away by the wind.

Deray howled and lashed out with his free hand, catching Grey across the mouth with the side of a closed fist. The blow was far more powerful than Grey had any right to expect from a normal man. The force of it sent Grey skidding across the deck toward the cabin wall. With a snarl, Deray leaped after him, slashing in a long diagonal line to try and catch his enemy between blade and wall. But Grey took the impact and went with it, shoving himself even faster and harder against the wall so that he struck and rebounded. He jumped to the right and the tip of Deray's sword scored a line through the wood.

Without pausing, both men closed in for their next attacks—Deray with another diagonal slash and Grey with a lateral cut that would have disemboweled the necromancer. However the combined speed of their attacks brought them together into a bone-jarring crash that truncated each cut. They immediately locked arms around one another to prevent a close-quarters slash, and grappling like that they went into a staggering dance across the wet deck.

It became immediately apparent that Deray's blow had not been a freak accident of angle or chance. As Grey had surmised before, he was immensely strong. It was like being wrapped by a steel band. The air was being squeezed out of his lungs and Grey could feel his bones grind. It was rare for him to fight someone substantially stronger and he knew that this level of strength could not be accounted for in any natural way.

It was twisted science.

Or, more probably, it was sorcery.

As they struggled, Deray's face was lit by a grin of delight. He was taking great pleasure in the surprise that must have registered on Grey's face. The necromancer leaned close until his lips were inches from Grey's ear.

"You are nothing, Mr. Torrance," he said. "You are less than a nuisance. You are nothing at all."

Grey tried to break the grip but it only tightened as they turned and stepped and fought for balance on the deck of the storm-tossed frigate.

As they turned, Grey nearly cried out when he saw that the deck—which had only been littered by the corpses of walking dead—was now filled.

A knot of figures stood by the freely spinning wheel. Pale faces in bullet-pocked clothes.

His men.

And her.

Annabelle.

The ghosts stood watching as he was slowly being crushed. There was no expression at all on their spectral faces. The two men turned and turned, and as they spun Grey heard Deray grunt in surprise. He'd seen the ghosts, too. For just a moment, the man was distracted, staring with wrinkled brow and a frown of consternation at the strange figures.

Grey took the moment, seizing the last chance he had.

He head-butted Deray, catching the man on the ear and then again on the corner of his eyebrow. It was a hard blow that exploded lights in Grey's own eyes. Deray flinched back, and that lessened the pressure by the slightest amount. Grey darted his head forward and clamped his teeth on the corded tendons on the side of Deray's neck and simultaneously brought his knee up to smash into the muscles of the man's thigh. Once, twice, again and again as he tore at the necromancer's flesh with his teeth.

Deray screamed.

He thrashed like a madman, no longer trying to crush Grey but going wild to try and escape him. Deray kicked back, catching Grey in the stomach with a sideways knee. The air whooshed from Grey's lungs and the impact knocked his teeth loose. He staggered backward, spitting blood and falling hard to the deck. Deray chased him, kicking Grey again and again, in the stomach, the chest, the face.

Grey felt his bones break. His ribs detonated like firecrackers. Bits of broken teeth clogged his throat and he collapsed sideways, dropping his knife. Deray kicked the weapon overboard and kicked Grey over and over again until Grey flopped back, bleeding and shattered.

Then Deray reeled in the opposite direction, blood boiling from a terrible wound. He dropped his sword to clamp his hands to his neck to stanch the flow of blood. From the force of the blood loss, Grey knew that he had nicked something important when he'd bitten Deray before. An artery.

Good. Let him bleed out like a stuck pig.

Even as he thought those words, Grey felt like he was drifting and for a moment he thought he'd fallen off the ship. But it was his consciousness that seemed to be tearing loose from his body.

I'm dying, he thought, and he knew it to be true.

So was Deray.

The ghosts began moving toward him. Toward both of them, their eyes filled now with a strange and awful hunger.

They're coming for me.

But they stared past him to the necromancer. Deray used one bloody hand to dig into an inner pocket. He produced a flat disk of polished ghost rock that was set in a silver frame. Strange symbols were carved into the rock and Deray began hastily muttering something over it in a language Grey had never heard.

"*Da'k gugt r'un ftaxung sha tsa't haaft shx ta'ans shas ha nax thunghiaa' shut latsuftansuaft ghu'ftg ang ta'a us ial un s'uftiasa,*" intoned the necromancer. "*Bx sha aftga' gugt I l'ax.*"

Above the ship, the storm suddenly intensified and in

his delirium Gsrey thought he saw strange, vast, impossible shapes leer at him from within the depths of the clouds. Monstrous eyes glared at him from a head that was lumpy and misshapen. Instead of a mouth and chin, there were dozens of writhing tentacles that whipped within the ferocious winds. Fires, ancient and endless, ignited in those eyes, and it seemed to set fire to the whole of the sky.

"Lu'g ur ghatsat ang 'angaantha," roared Deray, his blood gurgling in his throat, "haaft na su fta shx unts'ianans!"

Lightning, red as blood, slashed across the sky. Snakes of electricity crawled all over the envelope above the frigate. While behind the hideous face a vast pair of leathery wings seemed to reach outward, each one stretching for miles and filling the whole of the sky. Below, the fighting stopped and everyone screamed. Even the walking dead.

Grey used what little strength he had left to climb to his feet. He coughed and spat dark blood onto the deck, and inside his chest he could feel bones shifting in all the wrong ways. He stared at the great god of all monsters and spat at it, too. But the wind whipped it away, and the god did not even take notice of the dying gunslinger. Red lightning struck the ship and enveloped Deray, and for one mad moment Grey thought that the necromancer was somehow being consumed by his own dark magic. That fate had stepped in to rebuke the hubris of this madman.

But the fire did not burn Deray. It writhed over him and wherever it found a cut or a wound, it glowed like the deepest heart of a blacksmith's forge. Grey recoiled, throwing a hand across his eyes and crying out as the light burned his eyes. Even the ghosts by the wheel recoiled, and the glow seemed ready to wash them out of all existence.

Far below Grey heard Jenny cry out his name.

"Grey!"

Why she called him now was beyond his ability to understand. The light was so bright that it beat at him like hammers. Her voice though—just the sound of it—triggered a memory. Something that the vampire witch Mircalla had said to him. Something Veronica had repeated.

Worlds will turn on the wink of your eye.

The burning light began to dim, the lightning fading.

Worlds will fall in the light of your smile.

In the clouds, the face of the monster or god or whatever it was, also began to fade.

Deray stood there, wide-legged, blood glistening on his clothes, mingling with rain water. His chest heaved as if he had finished a great labor. The lightning, though gone everywhere else now, still burned in his eyes.

He raised his hand to touch his throat; he touched his chest with the other. The flesh was completely healed. The knife cut was gone. The bite was gone. He threw back his head and laughed. Exultant, triumphant.

Invincible.

Not merely a necromancer, but something else. Immortal. The unconquerable conqueror.

Grey turned and looked down at the crowd around the barricade. No one was fighting. They were all looking up at him. Jenny was not there. She was not standing where she had stood.

Looks Away was there, but he was alone.

Then . . .

No.

Not alone.

Looks Away, bloodied and exhausted, stood over a figure who lay in the mud. A slim figure with blond hair.

Lying there.

Broken.

"No . . . ," he said, but that single word had to tear its way through the wreckage in his chest.

No.

He wanted to scream it. But could not. It didn't matter, though, and he knew it. Jenny was gone. What remained was broken, ruined, half buried in mud.

Gone.

And that made him remember something else. Something Jenny had said to him not an hour ago as they prepared for this battle.

"*Don't worry,*" she had said so softly that only he could hear her. "*Death isn't the end.*"

Even as he remembered those words he actually heard them.

He turned his head and *she* was there.

Annabelle.

Standing there, her face bright as a candle. Her hair rippled in the breeze, but even though the wind was blowing her hair moved in a different direction. As if she stood in another place and was touched by some other, gentler breeze. It was so strange. Grey wondered if this was because he was dying.

"Death isn't the end," she said.

And as she said it he heard both voices.

Hers.

Jenny's.

Speaking as one.

"I'm . . . sorry," he said to both of them. "I'm so sorry."

Annabelle smiled, but he could see Jenny there, too. Like two images painted on glass, overlaid and then brought to life by magic. A shadow fell across her face and Grey turned, wheezing, gasping, coughing wetly, to see Aleksander Deray standing there, his clothes torn but his body whole. His power restored, immense, terrible.

"Now you understand," said the necromancer as he stepped close to Grey. As he spoke his breath blew against Grey like the draft from an open furnace. "Now you see why not even death itself can bar me from taking this world for my own. Now you understand why I can never be stopped. Now you grasp the full scope of your own failure."

"Yeah," said Grey. "I know."

Worlds will turn on the wink of your eye.

The words echoed in his dying brain.

Worlds will fall in the light of your smile.

Grey forced himself to stand straight. Despite the grinding pain in his chest, despite the liquid heat in his stomach, he stood tall one last time. He managed to smile. With split lips and broken teeth, Grey Torrance smiled at the man who had killed him.

"See you in hell, you son of a bitch."

He winked at Deray.

Then he wrapped his arms around the man and with the very last of his strength he threw himself over the rail, dragging Deray with him.

Chapter 89

They seemed to fall for a long time.

Deray screamed in terror. Real terror.

Below them the people of Paradise Falls screamed.

As Deray screamed red fire erupted from his mouth and nose. It enveloped Grey, it wrapped searing tendrils around them both as they dropped from the frigate down, down, down.

Grey had one last glimpse of the pale face of Annabelle looking over the rail at him as he fell. Annabelle looking at him with Jenny's eyes.

I'm so sorry, he thought.

And then the ground was there.

Even with all that rain and mud it was so hard.

So hard.

It crushed them both. Pulped them both.

But it did not kill them. The night and the storm and all of its dark magic were not done with them yet. With either of them. Grey heard them hit the ground. Heard the sound of bones snapped, of meat bursting. He felt the heat of blood. His and Deray's, mingling together. He felt the stab like a knife as one of Deray's splintered ribs speared him in the chest.

The world closed its eyes and there was a time of darkness.

Then there was a time of floating. Of nothingness.

Grey thought he felt himself still falling and he wondered how far he would have to plummet until he landed in the fiery depths of the Pit.

Would Deray be there with him? Would both of them serve out their sentences in Hell, chained together for all eternity? Was the universe that cruel? That perverse?

His eyelids fluttered open.

It was dark and the winds blew and the rain fell.

Grey saw a face come into focus as someone bent over him. He saw worry, and then saw that worry turn to horror as full understanding struck him. Looks Away closed his own eyes for a moment.

"By the Queen's garters, old boy," he murmured. "You've gone and done it now."

Grey tried to speak. Wanted to. Needed to. But there was so little of him left.

"Did . . . I . . . ?" he croaked. Hot blood choked him and he had to turn his head to spit his mouth clear. There was something wrong with his neck. The bones felt wrong. So wrong. "Did I . . . kill . . . him . . . ?"

Looks Away looked off to Grey's left. His expression was confused.

"This son of a whore is as hard to kill as you are, dear fellow," he said. He sneered at Deray, who lay beyond Grey's sight. Looks Away drew his knife and rain pinged off the bright blade. "I think I'll have to finish this myself—if anything at this point will end him. Let me do that for you, my friend. Let me make sure he goes first and—."

"No," said a voice.

And then another figure stepped into view beyond Looks Away. A tall man with iron gray hair, wearing a black vest and white shirt open to the mid-chest. A man who had a deep and dreadful scar over his heart.

A scar.

Not a chunk of ghost rock.

Not a bullet hole.

A ragged pink scar.

"No," repeated Lucky Bob Pearl, "he's mine." He held pistols in each hand.

Looks Away recoiled from the Harrowed, bringing his knife up, ready to fight. Lucky Bob shook his head.

"Don't," he said as he touched the scar. "We're not enemies anymore, Looksie. We used to be friends. Maybe we can be that again if the world doesn't end."

"Bob . . . ?" said Looks Away, stunned. "How?"

Lucky Bob knelt and placed his hand over Grey's heart. "He did it. He destroyed the ghost rock and freed me from the necromancer."

"But you're . . . you're . . ."

"Dead?" finished Lucky Bob, smiling a rueful smile. "Maybe. I don't feel dead. Hell, son, I've never felt more alive in my whole dang life."

"What about the . . . um . . . *other*?"

"The manitou?"

"I guess maybe we're both in here. Don't know how that's going to work out, but for right now I'm calling the damn shots. Me and nobody else." He tapped his own chest. "Heart's still beating. Wounds heal pretty darn fast. Don't ask how. Guess we're alive or close enough. And I guess we'll try and figure some way of getting along. Both of us sharing the same suit of skin and bones. Funny old world. Point is that this man— your friend here—saved us both. Me and the manitou. He could have killed us, but he didn't. And he tried not to kill any of us. He offered us a chance."

Lucky Bob stood up, and as he did so his smile went away as he looked around at the last of the undead. There were eleven of them, and each was covered with blood. Their eyes blazed with unbanked hatred.

"Well, come on, you yellow-bellied sons of whores," growled Lucky Bob. "This is my goddamn town."

The undead howled with blood fury and rushed toward him.

Grey could not believe what he saw, what he witnessed. The Harrowed Lucky Bob Pearl brought the guns up and fired.

Fired.

Fired.

His guns bucked in his hands eleven times. And eleven undead heads snapped backward from the impacts. Eleven pairs of feet lost all sense; eleven bodies crumpled to the ground. And all of it in the space of a few ragged heartbeats. The gunshots echoed like thunder and then faded to a ghastly silence.

"My goddamn town," repeated Lucky Bob.

Then the Harrowed turned from the pile of corpses and walked over to where Aleksander Deray lay crushed and broken. Ruined, but still alive, and Grey could see that the terrible damage was already healing. Soon the necromancer would rise once more.

"Tell me, you miserable piece of cow shit," said Lucky Bob, "how does one kill a necromancer? Hmm? 'Cause I aim to do it if I have to cut you to pieces or burn down this whole town around you. I *will* do it, I swear to whatever gods there may be. You made me kill my own daughter, do you know that? You made me shoot my Jenny in the heart."

Grey wanted to tell him—to insist—that Lucky Bob had not done that. The whalebone corset had deflected his bullet. But he looked at the ragged scar on Lucky Bob's chest. And he remembered the scar on Jenny's chest. It had been between her breasts, and in the heat of their passion Grey had kissed that scar.

That's when he understood. That's when he understood so many things.

Death isn't the end, she had said.

At the point of death a manitou could enter a body

and take possession of it. Heal it. Restore it to life, and then share it with the soul of the murdered person.

A manitou could do that. He'd seen it firsthand with Lucky Bob.

Was that it? Like father like daughter? The indomitable Pearls? Both of them . . . *Harrowed*.

And Annabelle? How did she fit into the picture?

Even as he wondered about it, Grey knew. She was every bit as strong as Jenny. And she was so much like her. In personality, perhaps in spirit. Had they bonded somehow? Become one woman? If so, then no possessing manitou stood a chance.

It had to be. After all, hadn't those lips spoken with the voice of both Jenny and Annabelle? Even as he thought that, he saw a pale shape rise from the mud behind Looks Away. Her face and hair were filthy and her clothes were torn, but her eyes were filled with a light that even death could not dim. She came to him, and Looks Away and Lucky Bob fell back in surprise. The Sioux looked close to breaking. Lucky Bob's eyes filled with tears.

Jenny paused and touched her father's face. "No," she said in a voice that was equal parts Jenny and Annabelle, "*we* will deal with him."

Deal with him.

"Annabelle . . . ," Grey said weakly. "It's okay . . . I'm ready . . ." He coughed up a gout of blood. "Whatever you . . . need to . . . do . . . I deserve it."

The Harrowed that was both Annabelle and Jenny stood there and smiled down at him. The other ghosts appeared around her. His soldiers, his men. His friends who he had failed. They were all smiling.

Those smiles were a terrible thing to see. They were without mercy. They were the smiles of beings that had walked too long in the valley of the shadow. They were the smiles of the dead.

"Take him," said Annabelle/Jenny. "Take him. Make it hurt. Make it terrible. Make it *last*."

The ghosts let loose a dreadful howl as they rushed forward. Grey wanted to close his eyes but he did not. After all the betrayal he could not deny them that. He nodded to them as they reached with cold, dead hands. The ghosts rushed past him. Aleksander Deray screamed as the ghosts fell upon him. The scream rose and rose and rose, filling the air, shattering the storm, tearing apart the clouds, rending the fabric of the world.

The ghosts did not touch Grey. But they tore the necromancer's soul from his body and dragged it down through the mud into the earth and down to Hell itself. Deray's scream lingered for a long time, a stain on the day.

It was done.

Done.

And Grey knew that he was done, too. Now it was his time to make that long journey down into the burning Pit. Like Deray, his time had come to pay for his crimes.

In his shattered chest, Grey's heart beat once. Twice.

A third time. Like the ringing of a fractured bell. Slower with each beat.

Brother Joe knelt beside him and made the sign of the cross in the air. He was weeping.

So was Looks Away.

And behind him was another figure, another woman. Voluptuous, with dark hair and emerald green eyes, and an inner light that burned with blue-white purity. Veronica.

Then *she* came and knelt down, pushing Brother Joe out of the way. She. Annabelle. Jenny. Both of them in one. She bent down to kiss his face, his eyes, his lips.

"Death isn't the end," she whispered, and then she said, "I love you."

He could only manage one more word.

"Love . . ."

It was enough. His heart beat again. And again.

And then no more.

Grey Torrance felt himself float free of the broken shell, and a curtain of darkness fell over him, over the world, over everything.

-1-

The summer burned away and fall came early to Paradise Falls. It was short and harsh and followed by a bitter winter. Snows fell deep and often and winds howled through the canyons and clefts.

But the winds were the winds. No spirits or demons lent their voices to those screams.

When spring came, it too was early. Rains fell heavily. No frogs or snakes. By mid-April there was green grass in the fields and flowers exploding along the sides of the trails.

The new bridge was strong and wagons rumbled across it every day, bringing supplies from all over the region. Bringing families of farmers. Bringing miners and a legion of scientists and their apprentices to work at the big factory Doctor Saint had built. Every store and building and house in Paradise Falls wore new coats of paint, and every person wore the finest of clothes. Larders were full and no one wanted for a thing.

The story of the richest find of ghost rock, gold, platinum, and other precious metals was news around the world. Hopeful prospectors flooded the town, but not a single one of them seemed able to find a good place to stake a claim. And no one in town seemed willing to explain just exactly where they'd dug up all those rocks and metals. Paradise Falls was a happy town, but a secretive one. It kept itself to itself.

Of a Sunday, though, everyone in town was in church, weeping for the dead, and thanking God for their salvation, and their bounty.

Thomas Looks Away did not go to church. He spent his Sunday mornings walking the grounds of his new estate. The damage from the attack had been repaired, and the vaults deep underground had been mostly emptied, their contents shared equally with the other survivors.

Mostly, but not entirely.

Even when he'd measured out equal shares with every man, woman, and child who had been standing after the battle, he still had a little over a ton of gold left for himself.

Life was good. And, if he spent a lot of time alone, talking to the shadows in empty rooms, no one commented. Not even when passers-by heard a woman's voice speaking to him from those very shadows.

Brother Joe had been restored to full office and now ran his rebuilt church with equal measures of fervor and humility.

-2-

On the sunlit porch of the Pearl farmhouse, Grey Torrance rocked slowly in his favorite chair and read the papers brought in from Salt Lake, Lost Angels, and even as far away as New York. It was a strange and busy world. Bad things were happening, but bad things always happened. There were wars and rumors of wars. There were fantastical machines. And there were reports of aborted coups in a dozen foreign countries.

He smiled and reached for his coffee cup. Like most

things he did, Grey lifted the cup carefully. Even now, seven months on, his body hurt in more places than he could count, and he knew that some of those aches would never really go away. Some hurts could not be healed.

Others though . . .

Well, there was less pain in some places than he had any right to expect. Less agony in his chest, his heart. His soul.

He laid his paper in his lap, sipped his coffee, and looked out at the day. A man walked down the street toward the house. Tall and pale, with iron gray hair and broad shoulders. He paused only for a moment to pass the time of day with Doctor Saint. They both glanced his way, saw him watching, and nodded. He returned the nod.

Then the little scientist headed back toward his lab and Lucky Bob strolled off toward Mrs. O'Malley's place, where dinner would be waiting.

That was a strange arrangement, mused Grey. Strange, but not entirely without precedent. And, after all, Paradise Falls was a strange little town. It always would be. How could it not?

"Penny for your thoughts," said a voice and he turned to see her come out of the house. Blond curls and blue eyes and a smile that held so many wonderful mysteries.

Grey laughed. "You can have them for free."

"And they are—?"

"Just that it's another beautiful day in Paradise."

Belle laughed.

That's what he called her. It had been what he'd started calling her during the long weeks when he hovered on the cliff between life and death. Not Jenny, not Annabelle. Just Belle. She'd accepted it. Or, *they* had accepted it. It became who this woman was.

Life was so strange.

She pulled her chair close to his and sat, taking his hand.

"Another beautiful day in paradise," she agreed.

They sat and watched white clouds sail across the sky. And every once in a while they glanced at each other and smiled.

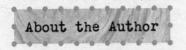

About the Author

JONATHAN MABERRY is a *New York Times* bestselling and multiple Bram Stoker Award–winning author, editor, and comic book writer. Maberry is probably best known for his Joe Ledger novels and his award-winning Rot & Ruin series for young adults. His books have sold in more than two dozen countries. He lives in Del Mar, California.

jonathanmaberry.com

TOR

Award-winning authors
Compelling stories

Please join us at the website
below for more information
about this author and other great
Tor selections, and to sign up for
our monthly newsletter!

TOR

—— www.tor-forge.com ——